A Stone's Throw

Lee Watts

For M

And all the others who deserved better

ACKNOWLEDGEMENTS

Thanks to my family and also to Maria and Carmel for their encouragement.

A Stone's Throw

A Stone's Throw

Chapter 1

A Trip to the Moon

It had been a warm but typically dull Belfast Sunday, and by late afternoon Martin McKenna and Brendan Price were thoroughly bored as they traipsed the quiet streets, discussing and discarding various options before deciding to relieve the ennui by booby trapping a telephone kiosk.

Brendan had a penchant for unsavoury jokes and laughed as he anticipated the coming fun, gleefully elaborating on his plan. His angelic smile, baby blue eyes and innocent golden curls concealed a thoroughly scabrous sense of humour, and this roguish spirit, fully shared by Martin, was probably why they had been friends for as long as they could remember. Their enthusiasm rekindled, they soon found the required material and a telephone booth they could watch from a short but safe distance. Waiting until there was nobody about, they entered and proceeded with the operation. Martin held the small plastic bag open and watched with fascinated disgust, nose wrinkling as Brendan carefully smeared a generous amount of dog turd around the receiver, then a little on the mouth piece using a twig as deftly as Rembrandt finishing a masterpiece. With a final flourish of the brown he was done. They then retired to an observation point on the corner to watch the results of their ghastly prank. A middle aged man in white shirtsleeves approached, digging around in his pocket for change with one hand as he opened the door with the other. Martin nudged Brendan with his elbow, both stifling their pent up mirth. Through the red panelled glass they could just about see the man lifting the phone from the cradle and reading a number from a crumpled piece of paper he had flattened out. He put the phone to his ear and immediately they saw his head recoil before he cautiously brought the piece closer to his nose. There was a loud scream of disbelief, and then furious cursing as the man crashed the phone down and tumbled out, wiping his ear and smelling his fingers. A woman passed him pushing a pram as he shouted, turning and searching as the perpetrators ducked back behind the corner.

"Ya filthy wee bastards! What the hell... if I find youse, I'll fuckin' skin ye!"

"Would you mind your language?" the woman snapped.

"Fuckin' smell that missus, see what some dirty bastard's done."

He jabbed a hand out to her, palm down like an impatient prince demanding homage from a recalcitrant peasant. The woman muttered something inaudible and carried on, her pace quickening. Martin and Brendan left the scene at a trot, holding their sides as a gale of reined in laughter was unleashed, only regaining their composure after several more minutes, both wiping away happy tears. Marty laughed again as he gave his schoolmate a playful shove.

"You're getting worse all the time so you are," he said. "I thought I was bad but you're bogging."

"It was worth it just for the look on your man's face, besides no real harm done and I didn't hear you saying don't."

Nearing the junction of Martin's street their intermittent giggling finally subsided. In the distance, to their mild irritation they could hear a faint tootling as some fool of an aspiring bandsman practiced on his fife.

"Will you be watching the moon thing tonight?" Brendan asked.

"Aye, I expect so. Who won't be?" Marty then remembered Brendan's place didn't have a TV. They would have to see it at the Lavery's next door.

"See you then." Brendan waved and carried on along the road as Martin turned right and continued homewards.

Like most streets in this part of Belfast between the Catholic Falls and Protestant Shankill it was typically red bricked and terraced, the houses for the most part accurately described as two up, two down. They were old, dating back to Victorian times. The red and cream paint on them was a bit scabby, flaking from the window frames and doorways of some houses, but most were well and proudly kept, the doorsteps uniformly red and clean. It all reminded Martin of Coronation Street on TV; even the cats lazing about on the tiles seemed to be the same, if somewhat stringier. He saw his younger sisters Patricia and Rosemary playing with friends in the middle of the road, Rosemary with her red plastic shoes and one lazy eye temporary patched, imitating every move of her bigger sister. One of the girls nearer his own age stopped her tennis ball in mid throw and followed Martin hungrily with her eyes as he passed.

"Aw, Pat, your brother's lovely so he is," she said only half jokingly. He blushed with pride and embarrassment, noting a few agreeing nods out the corner of his eye.

"Try living with him," said another voice tartly from the doorway. His elder sister Eileen was leaning against the frame with arms folded. Martin smiled fondly at her without answering as he brushed past. Glancing at him now Eileen had never thought about her younger brother as a 'looker'. He was merely a plaything as a baby, a pest and a bloody nuisance the older he got, and was now a cheeky just turned fourteen year old; but becoming handsome? Aye, maybe. He had his mother's features, was pretty tall and well built for his age with well groomed longish black hair, a winning smile, large navy blue eyes in an evenly proportioned face, and had that indefinable sparkle that people always found attractive. Eileen thought about this and his sometimes impish happy go lucky sense of humour which was definitely from their irreverent father Jimmy.

"Mary loves Martin, Mary loves Martin..." Patricia shouted after him in a childish sing song chant as he walked through to the kitchen. Jimmy looked up from his paper in the front room and snickered to his wife in a low voice.

"Aye, he's been looking more at tits than toys these last few years."

Their mother Bernadette took on her habitual frown. She worried and tried her best to get Martin to take more of an interest in school, and be more like his younger brother Thomas on whom she doted. With his innocent round face and open smile, Thomas looked his part as an altar boy and she even harboured notions of him carrying on and eventually become a priest. Jimmy was more realistic however and thought his eldest son, although intelligent was no academic, and as for Thomas and the priesthood, there was not a chance if he had anything to do with it.

Bernie shook her head at her husband, sat there smiling with his short nose, compact florid face, and eyes a shade lighter than his son's. Dress that man in green with a matching hat and he could pass for a leprechaun, bar his size and choice of language of course. Long ago she would have mildly censured Jimmy's careless use of bad language, not having been raised that way herself, but she rarely did these days. There was no malice in it; swearing came to Jimmy as naturally as singing to a thrush. She still crossed herself on hearing some of his more sacrilegious outbursts, but knew it was futile to try and reform him. Just last week she had revealed her wishes for Thomas, couching it in terms likely to appeal to her husband, of the priesthood being a good living and secure respectable employment. Jimmy had paused, eyes widening, his cigarette half way to his lips.

"Our Thomas, a priest? Have you been at the bottle?" he asked, his face caught between incredulity and mirth. "Catch yourself on! A steady job? I've never minded them being brought up in the church but I'll not have any of mine making it their life!" He had hooted at Bernie's pursed lipped face before inserting a final blasphemy. "Anyway you know what they say about getting on in the priesthood? Keep your mouth shut and your arse open and you'll do grand!" He then lit up, guffawing at his own wit. Bernie was stung, eyebrows snapping together in annoyance as she immediately retorted.

"No one I know would say such a thing. Only Orangemen and the foul minded like yourself, so now!" She had even stamped her foot as she said it and much good it had done.

Jimmy, although nominally still Catholic didn't really have much time for the church, although he didn't mind Bernie's piety and it was alright for keeping the kids good with promises of damnation for the naughty. In Jimmy's eyes, if Bernie had a fault it was that she took things too seriously. He enjoyed life as much as his limited means allowed, but as a practical man he had no time for dwelling on things he couldn't do anything about.

For her part Bernie thought Jimmy's problem was that he took nothing seriously, not God or politics or setting a good example. Like the rest of the family she loved his playfulness and sense of fun, but felt her efforts at instilling a respect for the church and their nation's history were being needlessly undermined by her husband's levity. Bernie came from an old and respected Republican family. Her Grandfather had fought for Irish freedom in the early 1920's against the 'Tans' and then against the pro treaty forces in the civil war, surviving English guns and Irish prisons, but he had never accepted the partition of his country. He and her grandmother had told of their own personal bad times in Ireland's proud and tragic history, of the times before, of war, of famine and being driven from their homes by land hungry Protestant settlers. Bernie had grown up with a deep understanding of Irish history and culture, being well versed from an early age about the time of the high kings, Brian Boru, Strongbow and the subsequent centuries of rebellion, and was trying to pass this on to her children. She felt it was no more than her duty to keep the Republican dream of a united Ireland alive. She wasn't bitter as some were. Unlike a lot of neighbourhoods, which were usually of either one persuasion or another, their street contained Protestant families at the other end, and although they had little contact, they got on well enough. The only time Jimmy ever made more than a fleeting comment on politics was when the subject of employment and job discrimination against Catholics came up. Unlike his wife, this was the only real grievance he felt living in Northern Ireland; that and those bloody Orange marches every summer.

George and Roy Ferguson approached the same street from the opposite end after wandering aimlessly in the centre, an earlier game of football having turned sour. The owner of the ball had stalked off in a dignified huff, his head held high, trying not to listen to the jeers, and haughtily ignoring the clod of dry earth that had struck his back. Jackie had arrived with his new leather football held high like a triumphant Atlas with an undersized globe, pleased at the way the other kids had surrounded him at the sight of the ball, reminding Roy of a film star ringed by adoring fans wanting an autograph. His popularity at saving them from the torpor of an Ulster Sunday hadn't lasted however. The game had been 'World Cup' and if he couldn't be either champions England or Northern Ireland then nobody could. The offer of West Germany had been rejected with righteous disgust and the ball withdrawn, leaving the rest of them name calling, which soon turned to head scratching and non committal shrugs as various other options were aired and rejected.

George and Roy had decided to walk into the centre. Although everything was closed it still beat going home and there was always the chance of some unexpected adventure, but as usual nothing out of the ordinary had occurred; in this part of the world nothing ever did. Now they were on their way home, picking up the pace a little on the approach to the Shankill, as tonight actually did have the promise of something completely out of the ordinary. Man was going to land on the moon. It had of course been a main topic of conversation now that the Twelfth was over and there were fewer parades. The march two years ago had been a proud moment in Roy's young life, as he had been lucky enough to hold one of the four strings that steadied the beautifully coloured swaying banner of the local Orange lodge. Everyone loved the Twelfth and its wonderful sense of belonging, the holiday atmosphere with everybody in high spirits and the flutes and drums that could so thrill the blood. Yes, everyone he knew enjoyed the Twelfth of July.

George booted a grease stained paper bag that sailed high into the air as they passed one of the numerous mission halls that proliferated in the area, along with their attendant gloomy billboard predictions and dire threats about the wages of sin. They weren't a particularly religious family, but did attend church sometimes. Roy darted a quick look at one of the boards, remembering how scared he had been when he was younger, one sermon in particular blighting his already colourful imagination with its talk of hell fire, garments of worms and other such delights for the wicked, dead and damned. Even at this formative age Roy was aware that the church seemed to be always on the lookout for sin and usually finding it too. George stopped, burped a blend of lamb and sprouts and gave an exaggerated sigh.

"I can smell that from here," Roy observed tetchily.

Glancing left George caught the distaste passing from Roy's features, so swallowing air forced out another long curling belch.

"How about that one then wee lad?" he mocked smilingly.

"Best not be late for tea," Roy replied. "You don't want to get in Da's bad books again do you now?" he crooned poisonously.

George was in a good humour so didn't pursue it. Teasing Roy wasn't a bad pastime when bored. He saw Roy as fussy and pedantic and precise, an easy target but one even if over a year younger he didn't take lightly. Although he had remarkable self control for his age and didn't usually bite, now and again his green eyes would bulge slightly, his face whiten and it was time to get ready, duck or run. George had learned this a long time ago; when playing he had pushed hard once too often and Roy had picked up his large, plastic red truck and simply crashed it into the side of his face. To be sure, George had given him a thumping and received a hard slap in response from Da, who was awakened too early after his five to midnight shift at the docks, but after that he took more care with Roy's temper. Looking at him now, George could see so much of their father in Roy, and not only physically. Roy was strong, wiry and of medium height, his hair close cropped and George envied him his best features, a regular square face with his Da's strong dimpled chin and sage green eyes. He also had good, white even teeth, which were not so common in the land of gobstoppers and boiled sweets. George had to make do with his mother's more banal darker brown hair, brown eyes and blunted less defined features. Also like his father, Roy couldn't always control his impatience. He was usually first to finish his dinner and chaffing to leave the table, or annoyingly would move other people's pieces on the Monopoly board in his haste; he also fidgeted constantly.

Their father William had never been one for sitting still and according to their Ma that was half the trouble with him. After a life on the ocean wave, roving the world in the Royal Marines with few worries, he was now stuck in one place with big family responsibilities: his wife Betty and children, George aged fourteen, Roy thirteen, John ten, and namesake William aged five, known lovingly if inevitably to all as wee Billy. William Ferguson took little pleasure from his job, which paid the rent and kept food on the table, including Sunday roasts of New Zealand lamb, and like most other men of his class and station he enjoyed a drink on a Friday night, and that was it. This frustration with his life, coupled with his own austere upbringing and naval background made him a sometimes ferocious disciplinarian, who could and frequently did lash out at his children's perceived failings. To him, a family without discipline and order was an unhappy family, where boredom and misbehaviour would breed and turn into anarchy. It couldn't and wouldn't be allowed. Mr Ferguson took no pleasure in this harsh regime, using verbal scourging, slaps and on occasion a thin bamboo cane. He wanted them to grow up straight backed with firm morals. Ulster Protestants were not a whining folk and asked favours of nobody; it was no more than his duty to instil what he called 'good Protestant values' into all his children if they were to become upright, upstanding and loyal citizens. If somebody had ever dared to tell William he was being stereotypically old fashioned in his views and behaviour, he would merely have shrugged and nodded. Proudly.

Although severe, his children never doubted his intentions, just his ways. He wasn't always strict and could unwind and be surprisingly tolerant and good humoured, especially taking pains with Billy. All the children bar wee Billy had felt their father's wrath at one time or another however, and had learned to detect the danger signs or at least avoid detection when making mischief. On one memorable day just last month however George had taken a pencil case from a school mate whose father worked with William. Saying he was going to return it cut no ice at all with his parents, their anger this time reddened with shame, and it was this that Roy was referring to.

As soon as their father came through the door that evening the whole family knew an explosion was coming, the atmosphere a charged and heavy precursor to violent storm. First, Betty was summoned to the front room and the door shut firmly behind her. The boys had sat at the kitchen table in silence except for Billy who noisily chewed on a piece of bread and mixed fruit jam. All had minor crimes on their conscience magnified by the smallness of a childhood world. All listened intently, heads cocked like forest deer at the first scent of danger to the low tones coming from the living room and wondered where the axe would fall. Seeing his brothers so preoccupied, Billy's grubby urchin brown hand helped itself to Roy's bread and began to consume it. His infant logic knew Roy wouldn't mind as he was Roy's favourite. Just then they all heard a low moan from their Ma as the door opened.

"How will I be able to look her in the face after this?" This was followed by their father's angry response.

"Ian just made a joke of it, but I'm not for laughing right now. George! Get in here this minute ye wee shite!"

His attempt at innocence was a forlorn hope. His father had looked at him with the angry disgust he kept for such occasions and told him he needed some physical chastisement, making it sound like a tried and proven medical cure. To their surprise he had then forced his son into a heavy duffel coat, thrust a bag of coal into one hand and a heavy clothes iron into the other and ordered him to run up the stairs at the double, all the while slashing at his legs with the bamboo cane if his speed slackened. After five trips up and down, George had tried concentrating on his Ma's best liked picture on the landing, a tacky printed picture of white horses running aimlessly against an unlikely red sky. Panting, with the sweat starting to bead his forehead and his neck chaffing at the rough material of the coat, he hesitated. His father, dissatisfied with the punishment, anger unabated and flavoured by humiliation at his workplace kept him moving. After a good ten minutes of stomping up and down the thinning blue carpeted stairs, time and again past the ceramic flying ducks on the wall, George began to cry. This was then taken up by Billy in the kitchen doorway, who was soon sobbing in distress at this bizarre and horrible sight, his face awash with a salty sweet melange of jam and tears. Only then had the punishment stopped.

George mused on all this as they turned left into their own street, the view of St Peter's Cathedral with its spooky Gothic spires by now a familiar one, although they had been resident here only a couple of years. It certainly had been an incident to remember and Roy's little homily about bad books was hardly necessary.

Roy was first to see their Uncle Sam's green Morris Minor parked outside their door. Both broke into a sprint to get indoors. Sam and his wife were welcome visitors to the Ferguson children, and despite half hearted protests from their mother, they spoiled the boys as much as they could. Uncle Sam was a police officer, large and jovial with receding dark hair and a loud laugh who always had a fund of new and exciting stories. His wife Heather was a well spoken and pretty ash blond; to the kids she was quite posh. They had no children of their own. Passing Sam's car they saw wee Billy behind the wheel, clutching it with both hands, eyes screwed up in concentration and making loud engine noises.

"Brrrrrrrrrrrrruh..... ehhhh.....brrrrrrrrrruuuum!" He looked up at them like a happy, just fed piglet, a fleck of toffee hardened at the corner of his mouth, a hint of possible good things to come.

The door was open and both marched into a front room already beginning to fill with a hanging cloud of blue cigarette smoke.

"Hello boys, good to see you," said Heather in her refined voice. Big Uncle Sam was sat on the sofa next to her with a bottle of stout. He used the more typical Belfast.

"Alright lads, what about ye?"

"Fine, thanks," they answered together.

Betty came into the room looking flustered, a strand of hair in her eyes, bearing a pot of tea with cups and saucers on a tray. Roy stole a glance at the crockery and raised his eyebrows: it was their Ma's best 'Pompadour' china, pristine white cups decorated with bright blue, purple and orange flowers. Setting it carefully down on the side table she addressed her sons.

"You'll have to wait for something to eat. I'll do sandwiches or something later."

William walked in from the back door, disturbing the wreaths of blue tobacco smoke which now eddied about him. On seeing his guests he broke into a smile.

"Och it's yourselves, are you at my stout already Sam?" he joked, taking his armchair and lighting up an Embassy Regal before adding in a slightly more formal voice, "I hope you're keeping well Heather." She smiled and nodded her thanks, accepting a cup of steaming hot tea from Betty.

"I thought we'd just pop round and see a bit of the moon landings and drink some of your beer," said Sam, stretching his legs out with a grin.

"You're sure you don't want to watch 'Z Cars' instead?"

"Aye, very funny."

"I heard they were going to make a TV series about our very own Royal Ulster Constabulary called 'No Cars'." Sam chuckled at the joke as Billy wandered into the room.

"When's tea Ma?" he asked plaintively.

Both Sam and Heather beamed at him as William swept him up and planted him on his knees.

"Are you hungry again wee man?" he asked affectionately as he ruffled his hair.

Betty was also smiling fondly and looking across at their visitors, noticing again the ache of childlessness behind their smiles. They had desperately wanted kids of their own, but it just wasn't to be, and although she and William had never really discussed it, this was probably why they both tolerated the way Sam and Heather squandered money on their boys. Sam spoke up.

"Tell you what, I'm pretty hungry myself and to save my sister there messing about in the kitchen why don't I get in some fish suppers. Sound good to you Billy?" he asked, seeking an easy and willing ally. Billy jumped from his father's lap with enthusiasm at this unexpected treat. Despite a lack of money but abundance of pride, William couldn't really refuse as he knew Sam only wanted everyone to enjoy the evening. There was no condescension in the man.

"Alright Sam," he said. "Who's for the chipper then? Any volunteers? No? Roy you've the food detail, let's see now, eight fish suppers and as the police are paying I'll take a battered sausage too."

Roy heaved himself up from the stool and waited for Uncle Sam to draw his wallet out of his hanging coat pocket. Sam opened it and carefully took out two pound notes.

"Here, that'll cover it!"

Roy smiled and started on his way to Reilly's chip shop. Walking along he thought about his Uncle Sam and how he always took an interest in how he was doing in school and what he was up to. As far back as he could remember his uncle had always been a source of good things and good times, taking them out for trips to the coast in his car, or fishing, or going along to Seaview football ground along with his father to watch Crusaders play and usually lose. As he walked past the familiar red bricks with the noise of squealing girls playing and the persistent chip chipping of a few sparrows he absentmindedly examined the green and lilac back of one note. There was a picture of a bank building surrounded by a Shorts aircraft, rolls of cloth, spools of linen and a cruise ship in the corner; all representative of a Northern Ireland that lived in a world of symbols, ancient and otherwise, of badges, flags and tribal colours. Roy laughed as he examined the ship, the most famous one built here of course being the *'Titanic'* but they'd hardly put that one on the note. He looked again at the ship and wondered what it would be like sailing on such a vessel to exotic parts, sitting on deck chairs, waited upon by white clad flunkies and drenched by golden sunshine. Maybe one day.

He reached Reilly's chip shop and immediately caught the strong smell of frying before he was through the door. There was only one customer before him who bore a strong resemblance to the Stormont Prime Minister Major Chichester Clarke. There was little other likeness.

"Give us a chip," he slurred. There was a whiff of stale whiskey.

That was definitely not the refined urbane voice of the Prime Minister who had lately been on the telly more than usual. He was served and weaved uncertainly past Roy with eyes glazed, hand delving into the bag for a hot chip. Mr Reilly was large, with a curious pear shaped head emphasized by sagging jowls. Red faced, he closed his till with pudgy hands and turned to Roy.

"Yes son, what'll it be then?"

"Eight fish suppers and a sausage please."

"I've only five ready," said Reilly letting out a quick smile. "You'll have to wait for the others."

Roy handed him the notes and collected his change, counting it, not that he didn't trust Reilly but because he didn't ever want his uncle to think bad of him if there was a mistake. Reilly watched him, lowering and multiplying his chins, his mouth turning down.

"Is it all there son?" he asked sadly. The door opened and he went to serve his next customer.

Martin sat at the kitchen table with its red checked plastic cover and watched his father trying to teach Thomas cribbage.

"Look, the aim is to get as many fifteens from that hand, or runs, or pairs." Placing his cigarette in the brass tray Jimmy began slapping his own cards on the table and sang out in mock Mississippi river boat style. "Fifteen two, fifteen four, fifteen six and two's eight. Why, this man's a winner again! Do you see?"

"But where does the two come from, there are none?" asked Thomas, his eyes flicking from one card to the next, frowning in concentration.

"Two points, two for every fifteen and two for the pair makes eight, see now?"

"So how many do I have?"

"Show us your hand then. Right ....no runs, no fifteens either, two for the pair of sevens, Jesus I want to play you for money Thomas!" He chortled through a blast of smoke.

"I need a pee," said Thomas getting up from the table. It may as well have been quantum physics; he just didn't have enough interest to take it in. His father's voice followed him as he went out the back door to the yard.

"It takes time son to become as good as me... or as modest!"

"I expect you're so good because you spend all day playing cards at work," said Bernie, clad in green apron and drying a last pan. "When you have work that is."

"I've work now haven't I?" Jimmy shifted uncomfortably in his chair before quickly changing the subject. "Are you making tea?"

On cue the kettle began to boil, the shrill whistle cut off by Martin who turned in his stool to stop the offending noise. Eileen entered and sat down with a sigh. A large brown pot was plunked down on the table, steam rising from its nozzle. After a minute Martin got himself a mug and filled it, adding sugar from the glass bowl with its casing of old grey sugar on the sides from a thousand careless spoons, and listened to his father teasing Eileen.

"Are you still grieving over that Davie Jones?" He winked at Marty. "Shocking so it is, Stopped Rocks guitarist found dead in the swimming pool." He shook his head ruefully as he carefully mangled the names. Eileen ignored him, poured a cup and wandered dreamily back into the living room. It was another funny habit of her Da's, deliberately changing words and names to their opposite.

"Anybody listening in on us'll think we're all loopers," Martin laughed.

"One of us anyway. It's easier doing a crossword sometimes than talking to you Jimmy," Bernie murmured, smiling wanly. She helped herself to one of his cigarettes and took a seat. Lighting it with a match she grimaced and coughed as she drew in and caught acrid phosphor. Jimmy's eyes roved the kitchen and fixed on the bread bin against the yellow tiles.

"Never mind that. Any father's disgrace left? I fancy a chip butty."

By which they knew he meant 'Mother's Pride' white bread, as the Stopped Rocks were the Rolling Stones and Davie Jones was in fact Brian Jones. Their neighbour, Mr Redstone was unfailingly called Mr Bluebrick and even Belfast's finest, George Best came out predictably as George Worst or simply 'Worsty'.

"Can I have some if I go get them?" Martin anticipated, knowing full well he would be going anyway but trying to extract a reward. Jimmy nodded, partly in acknowledgement at the cunning in the question.

"You can, and so can we all, chips anyway, we'll save the rest."

He pulled out a crumpled five pound note and held it up to the light in examination so they could all clearly see the words 'Ulster Bank Limited'.

"And where did that come from?" asked Bernie gently, folding her arms, her head to one side.

"Had a bit of luck on the dogs yesterday," said Jimmy, giving her a Cheshire cat grin. "I'm surprised you didn't find in my pocket last night."

"Jimmy, you said you wouldn't..."

"Ah, come on." He rolled his eyes in mock exasperation. "Jesus, I swear your Ma still has her confirmation money tucked away." He gave another smile. "Anyway you know I never bet big."

Bernie knew this was true. He was careful and didn't get drunk often either, or hit her, or do any of the other bad things that happened with grim regularity to some of the other wives in the neighbourhood. It was a small vice and she didn't begrudge him it really, accepting his oft repeated philosophy that a man without a vice is like beer without a head: flat, sour and usually bitter. She smiled slyly as she thought he was also after all these years still a tender and satisfying lover. Bernie was worried however about his influence on Martin and

Thomas who idolised him. She didn't like bad language and wouldn't get used to it even if her continual scolding of Jimmy seemed to have no effect whatsoever. His teaching Rosemary to point at her and say "shut your hole!" when she was learning to speak, in front of her visiting mother too, had led to a fine shouting battle, but for once, an apology from her husband. She felt that all the boys were learning from their father was a street sharpness but none of the things she herself thought worthy. She had been brought up in a small town in County Tyrone, her family originally coming from the Armagh border area where various cousins still lived on their small farms. She was of course a 'cultchie' to people from the city. Taking a last determined drag on her cigarette, she decided it would be up to herself to instil more of the good Irish moral virtues she had been brought up with in her sons.

Martin went to the chip shop. Sunday dinner was always a good feed, but he was soon hungry again. Today had been traditional cabbage and bacon with added mashed potatoes swimming in gravy, the only part of the meal his father ever made or ever could; it was his one culinary achievement. Fortunately, exposure to Jimmy's cooking was mercifully rare, his offerings were usually burnt, and even his fried eggs had black frilly edges as he tried and failed to get everything onto the table at the same time.

A few scrawny sparrows were scrapping in the gutter over a crust as he passed a group of boys his own age on the other side of the road, calling out to those he knew.

"Alright Stevie!" He nodded at another, "Patsy," and smiled at a third, skinnier but with a reputation at school for hitting first and not even bothering to ask later. "How ya doin' Mickey?"

"Sound!" and "Grand!" and "Alright, yourself Marty?" echoed back to him.

Martin was naturally easy going but not soft either, having learned at an early age to use fists when charm wasn't working. It was all so simple: around these streets people beat you up if they didn't like you, so it was best to keep them friendly. Better that than having to fight all the time, as win or lose, a punch in the mouth that brought blood and the taste of pennies was painful and something to be avoided when possible.

He approached Reilly's and noted with satisfaction only two customers. One of them looked familiar, from the other end of his street, having moved there not so long ago he was probably using Reilly's because his own regular chippy was closed. On seeing the other customer his pace slowed. It was Chris McCormick, known to all, behind his back at least as 'Beatle'. This name didn't come from any musical ability or devotion to the group, or any resemblance whatsoever to any of them bar a haircut he had once had. McCormick had tried to pass it off as being fashionable, but everyone knew it was a case of his Da sticking a pudding bowl on his head and drunkenly cutting around it to avoid the cost of a barber. Everyone knew the large McCormick family as rough and best left alone. Their father was a brutish layabout who spent his time in the pub or Crumlin Road jail for a variety of petty crimes. A shame to the Irish is how Bernie disdainfully described them, and Martin wouldn't argue with that.

Chris was a bad bastard. When they were younger his main occupations seemed to consist of ripping butterflies, chucking live frogs from tall buildings and roasting insects alive. Once long ago, he had seen him on some waste ground busy with a matchbox. Marty had been intrigued and wondered what the clicking noise was, and asked him if he had some jumping beans. A giggling Chris had told him it was a grasshopper he had put inside, and the clicking was it frantically springing and banging its head, a noise that increased in tempo as the box was lit before his horrified gaze. Later he progressed to birds, and even boasted of setting fire to a nest with chicks inside, oblivious to the disgusted or disbelieving faces of his audience. One kid in school had recently been foolish enough to be overheard using the name he hated and paid a heavy price. 'Beatle' had waited until the afternoon break and dragged the much smaller and now ashen faced Paul White behind the corrugated iron bike sheds where smokers congregated. The punishment was to be out of sight, but a public shaming too. First a slap, and then a full punch to Paul's mouth which made him spit blood. The sight of it had brought the first tears, his hands raised he wailed.

"Please Beat... Chris, I didn't say..."

"What was that? Please beat me did ye say? Fuckin' liar, I heard ye!"

Beatle had him by his blazer lapels and swung him against the rusty shed with a clang as his head bounced against it. Paul began blubbering which seemed to make Beatle angrier. He pulled the hands away and quite deliberately punched him again in the face, and then hard in the guts, which made Paul double over and slide down with retching noises; a fart punctuated his fall as he hit the ground. Apart from the distant playground shouting there was little other conversation, the dozen or so other boys there interested but neutral observers. Martin was one of them, and stopped his conversation with Tony Francis to see what it was all about. Beatle kicked the balled up figure on the ground, and then the corrugated iron which flaked rust down onto Paul's head.

"Right, you can make it up to me. Have you any fags?"

"No, I've none," said Paul, cautiously looking up from his cringing position.

"I'll take the fucking head off ye!" Beatle drew his fist back.

"I swear... don't!"

McCormick changed his mind and started going through his pockets: a couple of Blackjack chews, half a roll of Trebor mints, a half packet of Spangles, a snot rag, two cheap pens, an eraser, a chewed half pencil and finally a two shilling piece came out like an obscene version of the 'Generation Game'. McCormick took the coin and stamped on the mints but wasn't satisfied.

"I want some fags."

"I don't have any but."

"Tomorrow!"

"How... that's my last money."

"Well, maybe you better grow some, tomorrow now." With this last said over his shoulder Beatle had sauntered off, head and haircut held high. Aye, right enough he was a real bastard. So seeing McCormick here put Martin on alert as he entered. All the same he tried not to laugh at the back of that head, even from behind where he didn't have the benefit of Beatle's spotty, flattened suet face, he was one ugly overweight brute. He heard Reilly speak and then point with a grubby plastered finger to the other boy.

"You'll have to wait if you want a cod, he's first."

McCormick turned and stared at Roy, weighing him up. Roy, who was leaning against the wall straightened and stared back. Martin could see McCormick didn't like it, and so to avert a nasty scene which he didn't want to be involved in, but mainly because he wanted those chips pronto, he hailed McCormick like a friend using his best smile.

"Hey Chris, how's it going? Haven't seen you around," he said, as if with real regret.

McCormick dragged his piggy eyes away from Roy, and seeing Martin, half smiled as he answered. "Not so bad Marty, just in for a supper. Shouldn't have to wait but, if some people didn't hog it all for themselves." Then he deliberately added softly but still audible above the loud sizzling and crackling of the fryers. "Typical Orange bastard."

Roy stiffened and his hands came out of his pockets, which surprised both McCormick and Martin as he was smaller than both of them. Reilly looked up from his wrapping and snapped nervously.

"I'll have none of that language in here, or... anything else." He focused on Martin. "And what do you want?"

"Seven lots of chips please Mr Reilly, and don't spare the scraps!"

Marty turned and studied Roy, who although seemingly unafraid was keeping a wary green eye on McCormick as he waited for Reilly to finish wrapping his order. McCormick, dressed in a heavy beige sweater, dirt shiny jeans and boots despite the warmth, seemed unsure whether to take things further or just let it go and this amused Martin. He nodded at Roy, a small gesture of recognition to let him know he had no hostile intentions. Roy nodded back and collected his order, putting both large bags in his left, keeping his right free for any big 'taig' that wanted to try it on. McCormick let him pass, watching with narrowed eyes, thinking that if he saw him around his own street it wouldn't be just his cod that was battered.

As he left the shop Roy let out a deep breath. His heart was hammering and he wanted to get home quickly and not only so the food kept warm. That had been a close one. He knew the one boy vaguely from the other end of his own street, but not that other fat thug. Although the bastard called Chris was bigger he would have gone for him despite his fear, knowing from painful experience that getting in first was what counted when there was no choice anyway. He was relieved at the slight intervention, which had probably averted a split lip or worse, but that last insult "Orange bastard" had made him boil. Roy never questioned how they knew he was a Protestant, as most of the time his own could tell who was a 'taig'. Outsiders might laugh at this, but he knew it was true, and not just the old one about 'taigs' eyes being closer together or smelling different, it was just a sense; you didn't always need to know the last name or what school they attended. Normally around the Twelfth of July and the marching season Catholics made themselves scarce, this year though seemed even to Roy's adolescent mind a little different. Coincidentally as he got indoors, the discussion was following his own thoughts.

Roy was greeted by an ironic cheer as he passed the front room on the way to the kitchen, where he could hear his Ma clattering about getting dinner plates and cutlery ready. Betty took the bags and began unwrapping the cod, golden brown, still warm and steaming slightly, and making Roy's mouth water.

"Take those in to your aunt and uncle, they can eat at the table," she said as she handed Roy the plates.

Uncle Sam was already at the table, licking his lips and rubbing his hands together as if it was cold. Heather got up from the couch and sat next to him followed by his Da, who first crushed out a fag and blew ash from his front. Roy returned to the kitchen along with John, George, and an eager Billy.

"Can we sit on the floor and watch the telly Ma?" asked John.

"No, you'll sit properly at the table here in the kitchen, the telly can wait. You can eat out of the paper."

"Is there any pop?" asked George.

"No. There's water in the tap."

She checked Billy's fish for bones and pleased to find none put it out for him. The other children dived into the remaining bag and with good natured pushing claimed their own paper wrapped meals. She took her own and William's along with a salt cellar and went into the living room, where the children could hear the conversation amidst the clash of knives, and forks scratching on plates.

"Equal rights!" Their father exclaimed to Sam. "What do we have that they don't? Is my house any different to those down the street? Have you seen all the new flats built in Divis and elsewhere, and who's moved into them?"

"You don't have to tell me William, anyway this civil rights carry on is no more than a front for Republicans, you look at some of the people in it and you just *know*!"

"Equal rights my arse! Did we have any more chance than them? What are we supposed to be, privileged or something? Shite!"

"The whingeing of that Devlin and Hume make me sick. We know what they really want and they'll not be getting it!"

In the kitchen the boys could tell their father was getting annoyed as he always did on this subject and so listened with more intent, not that they disagreed one inch. Roy looked at their kitchen with its drab grey and white walls, the sink and tiles and the wooden shelf along the opposite side, a framed picture of the Queen peering down amidst all the other porcelain and brass knick knacks. No, he didn't feel privileged. Their house was exactly the same as all the others. In between the scraping of forks and clink of stout bottles their Ma joined the conversation in a scandalized whisper.

"Do you know what some fool asked me the other week when I was watching a parade in the centre? I think he was English but, he asked me why we have these marches all the time. So I says to him, why shouldn't we? It's our land and our traditions and the sacrifices made for it should never be forgotten! They just don't understand us!"

"Well said Betty!" Heather supported.

They heard the TV being switched on and the aerial being moved about to an optimum position, and then their father shouted through.

"Boys, it's starting soon!"

There was a satiated sigh from Sam as he sat back and then winked at Heather. "Would you drive?" he asked. "I'm not on duty tomorrow so I fancy having a crack at William's whiskey as this is such a special night." Heather nodded her reply to him through a mouthful of cod.

A further ten minutes of frenzied eating, straining and pushing to digest the chips disposed of their fish suppers, Billy struggling with his, but being helped by George and John who gleefully took most of his chips. Billy's eyes widened and he began a piping complaint, shielding his food with his arms.

"They're mine! I'm not done yet!"

"Stop your slabbering, you eat too much anyway."

"That's right, did you not know that eating too much chips at your age is dangerous?"

"Aye, I heard of a wee boy of six who took a heart attack after his supper!"

Billy looked worriedly to Roy for enlightenment. He laughed and shook his head and began gathering up the greasy wrappers with their astringent vinegary smell. Their Ma entered carrying stacked empty plates, the few leftovers, mainly from Heather, piled on the top along with the cutlery. She scraped it into the bin just as William called through again.

"Leave the plates till later Betty!"

"No, I'll do them now, it's only a few."

The boys filed into the living room in order of age and height, Billy bringing up the rear. Already yawning surreptitiously, he sat on the floor in front of the TV whilst the others sat themselves down at the vacated dining table. They watched the BBC extended news coverage, brainy scientist James Burke explaining to the thick of the world what was happening and how. William left but hurriedly came back into the room with two glasses and a bottle of Black Bushmills. Sam looked up as he reached for an ashtray, one of the many brass and metal ornaments that festooned the house, bought mainly by the boys on Birthdays and Mother's Day. He waved vaguely at the television.

"You haven't missed anything. What's this? Black Bush' no less, thanks very much."

"None but the best for the peelers!" William said, pouring a hearty two fingers into each glass and adding water.

They watched in silence as the space capsule touched down at last to everybody's relief. Then amongst all the chatter, flickering grainy images and high pitched beeping the dramatic words: "The Eagle has landed."

A short distance away the McKenna family were watching the same images. Thomas had given the top of the TV the flat of his hand, not understanding the poor quality of the picture.

"Get away from there you wee tube, it's supposed to be like that!" Jimmy shouted.

"This picture's rubbish Da." Thomas wasn't satisfied and tapped the screen with a finger nail.

"Am I talking to myself here? Sit down. Anyway what should I do about it? Ring Cape Canaveral and say our Thomas isn't happy with the view, can you do another one?"

Everyone laughed including their father's mate Gerry Fox who had called round whilst Marty was out. Marty sat on the couch and turned to look at him, dark brylcreamed hair above chestnut brown eyes, his thin grim mouth now smiling. A big barrel-chested man, Marty noted he was also as hairy as a monkey as he looked at the matted dark hair on the back of his hands.

"Like another beer Gerry, or maybe something stronger?" his father asked.

"I'm in tomorrow, but aye, as you're offering... what do you have?"

"No White Shrub," said Jimmy, ignoring Eileen's groan. "But I do have some Jamieson."

Gerry's brow creased a second in puzzlement before understanding came and with a snort he said, "Fine Jimmy, thanks."

Without waiting to be told, Marty heaved himself from the sofa and went to the kitchen to fetch the green bottle placed on top of the wall cupboard, out of reach of small hands. Standing on a chair he leaned forward and arm outstretched took hold of the half full bottle. Nothing much seemed to be happening on the moon, so unsurprisingly the conversation turned to events nearer home.

"...and how many of us is there working in the shipyard? I read somewhere about one in fifty, and they say there's no discrimination? My hole!" Gerry started guiltily, "Eh...sorry Bernie."

"That's alright," she said. "It gets to me too sometimes, especially this time of year what with the marches going on and on. It's an insult to us, like saying to your neighbour every year, remember when we came and took your land, nice weather by the way. It's not on and high time we stood up for ourselves."

"Ah! The elixir of the Celts," said Jimmy. He poured small measures and smacked his lips. Bernie took a sip and Jimmy lit a cigarette.

"I'm all for civil rights," Gerry continued. "Why should we be second class citizens in our own country? The way some of them look at you too, especially this time of year, like you've just crawled out of cheese or something."

Marty noticed that the more they drank the further their arguments went, especially this past year or so since the campaign began. Marty agreed with every word though. He disliked the parades and the blood chilling din of the great big Lambeg drums.

The coverage continued to disappoint the expectant children. Rosemary had by now fallen asleep and was taken gently in both arms by her father upstairs. Thomas and Pat were yawning, Eileen was curled up with a magazine and only Marty followed the conversation. Jimmy came softly back down stairs to hear Bernie speaking of sacrilege.

"What have I done now?" he asked tiredly.

"I was on about eleventh night and all those damned bonfires, and sticking a dummy on top dressed as the Holy Father. It's shameful, dancing around it like a lot of heathens. It's not funny Jimmy, I'm serious!"

"I know, sorry love."

Bernie took another drink which was unusual, watched curiously by Marty and Eileen who had looked up from her glossy pages. Gerry was nodding dolefully as she spoke.

"My family fought and suffered for this country, who are they to come and turf us out of our homes, starve and kill us, divide the country in two?"

Bernie's voice had taken on an unusual sharp edge, almost as if she had personally witnessed the last several hundred years. Jimmy poured himself and Gerry another, but Marty noted wryly that he kept the bottle at his side this time. The TV gave another high pitched beep which jolted Patricia awake. Bernie finished her drink, adding with some finality.

"My father was right. There'll be no real change until that line is gone from the map."

Roy watched the grey and somewhat fuzzy pictures on the TV but listened as Uncle Sam and his father talked politics, now a little tipsy from several whiskeys.

"...to be ruled from Rome and told what to do by a load of work shy nuns and priests. Is that why our daddies fought and died in their thousands on the Somme? They'd turn in their graves if they could see what's happening."

Roy had a momentary image of thousands of bodies all turning in their graves in unison like some macabre synchronised dance. He only half stifled a burp of laughter, managing to catch and turn it into a strangled cough at his father's sharp suspicious glance.

"Any true Ulsterman would rather die William. Spouting a load of mumbo jumbo at a mass like they do down south? That's what they're really after mark my words, to push us into a united Ireland. I'm telling you that Clarke will have to go and all, compromise is just the first step down that road."

"We've paid thousands of lives to prove ourselves loyal, what more do we have to do? We're as British here as the Scots, Welsh or English. It's blood and that's that!"

"That's what I can't understand, if they hate it so much here why don't they just go? The border's not there to keep people in."

"Because they're better off here and know it. Not that you'll see one admit it."

Roy and Marty stayed up most of that night, waiting for Neil Armstrong to make his move in the early hours before the dawn. Whilst they watched TV they listened to the arguments and grievances of their parents, and their parents before them, going back a long, long time. They had heard it all before of course, but it seemed that the centuries old deep tribal hatreds were stirring, sounding fresher and every day more relevant. It was not just about a single line on a map, but lines drawn much closer to home as they were soon to find out. Going to bed exhausted at about eight in the morning, someone was clearly to be heard practicing on a drum despite the early hour. Roy and Martin drifted peacefully to sleep with the sound resonating faintly in their ears.

Chapter 2

Wired to the Moon

Two weeks later Roy went to visit his Granny in the Tiger's Bay district. Granny Janet was his only living grandparent and hadn't been well lately. For this visit it was just himself, his father and John. Stepping from the bus and walking into her street, Roy noted that his father seemed concerned yet also resigned, only putting on a cheerful front as they got to her door. He hesitated a second before entering, his face deliberately lightening before letting himself in with the spare key.

"Ma? Are you in?"

They trooped in behind him and went into the front room, which still had a slight smell of bird seed, despite the fact her last feathered friend had died months ago and travelled the same watery route as those before him, briefly mourned, but no emotion wasted on his funeral. A simple flush and he was away.

"Where else would I be the way I feel at the moment?" she answered in a shaky, breathless voice.

As he bent to kiss her in the armchair Roy was saddened to see how much she had deteriorated since his last visit. Her face seemed drawn, tired and white, the hairy mole on her chin prominent, and he could actually hear a sound like somebody gently using a bellows when she breathed. Only the eyes were still lively, sharp, and the same green as his own, smiling at him now, even if the mouth did retain its usual straight and unbending line. The TV was on but unwatched. George Best was being followed around the park by lots of beautiful girls who just couldn't resist the aftershave he was advertising. "Always the best for Georgie," a voice punned with feeble humour. William used Old Spice himself and turned the irritating rubbish off.

"Have you been eating right?" William asked, his face now serious with concern. "A pot of tea and sandwich won't be enough the whole day. Is Mrs Roberts still looking in regular?"

"Yes, she's just away. Don't fuss so William, I'll get by. I've been through two wars, and survived half the town wrecked by the Germans."

William laughed, thinking what she would say if he *didn't* fuss. He went into the scullery to put the ancient kettle on. "You weren't seventy nine then but, and anyway I was here too you know."

"Aye, you were just a boy in the last one, and you didn't see the misery the first war caused around here."

She looked at the old black and white photos sat on the cabinet as if expecting agreement, the people in them real flesh and blood to her, forever in colour, and then at the boys sat opposite her as if comparing. Roy and John had both heard the stories and liked them too; Granny told them so well. Whatever was wrong with her it wasn't her memory. Roy glanced at the photos. One contained his Grandfather whom Roy remembered vaguely as an old and upright gentleman in a shirt and tie, shouting in a croaky voice instead of speaking. He wasn't unkind, but his grandchildren were nervous of him, sensing how their father, who appeared to fear nothing was almost timid in his presence. In this sepia photo he was a young man, standing straight and alone in his uniform, rifle and bayonet in hand, staring out proudly from within the oval frame. In another he was in a group of soldiers smiling and standing at ease in various poses, before what was either a trench or a newly dug mass grave. Roy looked about the room with its cream wallpaper, ornaments that were dustier than he could ever remember, and large picture of the royal family. William came back in with a plate of scones.

"There was hardly a house around here that didn't lose someone or have them come back wounded and changed forever," she said. "Everyone did their duty, you couldn't not go! Your grandfather lost a brother, this after three years and becoming stone deaf on the Somme. They still sent him back to the front." She smiled tiredly at them, taking a proffered scone from William with trembling gnarled fingers that reminded Roy of thin white tree roots. "Your grandfather was lucky, he went through it all. Wounded, gassed, a metal plate in his head too, and then taken prisoner. He didn't like Germans to his dying day."

Roy wasn't surprised. He remembered the story of how his grandfather was taken captive as he found it quite funny: he had gone to sleep exhausted and woken up in the middle of a trench raid to find himself surrounded by laughing Germans, his comrades either fled or dead. He remembered his grandfather visiting once and giving a satisfied grunt as he trod on some plastic soldiers they were playing with. There was little damage; George soon straightened out the mini grey German spiked helmets. They let Gran talk on, while William brought tea and poured. John daringly interrupted her.

"Can we see the medals Gran?"

She nodded, putting the scone down uneaten. Pointing with a shaky blue veined hand to the dresser she said, "In that drawer John, at the back. You may as well take them with you later William, they're yours to pass down."

John opened the drawer and rummaged amongst the pills, pens and other assorted bric a brac. He took out three medals, still brightly polished and attached to their ribbons, and another in a clear plastic bag. He handed them to her and she held one aloft for all to see, a bronze disc with an angel on one side and some writing on the other, its ribbon a broad red stripe in the middle, bleeding into other colours of yellow, green and blue at the edge. The other was much simpler altogether, silver with its ribbon of blue and red vertical stripes giving off a smell of Brasso. Roy wished he owned them or better still had won them himself. The last was his favourite even though it wasn't British. It was an Iron Cross dated 1915, taken by his Grandfather as a souvenir and fortunately sent home for safe keeping before his own capture. It had been carefully preserved as it was found, even now the dried muck, clay and rusty blood adhered to the edges and tiny crevices; it had never been washed. His Gran spoke again, obviously glad to see them with the chance to talk, but looking at them with a puzzling intensity. Roy had the feeling she was trying to leave them more than just medals.

"Don't forget either when this was happening in France what was going on in Dublin, rebels stabbing us in the back. During the last war too, helping German spies and flashing to bombers and submarines from rooftops!"

Roy had a brief mental image of somebody in a raincoat exposing his moon whitened genitals at a passing U Boat Captain, or his arse to dumbfounded pilots flying overhead. His Gran peered at him as if she could read his disrespectful thoughts.

"I've seen a lot and I see what's happening now. Always remember, those who died for this country, over hundreds of years to preserve us and what we have as we are. Don't let your guard down. Ever!"

Roy and his father nodded and John shook his head, unsure which was the right movement. He nodded too.

A couple of days later Martin stood in his doorway talking with Brendan who had a new record. It was a Friday afternoon and the street was unusually quiet, hardly any children were playing outside even though the sun had come out and was rapidly drying the pavement. Martin saw a dark blue curtain twitch across the road a few doors down and a vague shadow move behind the netting. Mrs Henderson, the nosey old bag. Nothing better to do than watch the neighbours thought Marty, tempted to thumb his nose, but remembering his Ma's warning to them just recently about not provoking the neighbours; the Hendersons were one of the few Protestant families to live on their end of the street. Jimmy had added his own contribution, for once quite serious. "That's right, don't be pissing anyone off, there's a queer feel right now."

Marty knew what he meant. By this time in August with the marches all but over things were usually getting back to normal, but it felt different this year. Last week there had been a serious riot when a Protestant mob had tried to get at the Catholic Unity flats complex and a few petrol bombs had been thrown. He had heard all about it from Frankie Saunders who claimed he was there, constantly moving from one foot to the other as he excitedly described how bricks and bottles had flown through the air, and one of the peelers had took a stone to the mouth and spat blood on the ground. Frankie had proudly shown him a grazed knuckle, telling everyone how he had been in the fight. No one believed that part of it though, as Frankie was a weedy specimen with glasses, buck teeth and freckles that looked like a spray of shit had caught him square on. He reminded Marty of the school bully victim in the comics they used to read. He was also known as a terrible spoofer and when they were small he had told a gullible Marty that his father was the captain of the cruise ship *'Queen Elizabeth'*. Marty had enthusiastically passed this news on to his father, who instead of saying "Wow! Really?" had laughed until the tears ran down his face and he collapsed into his chair holding his sides, the laughter only increasing the more Martin stamped his foot insisting it was true. Other gems from Frankie included the ownership of a solid gold sword, the secret location of some buried Armada treasure and even a win on the pools, all this when he had holes in his grotty school jumper. Since then, Marty had been sceptical of Frankie, but true enough, this time there had been a real riot. As for the knuckles, he had probably just fallen over in his haste to get out of the way.

"Come inside and we'll play it now," said Marty, opening the door wider and glaring across the street. Bernie poked her head out from the kitchen.

"Hello Brendan, how is it with your Ma and Da?"

"They're fine thanks, Mrs McKenna."

Marty hustled him towards the stairs before his Ma asked something embarrassing as mothers always did.

"Would you like some tea and biscuits maybe?" she asked as Jimmy and Eileen came through the door.

"Aye, dead on!" Jimmy answered. Bernie ignored him, still looking at the boys, her face questioning.

"No thank you Mrs McKenna."

This was followed by the drumming of their feet on the stairs. Bernie watched as Jimmy carefully took his boots off, standing stork like. They were caked with dry muck from the building site. He battered them against the side of the doorstep.

"You're early home today. Why's that?" she asked.

"We finished off." Looking up he added reassuringly, "Not permanent, there's a good few months to go yet. Now how about those biscuits and maybe a tin of Harp as it's Friday."

Upstairs Marty took out Eileen's battered red cased record player from under the bed and plugged it in. It was a cast off from an aunt and getting old, the case was dented and the red plastic skin was peeling and scabby but it still played. Opening the lid Brendan handed him the record with a bow and flourish worthy of a royal courtier.

"Honky Tonk Woman!" said Marty enthusiastically.

"Yeh, I love it. Bugger the Beatles, there's no contest."

Marty put the record on and they listened to Jagger and the boys laying it off about exotic women in distant Memphis and exciting New York. By the third playing an audience had gathered in the doorway: Thomas, Eileen and Rosemary as usual holding her cuddly brown bear 'Boo Boo'. Nearing the middle the needle jumped and slid across the record with a horrible scratching sound causing Marty to leap to his feet in alarm.

"Shit!"

Rosemary stared at him accusingly, "Ma said we weren't to use swear words..."

"I know, I know." Marty smiled as he cut her off, his voice wheedling in tone. "I'm really sorry, I promise I won't do it again. I'll give you a couple of Fizzers next time I'm at the shop O.K?" She smiled back at him mollified. Marty put Jagger back on for yet another spin. Eileen watched them amused.

"Aye, you two had better watch out for them honky tonk women," she said.

"What's a tonky woman?" asked Rosemary, eyes wide and blue as Delft.

"A bad girl," said Eileen bending down to her.

"Do they go to church?"

"No Rosy," said Marty gently, and then remembering his own father didn't go that often either added hastily, "but it's not that makes them bad, they're just naughty..." He tailed off and looked to Eileen and altar boy Thomas for guidance. Just then their Ma called up the stairs for Rosemary and saved him from more awkward conversation. He put the 'B' side on. 'You Can't Always Get What You Want'.

"No you certainly can't Mick," sighed Eileen philosophically.

"I wish I didn't have to go to mass all the bloody time!" Brendan blurted suddenly.

Marty sympathised, thinking about his confirmation and having to wear a suit which would have been fine had it fitted. Confession was worst, and Brendan was probably thinking about this, both now at an age where they didn't want to confess all their sins, especially the sinful thoughts of the flesh. And even worse these last few years, actual deeds. Last time in the box Father Callaghan had seen through his attempts at concealment. He half wanted to tell him about the dirty book with its exciting nudes, but instead settled for revealing he had "wicked thoughts," to which Father Callaghan had paused significantly, and then knowingly asked if he had gone any further with these thoughts. He had, several times in the quiet of the toilet, but admitted to only once and received his penance with relief, knowing full well he would be having the same thoughts again by evening. He couldn't help it. He was growing up fast and it was a wonder the old man couldn't actually hear his hormones fizzing and crackling like a bowl of Rice Crispies on the other side of the confessional.

"You don't have to go at all when you're older," Marty told him, then laughed. "You can always change religion, and as my Ma says burn in the afterlife." This last she usually said whilst looking at their father.

"Protestants are lucky. They don't have confession. They have it easy so they do," Brendan continued gloomily.

Marty wasn't so sure about that, and reminded him of the one time they had seen some sort of Presbyterian preacher giving a sermon. Their curiosity had gotten the better of them and they had managed to sneak past a spellbound usher. The man had shouted like a scarlet faced Old Testament prophet, roaring and ranting hideously as if representing the torments of the damned himself. They had fled in terror.

"Imagine having him in the box with you," Marty laughed. "He'd probably hear your confession and then beat the shit out of you!"

Putting the record on a last time, Marty's mind drifted to his first 'ride' last month. He had yet to tell about that one, not that it had lasted long. Maureen Veroni had let him go the whole way. She was thin and spotty, with her father's Italian complexion and dark brown eyes, but she had one redeeming feature and that was a willingness to drop her knickers. She was so sophisticated too, having her own condom which she had rolled onto his eager knob whilst he tried to control his breathing. In and out, all of a minute and he was there, leaving him feeling weak, foolish and a little embarrassed at his rapid fire performance. She had asked him if it was his first time and he had reluctantly admitted this, surprised by her evident satisfaction that couldn't have been sexual. Anyway, he had done better the next time: Maureen was a year older in age and a world away in experience and Marty was a well endowed and keen student.

"Will you be telling all at confession?" he asked Brendan, who shook his curly head.

"I won't be mentioning last week at the fair, if that's what you mean. Any road it was you that did it."

Marty was momentarily confused before he realised what he meant. The previous week they had gone along the coast to a fairground and enjoyed a memorable day out. They had met a couple of girls of their own age and awkwardness, and as it obviously wasn't going anywhere Marty had pulled a stunt that left them both sick with laughter. Climbing down the sea wall one by one with a small hang and drop onto the sand below, Brendan had watched one of the girls hanging uncertainly. He gallantly answered her call for assistance by jumping up and pulling down her skirt, pants and all, her outraged shriek drawing attention to her bare bum before she dropped in a crimson faced heap. It wasn't this he was referring to however; that had been merely the first course of mischief. They had argued and baited the stall owners without respite and swiped candy floss before the day culminated at the rifle range. The prizes offered were crap, so Marty and Brendan had both shot at these with the weakened air rifles instead of the paper targets, claiming the sights were crooked. The proprietor, a fat and sweaty travelling woman had brayed a warning, so Marty had used his last pellet on her ample arse when she bent down to pick up a newly damaged toy. They had run for it as fast as they could, laughing hysterically all the way.

By the following Thursday evening a lot had happened. William Ferguson sat in growing disbelief, his fists clenched in anger as he watched the latest news bulletins. It seemed to be getting out of control. He fumed at the pictures.

"Bloody rebels!"

The latest round had begun in Londonderry when the Apprentice Boys march had been attacked with bottles, rocks and whatever else came to hand by a Catholic mob. The police had also been attacked, this time with prepared petrol bombs from the flats there, and hadn't been able to put the insurrection down. That was what it was. A full scale rebellion was starting, the police were stretched and the Special constabulary called out. The 'B'men were feared by the other side and with justification. The attendant hatred was to their own side of no account, they were their saviours and needed now. It had gone on all day yesterday and then that bugger in the Republic, Jack Lynch, had poked his long ministerial Fenian nose in, and sent the Irish army to the border to "help" with field hospitals; probably to aid injured criminals thought William bitterly, or for something more sinister. Even worse this afternoon, troops, actual British soldiers had been sent onto the streets, not to quell the rebels and put them in their place, but to protect the bastards. Betty unclasped her hands and summed up William's own view in one word, shaking her head and lighting up a Park Drive.

"Unbelievable."

Everyone had been aware of the growing tension, it was palpable. And where they lived there could be no ignoring it. Lately people from the other end had stopped talking and become withdrawn, avoiding their end of the street as much as possible. Rumours had been flying about all this week, one after the other. It was said there were to be further demonstrations here in Belfast to support the Londonderry riots. Sam had called around earlier that day with the latest news, none of it reassuring. He had sat wearily at the kitchen table and drank the proffered glass of water in a single gulp, his hands grimy and nails black rimmed. A smoky scorched smell reached Roy's nostrils as he put the empty glass down.

"I can't stop long," he said. Betty and Roy looked at his tired features, bags under his eyes and a fresh graze on his cheek.

"What's happening Sam? Look at the cut of you, are you alright?" Betty asked anxiously.

"Been on the go all night, did you not hear about it on the news?" he asked, blowing his cheeks out and shaking his head. "It's serious Betty, last night the station got attacked by a mob, stones, bricks, a few petrol bombs. We went as support and they even had to bring the armoured cars out. That mob was wired to the moon, insane. Someone even fired a few shots at the car too. Anyway, I've been hearing things and you'd better tell William to keep everyone indoors tonight." He got up to go, but seeing Betty with her hand to her mouth he put a comforting arm around her. "It'll be alright, we'll soon sort this lot out. Now, see you later."

Two friends of Roy's, Andrew Dartnell and Adam Oakley dropped by soon after, Dartnell wide eyed and having difficulty keeping his excitement in as he fidgeted and shifted about. Betty answered the door, peeping cautiously around as if the mob had come with torches lit.

"Is Roy there Mrs Ferguson?" they chorused politely.

"Not right now boys..."

Roy's head appeared from behind her and said, "Just for an hour Ma, back before you know it!"

Just then Billy smashed something in the front room and began a wailing apology and Roy used the timely distraction to make a getaway before Betty had time to react, torn between the two problems. He swerved past her, like George Best with a half witted defender, waving and moving fast along the street, knowing full well even now his Ma wouldn't be so common as to bawl at him in public. Stay at home today and miss the excitement? Hardly.

William came back early, looking as worried as anyone could remember. He just had time to pick Billy up and give him a twirl that made him giggle high pitched and listen to Betty telling him of Sam's visit when there was someone at the door. Jackie Grant and Graham Campbell stood there, all dour gravity which seemed to suit Graham with his heavy bulldog features and bushy eyebrows. He removed his hat, revealing a head so bald and pink it looked like he had a shower cap on. William greeted them, waiting for one to speak, knowing which it would be.

"All right William? Have you heard we've been getting a community defence together?" said Jackie, pushing his fair hair back. "After what's happened in Londonderry and up near Ardoyne last night, we need to prepare ourselves."

"That's right, that smoke this morning was the show room, the only one of *ours* on the Falls going up." Graham waved an arm. "I've heard too that they've guns been taken out and it might be our turn tonight. You're ex military as are a few of the boys who're doing the organising. We'll be meeting at the garage around seven, O.K?"

It wasn't really a question and one wouldn't have been necessary anyway. William nodded his approval.

"Right!"

A little later, Roy came home breathless as groups of people gathered on corners and in little knots at opposite ends of the street. He had noticed a couple of boys collecting all the milk bottles they could lay hands on, dragging them in a small cart in the Shankill direction. George was eager for news, not having been nimble enough to avoid his Ma, and interrogated a slightly flustered Roy upstairs. John was listening with half an ear whilst playing soldiers with Billy, the various plastic mini platoons strewn over the bedroom floor.

"Adam was telling me he heard there was going to be trouble, maybe rioting round here tonight," Roy said heatedly as he leaned forwards cross legged on the bed.

"In our street you mean? How - who from, I mean who told him that?" George asked impatiently.

"From the Falls end, they might want to come up this street. I heard some places were attacked last night on the Shankill. Trevor McMaster was telling me the taigs are looking for trouble. There's already barricades going up in some places. I saw lots of people on the way home, we're getting ready so we are."

"D'ye think Da will let us help?" George asked hopefully, gulping. "I mean, this is it!"

Roy shrugged but doubted it. He watched his younger brothers playing with what had once been his favourite toys: grey plastic German infantry against green British, lots of miniature figures locked in a variety of action poses, firing rifles and machine guns and chucking grenades. There were even a couple of figures carrying a stretcher between them, forever and ever. He noticed with a smile that Billy didn't discriminate and had some Japanese soldiers in there and even a few Romans with swords. The ones he had personally always liked best were the green parachutists that even had a little drop box in the packet. John rolled a six. That was a kill and he cheered as he flicked over one of Billy's men. Billy tried to retaliate, but could only manage a one and therefore a second go, a two, nothing. Both boys watched, thinking about the coming evening, as Billy and John killed each other off one by one.

Jimmy and Bernie sat at the kitchen table later that evening, meal eaten, the washing up done and children safely indoors. They spoke quietly, like two people in a sick room. Jimmy hesitantly raised the subject on his mind.

"With the way things are it might be an idea for the kids to go and stay with our Niall for a while, what do you think?"

Niall was Jimmy's brother and only near relative who had room enough, or truth be told, was willing enough to put up a lot of children. A large friendly bear of a man who lived alone in wholly Catholic Andersontown to the west of the city, with a good job in the housing executive. Bernie sighed and lit a fag without answering.

"It's not something I want either," he continued, "but it's only for a wee bit, say till they go back to school. A couple of weeks at the very most, this nonsense will be over before then but."

"Have you asked him?"

"I have. He's fine about it. It's only for a wee while mind, we can make it a sort of holiday even." Jimmy tried to sound enthusiastic, but his smile was wavering before it was fully formed.

Bernie didn't know Niall as well as Jimmy of course, but what she did know was favourable. She liked him and the fact he liked the same things she did, an older more serious version of her husband. She was also impressed by his having a good job and felt some sympathy at his losing his wife so young and never remarrying. The times they had seen him he was always good natured and was very fond of Jimmy and the children too.

"Alright then, we'll see how it goes. Only if we must but."

William had gone at the appointed time and left strict instructions nobody was to leave the house that evening. He had emphasised this by looking everybody individually in the eye, lingering on Roy and George a second longer. He was worried, but personally didn't think matters would get too bad. They would be safer just staying indoors and letting the men protect the area, if it at all came to that. Not that it would. Of course not. This wasn't some banana republic, this was Britain.

For most of the day groups had been forming in various parts of the city, seemingly coming spontaneously together, fuelled by rumour and growing larger and more vocal in the gathering darkness. There had been incidents here and there, which became exaggerated and added to the general fear and anxiety now gripping both communities. In streets like their own, running roughly from the Protestant Shankill to the Catholic Falls it was particularly tense, both sides seeing any move in their direction as an enemy incursion to be repelled and righteously punished. A large crowd had congregated at both ends by dusk, leaving the middle of the street an empty no man's land.

It was dark in their bedroom except for a soft, orange strip of light where the curtains didn't quite meet. Billy and John were already asleep. John had to be threatened. Billy had merely yawned and nodded off without protest. There was shouting and catcalls outside, but as yet nothing serious. Roy and George cautiously poked their heads out of the window, looking first one way, then the other. Some doors were open and figures could be dimly seen, all watching, waiting.

"Rebel bastards! Fuck the Pope ye taig scum!"

Something rang out, a metallic tinkling on the pavement as a handful of big bronze pennies were thrown. It was the same as what had been done elsewhere, the insult was clear and the response the same.

"Orange bastards! Fuck you and your Queen!"

A first stone flew through the air at the Protestant side, followed as if this was the cue for the opening by tens, then hundreds of assorted missiles. A lot of the dark blobs at windows disappeared, Roy and George merely pulled back a little to watch the show. It was still a way off, their own side with their backs to them, no sight of their father as yet.

The two crowds slowly converged on each other in order to get a better aim, at first hesitantly, but then seeing nobody yet down or hurt, a little faster. The noise had become terrific, shouting, thuds and crashes mixed with higher pitched screams, squeals, clinking and smashing of bottles. A rock hit a metal post with a dull hollow clang, and then clearly audible came a first shout of pain as a stone hit home. Footsteps sounded rapidly on the stairs.

"Get away from that window!" Betty shouted. Seeing she had her coat on Roy looked questioningly at her. "I am not going anywhere," she said. "Just keep away from the window."

She gently picked up Billy, holding him tightly to her chest as he mumbled in sleep and took him to her own room. They both went back to the window, just in time to see the first petrol bomb flash through the air and crash with a 'whumph' near the head of the enemy line, figures jumped and scampered out of the way as a cheer went up from their own side. A second was thrown and several more returned, crossing each other on their way. Crude missiles and hatred filled the air. A new sound now was the breaking of windows, and in the distance the first sirens could be heard.

Just as it was getting dark, Jimmy and Marty spoke with some of the guys on the corner. They reckoned there was going to be trouble and were getting prepared. No Orangeman, peeler or 'B' Special bastard would come down their street and set foot in the Falls this night. They watched what 'preparations' actually meant with acute interest. A barricade was being assembled using whatever came to hand, and milk and lemonade bottles were being carefully filled with a mixture of petrol and sugar. Marty asked what flavour they were making, and then if they'd got the deposit on the bottles, causing the men to smile grimly without looking up from their labours. He looked at the white Tate and Lyle bag with its comic cartoon sugar cube on the front.

"Why the sugar?"

"So it's the correct *sweetness* eejit," said Jimmy with mock emphasis. "No, actually, sugar makes it burn better."

"Aye," said one of the men with a wicked grin. "It makes it stick better too."

Jimmy rubbed his chin and nudged Marty to move on, his Da now deep in thought as they walked home, debating what was best to do; it appeared to be more serious than he had first imagined. A crowd was gathered a few doors down from their home. They couldn't see past the press but knew that there was by now a similar throng at the opposite end. Jimmy came to a decision.

"I'll ask your Ma if she feels like going to our Niall's tonight."

The missile throwing had been going on for some time, the air stinking of petrol with an early tang of smoke. Bernie had been outside with Jimmy to assess whether it was safe to move and was nearly hit by half a house brick. It came over the mob just up from her door and missed her head by a whisker, bouncing with a dull thud as it hit the road and skidded away. She had felt it pass though and that decided her.

"In! In! We'll have to wait a bit until this dies down."

Stopping briefly to look around, Jimmy could already see several windows broken, including the Henderson's, but as there were no lights on he assumed they must have gone. More people were coming from the Falls direction to swell their numbers, some carrying sheets of corrugated iron between them and others with a variety of makeshift weapons. Bats, hurley sticks, pieces of piping and even one with a sledge hammer for breaking up the paving slabs. Jimmy noticed the rolling gait and bulk of Gerry Fox in amongst them just as he ducked indoors.

Bernie was already upstairs, urgently getting a few belongings together in their old brown musty suitcase, haphazardly throwing in clothes. Marty and Eileen were at the window, watching fascinated at the drama being played out before their door, light from the small fires on the street flickering dimly on their faces. "Get the others dressed to go!" Bernie shouted. "We'll wait for it to calm down then..."

Above the roaring outside there was a nearer sound of smashing as their front window came in. Bernie's hand went to her mouth and Jimmy went down the stairs three at a time to see the damage. Eileen grabbed clothing and shooed Patricia, wee Rosemary with 'Boo Boo' and a laggard Thomas into the back bedroom facing the yard. At the window Marty was joined by his mother who watched in disbelief, both hands now to her cheeks, as her own street became a battlefield.

The opposing mobs had come closer, the din even worse but improbably from time to time the shrilling of a flute could be still be heard. As they watched, a man from the other side stepped out with what looked like a round shield, in fact a dustbin lid. Fending off a rock that clanged against it, he then turned and like an over dressed Olympian spun it through the air like a monstrous discus to shouts and cheering. It clashed noisily against the corrugated iron fencing which was being held as a shield, and that seemed to send their own side mad as they began advancing behind the ridiculous yet effective cover. Stones were still being flung by the dozen and petrol bombs too. Small fires were everywhere, on the street and up walls where the fuel burned in golden vertical lines. They heard Eileen scream from the other room just as Jimmy came bounding back up the stairs.

"Holy Fuck!" he shouted on seeing a pool of fire in his own back yard. Another flaming topped bottle came over the wall but fortunately didn't hit the house, having been thrown blind.

Bernie stood mesmerised. Marty felt Thomas by his side pushing to get a better view. There were now a few people sitting or sprawled against houses, obviously hurt and receiving rudimentary first aid. Bernie came out of her trance, the fighting had moved further up the Protestant end.

"Jimmy! There's people need help there, bring them in!" she cried.

"They're not the only ones," he said, his footsteps again on the stairs. The door opened and the noise of human shouts and weird clanking increased momentarily.

At the other end of the street Roy, watched with his nails digging into his palms as he saw the bastards getting closer, looking as if they were winning. George leaned out and screamed a nearly incoherent "Bastards!" before Roy pulled him back in. A petrol bomb hit one of the corrugated fences and flames spread at their feet, making them shuffle about and dance to avoid the hot little tongues that licked at their ankles. "Yes!" he heard himself shout as if at a goal. Then they saw the first police arrive, armed with batons and shields, some 'B' men amongst them; Roy half expected to hear a cavalry bugle. With renewed cheers and vigour they surged forwards towards the opposition, Roy noticing some of the uniformed figures also stooping to pick up rocks. There was a rumbling whine and an armoured car appeared behind them. They gave way and it eased through towards the Catholic line which visibly wavered before the shields were dropped and the line disintegrated into fleeing knots of men, some heading back, others to the side, out of the way of the pursuing vehicle. The battle now became more vicious and hand to hand, the street filled with groups of baton and club wielding men, retreating towards the Falls end.

Jimmy had taken towels and dabbed ineffectually at head wounds as best he could but felt useless. He heard the shouting and fighting getting closer again, and a few people jogged past him looking back as they did so. He realised what was happening, stepped on a discarded pipe that twisted his ankle, but still managed to sprint the short distance to his own door, banging it shut and breathing hard. Upstairs Marty and Eileen watched with relief, which quickly turned to dismay at what was now unfolding before their terrible window box office seats.

A group of men stood directly below. The armoured car ignored them and swept past. Another group followed the car and came running at them with berserk screams, faces savagely contorted, mouths open and hair flying. The others braced to meet them, backs to the wall with one foot forwards, fists and clubs ready. Marty watched a running flying figure, the blue check lining of his jacket flapping open like a hungry bat as he sprang, kicking at chest height. With a sickening thud a man went down. Like wolves, several others immediately gathered round the prone writhing figure, trying to get their own kicks in. One of these was punched hard to the head and another received a heavy blow from a club across the small of his back, dropping him like a limp rag. The man with the club was swinging it wildly, two handed like a medieval knight on crusade, screaming noise but no words. A dull red brick to the back of the head felled him. Two men by the house opposite seemed to be doing an imitation of a playground dance, both having tight hold of each other by the collar, swinging around and around as they sought to throw their opponent to the ground by sheer momentum. Marty watched the helplessness of one lad in cold horror as he was caught in a headlock and repeatedly punched in the face before his howling, victorious assailant changed grip, both hands now holding him down by the collar, enabling him to kick savagely at his stomach. Another figure moved crablike rapidly on his back, legs flailing out, hands cut by broken glass, desperately trying to ward off his attackers, and now Marty could see even by this light the blood on the faces and on the ground. Individuals were leaping and hacking at each other, grunting with their efforts to hurt and maim.

It took less than a few frantic violent minutes before the mob moved on, leaving half conscious, battered and bleeding men breathing harshly where they lay. A new sound was then added to the night, sounding near the end of the street and heard clearly above the noise. A louder, sharper crash which was repeated almost immediately as someone fired a shotgun. More shots rang out and people began to scatter, into houses where possible, or just into the doorways, taking cover as best they could. There was a brief lull and then a harder crack, then two more as a nervous policeman opened up. The sounds of gunfire could now be heard all around. The sky was becoming illuminated as around the city the pain of their own street was replicated and one by one the houses began to burn.

Roy wanted desperately to go and join in, he could see figures moving about but uneasily thought of his father's command. He stayed put, he and George and now John joining in the excited discussion of what they had seen. They heard their own back door slam shut and the voices of men speaking loudly, and with relief they heard their father's joining in. Roy went downstairs as William's voice barked orders.

"Bring him onto the couch there! Easy now. Betty, go and fetch a towel. Now!"

Betty stopped staring and moved quickly, ignoring Roy who had come to the doorway. On the couch he could see a stranger. Another man, whom he recognised despite his dirty black face as Jackie Grant, was putting cushions under one of his legs, raising it higher and provoking a hiss of pain. Beneath the streaks of grime the stranger was as grey as the pavement he had just been lifted from, his broken nose the same red hue as the half brick that had come out of the shadows to hit it with such violent force. Roy looked properly at the leg, the brown trousers rolled up to the knee, the bunched cloth wet and dark and he could clearly see a grouping of small blackish holes in the shin, each one leaking and dribbling blood onto the cushions. His Ma came in with a large green bath towel. William took the towel and wrapped it tenderly round the shotgun wound. Jackie spoke as if to a sick child.

"You'll be alright there Davy, just a flesh wound so it is. Somebody is getting a car now, we'll have you in the hospital in no time."

Roy looked at his father who was fully occupied and took the opportunity to step outside. There was rubble, pieces of wood, bin lids, glass and battle debris strewn everywhere. Strangely enough it also appeared to be getting light, but then he realised with a shock that this was entirely due to the fires. He caught the smell of burning, there was a hell of a lot of smoke in the air and he saw with a thrill, houses further along on fire, the windows open, flames reaching higher and higher as he watched. He looked above the houses and noticed a glow, but not from street lights. No, the sky was beginning to resemble their Ma's picture on the stair landing; distinctly reddish. Roy leaned back against his front door and wondered if his Granny had seen it the same in her time.

The noise of fighting had passed further up to the very end of the street, now replaced by loud crackling, crashing and a tinkling of glass as more houses went up. The McKenna's could still hear shouting outside, but it was now more controlled. They gathered in the kitchen, apart from Marty who was told to watch upstairs with the light out and Eileen in the back room doing the same. They waited to see what further horrors the night would bring. They had packed their few valuables, money tucked away, each carrying what was precious to them. With a bit of luck they hoped it was over. Bernie was quietly praying.

"There's people coming up the street!" Marty shouted.

There was a banging on the door which made them jump. Rosemary didn't know what was going on, but was instinctively aware that this was danger and so held Jimmy's arm tighter.

"Youse have ten minutes to get out," a vaguely familiar voice spoke loudly. "We want you gone from here and that means for good!" Other voices joined in.

"Out you Fenian bastards!"

"Get out, now! We'll have no more taigs round here, we'll have it clean and Protestant!"

These last words were accompanied by cruel laughter and jeers and Bernie knew instantly that some had been drinking and were probably all the nastier for it. Marty and Eileen came down the stairs, just in time to hear a shouted, "Ye drunken eejit! Don't!" from outside, immediately followed by the now familiar crash, tinkle and whoosh of a petrol bomb. This time it was louder because it was in their own front room; the window already gone, futile slack curtains still closed, it became an inferno in a matter of seconds. Bernie put her hands to her head, standing stock still as she glimpsed their life built up over years being destroyed before her eyes. Marty reacted first, quickly shutting the front room door and with his Da, pushing everybody out of the back door. They emerged into the back alley with the sounds of their own home cracking and spitting. Once they were safely outside into the smoky throat tickling air, they each began to see the enormity of what was happening. They were silent apart from Patricia and Thomas who were weeping quietly. Eileen, Bernie and Jimmy stood open mouthed. Rosemary and Marty showed less emotion. Marty stared bleakly, his fists clenched painfully tight, his eyes reflecting the excited flames as a hot scorched breeze blew on his face, a uniquely Irish Sirocco. Rosemary had lost 'Boo Boo' and her face was blank as an unwritten page.

A day later the remaining residents of the street walked about, some of them clearly shocked, seeing for the first time the extent of the damage. It was as if a tornado had swept through the area: bricks, stones, broken glass and piping lay everywhere, the whole of the Catholic end was gutted, the fires not quite satiated and still smouldering, the windows no more than blackened eye holes. Twisting pillars of smoke still pierced the grey overcast sky. Two of their own homes had been lost totally as the fires spread along the terraced houses before being contained. William shook his head slowly to his wife, their own house was also damaged but not badly, the door a bit the worse for wear and one window through, but new glass and a lick of paint would do the trick. Not so for others.

"What a mess, it's got way out of hand," he said.

Betty was surveying the street and shoeing a thrown brick to one side and said with surprising bitterness, "That's all they deserve the likes of them, they started this so they did!"

"Betty, I heard there are people dead. Really. Dead." He repeated it tiredly as if convincing himself. "Five, six, I don't know how many but..." He raised his hands and then dropped them, unable to express himself adequately. "I'll tell you this. There's going to be change."

Later that afternoon change marched down the street, incredibly with rifles ready, steel helmets on and bayonets fixed. Roy and his family were watching along with almost everyone else as the soldiers marched in step to shouted commands, past the gutted buildings, faces to the front but eyes flicking to left and right, disbelief on some faces and disgust on others. They stopped, boots crashing down in unison. Order had come to the city.

The next day Bernie, Jimmy and Marty came all the way from Andersontown to see if there was anything left to salvage from their home, leaving the children under Eileen's supervision. There were soldiers everywhere, blackened buildings, barricades on the main thoroughfares and smoke in the air. There was little traffic; Belfast was in a state of shock. Approaching their street they actually had trouble recognising it. They found their own burnt house and looked at it numbly, knowing it had been a wasted journey. It was still standing as were most of the others, but they were no longer homes; gutted by fire, no door, no windows and in some cases no roof. Mere brick shells. Marty looked at the empty oblong window spaces, the edges like the doorways an alternate white and red brick checker design, now ugly and smoke blackened. He saw the same effect above every opening, black and scorched where the fires had burst outwards and upwards. The smell was horrible: burnt plastic, burnt wood, burnt wiring and hot metal. The stairs were gone, and a few charred heavy beams leaned at all angles. Jimmy went in for a closer look, glass cracking and scrunching underfoot. He shook his head slowly and carried on through what used to be the kitchen to the yard, stumbling over a beam and dirtying his hands on the crackle glazed blackened wood. He came back out and Marty noticed he had a slightly singed and dirty 'Boo Boo' in his hands. Bernie half laughed and cried at the same time as she took it from him. A voice called out to them provokingly.

"How's *that* for a Cookstown sizzle!"

It was Mrs Henderson standing just inside her doorway, large white apron and slippers on, fat arms crossed, head high with an expression on her fat face as if her finger had just gone through the toilet paper. She was a large woman who appeared at first glance not to have breasts at all but rather one single huge bosom, like a proud and enormous pigeon. Marty took a step towards her, face stiff and white with rage before his father grabbed him tightly with a shake of his head. He gave his son a gentle slap to get his attention and avert the hot stare to himself. Other people had stopped and were watching.

"Come on, there's nothing. Let's go, leave that bitch," he whispered urgently to his son. As they were leaving Bernie turned and said mildly but loud enough for Mrs Henderson to hear.

"I'm not from Cookstown." Then aside to Marty she hissed fiercely, "Never forget this! D'you hear me. Ever!"

Chapter 3

Poles Apart

Martin awoke slowly on this summer morning. It was already warm, and mundane sounds floated up from below. There was a banging and scraping of chairs, voices, Pat and Thomas arguing, his Ma admonishing and his Da passing various cheerful comments. The sizzling of rashers made him flare his nostrils like a Bisto kid as he stretched pleasurably, thinking how good it was to have his own bed at last and not have to share with Thomas. It was a narrow camp bed, and although he still had his younger brother in the room, it was a luxury none the less. And now they also had a tiny extra room, the partition probably not part of the original building but welcome. The girls shared a bunk bed on the other side and Eileen had the box room. Their parents slept in the front bedroom.

Marty put his hands behind his head and reflected that it was nearly two years since their move. Uncle Niall had been grand and put them up as best he could, but none of them had been happy in their short stay there. The place was pretty big but had a frugal untidy feel, obviously a single man's abode, having long before lost the female touches that made it a home. To their good fortune, within a few weeks they had somewhere else. Niall, using his job with the housing executive had found a vacated house in the New Lodge; there were quite a few vacant houses around this time, but not so many in Catholic areas. This one had been left intact by a Protestant family who no longer felt safe there. It wasn't the nicest of areas, but at least it was a house and not one of the dire flats of the district, which according to Jimmy were twelve stories of stacked shite, designed of course by people who wouldn't have to live in them. It was simply a case of moving in and taking physical possession of the place. At first it had been rough going, but bit by bit Jimmy and Bernie had filled the emptied house with whatever furniture they could lay hands on, Niall always on hand to help physically and morally with his bear like physique and cheerful mien.

Gradually, family life was restored to something approaching normal which was more than could be said of Belfast. As if to emphasize this Marty heard a helicopter droning faintly in the distance, a common sound now as the conflict grew steadily more violent. Things had changed beyond belief and were getting worse. The Brits, who at first were welcomed, were now seen for what they were: an army of occupation who shot unarmed men, searched and ruined homes, and were accordingly hated with a very Irish passion. They had their own army now, even if it was split into Provisionals 'Provo's', and Officials 'Stickies', who bravely engaged the Brits more and more in gun battles on these very streets. The first soldier to be shot dead was on the next road to their own in February, and Marty remembered the intensity of the shooting, the noise of British rifles cracking, and their own lads replying with an assortment of weapons from another age, but as lethal as ever.

Another sound that was becoming familiar was that of explosions, small blast bombs in riots, and larger devices left in the centre, the crump of which could be heard even at this distance. Marty was fully behind the Republican movement, preferring the more traditional 'Provo's to the left leaning 'Stickies' despite the fact that an intense looking Che Guevara had pride of place on his wall.

Marty took part regularly in the by now almost ritual rioting, starting mainly after school, with a short break for a hurried tea, that took place in the New Lodge itself and on the borders of Protestant areas such as the adjacent Tiger's Bay. The usual pattern was that he and others would form a crowd and throw stones at the Protestants who had formed up for the same purpose a short distance away. Eventually, soldiers would be deployed carrying riot shields and batons, sometimes wearing gasmasks which gave them a scary look like something out of Dr Who. The stoning would switch to the soldiers, who would duck behind their shields in Roman legionnaire fashion and fire rubber bullets, CS gas or sometimes make a charge to try and arrest some slow individual and give him a thumping. Marty hated the gas, dreading the long twisted ribbon of white smoke as the canister dropped from the sky, hitting the ground and spreading out in a puffy harmless looking cloud. The first time he took a good whiff he had been blinded by tears, his eyes stinging and then as it reached his lungs he had coughed until he was sick, the pavement receiving his tea and toast. They didn't seem to be using it as much nowadays, preferring rubber bullets instead, which at best were extremely painful and at worst could kill.

Marty had lately seen more IRA volunteers around, sometimes using the cover of the crowd for a quick pop at the Brits and good on them. The first time he had seen an armed IRA man in their street Marty had been nervous, but this soon passed to curiosity and then admiration, especially when he noticed the way some of the girls went for them. They were real live local heroes and he wanted to be a part of them. He was only dissuaded by his parents.

Getting up, Marty grabbed his jeans, checking the pockets and counting his money. No notes of course, in all a massive total of thirty five and a half new pence. He looked at the bright new decimal coins introduced just a few months ago, flipping them on his palm: a half penny, a couple of two's, a penny and three nickel ten pence pieces, all of them with crowns in their various designs and her fucking majesty on the front. He put the jeans on and the cherry coloured Ben Sherman shirt his latest girlfriend Roisin liked so much. She was pretty enough and much to his conceit had refused the attentions of some of the other lads, but he was still adolescently sensitive about her having a cast in one eye.

He followed the delicious bacon smell downstairs. Everyone was in the kitchen, bar Eileen who had already gone out to see her mysterious new boyfriend. Marty however had recently recognised him as he hurried up the street with another man before ducking into a house, both armed with vintage looking rifles. Thomas and Patricia were squabbling again as he took a chair. Jimmy looked up from his *Irish News* and rapped Thomas over the head with it as he addressed Marty.

"You're up then. Bit early is it not? Did you shit the bed?"

His Da had been at home a lot recently, work was harder to come by and so he was now on the 'Bru'. Marty watched his Ma turning streaky rashers over.

"Is that for me?" he asked, helping himself to bread.

In reply Bernie put a plate of bacon in front of him swimming in grease, which he dipped the bread into, after carefully filling it with the bacon strips and a dollop of ketchup from a gluey, red crusted bottle. He winked at Rosemary, who smiled back showing her missing baby teeth before going to the living room taking her bear with her. For weeks after their flight Rosemary had been a cause of worry on top of everything else; she had hardly spoken, had nightmares and wet the bed much to the discomfort of Patricia who woke up damp and complaining alongside her. With a child's resilience and acceptance she had slowly returned to her normal self however and even renamed 'Boo Boo', who given the smell that stubbornly clung to his fur was now appropriately called 'Smokey Bear.'

Marc Bolan crooned seductively about Hot Love from the radio and Marty thought of his last appearance on Top of the Pops, dressed top to toe in silver. Jimmy had rechristened him too: 'The Tinfoil Tube' which was only slightly better than "Who's that poof?" Bernie sat down, poured a cup of tea and lit a Park Drive, eyes narrowing through the smoke as she picked up the discarded paper and read.

"About time too," she nodded mildly.

She was referring to the moderate SDLP pulling out of the Stormont parliament. Two men in Derry had been shot dead by the army; no fuss, no enquiry. His parents confused him. They would get as angry as any other Nationalist but kept out of the conflict as much as they could, or were allowed to. It was especially strange considering his Ma's background. His father was more interested in the everyday practical things in life and always had been, so he understood that. Their reaction last week when he said he was thinking of volunteering had surprised him. Jimmy had shot an angry look at Bernie and they had then spent an hour persuading him to stay on at school. His father had spoken first.

"We know it's not easy son, what with all this going on, but you're still young. Things will change, believe me."

"That's right Marty, I'm proud that you want to fight for your country but please, there are other ways. You've the brains to go on and do something, there's more than one way of fighting back," his mother added.

"But I ..."

"Please son, don't. Not yet. Get yourself an education and a good living. Don't be ending up like me."

"There's plenty of time to join the struggle if that's what you have to do, but you don't have to pick up a gun to do it."

Marty had friends who were in the 'Fianna' or junior IRA, running errands and helping out, doing their bit. Frankie Saunders for example and Brendan too. Sometimes he felt guilty at their lack of activity. Lots of people were on a rent strike, known locally as 'Rent spent', but not his parents. She also never joined in the so called 'hen patrols' of local women to keep check on the Brit patrols and give them grief using whatever means they could. Come to think of it, he couldn't imagine his Ma using foul language, spitting abuse or saliva. He had even seen one woman hurling what looked like a sodden nappy from close range, and getting punched straight in the face for her trouble. No, she despised that sort of thing, but he knew she was Republican to her bones and hated the state she lived in and had not a shred of sympathy for the enemy. He had eventually been persuaded, reluctantly, but he still took part on the fringes, feeling that rioting was the least he could do.

Jimmy interrupted his thoughts as he poured another cup of tea. "Oh, I meant to tell you, that wee girl called for you earlier, you know, the one with her eyes at ten to two."

Five streets and a world away Roy had also just awoken, hot and sweaty after a weird dream featuring Jim Morrison, his Uncle Sam and himself twirling a baton at the head of a parade. The dream had taken a mad turn when he realised he was nude and Morrison had given him a flag to cover himself which turned out to be an Irish tricolour. He had then been promptly arrested by a grimly disappointed Sam.

Roy allowed himself a rueful relieved chuckle, his eyes focusing on the Glasgow Rangers poster on the wall, most of the team with fashionably long hair and sideburns. His ears picked up the sound of wings whistling and whirring outside. He glanced out of the window and watched two doves mating on the roof opposite. One hopped on the other and pecked away and Roy thought about last month and his first time. Her name was Laura, and she wasn't the typical 'Shankill Milly' whose usual first greeting would be "Shew us yer cack wee lad!" No, Laura was nice and gentle and had fancied him since they moved here a couple of months ago. She had become popular in recent years despite the fact her family was known for their less than clean house; her mother was slovenly, unwashed, unkempt and provided the neighbours with a good gossip. They were the local flea bags, only Laura developing into a pretty girl with long, light brown hair, grey eyes and a cute little upturned nose. She also had a good pair of tits, which Roy had groped in wonder as the nipples became as hard as his own cock bulging awkwardly in his jeans. The first time of course had been a non event, a lot of fumbling, heavy breathing, strange smells, wet fingers and his own quick coming. He had barely got it in. She didn't say much after but Roy didn't care, he felt great that he had at last done it.

He yawned expansively, poking his head out and seeing along the street the now familiar cranes of Harland and Wolf in the distance, silhouetted against some puffy white clouds. This house had been his Granny's, who had died recently leaving it empty. His parents had decided some time before when it became obvious she was dying, to move in here; with the way things were, with large parts of the city's population in periodic flux nobody was going to object. William was practical about it. Moving to the middle of Tiger's Bay was nearer to work for one thing, and their own street had become a shithole, even with a barrier sealing it off from the Falls. In reality this was pretty porous and the house had had windows smashed regularly, the sounds of rioting and drifting tear gas horrible daily reminders they were living but a short distance from a Republican ghetto. Subconsciously it was a move home for William. He had been raised here and it felt and surely was safer for them all.

There was little sound from downstairs. The radio was on of course as his Ma liked to keep up with the news and listen to music whilst doing the housework with a pink feather duster and hoover. The radio at the moment was just finishing a Doors number, one of several in tribute to Jim Morrison who had died last week. His father and George were both at work, George being fixed up with a job alongside his Da. The local news came on and Betty stopped to listen: a soldier of the Parachute regiment had been shot dead the previous day in Andersontown, there had been several bomb attacks overnight, a robbery of a post office, and other serious disturbances in several towns throughout the province. The sort of news that was becoming commonplace these last six months or so. Betty resumed her dusting of the cabinet and the black and white photos, now mingling with a few coloured ones of the family. She looked up as Roy stopped to greet her a good morning on his way to the kitchen.

"Good morning yourself young man. What do you have on for today, what's left of it that is?"

"Nothing."

Nothing was about right. School out, exams done and now he had to wait on the results to see what his options were. Probably more schooling and then Uni with a big fat grant with any luck. After that, Roy had a vague idea of joining the RUC, or maybe the Army, maybe even as an officer or something.

He opened the bread bin and took out a couple of slices, stuck them under the grill and looked around for the butter dish, pursing his lips in irritation on discovering it was all but gone, with only a few ridges and dabs of yellow at the bottom. He angled the knife and scraped away, getting enough for one thin coat on the bread. Chewing his toast, Roy thought about things in general. Listening to the radio he knew from firsthand experience what "serious disturbances" meant. What a typically posh BBC term. If in the mood, one could go along to a serious disturbance anytime one chose, usually at the border with the Catholic New Lodge area, where one could throw stones at one's enemy, hopefully causing serious injury to the objectionable swarming Fenian trash that inhabited said area. He and George had been to a few riots, but careful not to let their father know, as he would go absolutely mad if he found out, the thought of the consequences keeping them both low key in their attendance. But what were they supposed to do, just let the Fenians do as they pleased? Roll over and not fight back?

Roy along with just about everyone else in the province had shared in the revulsion of a few months earlier when three young off duty, unarmed soldiers had been murdered after being invited for a friendly drink. Two of them were brothers only seventeen and eighteen, shot down like dogs by terrorist cowards and left at the side of a wet lonely road. Just last week the bastards had even put bombs on the route of the 12th day Orange parade, trying to stop them enjoying even this. It was great to hear the various bands tuning up, and then the deafening sound of the Lambeg drums, huge things two feet deep that could only be carried on a neck harness, and beaten with Malacca canes which vibrated the air. This was accompanied by the distinctive shrilling of hundreds of flutes and fifes and there was no better sound in the whole world. George had joked about those Malacca canes, saying that if he caught them throwing stones, their Da would probably beat them both like a Lambeg. His Ma addressed him again.

"If you're going out don't be late back, your Uncle will be visiting tonight. And be careful."

She always added this last, and for Roy wholly unnecessary bit of advice. He wasn't stupid. Although still young, Roy had learned fast about the facts of life. His father was an excellent tutor as negligence in thought or deed had often proved a painful experience, and as his father often quoted, "There's no substitute for experience." His Ma had a few sayings which she aired regularly too, like the one about manners costing nothing, but it had been his father who had proven the point by showing them with a slap that not having them could be expensive. Roy had learned to control his temper too and think before opening his mouth, knowing even now that the difference between saying something clever or speaking shite was about two seconds thought. His father never tired of drumming this into him, the importance of self control, and it was about as close to an admission of his own personal failing as he would get. Roy finished his toast quickly and decided to go and see what his friends were doing.

Mickey Flynn, known locally as 'Farrar' sat on the couch and took a cup of tea from Eileen's Ma.

"That's grand Mrs McKenna," he said, sipping it cautiously and smiling his thanks.

Eileen sat next to him and brushed a piece of nonexistent fluff from his arm; any excuse to touch him would do. Jimmy watched this and glanced at Bernie with an amused but fond expression. Marty was watching TV. Bernie was looking at Mickey, examining him, as yet undecided on an opinion, after all they had only seen him a few times and he had been courting Eileen now for several months. His hair was a dark auburn, not too long, with blue eyes, an oval face, slightly hooked nose but a good open smile. What they knew of him was little enough, only that he was born and raised in nearby Ardoyne, from a decent hard working family, obviously keen on their daughter, and that was about it. Bernie and Jimmy had asked around and both now had their suspicions. They decided to invite him more formally for tea and interrogation. Eileen was nervous and ill at ease.

"We want to get married," she said suddenly.

There was a clatter of crockery as Jimmy dropped his empty cup.

"You're joking me! You're only...eighteen, for fuc..." Jimmy was spluttering in shock, before a look of suspicious doubt narrowed his eyes. "Oh for the love of God you're not up the duff are ye?"

"No, I'm no such thing Da!" Eileen spat at him her face flushed with embarrassment.

Jimmy picked up his cup, not bothering to hide his relief. Bernie showed no shock but merely began probing, gently and practically. Had they really thought it through, how long would they wait, had they told his parents? Jimmy asked how they were set for money and where were they going to live. Both had thought about it and had the answers rehearsed. Everything was planned. They would live initially at his Ma's house which had a spare room and then find a place of their own. Jimmy seemed satisfied, looked both of them in the eye and asked them one last time were they absolutely certain this was what they wanted. Then he gave a handshake and hug and so conferred his blessing. Bernie was still deep in thought. Marty had stopped watching the TV; this was much more interesting than Valerie Singleton making things from rubbish on Blue Peter.

"How did you get the name 'Farrar'?" he asked. Mickey hesitated then gave a sheepish shrug. Patricia, Thomas and Rosemary came in and sat in front of the TV, jostling for position.

"I've only had that the last years, eh... well, you know yer man Farrar-Hockley? Well, there was a wee bit of bother and there he was slabbering in front of the cameras so I lobbed a wee stone to shut him up."

Jimmy laughed delightedly and slapped his knee but Bernie said nothing. They knew of course who he was referring to. Major General Farrar-Hockley who was one of the top Brits and therefore a figure of hate. With quick fitting Belfast wit he had been almost overnight renamed as 'Horror- Fuckly' and it was this as much as anything that Jimmy was thinking of when he laughed.

"Did you hit him?" he asked with a grin.

"No, maybe next time Mr McKenna."

"Will there be a next time?" Bernie asked softly, sipping from her own cup. Her face was neutral, but there could be no doubt what she meant. Eileen fidgeted and Mickey carefully put down his own cup, and answered in the same coded way.

"I'll put it this way. If someone comes into my house and tries telling me what to do I'll put him out whatever way I can." He said it flat and unblinking. Bernie stared back and nodded twice, slowly. She looked at Eileen knowingly and pitied her for what life she may have chosen but sighed an acceptance.

"Aye, I understand that," she said sadly. Then more brightly, "Would you like another cup?"

George was out with his girlfriend Julie, a small shapely blonde with a loud laugh and slightly chubby face that Roy secretly fancied, but he knew better than to reveal this as the slagging he would receive would be relentless. Roy was sat on the settee with John and Billy watching Top of the Pops. Sam sat at the living room table, laughing with William and another man called Robert Allen, whom Roy had guessed immediately was a colleague of Sam's. They were reminiscing on some of the things that had happened down the years at the docks.

"The time with the pig had to be the best one Robbie," said Sam.

"Aye, I was on the gate one night years ago and we stopped one car with two in the front and three in the back. I was just about to let it go through, but Dave says to me to hold on a minute, it's not that cold is it so why is your man there in the back dressed up for the winter? He was too, overcoat and all with the collar up, hat over his eyes and a pipe in his mouth. A right ugly bugger to boot, but then he would be: it was a whole dead pig that those thieving devils were trying to smuggle out dressed as a man!"

Sam burst out laughing at the memory. "The best part was that when we told Alex, the eejit said he'd seen the same fella going out regular like that week and he'd felt sorry for him being so ugly and all."

Roy watched as Jimmy Saville introduced the next act, a leggy blonde in hot pants accompanied by three right clowns dressed horribly, all in brown and yellow like rotten bananas. Roy looked around and saw that Billy was busy excavating his nose. His Ma came in with a few bottles of stout, and noticing Billy, finger in one nostril almost to the knuckle she grabbed his hand.

"Mucky pup, go and wash your hand this minute."

He stamped out grumpily. William took the bottles and opened them. They clinked together, "Cheers!" Billy came back in and sat down, suddenly asking as he often did out of the blue.

"What's polarisation Da?"

They all stared at him curiously, conversation stopped. William was intrigued.

"Where did you come across that then?"

"On the telly I think, I don't know. Just heard it somewhere."

His Ma tried to answer him, to make him understand in children's terms but somehow protect him even temporarily from harsh reality. "You know a bit about how the world looks Billy? There's a North Pole and a South Pole, well they're at opposite ends aren't they? It just means when two things are opposite each other." She sat back pleased with her answer.

"They're still part of the world though aren't they?" he asked.

"Yes, of course."

Billy seemed satisfied. He had thought it was something to do with everybody getting colder, or to do with the soldiers and shooting and all but hadn't said so as John would only laugh at him. Roy smiled and ruffled his hair, thinking it was better than some of his questions, like the time last week when they were all sat watching a film and he had staggered everyone with an innocent, "What's syphilis?" There was a huge embarrassed silence. His Ma carried on watching as if deaf, John scurried to the toilet and Roy had sat there pinching himself trying desperately not to laugh. Billy had asked it again, but the only answer was his Da shifting in his seat and breathing out a stream of smoke heavily through his nose like a disgruntled dragon, a sure sign, which Billy, although still puzzled understood meant shut it.

Top of the Pops was finishing. Billy had found something interesting on the end of his finger, but before he could flick it at the back of John's neck Betty took him gently by the ear to the kitchen sink to brush his teeth before bed.

"Polarisation? Well, that's one way of putting it," said Sam thoughtfully.

"Have you heard anything recently Sam?" asked William. "I've been hearing all sorts of rumours about bringing back internment, and not before time."

"With how it's going I don't think there's much choice, not a matter of if but when. It's at the stage now where we can't enforce the law in some areas. Look what happened recently just over the Ardoyne with the two officers."

Roy knew what they were referring to. Internment without trial, the only way to sort it out even if a bit heavy. As for the policemen, both of them shot dead on the street for trying to do their job. Robert added his own view, getting up to leave.

"When Faulkner came in I'd say it was just a matter of time, getting the intelligence together and lifting the bad boys in one go. That should stop them in their tracks."

"Right then, we'll be off," said Sam. He raised an arm in farewell, winked at Roy then shouted through to his sister, "Thanks Betty, see you soon."

Robbie nodded and smiled his own thanks and they were gone, Roy seeing them to the door. He noticed how they peered carefully through the drizzle either way up the street before going to Sam's car; even though this was a Protestant area they remained cautious. He took a last glance, noticing the street lights come on in the gathering gloom, the orange glow making the wet red bricks glisten before he closed the door.

Later they sat watching the telly, as usual in the dark, William maintaining it made the picture better, just like the cinema and saved electricity at the same time. The light flickered shadows across the wall. John was in bed and Roy noticed his Ma kept checking the clock with a worried frown. William was also quiet and not making his usual scathing technical observations, despite the fact they were watching a Hollywood war film. He had seen real active service in Malaya and Cyprus. His Ma broke in over the muted battle sounds and low steady clicking of the clock.

"He knows he's work tomorrow, did he not say he'd be in by now?"

At that moment there was a banging on the door and a girl's high pitched voice, crying, almost on the point of screaming. There was also a man's voice and what sounded like George, by which time William had jumped up and was at the front door, opening it as a nightmare invaded their home. Roy was on his feet and his Ma had her hands to her mouth in horror as three loud, bedraggled figures staggered into her front room. William was shouting questions, putting the light on which made the scene even worse. It was Julie, her hair tangled, wet and witch like as if it had been ripped and pulled, a graze on her forehead where she had fallen and crying freely now, her face no longer pretty, but stretched and blubbering, the mascara black and smeared. Another man they vaguely knew from the area was gently lowering George, now assisted by William, onto the couch. Blood was dripping lethargically onto the grey carpet from a gash on his temple, and his nose was crusted with more blood and puffing up even as they looked. William quickly examined the gash and checked his head, running his fingers through his son's hair. Betty rushed to get a basin of water and the first aid kit they had bought recently. George groaned and put his hand to his mouth, his lips swollen and split and he spoke with difficulty, like a drunk in the last stages before sleep took hold.

"Got us on way home, 'our or 'ive o 'em. Hit Julie too, 'asards!"

Betty was grimly dabbing at the head wound which luckily wasn't deep, her jaw clamped. Roy noticed the other man, tall and apparently in his thirties with dark unfashionably short hair. He had an air of menace about him, not his size so much but his eyes, which were small and black as two currants. He spoke for the first time, his voice rough and gravelly.

"That's right, the dirty taigs must have seen them crossing over and knew they were Protestants. They just laid into them without warning. Me and some others chased them off but. They even took a swing at the wee girl there the bastards."

William thanked him as he went to leave, discussing whether it was worth calling the police, knowing that it wasn't. It could wait until morning, as it looked like George, although battered would be alright, and he doubted if the police would be going door to door in Republican New Lodge tonight. As he left, the stranger called to George.

"You take care son, my name's Eddie Frazer, from Canning Street."

George mumbled a feeble thanks and he was gone. Roy stood watching, the anger in him seething and roiling. He felt adrenalin flooding through his stomach but kept it under control. There was nothing he could do anyway. He noticed the man Eddie had said his name as if they might have heard it before; he would have to ask about. Julie had calmed down but was weeping gently, kneeling before George who smiled for the first time and revealed a missing front tooth, which set Betty off into a flood of angry tears. He ran his tongue over the gap, surprised at the lack of pain, but knowing it would come later. William was standing shocked, angry and like Roy frustrated, but not knowing what to do in these changed times. He indicated Julie with a flick of the head and spoke to Roy.

"We'd better get her home, I know it's just around the corner but I'll come too. Just in case."

George closed his eyes a few seconds, his tongue again running around his mouth, feeling for any other damage, his hand touching his nose which had a curious numb feeling as if he was feeling somebody else's flesh. His father might not know what to do, but George now had no doubts at all. It was simple: they had to defend themselves.

It was still dark as Lance Corporal Andy Miller sat tensely alongside the other members of his section, SLR between his knees, the barrel pointing at the roof in the back of a one ton Humber armoured car, waiting to go on what with typical army bullshit was known as 'Operation Demetrius'. In other words, a roundup of all the guys in the IRA they could lay hands on. Internment. Each section had an address and a name to go with it from the local police files. He thought with a sour tinged wonder, that all over Northern Ireland thousands of squaddies were doing the same thing right now. His company had some poxy shithole of a street in the New Lodge, three separate houses with their hopefully sleeping terrorists to take in. Andy looked at the others, like himself wound up with excitement and apprehension, as the Humber, known because of its ugly appearance as a 'Pig', gave a lurch and whine and began to roll. At last they could pay off a few scores.

Private Broughton peeped out of a window slit, watching the red bricked houses go past, some parts reminding him of his native Bradford. His face a deliberate blank he turned to listen to Andy, a typical brash opinionated Londoner sounding off and an Arsenal supporter too; doubly annoying.

"Right! No fuckin 'abaht lads, we wanna be in an' aht as quick as possible, grab our bloke, make the search snappy, before the locals gets a chance to take a pop at us!"

Andy was keen to get this over. In fact he was keen to get out of Ireland altogether. They had been here for several months and were sick and tired of all the crap as this wasn't real soldiering; riots with everyone chucking bricks, petrol bombs, kids as young as five or six joining in, the women gobbing off all the time and you had to stand there and take it. He hated Ireland and the Irish. They hadn't had anyone killed, yet, but two blokes had been hurt badly, one shot in the stomach and another with a burst ear drum from a blast bomb. He had seen the guy who was shot gasping in pain as if winded, rolling on the pavement with his legs drawn up and that hellish crowd where the gunman had fired from jeering and laughing as he was put in an ambulance. Some of them had even done a sort of mocking childish dance, the bastards. Then they had stoned the ambulance. Just about everyone else had been hit with something and they were all pissed off with it. It wouldn't be so bad if they could just shoot a few of the cunts, but no, no, it had to be within the rules, yellow cards of instructions and rules of engagement and shit whilst the IRA were free to have a go, just to keep some suited political wankers in Westminster happy and guilt free. He would like to get hold of some of those MPs who were always bleating about human rights, stick a rifle in their fists and shove them out on patrol, and see how far they got preaching peace with a baying mob. Arseholes. There was intermittent radio chatter, call signs and static. Their driver Paul Jackson, another Northerner like most of the regiment turned to announce cheerfully in broad Yorkshire.

"Almost there lads, everyone ready for t' show?"

The announcement was redundant. They could all tell where they were by the amount of noise coming from outside, a weird cacophony of bin lids, whistles, shouts, both military and higher pitched now interspersed with the banging on the roof and sides of their vehicle as stones hit. 'Smudge' Smith gave a tight grin.

"D'you think they know we're coming?"

Their vehicle screeched to a halt, throwing them momentarily forwards and then the door was open and everybody was piling out, some deploying with rifles high, scanning the street to cover the arrest teams. Andy jumped out into the din and half light and was greeted by a large stone that just missed his face, glancing off the metal door of the Pig with a loud clank. Other soldiers were shouting and there was the sound of a rubber bullet being fired, and then another. He noted with satisfaction they were right in front of their own target, number 36. Sergeant Grey who was in charge of the section was already at the door. Not a small man, he took up the sledge hammer he was carrying, which made him look like a uniformed angry Thor, and with a smashing blow hit the door at the lock. There was the sound of splintering wood as he dropped the hammer and kicked at the door which flew open. He charged in followed by the rest of the team who fanned out into the front room and kitchen. Andy, Sergeant Grey and two others ran up the stairs, to be met by a woman in the act of putting on a crumpled pink dressing gown and switching on the light, three small pale faces appearing behind her.

"Get out! Out! Now! What..."

They brushed past her angry protesting face, disregarding her completely and went straight into the bedroom. A fat man was sat up in bed, white faced, greying hair awry and spiked at all angles like a deranged Einstein, his eyes wide and owlish. Sergeant Grey stood over him, ignoring the screamed abuse, tried to remember the formal words of arrest and could not.

"Seamus Gillespie?" The man nodded. "O.K get your clothes on, we want you for questioning."

Andy began a cursory search of the room, drawing the curtains back to reveal the show outside where the street was full of uniformed figures running about, some already with their captured prey, putting them into the back of an accompanying Saracen. The noise was getting worse. Grey had flung back the sheets as Gillespie found his voice, unsteady with shock and disbelief.

"You've got it all wrong."

His wife pushed her head past the soldier at the door and screamed, "He's a heart condition, leave him be ye bastard!"

As he searched in the drawers, Andy glanced up at him and thought she might not be wrong; he was a fat fiftyish fucker, not at all what he was expecting. Grey picked up some clothes from a stool and flung them at him.

"Come on, we don't have all fucking day!"

Andy went through the wardrobe, quick as he could, pulling out everything onto the floor in haste and spite. There wasn't that much in the room: a dressing table with scattered coins, a clock, a tin ashtray nicked from the pub and a packet of Number Six fags. They waited for Gillespie to dress, noticing for the first time the cabbage damp smell of the room and the dark patch of mould that stretched down from the corner of the ceiling to the floor, staining the wallpaper with its incongruous pattern of stalled coloured racing cars on the off white background. He could hear the others in the next room, and downstairs the sound of breaking glass. As soon as he had his trousers on, Grey was pushing Gillespie to the door and down the stairs as if he were late for an important meeting. Andy followed, accompanied by the shrill abuse and feeble slapping on his flak jacket of Mrs Gillespie.

Through the fractured door Andy caught a glimpse of the rest of the house where the others were still searching and gave a satisfied smirk. The front room was a mess, with broken ornaments all over the floor where they had been swept by an angry hand from the mantelpiece. A marble 1920's style clock lay cracked and mixed in with lumps of coal from the upended scuttle by the fireplace, and there was frosted glass on the floor from the living room door. The TV was also upended, but the screen strangely unbroken, as was a Formica topped table, its stilted legs pointing upwards. The settee had been tipped and the sacking bottom ripped and gutted. In amongst the debris strewn floor lay the contents of a child's board game alongside a fractured vase, its pieces now an abstract mosaic, red flowers adding another splash of colour. In the kitchen it sounded like the floorboards were being ripped up. Private Johns came through, his hands white with flour and tut tutting with a malicious gleeful smile. He shook his head.

"You'd think t'house was hit by a bomb!" he declared vengefully.

Marty and Jimmy had been awoken like everyone else by the unholy din and known almost immediately that internment without trial was in. It wasn't unexpected. Mickey had been on about it last week saying it would come soon. So now they watched as what looked like several houses were raided. There were troops all over the place. To their shock they saw Seamus Gillespie being put into the back of a Saracen, half dressed and bewildered looking. As far as they knew, Seamus hadn't been involved in anything since he was young and only then a bit of Sinn Fein stuff. Next in was young Liam Mullan, who was being dragged kicking and shouting by four of them, one on either arm, another at his rear and the lead soldier striding forwards with Mullan's luxuriant long hair wrapped cruelly in one fist, arching him forwards in a buckled half run. The only surprise there was that he was still around, as he was known by many as an active helper on the fringes of the IRA if he hadn't already progressed to full membership. They threw him into the back, one of them giving him a helping boot in the arse on the way, his mother following up the road, face raging red and screaming. Then at that moment they heard more commotion above the growing din from three doors down and ludicrously saw

Frank Richardson being escorted out, a soldier either side of him. Frank was leaning on one of the soldiers and walking slowly as he always did. He was a small man, balding with a big grey moustache and had a lung complaint. His woolly green cardigan flapped loosely as he shuffled along. As if to emphasize his frailty and the lunacy of his arrest, his wife Alice came up the road in her slippers and handed him a little brown pill bottle and his glasses with thick pebble lenses. They watched as an officer, hands on hips, disbelievingly questioned one of the soldiers and looked at a piece of paper, his finger running half way down the page before stopping. Shaking his head he helped Frank into the back of the arrest vehicle just as a fresh shower of stones was beginning to come down. Shouts and vicious insults were hurled at the departing uniforms.

"British Bastards! Get out of our country! Out to fuck with ye!"

"I hope youse all die of cancer and your children too!"

Jimmy ducked back in, pulling Marty with him. He was genuinely shocked.

"Would you bloody well believe that? Frank Richardson? Aye, I can see him being a top marksman." Bernie took her hanging checked coat from the banister and put it on.

"I'm going to see Alice, see if she's alright," she said.

Alice was sitting in what was left of her living room. Other neighbours were already in attendance, fussing round with soothing noises either side of her chair. Another brought her a cup of tea from the ruined kitchen. Bernie looked around the room, saw with angry bewilderment and gritted teeth the broken crockery and ornaments, the door hanging off its hinges and even the fire place tiles deliberately cracked and chipped. She picked up a damaged holy statue, defiled now by those people and saw the shaking hand as Alice put the cup of tea to one side on the only untouched little table, still with a few yellow cake crumbs and tiny fleck of jam.

"Why? Why? What did we do? Frank doesn't even go out. Why?" she asked in a small voice.

"Don't you worry Alice, Frank will be home in no time. It's a big mistake is all by those fools. It'll be alright, you'll see. We'll clear up here and get down to... and sort this out," said Brenda, her immediate neighbour, realising they didn't know for sure where they would be taken.

Bernie spoke for the first time in a low whisper but loud enough for them all to hear, her voice shaking with anger. "Our day will come." Then in Irish "Tiocfaidh Ár La'!" before adding to the delighted surprise of all who knew her, "I want them bastards to pay. The whole bloody lot of them."

The rioting had gone on all day unabated. The intermittent cracking and banging of shots could be heard with little respite, the city was covered in clouds of smoke from an assortment of barricades, burning tires, burning buses and again burning homes and buildings. Belfast was on another round of its own version of musical chairs, but played with houses to the music of crackling fire and violence. A new record was set in that fourteen people had met violent deaths in a single day and hundreds were injured in the eruption following internment. By evening several thousand people were on the move, both Catholic and Protestant.

On the news that evening the Fergusons sat silently watching what looked like their country descending into civil war. The rumours had been going all day and they had seen with their own eyes the scale of the destruction by the amount of smoke in the air and sound of gun battles. Where they were was pretty safe, as graffiti on one wall crudely but accurately stated, 'No taigs here.' The local defence association was ready and the army was everywhere so they felt secure enough for now. They watched the images on the BBC, recognising one of the roads almost totally ablaze. People, *their* people, moving out with their possessions piled at the side of the road, the anguish, fear and hatred etched on their faces as they waited for transport to take them God knows where. William thought he'd caught a glimpse of his workmate Derek Blaine amidst all the chaos and pointed.

"Was that Derek there Betty?"

"I didn't see, but that car looked like his. What was left of it."

William sat mutely, glowering. Roy got up to go out, followed by George whose bruises had now turned yellow from their original black and purple.

"Where do you think you're going?" Betty asked abruptly.

"Just out, we won't be far Ma," George answered, keeping moving. Their father looked up but didn't stop them.

"Alright, but don't be going as far as the gardens, stay away from the Antrim Road too, and be in well before dark. I mean it!"

They 'yes Da'd' him out the door, hearing him say to Betty that they couldn't be kept cooped up all day and night and it would be OK where they were. All very true, but only if they obeyed and they were both now regularly if still carefully ignoring their father's commandments. To their relief, John was barred from going with them and told to go and see what Billy was up to. They didn't want him with them on this little expedition as he was still too young. The last time they had taken him only because he had overheard them speaking of the riot, his face splitting into a huge crescent smile as he immediately turned blackmailer. They went out, waving to Billy who was bouncing around the street on his new Space Hopper that Uncle Sam had brought last visit.

"Can I come?" he wailed,

"Not this time," Roy grinned back. John came out, this time with a downturned horseshoe mouth and gave the Space Hopper's orange dirtied face a frustrated kick. They carried on, turning the corner and walking quickly towards the sound of the distant crowd.

The rioters seemed to be taking a breather as the two sides stood off from each other on either side of the intersection with just an occasional thrown missile, too far to cause any significant injury. On one side there were a few Union and red hand of Ulster flags and on the other Irish tricolours, technically illegal, but no one was in a hurry to go and get them. An RUC Landrover was parked further up, the officers wary and watching, knowing there was little they could do without backup from an already stretched military. The whole place stank of smoke, and from afar the city must have looked like it did in 1941 after a heavy German raid. In 1971 the damage was all self inflicted. There was no traffic. In the middle of the road two cars were burning, their paint scorched off but still identifiable as a Volkswagen Beetle and a Mini, their owners having been stopped and pulled out, then pushed and booted up the road without ceremony or much complaint. A large man came over to their group flanked by two others and addressed them.

"Alright lads? Come to join us and watch the fun?" asked Eddie Frazer.

One of the others said something quietly to him and Eddie shook his head, replying in a low voice what appeared to be instructions. The other man disappeared into the crowd. He smiled and offered them a cigarette each. Only George accepted. His unwinking flat little eyes studied them as he put the packet into his pocket and gave George a light. They looked past the cars at the hate filled crowd wobbling through the heat haze.

"Terrible so it is, there'll be no going back after this. Did you hear what happened up near Ardoyne? Whole streets of good Protestant families burnt out, nowhere to go. Same in New Barnsley, we've had to evacuate the whole estate."

They listened and George agreed with a curse. Roy, although of the same view couldn't help noticing that Frazer said it all a bit dispassionately, like he wasn't really too bothered. He finished his fag and flicked it away.

"Well, if you want to do more for your country and community than a wee bit of stone throwing let us know. We're getting organised." He waved a contemptuous arm at the enemy opposite, "That shite there won't be getting away with it anymore! See you around."

He sauntered back to the crowd which opened to make way for him. George stood gazing after him clearly impressed. Roy scratched the side of his nose intrigued, and wondered who exactly 'we' referred to. A part of the mob opposite were on the move and the noise picked up again, more stones were thrown and then one of the taigs suddenly ran out into the middle of the road and threw a petrol bomb which arced through the air and exploded, catching a few of their crowd who couldn't move quickly enough, hemmed in from behind as they were. There was a frantic flapping and rolling on the ground as one guy tried to put the fire out on his legs, now assisted by others with items of clothing to smother the flames, accompanied by renewed whistles and jeers from the other side as they hooted their jubilation. This appeared to be the signal to restart the fight as both Roy and George threw their stones with as much force as they could, shouting as they did so. Through the haze Roy caught a glimpse of a familiar looking face that had the same momentary puzzled look as his own before it disappeared again into the crowd of arm swinging, roaring people. He couldn't place where he had seen him before though and swiftly forgot about it as they reached down for more rocky ammunition.

The Catholic mob suddenly turned in the other direction, and looking themselves they saw why as a convoy of Army vehicles came to a stop a hundred yards away, disgorging the uniformed passengers who deployed either side in doorways and behind their open armoured doors, weapons ready. A volley of gas canisters popped into the air as an upper class English voice was heard through a loudspeaker telling them to disperse. The crowd ignored this, the sight of uniforms sending them into a frenzy as they threw everything they had at the new targets. Roy watched fascinated as something was thrown that was clearly not a stone. A flash and small explosion followed that echoed briefly: a blast bomb. A soldier ducked down and retreated holding an injured elbow, reflexively pulling out a bent four inch nail and throwing it with a dull ring onto the pavement along with a few red droplets. One of the others fired a shot into the air which made everyone flinch and lower their heads. There was now a cloud of white gas hanging about. Someone with a handkerchief wrapped around his face like a highwayman ran out to the cheers of his own side, kicked one canister away and picked the other up, flinging it any old how towards the armoured vehicles. A burst of shots rang out, the strike of them on the road in front of the nearest Saracen creating puffs as they ripped into the tarmac, followed by shouts from the soldiers searching where the fire had come from. The crowds scattered a little, retreating into their own tributary street entrances that branched on to the main road. Another rapid volley came, striking the nearest armoured vehicle like a handful of marbles on a tin roof. Roy watched from the corner, able to tell from past experience that it was a Thompson being used. Someone next to him pointed at an upstairs window further down and opposite, the netting billowing out. The soldiers had spotted it too, and within seconds chips of white painted woodwork were flying from the frame as the glass dropped out onto the road with a crash, the high velocity rifle shots cracking loudly. He felt George grab at him, swearing with the excitement.

"C'moan ta fuck!"

They turned and quickly walked back, weaving through the crowd, as if exiting a football match.

Chapter 4

Crystallised Calcified Petrified

Months passed and the conflict worsened. Instead of putting out the fires, or at least damping them down, internment had acted as an accelerant, as if the authorities had mistakenly used petrol instead of water. Each month brought fresh statistics, the levels of violence, of shootings, bombings, deaths and injuries continued to rise which caused more hatred which caused more violence. The flames were kept well fed throughout the year.

Marty was up early on this particular last Saturday before Christmas, as he wanted to see Brendan in town later but had a few chores to do around the house, the first of which was getting a fire going. A real fire was a lovely cosy thing to come down to and made any place home; the trouble was it was such a pain in the arse getting it going. It was his turn and he hated doing it, scraping out the ashes from the grate and taking them outside to the dustbin. It was still dark and the cold was bitter enough for him to sharply suck in his breath as he hurried back into the living room, stopping only to collect a wire knotted bundle of kindling wood and greasy paraffin fire lighters. Outside he heard the hollow clink of empty milk bottles being collected, accompanied by a half hearted whistling from the milkman. Marty searched about for old newspapers, glancing at the headlines before crumpling the sheets into balls, adding newsprint to his already grimy hands. India and Pakistan were slugging it out thousands of miles away, warmer there than here at least and then a headline much nearer to home. He screwed up the page describing the horror of last week's bomb attack in the Shankill which unsurprisingly no one had wanted to claim. Everybody knew who had done it however. Four people had been killed when a building collapsed onto the road. What had made it particularly bad was that one of the victims had been in a pram and another was a toddler. That had been a response to the previous Saturday's Loyalist bomb in the *Tramore* bar, which had set a new record of fifteen dead in one go. That bomb they hadn't needed to read about in the paper as most of the victims were from around the New Lodge. Bernie had known one of them personally and Jimmy several as nodding acquaintances. Now they were statistics, smeared newsprint to be cast again onto the fire. Marty crumpled more paper, hearing the first movement above him as someone put a heavy foot on the floor.

It was sometimes not so clear anymore. He knew where his allegiances lay and never doubted the rightness of the cause, but he had a worm of unease when people got killed that shouldn't have. He had asked Mickey on one of his infrequent visits to the house and hadn't liked the answer much. "In war regrettable mistakes are made, people get hurt but the movement has to continue," he had said through a hurried mouthful of crisps, sounding like he was reciting from a book. Eileen was still besotted and proud of her man, and his Ma was always ready to serve him a cuppa or do a corned beef sandwich no matter what the time, his visits being at all hours due to his activities. Jimmy on the other hand seemed to have cooled in his initial liking the longer the campaign continued, and had been openly critical when it came to bombings.

Marty had continued at school, unwilling but respectful of his parents' wishes and this reluctance had shown in his grades. It was difficult to concentrate on boring things such as literature and history when there was so much excitement all around. How was poetry relevant? 'My love is a red, red rose'. Aye, he could see himself quoting that during a riot as a baton connected with his head. As for history, that was happening now and he should be helping make it rather than just reading about it. Life was frustrating.

Jimmy was first up and Marty could hear him humming 'Strangers in the Night' as he pottered about in the kitchen, the sound of the bread bin opening and then a low roar as the grill was lit. After a couple of minutes he sauntered in sloppily dressed in old jeans and string vest despite the cold, a happy smile on his face at the sight of the fire catching hold.

"Good morning son!" he boomed, two pieces of toast in one hand. "Will you be making a pot of tea to go with that lovely fire?"

Marty rubbed his hands and nodded, amused as ever at his father's steadfast good humour. Jimmy sat down, carefully putting the toast on the side table, spreading blackened crumbs and casually picking up one of Marty's literature books.

"What's this now? Auld Billy Shakespeare no less. Henry Vee. Who's he then?" he asked, eyebrows raised in mock enquiry.

Marty laughed as he went to make tea, passing his Ma as she came down yawning a good morning to him. From outside came the unmistakable diesel whining of army vehicles going past and the faint tremble of the house as a heavier Saracen rumbled by. To their surprise they heard them stop and then came the sound of doors clanging open and shouting. There was radio static just outside the window and a dog began barking further along the street. Jimmy and Bernie looked at each other, instantly alert as the first heavy hammering on the door began, followed a second later by a tremendous crash as it was smashed open. Two soldiers came quickly into the room bawling orders. Others ran upstairs and two more went into the kitchen.

"Get your hands on your heads!"

From upstairs came the shriller voices of the children and a lot of noise and clumsy banging. Bernie made an instinctive move towards the stairs, stopped by one of the soldiers just as an officer stepped in. From above came further shouts.

"All clear sir!" and from the bedroom, "No one except kids sir! He's not here." The officer came forwards and placed his hand on Jimmy's shoulder.

"Are you James McKenna?" Jimmy looked down at the hand then nodded. "I am arresting you under the Special Powers Act. We wish to question you concerning terrorist crimes in this area."

Before Jimmy had time to think, the officer had repeated the performance with Marty, his Mother gasping a startled "No!" as they were pushed and shoved, hands aloft, Jimmy still holding on to a piece of toast before one of the soldiers saw it, and cursing, knocked it out of his grasp. As they went outside into the chill they could hear Bernie starting to shout above the noise of Patricia crying. Looking up Marty caught a glimpse of Thomas and Rosemary's scared white faces in the bedroom window before his head was pushed down and they climbed into the dark interior of the vehicle. All told it must have taken less than a couple of minutes before the arrest team piled in after them and the Saracen pulled away, smelling of oil, sweat and boot polish.

Marty sat opposite his father, both still wide eyed in disbelief. Looking around at their travelling companions Marty was far from reassured; he lingered briefly on every face seeing the same narrowed eyes, set mouths and raw hatred. One of them returned his glance with penetrating hot eyes.

"What the fuck are you lookin'at? Face your front you Irish twat or I'll punch your fuckin' lights out!" He snapped at him.

Marty was frightened and looked away and down at the floor, feeling his father's hand squeeze his knee.

"It'll be alright son. It's just a mistake."

There was a sudden flurry of movement and the meaty thud of a fist hitting flesh as the same soldier lashed out as hard as he could in the confined space, hitting Jimmy flush on the cheek.

"No talking!" he screamed. Marty let out a shout of pain as the soldier next to him suddenly rammed his elbow into his side. "I said no talking, didn't I? Are you all thick here or what?"

Jimmy gave a slight grunt of discomfort and this was rewarded by another punch to the side of the head and more shouted instructions not to speak. In the dim light Marty could see the soldiers were enjoying this game as the Saracen rocked and lurched, speeding to its destination. The initiator of the game was now grinning, his loose lower lip stuck out as he rasped at Jimmy. The anger however was clearly real.

"Yeh, that's right. It's all a mistake and you don't know nothin' do ya?" He turned to his companions. "You all hear that lads? They're innocent. That's almost funny. They always are aren't they, when we drop one of theirs it's always the same story, going for a loaf or pint of milk usually at midnight and no fucking shops even open. Buggered if I know who's bin shootin' at us eh?"

There were a few laughs at this sally which encouraged him to go on, now shouting suddenly at Jimmy's bowed head, his face only inches away as if trying to push his words physically into his skull. "Thirty odd soldiers dead this last four months, half of them in this fucking dump! An' you got the brass fucking neck to come out wi' that fucking shit!" He raised his head and shouted to the driver, "Oi! Geoff, nobody shot Pete in the back last month and left him bleeding on the street! Everyone in that crowd that started singin' an' laughin' about it they was all innocent too." He gave Jimmy a final slap, anger momentarily satiated.

They continued their journey in near silence, the only noise being the creaking and whine of the vehicle and vague muted street noises from outside. Once there was a sharper clang, probably a stone hitting the roof and this acted as the bell for another round of abuse, this time a vicious verbal lambasting as the soldier next to Jimmy tried his best to bait and humiliate his captives.

"Why are you all so fuckin' filthy over here?" he asked in a pained voice as if genuinely seeking an answer. One of the others joined in.

"Beats me Rick, all I know is I hate searching houses here. Never know what you'll put yer 'and in. They're just born dirty I reckon. You allergic to water or what Paddy? Or is it just soap?"

This last brought spiteful laughter. Marty felt humiliated, scared and burning with anger at the same time at their helplessness. He stole a quick glance at the last voice and was surprised to see face with the blond crew cut under the beret could only have been a few years older than his own. Rick tapped his father lightly on the shoulder and leaned towards him, whispering almost confidentially.

"Know what we found in one of your shitty hovels last week pal? A fuckin' jam rag under the bed, a used bloody tampax in an old frying pan under the bed. How's that for minging then? Every place I've been stinks pissy too. You people turn my guts."

Jimmy looked up at him slowly, thinking of his own spotless house, one cheek already red and puffy and said in a calm deliberate voice, "The only dirt here is youse."

He lowered his head again. For a second there was no reaction, and to Marty's surprise no fists. Rick peered out of a slit and then sat back with a nasty knowing smile.

"Nearly there," he announced in a dead tone. "Somebody else's turn now. I'm sure they'll be interested in what you have to say. Have fun."

The Saracen turned sharply and came to a stop, the doors were flung open, the shouting and bawling resumed, then father and son found themselves being hustled out of the back of the vehicle, jumping down into what Marty at first thought was a school playground. It was in fact a parade ground of the barracks they had been brought to and for the first time Marty began to feel the cold. He noticed his father had his arms crossed tightly and was shivering in his string vest. He also had only socks on. They were hurried into the nearest squat red building and found themselves in front of a desk where a large, bald and bovine looking Sergeant slowly took their details: name, address and age, checking with ponderous deliberation against his own list. He leaned back and looked at Marty speculatively, his pen tapping his bottom teeth.

"Where's Michael Flynn?" he asked slowly. Jimmy, looking at his chevrons spoke up, seeing a chance to get his son out of this.

"Sergeant, we know nothing about this. Martin is still in school, he shouldn't be here now you know that," he said in as reasonable a voice as he could.

Something hard and cold jabbed into his back making him jump. The sergeant raised a hand slightly, like Caesar in the coliseum and the object was removed. Just then a door opened behind them and the sergeant jumped to attention. A Captain came into view, followed by somebody in civilian sheepskin coat and black trousers. Marty studied the face of what was obviously a copper with his neat trimmed moustache, dark hair, pale skin from too much paperwork indoors and unsmiling, cold pale eyes like something found on a fish monger's slab. The officer spoke first, a slim, elegant figure with sharp almost foxy features, sitting himself on the corner of the table and smoothly taking control.

"Very well Sergeant, all processed properly? Pity about Flynn but never mind." He turned to Marty. "Look, we know Flynn is at your place all the time, we do have intelligence, where is he now though?"

Marty stood tight lipped, staring at the polished floor and the officer's shiny shoe as it swung back and forth, in and out of his line of vision.

"We can hold you both here for a long, long time you know. As for your son's relative youth, well we've had younger activists. Indeed they can be held indefinitely, it's called at her Majesty's pleasure. We can avoid all this unpleasantness if you just tell us... a few things. You can help us. And yourselves."

He smiled at them reassuringly, like a cartoon fox in front of a hen coop trying to convince the occupants of his good intentions; the chicken's friend.

Jimmy sighed and spoke, "Catch yourselves on. Yous've made a mistake, we don't know anything. Intelligence? Aye, what about yer man Frank Richardson? Anyway if you've so much intelligence why the fuck don't you know where that other fella is?"

The leg stopped swinging. Marty looked up and saw the officer now with his lips puckered in annoyance. The cop had not taken his mackerel eyes from Jimmy, but was now smiling and nodding as if in approval. They went out together and Jimmy turned his head to Marty and shrugged.

"I could use the toilet," he said.

"Me too Da. Can we go to the toilet please?"

"No. You'll have to wait." The sergeant moved his weight slightly and grimaced. "I want to go too." Jimmy's absurd humour couldn't resist the opportunity.

"Let's call a taxi, then we can all go."

The soldier behind him gave a quick savage punch to the kidney which winded him, the one behind Marty grabbed his arm and twisted. Leaning over Jimmy's gasping doubled over figure he screamed at him.

"Comedian are we? Find that funny did you? Do you think we're playing games here?"

Just then the officer and cop came back in, making the soldiers jump to attention again like naughty school children when teacher returns. The officer eyed Jimmy impassively as he tried to get his breath and the cop spoke up in a high pitched icy voice.

"We will be separating you and your questioning will begin in an hour once the doctor has taken a wee look at you first."

Marty was right, he was a peeler and by the sound of his accent local, and therefore one to be wary of. They were taken out and along a white painted corridor with doors either side every few yards. They stopped near the middle and Jimmy was pushed into one and Marty the other opposite, the doors were locked after them. Marty moved his eyes around the small square room, smelling of disinfectant and stale cigarette smoke, all creamy white bricks, a grilled high window opposite and simple wooden table in one corner. That was all. Marty sat down shakily and waited for the doctor to come.

It was near the end of winter, but there were still icy mornings when Roy didn't want to leave the house. This particular Saturday was another chilly one and Roy lingered in his unheated room thinking about his future. New Year had come and gone and another birthday too. At school he was doing well and expected to pass his exams, but after that he still hadn't made up his mind. An army career interested him, but he hadn't decided for certain. One thing he did know though was what he *didn't* want to do, which he regarded as decision of a sort. Roy knew there was no way he was going to be joining his father and George at the docks. The more he thought about it, the more the forces appealed to him, the chance to travel and do different things every day had a lot going for it. The discipline and taking orders that went with military life he wouldn't mind at all, it was what he was used to; in fact, compared to the regime his Da ran it would probably be easy.

Although he would never admit it, even to himself, Roy still had vaguely romantic notions of martial heroics, this despite the last few years of harsh reality on the streets of his battered city. Thinking about the troubles made him think uneasily of the last few grim months and how it was affecting his own family too. George had become involved. Roy had not, still fearing and respecting his father's wishes, not to mention Uncle Sam's. At least this was what Roy told himself. He had even stopped attending riots. It had started as usual with another atrocity last September: the IRA had bombed a pub on the Shankill, blowing two innocent men to oblivion and injuring a lot more just back from watching the Linfield match. Roy had watched in silence as the coffins were escorted by the crowd and members of the Orange and Black institutions, and it was here that they bumped into Eddie Frazer, black leather jacket and black tie matching his shining black little eyes as he nodded a greeting.

"A sad day, lads."

He eyed them and then lightly took George by the arm, guiding him a little to one side and speaking so low that Roy couldn't hear. He had taken an instinctive distrust to Eddie, sensing no real warmth in his smile. He had also seen him with his wife, who looked rough and haggard and beaten, both physically and mentally, noticing the small white scar on the bridge of her nose from an obvious and not too distant break. He knew what sort Frazer was then and avoided him. Although intrigued, Roy didn't move closer. Eddie clearly wanted privacy so he would simply ask George later what it was all about. After a minute another man, also in black, stood next to Frazer, patiently waiting for him to finish. Eddie shook hands with George, gave Roy a slight wave and moved off.

"What was that all about then?" Roy asked as nonchalantly as he could.

"Mind your own business!"

Roy turned, shocked at the vehemence of the answer. Not only that, but the fact that George was keeping it secret, something entirely new in their close fraternity. He left it for the time being but despite repeated questions later, nothing was forthcoming. George was changing since the beating he had taken. Although on the surface he retained the same affable nature Roy felt he was becoming a little withdrawn, not so spontaneous and perhaps a mite secretive. He now even had his own small closet wardrobe which he kept locked, insisting on a "wee bit of privacy."

The months went by, the violence got worse, more people died and life went on but definitely not as usual; daily gun battles and the crump of explosions could never be termed normal. George was out a lot without Roy and rarely said where he had been. He was always at work in the morning though, and this satisfied their parents who didn't seem to notice anything odd. Roy had his doubts but typically kept them to himself.

Roy went downstairs to the warmth of the living room fire. His father glanced up at him from his fireside chair, lowering his newspaper slightly and grunting a good morning.

"Morning Da!" Roy said brightly.

"Are you going to the football this afternoon?" he asked.

"Aye. Uncle Sam'll be round later and we'll go together."

"You never know we might even win a game this season. I was just reading the next international Northern Ireland play at home won't be at home. It'll be played in England instead, it seems things are that bad other teams won't come here."

William shook his head tiredly and raised his paper again. Roy shrugged, and smelling sausages frying went into the kitchen. His Ma was at the cooker jerking the pan back and forth to keep the contents from sticking. John and Billy sat expectantly, knives and forks clutched upright on the table like two medieval statues, plates in front of them, loaf of bread and 'Daddies' brown sauce bottle at the ready. Their eyes were fixed on the pan, their salivating near audible.

"Morning all."

Only his Ma answered. "You're late up so you are, you'll have to wait until I've these fed if you want a sausage."

"That's fine Ma, I'll make my own later. Do you need anything at the shop?"

"No," she answered, before wrinkling her brow in thought. "Yes. Get some fags for your father, there's money on the mantelpiece."

As he went through, Roy affectionately ruffled Billy's already tousled hair. He didn't even seem to notice, his eyes riveted on the frying Cookstown Sausages. Roy laughed at their earnest expressions as the food was put on their plates and they fell to, making sauce spread sandwiches, the sausage filling piping hot and causing them both to breath out heavily but with obvious pleasure. Breakfast in the Ferguson household was always substantial even in lean times, it being an unspoken parental rule to start the day with a good feed. On some occasions William himself would make an 'Ulster Fry' as a special treat: bacon, sausage, egg, mushrooms, tomatoes, black pudding, soda farls and sometimes potato bread. Basically it was anything that could be fitted into the pan and cooked, dripping with grease.

Later that day Sam made his appearance, Betty giving his large frame a hug and a kiss as he entered. William was half watching Grandstand on the TV. He leaned forwards and poked the glowing coals in the fire.

"Sit yourself down Sam, how's it going this weather?"

"Not so bad."

He looked weary and Betty too had noticed his usual good humour was not what it once was, commenting on this to her husband just last week. It was hardly surprising thought Roy with the way things were, the risk of getting shot or blown up on any given day was increasingly very real and had to be taking its toll. Betty worried about him as much as Heather and although they were all proud of him for doing his duty, the tension was there always, a lurking dark shadow under the surface, still as yet in an undefined shapeless form. He rarely spoke now about the job, and then usually in hushed tones to William over a glass or two. He saw Roy and his face immediately lightened.

"Ready for the big match young fella? We'll give Coleraine a pasting today!"

"Huh! Who do you fancy for the title now?"

Sam made a pretence of thinking at the by now ritual question before answering, "Linfield or Glentoran, but only if Crusaders let them." Sam raised himself from the seat. "It's still bloody cold out Roy so get a warm coat on you."

Roy thought about this and standing on the terraces for a couple of hours. He would have to borrow George's new leather coat, that was heavy enough and his brother wouldn't mind. Running up the stairs he saw straight away the closet was locked, but then remembered with a wicked grin where he had seen George hide the key, watching him silently through the door jamb as he furtively placed the flat key under the carpet at the corner. He retrieved the key with a chuckle, opened the closet and put on the heavy black jacket, grabbing a scarf and hurrying back downstairs where Sam was already at the door, looking up and down the street.

They went out together, breath hanging in the air despite the weak sun that poked out from time to time, seeming to dither as to whether it was worth the effort to shine this day. Sam quickly unlocked the door of the car, and as he got in and put the seat belt on, Roy felt something inside the breast pocket of the jacket, something heavy. Roy put his hand in and felt a cold, hard, metallic long rectangle, and just as he was about to pull it out for a better look he felt one open end and experienced a thrill of real horror. It felt something like what a magazine for a pistol might feel like and the knowledge stopped the breath in his throat. Sam was talking as he pulled away.

"...too cold to snow he says. What an eejit! Do you think Captain Scott thought that down in the South Pole? Aye, I can see it now. All sat round in a tent minus fifty degrees and your man Oates says he's stepping out and may be gone some time. Oh don't worry Oatsy, it's too cold to snow, you'll be fine. Close the flap on the way out." He guffawed and glanced at Roy's rigid blanched face, registering something wasn't right. "Are you still there? Did you go for a pee before we left?"

Roy nodded, praying that what he had was something innocent but knowing different, his mind racing as his sweating hand felt a bullet, confirming his discovery. He could only think over and over again the same word. 'Fuck! Fuck! Fuck! Fuck! Fuck! Fuck! Fuck!' Like some weird satanic chant in his head. His imagination was now going full throttle with dread thoughts, as possession of this could mean years in jail. Sam was speaking again and Roy tried to follow the words, forcing himself to look at him, glad he was sat down as his legs felt suddenly weak.

"I said have you decided what you'll be doing after your schooling?" He glanced at Roy quizzically. "You look like you've just seen a ghost." His policeman's antenna was now twitching and scenting something was definitely amiss. Roy answered trying to keep his voice natural, but Sam was now attuned and picked up the slight quaver.

"I... still don't know. Not yet for sure anyway."

Sam gave a grunt, driving in silence for a while, obviously in thought. It wasn't too far and luckily as they weren't heading into the centre there was no vehicle stop check. Sam would have only to have shown his ID to proceed but Roy wasn't thinking straight at this particular moment, and could only imagine with renewed terror that made him flush being dragged out along with his uncle and ending up in Crumlin Road jail. They pulled into the car park and came to a stop. There were a few people about, heading like themselves to the game. Sam slowly and deliberately turned to face Roy who was still paper coloured with shock.

"Now. What's going on? I'm no fool Roy, I've known you all your life and I know guilty faces when I see them too so out with it!"

Roy's hand involuntarily moved to his jacket pocket. Sam's eyes narrowed and with surprising speed and violence he grabbed the lapels, dragging Roy over in the confined space. His hand went into the pocket and came out with the full magazine, blue black and heavy. Sam stared at it in astonishment as if he had a tarantula on his palm for a full five seconds before putting it into his glove compartment, slamming it shut in anger. He then did something he had never done before. He slapped Roy across the face with the flat of his hand.

"You stupid, stupid wee bugger!" He roared. "Have you any idea what could happen if you're caught with this? Well? Eh? My God! Is that all there is, tell me, the truth now!"

He grabbed Roy roughly by the cheeks showing a strange blend of violence and affection, begging him as well as commanding. Roy had no intention of squealing on his brother despite his anger, feeling in the other pockets and then shaking his head. It was this uncertainty however that Sam immediately noticed and with a flash of intuition knew the truth.

"That's not your jacket is it? Bloody George!"

Sam raised his hands and exhaled deeply, bringing one fist down heavily on the dashboard. Outside a couple of white faces turned to stare before carrying on their way. Roy found his voice.

"Please don't say anything! Our Da will kill him, skin him or disown him or..."

"Aye, whichever comes first."

Sam was confused about what was the best solution. He was a member of the Royal Ulster Constabulary and this was a very serious crime, family or not, and failure to report it would be a gross neglect of duty and Sam believed in his oaths. He rubbed his forehead with both hands, running them through his receding hair, deep in thought. As well as getting George into a lot of trouble it would break his sister's heart. He knew then he couldn't do it according to the book, but obviously he would have to do something, tell William or just privately scare the hell out of George, one or the other or both. He then hit upon another idea, trying to wring a drop of good out of the situation. He spoke again, now patiently as he calmed down, wanting badly for his sister's son to understand.

"I know it can't be easy for any of you, living where you do in the times we do. I sometimes want to get even with those murdering bastards myself but, there has to be laws Roy, it's as simple as that."

Roy found himself shaking his head and said, "The law isn't stopping it though."

"No one said it was perfect, but you've to think of those laws as a fence." Sam exhaled heavily and continued. "Aye, sure enough there'll be holes here and there some clever lawyer can crawl through and bits rotten that have to be replaced now and then, but you start ripping it all down and eventually you'll have no protection at all against chaos and evil."

"What about George?"

"I'll have to think about it, we can't just pretend this hasn't happened. One thing though I want from you, O.K?" Roy nodded his agreement eagerly, relieved that this dreadful little episode might just turn out alright. "I want you to give me your word, promise me here and now that you won't take the same road. I want your solemn oath, on your mother's life. As a true and loyal Ulsterman. You won't ever get involved with any illegal organisations. You know who I'm talking about too, you stay within the law and never do anything I can arrest you for, right?"

Roy looked at him, seeing really just how much his uncle did care about them, knowing what being a policeman meant to him and how agonising it must be for him to compromise his principles.

"I swear," he said simply and quietly, taking his proffered hand. Sam held his stare for a long couple of seconds and gave a single nod.

"Alright then."

"What will I tell George?"

"The truth. Tell him he has to stop right now, I'll say nothing this time but that's it." Sam sniffed hard and rubbed his chin, again thinking solutions. He stabbed a finger at the glove compartment with its unwelcome contents. "If he's any sense he'll tell the owner of that the same. They'll know better than to push it. They're just as bad as the other lot." Sam seemed satisfied at this which in turn reassured Roy. "O.K, you can tell George I'll be round for a word sometime in the week. Now, let's watch the game."

George arrived home later that evening, and after a cursory greeting to the rest of the family immediately went upstairs, followed casually by Roy. George was staring at the coat lying on his bed when Roy came up behind him.

"Looking for something?"

"Where is it?" he hissed at Roy, spinning around, his cheeks flushed.

Roy didn't answer, coldly letting him sweat a bit as he had this afternoon.

"I said where is it?" George raised his voice a little, but not enough for anyone downstairs to hear.

Obviously his Da didn't know anything as he would have pounced and beaten him half to death the moment he walked through the door, so Roy must have it. Roy related the events of the afternoon all except his own promise. George sat heavily on his bed next to the guilty coat, staring at the floor.

"I was just holding it for... someone. Shit! What'll I say? Sorry, but my brother went and squealed on me and my uncle's got it now? Oh, and by the way did I mention the fact my uncle is a peeler?"

"No one squealed, you fool!" Roy retorted quietly. "Sam'll keep it just between us. Probably. Anyway he'll be wanting a wee word with you for sure. You could have gotten me jailed so you could ye prick!"

"Shut up to fuck! Why d'ye think I had the door locked in the first place? If it's anyone's fault it's yours ye thieving nosy bastard!"

"Why did you take it? Why get involved so?"

George looked up at him, his mouth curling with distaste. "In case you hadn't noticed there's a fight going on here, we're all involved whether you like it or not." He turned away. "Most of us that is."

Roy wanted badly to hit him for that, the two of them trading whispered insults for the next ten minutes, ears alert for any movement on the stairs but getting no further. Roy was sad and exhausted at the end of it, realising that a barrier had come between them. He lay that night, hands behind his head thinking about it, unable to sleep. Now he understood when people spoke of a crossroads; he and George would be taking different paths. He considered telling his Da, but only for an instant. The result of that would be unpredictable and would lay him open to accusations of betrayal, and he had heard enough of that for one day. He just hoped his Uncle Sam could talk sense to him.

A few weeks earlier Jimmy had been released from custody and came back to a changed home. It had been repeatedly and brutally searched in his absence and much superficial damage done. Not that Jimmy took much notice as he was a changed man after his weeks of internment. Martin had been released soon after his arrest, but they had held Jimmy and questioned him relentlessly. The intelligence was faulty, but how to explain you knew nothing to people who were convinced you knew plenty? It took time to convince them. Sometimes they wouldn't listen at all.

Martin brought his father a cup of tea and some digestive biscuits, gently putting them down beside him, knowing not to give the cup directly as his father's hand would quake embarrassingly. Jimmy looked briefly up at him like a scolded dog, the fear and shame still raw in his eyes. Martin turned quickly away, feeling the rage welling up inside, so bad it sometimes made his head hurt and his cheek muscles ache from gritting his teeth; he felt as if his blood was going to boil and burst hissing out of his veins. He walked swiftly back into the kitchen, eyes again stinging and stomach queasy from the acid of his hate, wanting to smash and kill the people who had done this. He sat at the table, fists balled and remembered.

He had sat for a little while in that room, bare except for the table waiting for the interrogation to begin, his imagination doing its best to frighten him. His logic told him that was probably why they made him wait; they would let his own mind do their work for them. This thought, and the fact he could still think clearly at all gave Marty some comfort. He started counting the creamy white bricks and wondered how many others had done the very same thing. His thoughts were interrupted by sudden shouts from outside and with a stab of concern he recognised one of them as his father, not just shouting but sounding like he was in pain. He jumped up and crashed into the locked door, slapping it with the flat of his hand.

"Da!" The echoing noise on the other side of the door continued, gruff shouting mixed in with his father's own.

"Whadda ya fink of *that* then Mr McKenna?" a sharp voice demanded, just like a salesman proud of a special offer, followed by the sound of muffled banging and scraping. It continued. "Keep standing! Fingertips only. Leave that fucking hood alone!" He heard his father shouting defiance.

"Fuck youse! You're bloody fools..." before it turned into a bellow of real anguish that went on for what must have been all of five seconds, fading into a retch and whimper. Marty froze, eyes wide, horrified not knowing what the hell was going on just ten feet away from him in the opposite room. There was more shouting.

"Get him up! Against the wall."

More banging about, gasps and grunts. Another shout of pain and with sudden clarity Marty was remembering an incident when he was a kid. He had secretly heated up the metal handle of a knife over the gas flame in the kitchen, watching fascinated as he held it under the tap and watched one by one the water drops dance and sizzle. On the second heating his father had unexpectedly walked in for a sandwich and had picked the knife up before a shocked Marty had time to warn him. It had blistered his hand and his scream had sounded all down the street. It was the sound Marty was hearing now and he thumped again on the door, his tears blinding him.

"Stop it! Stop it! Stop it!"

It went on and on as Marty slid down the wall and held his head in his hands to drown the awful noises out, not believing it possible in this day and age in what they called a part of Britain. He put his fingers in his ears, face now resting on one hand against the ground and concentrated on the cracks and gouges in the rough concrete floor that were illuminated and shadowed by the feeble sunlight coming through the grilled window, like so many miniscule valleys and fissures. He lost track of time but eventually raised his head, cautiously removing his fingers. There was quiet. No, he could just make out what sounded like low moaning and whispered voices. Questions. Footsteps sounded and his door was flung open with a creak and a bang, making him jump. A smooth educated sounding voice coated in happy malice spoke.

"Somebody told me the Irish were a tough lot, well that's a load of bollocks isn't it? Is there anything you want to tell us or the good police officer here? You know, help us put away some murdering scum perhaps, stop more children being blown to small pieces, that sort of thing?"

Marty brought his head a little higher taking in more of the hated uniforms and looking past them, seeing his Da against the wall in the opposite cell, hooded head slumped, naked and humiliated. He looked into the cold eyes of the peeler and numbly shook his head. The soldiers looked at each other, one of them shrugged.

"O.K, your choice. We'll be back for a chat later. Bye!"

Marty curled into a ball and cried himself to sleep. The hours had dragged and Marty awoke cold. He listened but heard little, a few distant laughs and talking. It was now dark outside. The door was opened and steaming food brought in, plunked down on the table with a plastic fork but no knife. Marty was hungry but decided not to touch the sausage, egg and what looked like mashed potatoes the same colour as the walls. It was a futile protest, but it made him feel somehow better.

Hours went by with occasional shouts and noises from the opposite cell, each one making him jerk, his heart leaping in his chest. This had to be the worst and with a start that made him blink he understood. This was part of it, like making him wait to let his mind conjure up all sorts of nightmares about what they were going to do and he'd be only too glad to tell them what they wanted. They could only go so far, surely? The law was still the law, wasn't it? Marty then thought about his Da. That was a real enough nightmare and he began to doubt again. These were really angry men and had seen some gruesome sights and wanted the people behind it, they might stop at nothing. The thing was he had nothing to tell anyway and after this day never would.

It was daylight. He sat on the ground directly opposite the door waiting. The door opened again with its usual creak and bang. The sergeant and another soldier in a green track suit were back along with the policeman.

"On your feet."

Martin complied as slowly as he dared, dragging himself upwards against the wall. The sergeant moved to one side, giving Marty an unobstructed view into the opposite cell. What he saw burned into his mind. His father was no longer hooded or positioned against the wall, he was on his hands and knees in only his underwear, a cloth in one hand and a bright red plastic bowl at his side, slowly cleaning up a puddle, his face bruised on one side with the mouth hanging slack and bloodied, head bowed.

"What a wanker," a voice jeered from one side. "Pissed himself. Get it cleaned up!"

"That's enough, shut it Jones will you?"

His father momentarily looked up, seeing the faces of his tormentors, one or two not bothering to conceal their enjoyment, others sickened that they were witness to this ultimate abasement, amongst them to complete his shame, the white staring face of his son, mouth open at his degradation. Marty watched as his father's head dropped and his shoulders began to twitch and realised he was seeing his father cry. Another soldier quickly shut the door, red faced and obviously angry at his own unwilling part in this humiliation of another human being. The policeman stepped in front of Marty, his eyes betraying no emotion.

"Sorry about that lad," he said in his curious high pitched voice. "Is there anything you want to tell us?"

Marty stayed silent, hardly hearing the question, his mind still stunned by what he had just seen. He felt ill, nauseous with what they had done and then the anger began, he could feel it beginning to burn, running through his veins and making his face hot and his body tremble. The officer took a step back and the others straightened their postures. Marty struggled to control himself. He shook his head both in denial at the question and what he had witnessed. The policeman watched him for a couple more seconds, the cold fish eyes unwavering as they scanned him.

"Very well, as soon as we have completed some paper work you are free to go."

The whole family had rushed into the rainy street to meet him, hugging and dragging him into the dry warmth of the house. Bernie alone had stood in the door, arms folded, looking behind him and along the street, searching. Marty suddenly felt so tired and wanted to cry, just let it all go, but knew he had to keep controlled, not wanting to distress his Ma any more than she was already. They asked him what had happened so he told them, carefully tailoring his story so as not to worry them. The first question from Patricia and Rosemary of course was when Da was coming home. Marty lied, telling them he was still joking as always and would be back soon which had satisfied them. He stole a glance at his Ma and knew she wasn't fooled, but she joined in the subterfuge knowing how it might affect her younger children, especially Rosemary if she thought her Da might not be home for a long time. It was better to put things off and hope for the best, after all Jimmy was innocent of anything so should be released any day. Privately she was extremely worried. To the outside world her husband was the same as always, jesting, laughing and carrying on, a man that seemed to be able to shake off the problems and troubled times like water from the proverbial duck's back. Nothing appeared to get him down. Bernie knew differently, knew that he wasn't so impervious, that the last years had weighed heavily on him, pressuring and straining as they strived to bring up a family in evil days. Only she saw just how much of a toll it had taken and how tired and weary he really was.

When Jimmy finally did come back in the New Year it was obvious to everyone that he wasn't the same man. There was no laughter, his eyes seemed remote and lifeless and physically although it had only been a matter of weeks he looked years older. Bernie had embraced him at the door and Jimmy had hardly moved, his hands staying unresponsive at his side, mumbling a hello and shuffling to his armchair by the fire. They were all so happy to see him again, the children crowding around his chair, faces smiling and shining. Jimmy did his wan best to appear cheerful, but it was so obviously forced that Bernie soon chivvied them out, saying their father just needed some rest and things would soon be back to normal. Later that night in bed Bernie realised just how badly Jimmy was altered. He lay next to her in the dark, whispering and again crying, shocking Bernie to her core at the change in him as she raised herself on one arm and listened. She was frightened and consoled herself that perhaps in time he would recover.

Marty eventually got up from the table and went to check on Jimmy. His Da hadn't moved. A biscuit lay where it had fallen, but he had drunk a little of the tea. He thanked Marty softly and held the cup out in a trembling hand, not looking at his son. He wasn't getting any better and the doctor had put him on some sort of pills, which as far as Marty could see only made him sleepy and withdrawn. His humour was totally gone and he neither told jokes nor laughed at anything; it was like having a stranger in the house. His brother Niall had been upset and tried to shock him out of it, shouting at him to pull himself together, even going so far as to gently slap him, but the only result of that was to start Jimmy crying again. Niall had stood mouth open and blinking, stunned before taking him in his affectionate bear hug. It was Niall that had made him to go to the doctor. Marty took the cup gently from his father, and going into the kitchen, opened the back door and with all his might smashed it against the ground into a hundred tinkling shards.

It was another bitterly cold daybreak as Sam sat sipping hot sweet tea in the canteen. He looked around at his fellow officers and listened to their early morning banter, most of it he noticed having very little to do with traditional crime; these days it was all terrorist crime. He also noticed with satisfaction that when he was around there were no more derogatory remarks about Catholics. He had verbally lashed one younger constable just last week for this, in his view they had to be as impartial as possible if they were to do their job properly. Young Trevor Green came and sat opposite him, fiddling with his holster, hat or anything else in range of his restless hands, impatient as usual to be doing something. His newly commissioned eagerness tickled Sam who smiled, remembering his own zeal many years ago. He had learned patience since then, knowing crime wasn't going to vanish any time soon leaving them all redundant.

"Are you ready Sam?"

Trevor was chaffing to be away, his fresh freckled face questioning with the bright eyes of an alert squirrel. Sam finished his tea and slowly got up as Trevor abruptly stood, dropping his hat as he did so.

"For goodness sakes ease up would ye, you're jumping about like Elvis with worms. There's no rush, the break in must have happened last night according to the report. We're just following up is all," he said.

He took his overcoat from the back of his chair and put it on, carefully buttoning it up as Trevor watched impatiently. They stepped out into the icy cold, Sam pulling a face like he had just bitten a lemon.

"Jeeeeesus! That's cold but!"

They got into their unmarked black Cortina. Trevor elected to drive. They were going to investigate a break in that had apparently happened the previous night at a cafe in the Ormeau Road district. It was a mixed area, and quieter than most, but Sam was always cautious. He knew the cafe. *The Sunspot* was a greasy spoon type of place, friendly and unassuming but did a great bacon sandwich, the fat crispy and melting in the mouth. He had used it himself on occasion. Trevor he noticed was driving as fast as possible, the novelty of being in uniform not having worn off yet. Give it time thought Sam as he lurched in his seat and tried to rub some heat into his hands. He looked at the orange disc of the sun just up, squinting at it as it became brighter but not in the least warmer. Before they reached the turnoff for their destination Sam spoke casually.

"The cafe is on the right hand side about half way along, opposite the junction with Gibbon Street and the chemist on the corner. Drive past it first for a quick look, then park up the end. We can walk from there."

Trevor grunted an acknowledgement, his mind obviously elsewhere, probably on super instinctive detective work, hunches and heroic arrests. They turned into the road and stopped almost directly outside the cafe, Trevor leaving the car almost before he had come to a stop. Sam frowned and clicked his tongue in annoyance as he wearily got out and called after Trevor who was already nearing the doorway, but oddly the cafe was closed and empty.

"Bloody well wait will you?"

Trevor stopped and turned. He raised his hand to his hat as if saluting, but really he was shielding his eyes from the low winter sunshine. Sam looked past him and saw movement reflected in the cafe window. He turned to see what Trevor was looking at. His hand went automatically to his own hat in imitation of Trevor as the sun glared directly into his own eyes, half blinding him. It happened in seconds and lasted the rest of his life.

Three men had come out of the small chemist shop on the corner, the bell tinkling lightly as they opened the door and moved very quickly across the road towards the policemen. They were dressed almost exactly the same in light green heavy parka coats, blue jeans and black Dr Marten boots. All were hooded, like executioners. Sam knew immediately what was going to happen, not needing to see the guns they held, now levelled at them. Time slowed and there were a lot of loud bangs. Sam felt a hard punch in the stomach and then another to his chest which felt like somebody had pierced him with a burning poker. A shot to his left elbow threw his arm up in an involuntary spasm, and then he saw the black tarmac of the road rushing up at him and realised in a disconnected way he was falling. The shooting went on and on and he thought he could hear Trevor shouting and then screaming, cut short by more shots. He felt little pain now, but breathing caused a slight stabbing sensation. His cheek was on the cold road, and briefly focusing he saw Trevor spread-eagled a few yards away, coat open, hat flat next to him and blood coming out of a black pit in the side of his head like red water from a bottle. It lapped rapidly into small lake, a tributary now dribbling towards him from the slant of the pavement. He saw with a mild detached interest that the scarlet pool was slightly steaming and smoking because of the intense cold. He could hear distant shouting now and a woman's higher pitched screaming. A couple of pairs of jeans ran past him and then a pair of shiny new boots appeared in front of his face and Sam could see every little detail. The scuffing on the toe, the small wrinkles in the glossy leather where the foot bent and red blood splashed and caked on the looped yellow stitching above the sole. He could even vaguely make out his own dim reflection on what was left of the shine. There was another horrible crash in his ear and then darkness.

Later that evening William and Betty were ushered into a waiting room at the Royal Victoria Hospital. Robert and another colleague had called around that afternoon to break the news: Sam was alive but in a critical condition. They hugged a tearful Heather who sat next to a waste bin that contained dozens of crumpled sodden tissues. She looked exhausted and sagged in the chair. After several hours a doctor appeared and gave them details. He was blunt but not rude, speaking first to Heather, very doctor like in his white coat and holding a clipboard in one hand, pushing his steel framed glasses up with the other.

"Mrs Black? The good news is that Samuel is out of immediate danger, but I must emphasize he is still in a critical condition. We have operated and removed several bullets and fragments. He's a lucky man and a strong one."

Heather looked up him with her tear stained face but it was William who replied. "We were told he had a head wound, what...eh ..." He lifted his hands, unsure how to continue.

The doctor touched his glasses again and shifted to his other foot. "Yes. We can't be sure of the full extent of the damage. It's still very early you understand." He hesitated, undecided whether to continue. Heather stood up, bracing herself, unwilling to ask but having to know.

"Is Sam going to get better?"

The doctor studied her for a second and said, "It's really too early Mrs Black, there may be permanent damage. We just have to wait and see." Heather's shoulders fell. "I'm very sorry."

"Can we see him?" Betty asked.

The doctor again hesitated, asking himself what the point was, but then gave a nod. "He's still unconscious, but yes you may. Please, wait here and someone will be along directly."

Later they were led for what seemed miles along anti septic smelling corridors, they knew which was Sam's room when they saw two bored soldiers sitting outside the door. They were allowed to look in and William wished they hadn't. Sam lay on a bed, arms at his side, covered to the chest with a blanket in what looked like a plastic tent. They couldn't see much of his face as it was masked and half bandaged. There were tubes protruding from him attached to various machines and drips. Looking at the masked silent face William was reminded of a Russian cosmonaut. Betty and Heather began to cry again, so William led them out hanging on to one another, knowing now why the doctor had been so reticent, and taking a last look at Sam he doubted if he would ever wake up.

The troubles intensified into a storm as fresh gusts of fear and hate buffeted the province. Hardly a day now went past without some new act of violence, a bomb, a shooting, a riot. People were being injured, killed and mutilated. Soldiers, policemen, paramilitaries from both sides and more than ever civilians in the wrong place at the wrong time: the Ulster lottery. The Parachute regiment had shot thirteen civilians dead on 'Bloody Sunday' stoking the fires further. The British embassy in Dublin had then been burned to the ground, and the IRA then bombed the Para base at Aldershot, managing to kill some women cleaners and the regimental chaplain. In March, the *Abercorn* restaurant in the centre of Belfast, crowded with afternoon shoppers having a snack and a coffee was blown up resulting in yet more grisly carnage. Another bomb in the centre had killed seven a few weeks later and that was enough for the Government in Westminster. Direct rule from London was introduced to the joy of Catholics who saw it as a victory, and fury of Protestants who saw their own cherished parliament scrapped with a pen.

It was a sunny spring morning and Mickey Flynn was out on a job, namely being one of the shooters on an ambush. Mickey settled down into his firing position and began the wait. He wasn't keen about this particular job for several reasons: firstly, because he would be working with people who were relatively new to him, two of his regular team having been arrested the previous week. They were still members of 3rd battalion and knew the Ardoyne as well as himself, but still, it was a different element and made him uneasy. Colm Johnson he knew well enough, a big dark lad with a distinctive Mexican style drooping moustache, known locally as 'Pancho'. The other volunteer was Joe Quinn, who had earned his moniker of 'Frazzle' a couple of years earlier when he had mishandled a petrol bomb and burnt a large scar onto his right hand. A decent enough fella but his evident nervousness, continually gulping and swallowing air made him look like a distressed puffin, putting Mickey himself on edge. He became aware of a slight dampness under his arms and behind his knees. It was one of Joe's first big jobs so he was left to do the driving. There was also the fact they were doing the deed in daylight, which although not uncommon was not to Mickey's liking. He preferred the blanket of the dark if something went wrong; he knew these streets and the Brits didn't. Lastly was the fact that this particular job had been planned a bit too hurriedly for his liking, the C.O insisting on immediate retaliation to show the arrests had not diminished his battalion's effectiveness. They would send a message to the Brits by shooting one or two of them.

It was early and the street was pretty empty, most of the residents by now aware a shoot had been set up. Mickey hunkered down, occasionally peeping out for the signal from behind the fallen masonry of the half destroyed corner house as he stroked his M1 carbine's pale wooden butt. He would use the chest high brickwork as a rest. Standing next to him, Pancho was dressed in an olive green combat jacket and was also looking through a hole in the wall, several bricks having been removed earlier. Behind them, just out of view was the car containing Frazzle, who remained hunched over the steering wheel, gripping it as if trying to push it into the engine. Any approaching foot patrols would be reported by strategically placed spotters, to either prepare them to get ready or warn them of danger. That was the theory and most of the time it worked, but there was always the risk of the unexpected. There was little noise, a car honked its horn somewhere in the distance and a dog kept up a monotonous barking in the next street. By now the Brits had become wary if it was too quiet or too empty, learning from bitter experience what might follow such stillness. A blackbird sang above them, unaware and uncaring of the ugliness below.

Mickey moved a piece of charred wood to one side and briefly let his concentration wander, thinking of Eileen and their secretive and hurried recent marriage. No time for much of a honeymoon, but the time they did manage to spend together was pure bliss. He might be able to see her tomorrow with any luck. He also thought about her brother Marty who had recently asked him about becoming a volunteer. He might even be working with him one day. He didn't visit Eileen's home that much anymore and not only because of the obvious danger of being spotted, arrested or shot. No, to tell the truth he didn't feel comfortable there. Although no one had blamed him for what had happened he couldn't forget it was himself the Brits were looking for when they arrested Jimmy and Martin. It wasn't guilt he felt exactly, but every time he looked at Jimmy sat there in his armchair seemingly all bloody day he felt a twinge of unease. Eileen sometimes talked about her father too, and always sadly. Where once he had been so full of fun and mischief, now he was withdrawn, morose and sometimes bitter. She said that it used to be her father could brighten up any gathering and bring laughter to any room. Not anymore; as far as Mickey was concerned, her father now brightened the room by leaving it.

He sensed Pancho stiffen beside him and then bring his weapon up, looking to the far end of the street as a woman in a red top walked quickly past and out of view, the signal a foot patrol was on the way. Sure enough, around the corner came the first of two four man 'bricks' as the army called them, two running across the road covered by the others who briskly walked up to numbers 7 and 9, crouching down in the doorways, searching and scanning the street for danger. Shots crashed out from above him as Pancho let fly, making Mickey jump and curse as they were supposed to wait until the soldiers had gotten to the door of number 15. Too late he targeted a soldier who had flung himself down on the pavement behind an old scuffed black Morris Minor, letting a few rounds off, the recoil jerking his shoulder and then not as the rifle jammed.

"Shit!"

A bullet cracked into the masonry and tumbled bricks in front of him, raising a small pinkish dust cloud, then another. The reaction had been much faster than expected. Pancho was already sprinting towards the car, the driver's taut white face shouting, the words lost to him. Mickey scrambled away, breathing heavily, then ran to the revving car. Pancho watched as more shots crashed out and Mickey seemed to stumble and then fell flat, the carbine clattering on the pavement. He was down and finished, his last view that lasted a split second was that Mickey's head had sort of ballooned outwards as he fell before final panic took hold and they screeched away in a cloud of blue exhaust and burnt rubber. A minute later the body was ringed by soldiers. One of them was excited, breathing hard with the adrenalin still coursing through him. It might have been his shot and the gun was still there by the body so it would be all nice and legal. He toed the corpse and bent down, angling his head to one side for a better look, careful not to step in the blood pooled beside the shattered head.

"Fuck me! Humpty Dumpty or what?"

"No open coffin for this boyo," the radioman said flatly. He glanced at the body and quickly looked away, appalled at the damage. The mouth was open in a slack 'O' and everything below the bridge of the nose was still there, but above that the cranium had been emptied. The whole head seemed split and flattened like a torn rubber mask tossed carelessly on a blat of crimson and grey brain matter. People were starting to come out of their houses as the first outraged shouts began.

Marty was upstairs rummaging about in his record collection when he heard someone coming to their door early that evening. To his surprise it sounded like Gerry Fox. There was the sound of hushed conversation and then a scream.

"Noooooooooooo......."

It was Eileen, howling her awful grief, dog like in a high pitched keening that went on and on, freezing Marty's blood and rooting him to the spot. The sound of his sister's raw and sudden terrible pain, the sound of a banshee. He took a deep breath and went downstairs slowly, scared of what he might see.

Eileen was being fiercely held by his Ma, her shoulders heaving in giant sobs. The screaming had now subsided to a low moaning through tears as his Ma stroked her back before gently lowering her onto the armchair, kneeling in front and cradling her head in her hands. Gerry Fox stood head bowed whilst his Da just looked blankly at his wife and daughter, mute and uncomplaining. Gerry raised his head and looked directly at Marty, the eyes unblinking and contemplative rather than sympathetic, like a baker checking to see if his loaves had risen. Marty held his stare for a long moment before he turned away.

In the Ferguson's darkened living room a TV presenter made an announcement as if this was what mankind had been waiting for.

"... and now, live from Norwich! It's the quiz of the week! Sale of the Century!"

This was followed by a suave and smarmily polite Nicholas Parsons presenting a game show that nobody in this particular household was paying the slightest attention to. William and George sat deep in their own thoughts, both staring at the show blindly, the beautiful hostess unseen, the prizes unregistered.

Roy was sat at the table sipping a mug of tea and thinking about the events of this dreadful day, his anger and hatred flashing on and off as he thought about it. On the table lay the *Belfast Telegraph*, its headlines *'Bomb a minute blitz in Belfast, many injured'*. It didn't tell the whole story: as well as the injured, mutilated would be more accurate, there were nine people blasted into travesties of human beings; the IRA had caused people to be scraped up from the street like so much burnt jelly. His Ma and John were at the hospital visiting Billy.

The day had started with a bright air of anticipation. It was July 21st and after weeks of nagging Roy had finally been given permission to visit Uncle Sam, now home, recuperating and apparently out of danger. His Ma had been strangely reluctant to let them call and the younger children in particular had not understood why, as he had been home now for some time after a surprisingly rapid recovery. Eventually there had been a whispered parental conference, the tail end of which Roy had picked up ending with an ambiguous "...may as well be now as later."

Originally Roy had intended to go with John, but Billy had heard and started whining and demanding to be included. His Da and George were by now away to work on this overcast but warm Friday morning. Betty was hesitant to let him go along, but Billy's pleading and Roy's promise to keep him safe persuaded her. She had faith in her son's judgement despite his youth and decided to show this, albeit with a little unease which showed clearly in her eyes and frown. Roy couldn't as yet fathom the reason but instinctively felt something wasn't right, which was confirmed as they were leaving. She gave Billy a kiss which he indignantly rubbed off as 'sissy' and spoke to them as they opened the door.

"You know which route to take?"

"Yes Ma, it'll be longer but safer and we'll be getting a bus from the centre."

"Alright then." She hesitated, then spoke again. "Roy, you can't expect too much now. Your Uncle Sam is still... not the best but."

By now Billy and John were starting to jostle impatiently in the doorway. Roy gave his Ma his best toothy smile.

"Don't worry Ma, we'll be fine. See you later."

Sam and Heather lived across the river in a nice part of East Belfast, just off the Upper Newtonards Road. This necessitated a fairly lengthy journey, first on foot and then with a bus ride. By the time they arrived in the centre, Billy was complaining of tired legs and Roy was relieved to get on the cream and red bus, thinking maybe they would slow the pace on the way back. Billy was pressing his nose against the grimy window, ignoring John's teasing which stopped abruptly when Billy dug a half packet of fluff covered fruit Polo's out of his pocket and proceeded to eat them. Roy let out a burst of laughter when Billy turned to John with a victorious piglet smile and popped the last one into his mouth without offering a single one to his tormentor.

Sam and Heather's place was the second house on the left of the tree lined avenue, a fairly large detached affair, white painted and with a well maintained garden and lawn complete with rose bushes and a plum tree. It was a pleasant neighbourhood and reflected the comfortable status of those living there, professional and middle class types not at all like where they lived. Roy pondered this as they made their way up to the porch and knew that one of the reasons Sam and Heather had always been on such close terms with his own family was because they never made a big deal of status or money, and were never patronising or condescending as some others. It reflected his own parent's view, William once telling them that money was to be respected but not too much. It could open more routes on life's highway, but didn't guarantee a happy final destination; you could still choose a wrong path and follow it to misery and be carrying a suitcase full of cash. Roy had liked that analogy. He looked at the trees swaying gently in the breeze, listening to them rustle in the alien quiet of the avenue and then at the plum tree which always brought forth delicious violet globules. He had happy memories of summers past, of other visits with laughter, shouting and lawn games, eating the plums, the only danger the competing wasps.

"What's that there for?" said John, pointing downwards before the door.

Roy looked and saw a small wooden ramp. There was fresh scuffing and a few dents in the door frame. Unsure, he ignored him and rang the bell. The netting moved at the window and a moment later they heard the rattling sound of chains being loosened and snap of bolts being drawn back. The door opened and Heather peered out at them.

"Hello Auntie Heather!" Billy piped brightly.

She looked at them blankly for a moment before attempting a smile and opening the door to let them in. Roy noticed the change in her appearance, she looked tired and drawn and for the first time that he could remember there was no trace of makeup. There were wrinkles now that he hadn't seen before and her once so neatly kept hair was showing a few loose strands. She stood before them smiling weakly.

"It's good to see you all boys. Sam will be thrilled. He's not a hundred per cent yet so don't be disappointed. He can't talk... much." She stopped, searching for words. "The doctors say it might get better with time. I'll just get him ready," and with that she went into the front room. They looked at each other with growing unease. "OK you can come in now."

Sam was sat in a wheelchair by the window with a red tartan blanket over his knees and looked to Roy to have aged about twenty years in a few short months. John gave an audible intake of breath whilst Billy just stared. Heather stood at his side and Roy couldn't help noticing she spoke to him like a child.

"Look who's come to see you Sam! Isn't it great?"

It was hard to tell if Sam knew what the hell was going on. He made a gurgling noise like someone trying to breathe through their nose with a heavy cold, and to his shock Roy saw a thread of saliva dribble slowly from one side of his twisted face. He looked further and noticed the claw like hands and the legs beneath, the feet tucked into carpet slippers. Roy couldn't believe that his uncle had been replaced by this wasted figure, it was just too different. That was another thing, looking again at Sam's face it was as if the whole shape of his head had changed somehow and with a start he saw this actually was the case. Against the brightness of the window he could see Sam's head was curiously flattened on one side. When he looked at the eyes he instantly grieved again, his heart suddenly heavy. They were vacant, dull and dead. The others had taken this all in and the silence was broken only by Sam's laboured breathing. Heather spoke.

"He tires easily I'm afraid. I'll go and make some tea, please, make yourselves comfortable," and with that she swiftly left the room. They sat down and Billy looked tearfully at Roy.

"I want to go home," he whispered.

"Wise up, we're only just here!" said Roy, keeping his voice low. "What'll they...she think?"

So they sat for several of the most uncomfortable minutes Roy had ever experienced, trying desperately to make some sort of conversation with what was once a fine man, but now little better than a vegetable. To their great relief Heather hurried in bearing a tray, trying to keep some sort of normality going, her smile tight and face strained as she talked on.

"I know Sam's been so looking forwards to seeing you again, did it take long to get here? Help yourselves now boys. Any plans for the school holidays then?"

Roy could see she was struggling, the pain clear in her face and eyes and the way her voice now drifted and faded. At that moment there was another noise from Sam which made them stop and stare. What might have passed for a slight smile was on his frozen face and then came a wet, slow bubbling sound from under the blanket. Within seconds the room was filled with a smell of old cauliflower. Heather reddened and stammered.

"I'm sorry boys, it's not a good time right now..."

Roy got up, unable to witness this further descent of a man he had admired and loved his entire life. John and Billy followed him out, heads bowed where they said a hurried and embarrassed farewell to Heather who merely lowered her own head to hide her watering eyes. She hugged Billy and went to attend her husband. They saw themselves out in silence.

The bus ride back to the centre was made in a state of incomprehension. Billy said nothing, nose pressed to the window again, seeing little through the grimed glass, whilst Roy and John exchanged brief and shocked comments.

"I can't believe it! There's nothing there of him," said John.

"I know." Roy's voice cracked slightly as he replied, a pricking behind his eyes. "I don't think he even knew we were there. The bastards have killed him."

On reaching the centre and alighting from the bus it became immediately apparent that something unusual was happening on this busy Friday afternoon. They had left one horror and now stepped into another.

Several bombs had just gone off and policemen and soldiers were busy trying to shepherd people away from fresh warnings and danger, raw fear in hundreds of faces. As they stood watching, another bomb exploded, this one not too far away, sending a vast puff of dirty smoke into the air, the sudden crash of it making everybody flinch with an involuntary ducking of heads into shoulders. Roy grabbed Billy by the arm and followed the crowd. Another bomb, this one to the north but still loud enough. Then one to the south around Botanic way. There was a lull of a few minutes and then it seemed bombs were going off all over the place, screams and shouts could be heard and the crowds were becoming panicked not knowing where or when the next would come. The sound of sirens now filled the air along with more distant human wailing and guttural shouts. Roy, John and Billy followed a gaggle of wide eyed, white faced people up the road past shops and stores, people standing hesitant in doorways as if wondering whether to venture out into some rain. The people in front of them slowed near the end of the road and Roy raised himself on tip toe behind a woman and pushchair to see what the obstruction was. Two policemen were walking quickly towards them shouting something, arms outstretched like protective wings to stop anybody proceeding further. Some of the crowd turned and began to walk faster in the opposite direction, a few now running past the boys, their eyes huge and close to panic. The woman with the pushchair was trying to calm her crying child as she struggled to turn it around, the policemen drawing level.

"Quickly now, move away! We have to clear the area!"

Roy again took Billy's arm and turned to go. At that moment it seemed there was a micro second of utter silence followed by a massive crashing roar as a bomb went off, this time much closer, in fact where they had been heading, sending debris, bricks and lethal glass shards flying in all directions. Roy was shoved off his feet by an invisible hand, his ears singing. Quickly sitting and then getting to his feet he noticed the dust in the air and an amazing amount of rubbish strewn around. Others were also getting up, dusting themselves down, checking for injuries. Some seemed dazed in shock, standing staring and then the screaming and sobbing began. Roy looked around trying to take everything in, his senses still befuddled as if coming out of a deep sleep in a split second. One of the police officers had slowly pulled himself up and was kneeling in front of the pushchair, the child wailing and tear streaked but otherwise unhurt, her mother was sitting close by amidst shards of glass. Incongruously Roy at first thought she was wearing a necklace of rich red garnets on her pale yellow summer dress, but then understood with a jolt she was cut and bleeding. He could see more cuts and grazes to her bare legs and what looked like a garnet earring, one that grew and dropped onto her yellow shoulder as he watched to be quickly replaced by another. A scarecrow limped towards them and lurched past before they realised this hatless figure was a policeman, covered in dust, his trousers shredded as if a spiteful child had taken a pair of scissors to them. Roy turned to see John standing unhurt and trying to talk to Billy, whose hands covered his face. With a sudden cold thrill that stabbed his guts like an icicle Roy noticed blood on Billy's hand as John pulled them from his face. The sight of this blood set Billy crying and they saw that he had been hit by glass too. John put his arm around him and tried to see the extent of the wound. It was now bleeding freely and Roy swallowed in horror; Billy had been hit in the left eye which was already puffed.

"My eye! My eye! My eye! My eye!" was all that Billy could scream out as he began to jump up and down in pain and panic. The policeman came over and placed a handkerchief over the wound. Roy was now by him and doing his best to calm his little brother.

"It's O.K Billy, the ambulance is on the way. You'll be fine, we'll come with you."

Billy's hysteria was replaced by racking sobs as Roy took him and hugged him close, repeating over and over, "It'll be alright Billy, be brave now, it'll be alright."

Mercifully the ambulance came in a few short minutes and took them away. Billy was kept in hospital for a few days and stitched up, thankfully not blinded but he would carry a scar for life. They all would.

Chapter 5

Both Sides of the Chasm

It was raining softly but steadily, the drops pattering gently against the bedroom window, the grey early morning dimly lighting the room through thin blue curtains. Martin was fully awake and listened to muted laughter and clicking heels as a couple passed by outside, and then to the ticking of the clock and the soft snoring beside him. He turned onto his side and raised himself on one elbow, looking with a fond smile at the form laying there half curled, with short blonde hair and bare pale shoulders.

It was good to be home again. He casually stroked one arm, and then with growing interest gently slid the sheet down, revealing more of the sleeping body until it was naked to the top of one shapely thigh, the curves perfect and her buttocks beautifully round. He sighed deep in his throat as the figure stirred and gave a muffled chuckle, taking a handful of white sheet to cover herself. He felt himself quickly hardening, but then with a harsh ringing the alarm of the clock shattered the stillness, abruptly cut off by Martin as he banged his hand down, causing it to clatter to the floor. He lay back again and looked at the ceiling with its chintzy hanging lampshade. The angelic form besides him turned and focused with large, oval, slightly slanting blue eyes, the delicate eyebrows arched, and the small red mouth pouting and then curving in a mischievous self satisfied smile.

"Good morning, did you sleep well?" she asked knowingly, the voice alone husky and sexy enough to restart Martin's erection.

Before he could act on it she had rolled away and stood at the side of the bed, searching for last night's hastily discarded clothing. She frowned slightly at her feet, not entirely happy with their shape, the toes long and separate: Botticelli toes. Martin watched her entranced, not wanting her to cover the perfectly proportioned little body that gave him so much pleasure as she snapped on a black bra and then her knickers. She stretched, yawning widely, arching herself and Marty mused again on how the word feline did indeed fit some women. This one also had pretty sharp claws that had given his back a severe raking last night.

"I've to be away," she said, looking at him speculatively. "Will I be seeing you later then?"

Martin grunted "Aye," before smiling back at her. Watching her dress was not nearly as good as the other way around. She gave him a quick peck, and giggling, a squeeze through the sheets. She left and after a minute the toilet flushed and he could hear her pottering about downstairs before the door opened and slammed shut. Her quick footsteps on the street outside receded and Marty stretched for a cigarette from the table. He thought about what she had just asked and immediately tensed. Today was a big day and he hoped he had given the right answer. He lit up, remembering their first meeting and after a few puffs felt his tightened stomach muscles relaxing.

He had met her several years ago at a ceili he had gone along to with Brendan. He wasn't keen, but Brendan had insisted, so he had trailed along with his friend chattering away to make up for his own lack of conversation. By the time they arrived through the darkened streets, past the by now familiar but still hated foot patrol to the hall, the ceili was in full swing. Brendan was still talking, pushing his own blond locks back and rubbing his hands in anticipation.

"Plenty of talent here tonight Marty eh?" he shouted above the noise.

"D'ye reckon?" he answered not too enthusiastically, leaning with both elbows on the table, avoiding the spilled drink, looking carefully around them through the smoky hall.

"Jesus you're a miserable bastard." Brendan had snickered.

He looked at Marty to see his attention fixed on a table at one side. His eye caught a couple of girls in the process of fending off the drunken and obviously unwanted proposals of some big lad who was full to the gills and gripping their table to hold himself steady. One girl was laughing, her dark red hair and freckles evident even in this poor light. The other he noticed was coolly watching Marty, petite, blond with a pert nose and cute mischievous smile. He didn't recognise either of them and was about to comment when Marty got up, drink in hand and went towards them. He followed, pushing carefully through a few weaving bodies as Marty took a vacant seat opposite the blond. He sat next to him just as the drunk admitted defeat, turning and staggering away laughing and whooping wildly.

"Have a seat why don't you?" the red head asked with mock indignation. She eyed them up but wasn't displeased, waiting for a response. Brendan laughed and Marty gave his sparkling grin but more or less ignored her, speaking to the blond.

"Do you come here often?" he said in an innocent voice, knowing the most unoriginal chat up line in the English language along with the cheeky smile would make them laugh and get things moving.

Before long they were deep in shouted conversation, ignoring those around them. Brendan pulled a questioning face at the red head whose name was Anne and took her off for a dance. Marty looked the blond up and down trying to think of whom she reminded him of, and then with a laugh it came to him from childhood memory how much she resembled 'Tinkerbell'. He commented on this and was amused at her answer.

"You look bugger all like Peter Pan I can tell you, what's your name?"

"Martin."

"There's a coincidence, I'm Martina. Marty and Marty!"

Just then there was a commotion as the drunk crashed to the floor, banging his head on the way down, laying there out for the count. Most people just ignored him and shuffled around the prostrate figure, apart from a thin dark girl in jeans who came swaying over to tend to him. To Marty's surprise he saw it was Maureen Veroni, pawing at him ineffectually, one hand resting unconsciously on his crotch. Martina noticed his look of recognition and curled her pretty lip.

"Do you know her?"

"I used to."

"Nice of her to help the poor eejit."

Marty gave a cackle as he noticed the look of earnest concern on Maureen's face. "Help? She's probably trying to get a last hard on out of him!"

Martina joined in the laughter, his forthright earthy humour appealing to her. He found out she was not from around here but from just off the Andersontown Road and was just visiting, staying overnight at an aunts nearby. He didn't know the area all that well despite staying with his Uncle Niall that time, but remembered the houses there were much newer and better than in his own neighbourhood. It was also a district with a fiercely Republican population and as dangerous for crown forces as any in the province. Like him she was also thinking about university, where she wanted to study literature. They talked and talked, and when the evening was drawing to a close talked all the way to where she was staying, oblivious of the mundane and ugly surroundings. They focused for this moment only, on the beauty of mutual attraction, walking now with his arm around her waist which she had encouraged, leaning into him and wrapping her thin coat closer despite the mildness of the weather. It was strange, he was so relaxed in her company, he felt he had known her all his life. He hardly noticed as a foot patrol came in the opposite direction, each man dashing from one shaded doorway to the next, seeking as much meagre cover as possible, as if connecting dots on a street map. They hardly heard the wolf whistle and accompanying "Go on mate, give her one for me!" which was quickly hissed into silence by the patrol leader. They reached her aunt's house and saw the front room light was still on.

"I'd better be getting in," she said simply in that curiously husky voice, looking up at him with big eyes and long lashes.

"I'd like to see you again," he said.

She stretched her neck, lifting her face ever so slightly which was all the invitation Marty needed to take hold and kiss her for a long minute.

"Great, are you doing anything next Saturday?" she asked. Marty shook his head emphatically. "Call round about two then. Oh, and don't take any notice of my Ma if she's there but. She'll give you the third degree but she's sound."

With that she turned and went indoors. Marty walked a little further before suddenly jumping into the air, punching the night sky as a resounding, "Yes!" echoed up the street.

At this time Marty had been increasingly active, not to the extent of actually joining the Provos, but helping out on the edge, as for the moment they had more than enough recruits anyway. By his own lights he had kept his promise to his Ma, but that didn't stop him helping out in other ways. He had acted as a messenger and a lookout, and had once picked up and delivered a sealed bag to an address on the Falls, being stopped and searched by a random foot patrol, fortunately on his way back, their attitude and casual insults as they frisked and questioned him serving as all the justification he needed. He had looked at the soldiers with drab loathing. Didn't they realise what they were doing? How the fuck would they like it if a foreign soldier stopped them in the middle of the street in London or Birmingham or whatever slum they came from?

Predictably though as his relationship with 'Tinkerbell' or 'Tinks' as he now called her developed, he saw more and more of her and less of his friends, so this activity decreased and what is more he didn't care. He thought maybe he was in love and had the fantastic feeling that she loved him just as much and what could be better in life than this? There would be time enough to join the struggle which didn't look like it would be over any time soon; the struggle could wait and love could not. On the visits to her place he grew to like her Ma, who had a well deserved reputation in the area for fearing no one and speaking her mind. In a way she reminded him of Jimmy in better days, a strong character who didn't go to church, but had her own set of morals. Martina's father had died some years before and her only other sibling was a younger sister Irene, who naturally adored Marty at first sight as younger sisters always did. One huge advantage to her Ma's liberal 'screw the church' attitude was that she let him stay over some nights to the absolute scandal of Mrs Healy across the road. A disadvantage though was her Ma's encouragement for Martina to go away to study, to the mainland in fact and after a wonderful summer this was what happened. When she told him she had a place at Durham university he had been shocked and then angry, even though he should have expected it. Marty had also felt a twinge of jealousy as he had messed up his own exams.

"Why? What's wrong with Queens here in the city or even Coleraine?"

"I want to get away Marty, see somewhere else, you can still visit and I'll be back here in the holidays. I want to be independent," she said pleading with him.

He knew then it was over and felt instantly miserable, but there were no tears. He had grown up fast in this place and hardened his attitude, shrugging off the sting and disappointment. He wouldn't let it show. He smiled, turned and walked away tossing her a nonchalant farewell.

"Fine. See you round then," he said over his shoulder, glad to see the hurt on her face to repay some of his own pain.

It was soon after this that Marty had surprisingly decided to go to London. The invitation had come out of the blue a few days later from old school friend Tony Francis, who had been living and working in Stockwell for the last few months; he could get him a job and they could share the rent on a flat he had there. His Ma worried but consented, he was so young to be leaving home even if it probably was the safe move. At that particular point, to Marty it seemed a good idea, he was still vexed with Tinks and he had also recently witnessed the aftermath of a premature explosion, what the Brits laughingly called an 'own goal'. There had been the usual loud bang and a part of the main road had been sealed off. Later he had gone for a look and seen the remains of the car two volunteers had been transporting a bomb in. It had exploded on the way to the target and they had been blown to bits. There was very little left of the car, two flattened front wheels, some ripped bodywork, the buckled steering wheel and the engine, the torn wiring and entrails exposed humiliatingly. Martin had stared at it pensively and heard later that one of the passengers was a guy he knew vaguely. He wondered fleetingly how they sorted out the pieces, who was who and which family got what.

So he had gone, arriving early on an overcast morning at Victoria coach station and making his way to Tony's place, and after a boozy celebration in the *Swan,* Marty had tried to settle down to a new life.

Employment had been easy to find, building work for the most part. Being a plasterer's assistant was physically hard but well paid, and they enjoyed the immensely varied nightlife that such a metropolis had to offer. And of course the women, who to Tony's delight seemed drawn to Marty like a magnet, his boyish irresistible charm increasing his own chances which he made full use of. Marty enjoyed himself. He was young, handsome, and now physically a fine specimen from his work and had money in his pocket, but every so often he would stop and think about home, which despite everything still retained a strange pull for him. Brendan visited a few times and kept in touch but wouldn't stay, and Marty missed his company. In all he had spent nearly three years in the capital before his last visit home when events occurred that decided him irrevocably to stay.

He had been back only a few weeks, his family glad to see him, his Ma hugging and kissing him, trying to keep back her tears of joy, his sisters happy and laughing and Thomas, grown up now and more serious, giving him a friendly slap and grin. Even Jimmy wasn't too sour and seemed to have picked himself up a little from his depths. At least he wasn't drinking cheap spirits anymore which was a definite improvement. He gave his son a quick hug and brief but heartfelt, "Nice to see you Marty, really," before sitting down again with a beer and resuming his scathing comments on the TV. *Are You Being Served* was on and Jimmy pointed.

"What's so funny about some bloody poof mincing about would you tell me?"

He bumped into those of his friends that were still on the streets. Some had gone away or been jailed, or in a few cases were dead. Brendan came around the first week and they had a happy reunion, made all the better by the fact that he was just after finishing a short jail sentence for his part in an affray which had resulted in a bus burning.

The Troubles were still there in the background, the army and police, the roadblocks, security barriers, searches and harassment, the almost daily irritation. The whole situation was sort of like a toothache. Sometimes you wouldn't feel much at all and could even forget there was a problem, and other days there would be a dull persistent ache or a sudden sharp but short pain. Other times, the bad times, the pain would be almost unbearable. Although a ceasefire had come and gone and internment had finished, there was still the fear of being abducted if found walking the wrong street at the wrong time, to be slashed and butchered by sectarian murder gangs, and discovered early in the morning by a gaping milkman or postman, dumped like so much rubbish in an alleyway.

Marty decided to look up Martina, and did this by casually bumping into her near where she lived, pretending to be visiting his Uncle Niall who lived not too far away. He had of course asked about first and been excited to discover she had just finished her studies and was back living with her Ma and sister. She knew it was no coincidence and didn't care. For his part he hadn't dared hope it would be so easy, but within minutes it was just like old times as they chatted and held hands across the cafe table where they had gone to get in from a summer shower. She told him all that had happened since they had last met, and Marty noticed with not a little amusement his style of parting still piqued her even now. What surprised him was how politicised she had become, talking about the movement and such, whereas before she had avoided politics whenever she could. It was strange, but didn't bother him; although he didn't yet know it, he was about to become involved again himself.

The next day, feeling good and walking along the Antrim Road in the heat of a sunny afternoon he noticed police and soldiers on a joint patrol, nothing unusual but he instinctively slowed his pace and then crossed over. He just wanted to get home and avoid the hassle of being stopped and questioned before being let go. One of the soldiers however had noticed him cross and had other ideas.

"Oi! You! Stop there a moment."

Marty halted wearily, his annoyance clear to see, which seemed to antagonize yet please them at the same time.

"Name and address!"

Marty told them.

"Do you have any identification?"

He didn't. The soldier smiled grimly, his mustachioed face red, beefy and sweating in the heat.

"Well we'll just have to check you out won't we? So sorry." He didn't look it. He turned to the radio operator, "Alright Baz, run a check." He faced Marty again. "OK you, against the wall there and spread 'em, I'm sure you know the drill." He did, and hated it.

They searched him roughly, he could feel the soldier's breath at the back of his neck and smell the spearmint gum as they frisked him, then a quick punch to his kidney when he tried to turn around before they had finished. He noticed the look on the policeman's bored face, like they were handling dog shit and he felt humiliated and soiled, all the submerged rage coming swiftly to the surface. There was a crackling all clear on the radio and he was released with a contemptuous dismissal.

"Alright, you can piss off now."

Marty walked away, his legs unsteady from his hatred, frustration and humiliation, white faced with a futile fury, knowing that there was nothing he could do about it. He got home eventually and discovered more misery waiting to give him that final push. Thomas had been arrested. He couldn't believe it. His Ma was too distraught to tell him about it and was upstairs lying down, her favourite son and the dreams she had attached to him were now destroyed. It was Jimmy who stonily gave him the details.

"He was in a car along with that so called friend of his Peter Fallon and some other lad when they were stopped near the centre. They found pistols and ammunition, so I've been told." Jimmy rubbed his forehead with both hands like he had a massive hangover, eyes closed. Marty slumped heavily into the settee.

"D'you think it's true Da?"

"No. Not our Thomas, as for the other two who knows and what does it matter anyway?"

He was right, Thomas would be going away for a long time and they both knew it, Marty could faintly hear his Ma's stifled crying. She knew it too.

Marty had become a volunteer the day after Thomas had been arrested. It hadn't been difficult; he had simply gone to see Brendan, who had recently volunteered himself for operations. He shook his hand and later took him to a disused garage. It had that peculiar stink of old oil and damp. The man responsible for recruitment in Marty's area turned out to be John 'Bunny'

Hughes, a broad and balding man approaching middle age but not yet run to fat. He had done time and was known to Marty who didn't really like him, knowing him to be ready to beat the fuck out of people and not always when sanctioned. Marty kept his thoughts hidden and faced Hughes with his fringe of what was once curling hair, deep set eyes and a noticeable overhang to his mouth, hence the nickname 'Bunny'.

"You're welcome Marty, I heard what happened yesterday." He paused, searching Marty's face for a reaction before continuing portentously. "Are you ready to take up arms, to strike a blow Martin? If necessary take a life? To fight for Irish freedom. This is not the same as doing a few errands but." This last was said with a just a tinge of amused contempt. Marty noticed Brendan shifting, slightly embarrassed. He'd heard enough from the pompous bastard.

"If I wasn't I wouldn't fucking be here now would I?" he said calmly. Hughes frowned briefly before continuing.

"O.K, just so we know where we stand. Anyway we need all the volunteers we can get these days. You'll be contacted soon and we can get things sorted formally and begin training." He shook Marty's hand and was gone. Brendan was happy.

"Good on ye Marty!" He clapped him hard on the back, enthusiastic in having his best mate alongside.

A week later and Marty had been sworn in and what was tenuously called 'training' began. Earlier recruits had more extensive training in actual camps in remote parts of the Republic, including live firing, explosives preparation and such like. He was promised this at some later date, but right now he had to learn the basics of weapons and maintenance on the job. The Brits had been making inroads in recent years, arresting a lot of volunteers and disrupting the IRA structure, which was only now beginning to transform itself away from the old battalion, brigade, company format into smaller cells, limiting the damage if one member of the chain was caught and talked. Confessions under pressure were bad but could be rectified if the confessor came clean, but the worst weapon in the Brits armoury was the informer, the despised 'Tout' who was hated and feared, and of course, if discovered merited the highest punishment.

The training went quickly and Brendan was there to help along with the other members of the group he had joined, and over the next weeks he began to feel as if a missing piece of his life had fallen into place. He had sometimes hated his indecision and dithering and now he was finally committed he felt useful and important, a part of something bigger.

The feeling on holding a pistol was one of surprise at the weight when loaded, and when he grasped an AK 47 assault rifle for the first time he felt strange. He realised he was somehow empowered, for what he held was indeed power, the power to give instant death, power in its simplest form, crude and raw. 'Dixie' was one of the other volunteers, and barked a laugh at him holding the AK with its singular curved banana magazine, knowing precisely what was going through his mind. Marty had laughed himself, shaking his head, acknowledging Dixie's intuition. Dixie was a few years older, of middle height, dark scruffy hair with a blotchy face and quick wit not unlike Marty's own. His real name was Barry Dixon but this had of course been shortened to 'Dixie', as his father before him had long been known. The other volunteer was Danny Gardner, a gangly fellow who was likeable enough with his mop of carrot coloured hair, nervous manner and uncertain smile, but a little immature and extraordinarily clumsy. He was also new. Soon they were ready for their first operation.

They had been started on something small, a robbery for funds. It was still dangerous of course if they happened to bump into an unlucky patrol, but with a bit of planning should be alright. The target was a betting shop in Ballysillan, out of their own area, but one that amazingly hadn't been turned over before. It had been checked out and security was surprisingly skimpy so the go ahead was given and away they went.

Marty, sitting in the passenger seat pressed against the door thought he could hear a dull thumping and realised it was the feel of his heart. From behind him came a waft of warm leather and onion as Danny turned in his seat. This odour of sweaty fear strangely relaxed Marty, he wasn't the only one nervous and he found his own anxiety was gradually replaced by a cold calm. Brendan was driving and they carried nothing in the car, the gear would be picked up at an address nearer the target where Dixie waited. They drove along past houses and lines of shops with here and there a gap where one had been burned out, past pubs with concrete filled barrels in front to stop anyone parking too close with a bomb. These were at first painted green, white and gold, before changing like the kerbstones to Unionist red, white and blue: enemy territory. To Danny's annoyance Brendan pulled into a petrol station to top up.

"Could you not have done this last night?" he asked.

"Yeh, maybe. So what, we're clean." He turned to Marty sheepishly. "Have you any money on you?"

Marty said nothing, but shifting onto one buttock, dug into his pockets. He looked at the prices, 76p a gallon and calculating briefly, handed Brendan two pounds.

"Don't forget the change now. Or the green shield stamps."

"Dead on Marty, I'll pay you out of our winnings."

They arrived at a house where a tense Dixie came out of the door with a carrier bag and jumped into the back seat. Marty and Danny would do the actual robbing, Brendan the getaway and Dixie would dispose of the money and guns which he now handed out along with two black woollen hats that when rolled down became balaclavas. Marty looked at his. It was an ugly old

Webley revolver, like a bigger and heavier version of the toy gun he used to play cowboys with, but instead of caps there were fat bullets in the chambers, and instead of flaky painted silver this was a dull greyish black. Danny had a vintage but reliable German Luger.

They drove into a quiet side street where Marty and Danny jumped out and quickly walked to the betting shop, pulling down their hats and taking out the guns just before entering. It took a few excruciatingly long minutes, but was easier than Marty had thought possible. The cashier was gibbering and scrambling to put the money into the proffered bag as quickly as he could, it hadn't been busy and everybody had frozen the instant the two hooded figures entered. Marty had said two words, "Fill it!" whilst Danny covered the few customers and then they were gone, but not before Danny had dropped his gun with a loud clatter, cursing as he picked it up.

They were all safely back and counting the proceeds before dark. In all they had just over two thousand pounds, more than Marty had ever seen in one place, a good haul and so, so easy. Marty took his two pounds back before another volunteer came to collect the money, passing on the praise of Bunny and the news he would have more to do for them soon. Marty had a warm feeling of virtue and sighed as he handed it over with a wink.

"Easy come easy go."

That had been six months ago and was why Marty lay in bed now, the blue smoke from his cigarette slowly curling towards the ceiling, thinking about his brother and what he was going to do today. Since that first job Marty had been involved in two other robberies, a bit of scouting and a fire bombing of a hardware shop in the Protestant east of the city, all successful, all easy, but today was different. He finished his cigarette, got out of bed and looked at the drizzling sky above the drab houses outside, and realised this was the biggest step yet in his own personal war: this day he would kill.

He had heard the plan just yesterday and it really was quite cunning, involving the use of a booby trap bomb and a couple of shooters. It also involved the ruthless use of another human being. An intelligence officer had called and given them details.

When he had arrived, Marty was at first speechless and then gave a shout of laughter; it was none other than Frankie Saunders, taller but still with his buck teeth and glasses. He hadn't shown any surprise himself and greeted them coolly, getting down to business, explaining it to them in Dixie's kitchen.

A derelict half gutted house at the end of one street would have a small bomb placed in it packed with nuts and bolts. The command wire would be as short as possible to avoid detection, the firer wouldn't actually have to see his target, the signal to detonate being the first shots by Marty and Brendan at the expected patrol, some of whom should be in the building by then. In the confusion they would make their escape. Dixie, who was to do the detonating nodded appreciatively, he would be unseen. Marty had seen the flaw.

"There's one thing missing. How are you going to get them inside the house, you well know they avoid that sort of scene like the plague. If they think there's something up they'll just seal the area off and take their time, the wire's sure to be seen."

"That's where the beauty of this plan comes in." A sly oil on water smile had spread across Frankie's thin face. "They'll go into the house quick enough if they hear somebody laying there maybe dying, say with his knees shot off and screaming in pain."

Danny had been silent up to now but let out a gentle, "Fuck sake..."

Frankie inched his head up, slightly flushed. "You've no need to shed any tears over who we'll be using. He's a fuckin' tout and anti social, been robbing for himself so he has. We'll be doing the community a favour." He smiled slickly again, "Killing two birds with one stone if you like!" There was another silence before Brendan had another question.

"Who's going to plant the bomb?"

Frankie looked at Danny who gave a resigned nod. Marty had thought about this with a shiver at how clumsy Danny was. His hands reminded him of those things in the fairground that were supposed to grab a prize, the metal claw going along and down before weakly grasping an object only to drop it. Just so long as he wasn't with him when he was placing it. He had looked again at Frankie, wondering at this coincidence and face from the past, not knowing that yet another old acquaintance would soon be helping out in his own inimitable way.

Marty now washed and got dressed, deciding against another cigarette and looked again at the clock. It was time. Just then Brendan pulled up outside in a 'borrowed' car, a metallic green Capri, its breaks squealing. Marty was ready and went out, climbing in beside him.

"Who do you think you are, the 'Sweeny' or what?" Brendan didn't laugh. Marty scanned him quickly. "Everything OK?"

Brendan just nodded, concentrating on driving, but thinking about who he had just heard was coming, the other component of the operation, the man who would be leaving the 'tout' in the building minus his knees. It was the face from the past and he knew Marty wouldn't be too happy about it either.

Chris McCormick was still known as 'Beatle' even though he had long hair now that hung down to his shoulders in thick greasy strands, having only the barest acquaintance with shampoo. Only the older and more senior called him by his moniker, everyone else feared him and with reason. Beatle had a well earned reputation for vicious, brute violence and wouldn't hesitate to maim or even kill, indeed he seemed to take a sadistic pleasure in it all. For Beatle the current situation in Belfast was a Godsend. Others in the movement such as Brendan were uncomfortable with him, wondering why the IRA needed to use such an animal. One volunteer had even been rash enough to voice these doubts. His company commander had simply asked him who he wanted to take his rubbish away or clean the road, some weedy handless professor or a proper bin man? *Anybody*, he emphasised could make a contribution, and certain people were useful for certain things. Word had gotten back and the volunteer had been grabbed from behind one night as Beatle stepped out of the shadows and administered a painful beating in the dark. No disciplinary measures were taken, simply because higher up the ranks it was realised that Beatle's savagery could be put to good use. Although no academic, he was devious, apparently committed to the cause, and could be relied upon to carry out any orders no matter how morally suspect. The Troubles had given Chris McCormick a ready excuse for his unusual talents; he had never felt better.

He strolled along on this fine wet morning, hopping playfully to avoid an iridescent oil stained puddle whilst whistling an Abba tune over and over. He loved Abba and stole every new album. He had taken part in a number of official punishments for those who stepped out of line using a variety of weapons: baseball bats, hurley sticks, metal piping and sometimes his boots which he thought added a more personal touch and felt very good. If he ever got the chance he might try something out of a gardening kit, maybe a spade or hoe he mused to himself. Now and again he used a 'short', which was reserved for knee capping, and on one memorable occasion to put a tout into the next world.

He had been with another guy called Stevie, a nice lad who he unfortunately hadn't had a chance to work with again, as for some reason he always seemed to be unavailable. The tout had been trussed up with electrical wire, hands behind its back in a disused store house, sat on the bare concrete floor, stinking of fear and breathing heavily, the sacking on its head going in and out as it took deep and rapid lungfulls of air. Beatle had almost laughed as it was so comical. Their orders were to get any last information before 'nutting' him. Stevie had finished the last interrogation and shook his head slowly at Beatle. "My turn!" He had shouted eagerly like a confident child taking the dice in a board game, walking slowly around the figure on the floor, its blind head jerking around to follow the footsteps. He put the cold metal of the gun gently on its neck, thrilled as it gasped and shuddered away, now sounding like it was crying. Stevie turned away as Beatle started singing softly. First a bit of Abba mockingly.

"Can you hear me darling, can you hear me S.O.S.?"

Stevie's mouth fell open and he felt the sweat start out and turn cold on his spine as he realised that this guy was a fucking lunatic. Beatle then switched to

'Bohemian Rhapsody', all the while stretching his arm out at the figure now slobbering and rolling around in pure terror.

"Put my gun against his head, pulled my trigger now he's dead!"

Gunshots echoed hollow, bouncing off the walls, abruptly cutting off the whimpering. The tout wasn't moving, the hood now with holes and a spreading stain of red as it filled. Beatle looked at a thoroughly shaken Stevie and winked, blowing an imaginary wisp of smoke from the barrel like an old time Wild West gunfighter.

"I've been wanting to sing that for a while, the first thing that popped into my head so it was when I first heard it. You know, doing it for real."

Suddenly he began giggling which made the hairs on the back of Stevie's neck stand up. Beatle pointed at the still figure on the ground.

"That's funny when you think what the last thing was to pop into *his* head! D'you think ol' Freddie Mercury will mind any?"

So here he was again, this time to leave the victim alive but hurt as badly as possible. He hadn't been told all the details, these he would receive at the house, but did wonder why the fucker was being allowed to live. If it was up to him he'd be getting the OBE and no mistake. He smiled, thinking about when he had first heard that particular expression, OBE or more accurately, One Behind the Ear.

Beatle didn't approve of theft, not from your own people anyway. His father had instilled this into him when he was younger, when he had tried to pilfer some loose change from his Da's jacket pocket after he had come home pissed one night and fallen asleep in his armchair. His Da had awoken and caught him red handed; a minute later he really was red handed as his Da had seized him by the scruff of the neck, thrust the offending fingers into the door jamb and then booted it shut. It was a very effective lesson.

Looking around he noticed the quiet, kids at school certainly, but quite deserted, a few windows open and then he guessed there might well be an ambush involved and the residents had been warned to stay in and open windows to reduce blast effects. Maybe. He knocked on the door and when it was opened by Danny, he loped straight past him to the kitchen.

"Howdy, partners!"

He beamed at them sat around the kitchen table. The faces looked up and he immediately recognised Marty and Brendan. They raised hands in greeting, giving him tight stretched smiles. Obviously they were a bit nervous, job in hand and all that, he would have to put them at ease, what, with receiving his initial instructions from Frankie it was just like old times. He smiled again, to reassure them.

"Alright lads, where's my shooting chum?"

Marty looked at his watch, he should be there by now. "You can go with Danny there Chris, Dixie will have him ready," he said.

Danny gave him a single nod and they left the house, gingerly taking what resembled a large shoebox from the dustbin on the way, across the street to the derelict, the bag of shrapnel already there. Brendan and Marty then went to the front room upstairs to prepare, relieved that Beatle was gone. They had heard the stories about him and knew in his case they were probably true. They both disliked the idea that they were part of an organisation that contained a bastard like that. They checked their weapons and waited, standing a little back from the window they took it in turns to watch for the arrival of the patrol which ought to come via the waste ground the street led to.

On the opposite side and a half dozen houses further along was the derelict at the end of the street, the windows and door long gone, boarded up, but the doorway open to the elements. The roof was also burnt half off and blackened skeletal beams could be seen through what few slates were left. In the gloomy interior Neil Mallon sat uncomfortably on a blue plastic beer crate, his hands tied in front of him and connected loosely with a metre of slack to a heavy iron wall radiator. The hard edges of the crate were digging into his buttocks. He was just twenty and at this particular moment scared stiff.

He had been taken away the previous night, dragged out of the club and slapped about before being told he was to be made an example of for crimes against the Nationalist people. He felt himself go hot all over and his mouth went instantly dry, relief flooding through him when they added he was to be shot through both knees as punishment. It wasn't his first offence and he thought this time they might do him in, especially as the crime was robbing a shop in his own area. They had let him off with a beating and dismissal from the movement last year when he had confessed to naming people during an interrogation, which explained his relief at today's sentence. He was however uneasy at being hooded with a slightly soiled pillow case that smelled of lavender and aftershave. Dixie leaned against the grimy wall next to him and decided on a bit of reassurance.

"You're one lucky bastard so you are to get off so light."

He lit a fag and then another using the first to set it smoking. He lifted the pillow case and handed it to Neil who grasped it gratefully two handed.

"I know. Fuck! I almost dirtied myself when they took me off. Didn't even finish my drink but!"

He laughed nervously as he took in his surroundings, noticing the dank smell and graffiti on the wall opposite. He took a deep draw on the cigarette as he read. It was poetry of some kind. 'If you could keep voices like flowers, there'd be shamrock all over the world, if you could keep dreams like Irish streams...' Then he read the critical response scrawled through and over the rest of it. 'Fuck off hippy twat.' Just then they heard footsteps and someone trying to whistle what sounded like 'Mama Mia' but very badly. Beatle sauntered in booming a hearty greeting.

"What about ye?" He looked at Neil speculatively, then leaning down to him he asked quietly, "Are you ready for your big moment?"

Neil's face paled, his eyes blinked and his nose twitched like a nervous rabbit as he dropped the cigarette. Beatle adopted a strange Alabama plantation accent.

"Ya'll know whut you done boy. I do declare it's time. Are you ready Suh to pay the price, yo' moment of truth is heah!" Then stepping on the smoking butt he became business like. "Alright you, on the deck."

The hood was replaced and Neil did as he was told as Beatle resumed humming his tune and checking his lovely Browning pistol. Danny came quietly in with a plastic bag full of bolts and scrap metal and the shoebox full of explosives. He put the box on the floor as tenderly as a mother putting a baby to bed, not wanting to wake it, and carefully snuggled the bag around the base and on top. Dixie was busy splicing wires, and then as quickly as he could he trailed the command wire along the skirting board and out the back. Danny meanwhile had gently placed the crate over it all. He stood back. It would survive a cursory examination, especially with that poor bastard providing a noisy distraction across the room. Beatle watched it all with growing interest. Dixie put a finger to his lips and pointed at the shivering form on the floor and whispered, "Wait twenty minutes." It all became clear. A huge satisfied grin formed on his face as the other two quietly left the room. What a wonderful idea. He stroked his gun in anticipation.

Across the road Brendan and Marty were watching out of the upstairs window, Brendan sweating visibly and obviously scared. To his surprise, Marty felt calm and cold, alert but not in the slightest bit afraid and was briefly thinking about this when there came the sound of shots, sounding at this distance no louder than paper bags bursting. Brendan swung to him startled.

"The bloody fool, it's not time yet!"

Just then there were two more pops, and then two more. Marty was thinking furiously. The call would not be made for another ten minutes and the arrival time would be soon after, it was too early and there was a chance the bait would be unconscious or have bled to death. This put the whole operation in jeopardy, all because that fat fucker couldn't wait to shoot somebody. There was also the matter of those other four shots. What had he done? They daren't go and look, they would just have to hope Mallon was still alive. Just then he caught a glimpse of Beatle through a gap in a fence at the back of the houses walking unhurriedly away. He would have liked to have shot the stupid bastard there and then. They decided to wait as planned.

Half an hour later they saw a couple of army Humber 'Pigs' and a Landrover approaching across the waste ground, the Landrover parking some distance away. One of the Pigs pulled up next to the derelict house, partially obstructing the view, the troops quickly clambering out and taking up covering positions.

They were cautious and with reason, always suspecting a trap. Two members raced across to the end of the street and covered two more that dashed forwards, panting in their combats and heavy olive green flak jackets. They were at the entrance of the house but didn't go in, they waited and watched, scanning the houses and windows for movement, sensing the same unusual quiet as Beatle had done and drew the same conclusion. There was no sound from inside the derelict, no calls for help or shouts of pain. More soldiers moved across the ground, spreading out and then Marty noticed a Saracen armoured car arriving and decided they would just have to go for it before the whole area was sealed off. He nodded to Brendan who gulped, trying to get rid of the constriction in his throat and uncomfortable drumming in his chest and almost simultaneously they opened fire through the glass. The noise of the gunfire and breaking glass in the confined space was terrific. Brendan fired a whole magazine in a few brief seconds, spraying the Pig, bullets tanging against the metal, the derelict house and ripping up the tarmac in a dozen places, failing to hit a single soldier. Marty had selected a figure that had ducked down nearly out of sight behind the heavy front grill of the vehicle, calmly firing two aimed shots despite the mayhem. The figure disappeared and Marty felt a delighted jolt, sure he had hit him. Just then the front of the house seemed to fall out into the street, the boarding flung all ways by a violent explosion that covered the soldiers in bricks, dust and debris. Brendan was already halfway down the stairs with Marty sprinting behind him, out the back door and running to the waiting car.

Late that afternoon they sat around a table in the upstairs front room of a house near their own area, a typical red brick affair with a barbers shop below. Danny was peering out of the window, lifting the netting to one side like a nosy old curtain twitcher. Marty was pouring steaming hot tea for them all.

"Danny, get away from the window. It's safe enough here but it won't be if too many people see you gawping out. Sit down and get some tea inside you."

Danny obeyed. Something had changed and they sensed it in Marty's calm manner throughout the operation and deferred to him without thinking too much about it. They had listened to the local news on the radio, everyone tense and excited as the precise cold voice gave out the details.

"A combined gun and bomb attack this morning in the Ardoyne area has killed one soldier and injured several others, although none seriously. An as yet unidentified body was also found after the explosion which happened in a house close to Brompton Park. An army spokesman has condemned the attack, and believes the terrorists deliberately used the body to lure soldiers to their deaths. The murdered soldier, from..."

Marty turned the radio off. He had heard enough and wasn't the slightest bit interested in any personal information. So, he had got one. His only emotion was one of regret, not for the soldier, but at the fact there had only been one killed. He didn't want to think of them as humans anymore, as fathers, brothers, sons, husbands who were loved. Now they were just targets, an enemy to be destroyed. He had one other thing on his mind as he switched off the radio: Beatle.

A few days later Marty was surprised to be driven to a place on the Malone Road, one of the nicer parts of Belfast and home to well off professionals and the middle class. As he was dropped off Dixie pointed to a large detached white house.

"They'll be expecting you, I'll pick you up about two." He drove away.

Marty stopped a moment to look; it was nothing like the sort of places he had lived in. He walked past the low, grey stone garden wall with its well trimmed hedge and neat piece of lawn, a rosebush in the middle and saw movement in one of the jutting bay windows. The door opened before he had rung the bell. Bunny gave him a brief welcome, looking behind him and down the road before quickly closing the heavy glass panelled door and leading him through to a spacious and light back room, all in white and pale blue, complete with glass conservatory. Marty glanced out at a large square garden lawn with a small fish pond, a light wooden fence on two sides, and tall leylandi trees on the other, all very private. The house was owned by a sympathiser in the building trade, who allowed them to use it for debriefings such as this, meetings, and as a place to lay up in nice surroundings whilst he was on holiday or away on business. The only stipulation was that no weapons were allowed here.

An unexpected guest sitting at the large polished dining table was Gerry Fox. There was also another man Marty didn't recognise. An unwelcome sight was the figure of Beatle sat in an armchair to one side sipping a can of coke.

"Alright Marty?" he asked with a smirk.

"Well done Martin," said Gerry, giving him a quick handshake and pat on the back. "You were unlucky not to get more but it was a good operation."

The other man stood up, middle aged, tall, thin and nearly bald with a long neck, pale face and small round glasses. He looked more like a science teacher instead of a senior Provisional. He gave Martin his bony hand and introduced himself in a refined Dublin accent.

"I'm James O'Mahony. The main thing is, all volunteers returned safely after a successful attack; that's the important thing, well done."

Behind him Marty caught Bunny's beaming reflection in the window as he put a hand on his shoulder, looking like a master with his prize winning pupil. O'Mahony cleared his throat, sounding a little uneasy.

"What do you think yourself about the attack Martin? I've heard rumours and we need to co operate and clear up any... misunderstandings. You're a little annoyed that it didn't go totally to plan? "

"You heard right." He looked coldly at Beatle, who held his stare but looked uncomfortable. Marty felt himself getting angry as he thought about what had happened. He pointed at Beatle. "That stupid fat fucker could have gotten us killed. There's more brains in a wig! He was supposed to wait. He didn't. He was supposed to leave Mallon alive, he didn't!" Beatle was by now on his feet, dropping the coke can and spilling the contents all over the thick white carpet.

"He was alive when I left him!"

"So why did I hear six shots instead of two? Are you that bad a shot?"

"No!" Beatle retorted, stung. "I done his ankles as well... and his arms." He reddened at the looks he was getting, glaring now at Marty. "He was still alive but! Ah, fuck you Marty..."

He was cut off before he could finish as Marty swung at him, throwing a punch that landed square on his nose, sending him flying back into the chair. All at once the others were holding on to them and Gerry was shouting.

"Enough! Catch yourselves on! Any more of this and I'll beat the shit out of the both of youse!"

O'Mahony jerked his head at Bunny who was calming Beatle, indicating to take him away. They left with Beatle muttering threats under his breath as he was ushered out. O'Mahony shook his head slowly, as much it seemed at the brown stain on the carpet as anything else. The front door closed.

"Alright, Martin. Calm down now and sit," said O'Mahony. He watched Marty carefully. "We can't have this sort of in fighting, it helps nobody but the Orangies."

"That's right Marty," said Gerry. "You've seen what can happen if these things get out of hand. We don't need it in our own ranks."

Marty knew he was referring to the various internecine disputes of recent years between the Officials and Provisionals, and then the savage splintering that came with the forming of the INLA from the Officials. A lot of people had died as a result of this fratricidal in fighting, and it had been lapped up by their enemies glad to see them do their work for them. Marty understood but didn't see it as relevant to Beatle.

"I'm not working with that psycho ever again. I'm serious. Christ sakes you must have heard the stories about him?"

O'Mahony and Gerry looked at each other. Yes, they had heard, but Beatle had friends who didn't care about any of this, such unquestioning violence had its uses. They also knew that Beatle was unlikely to let someone get away with flattening his nose, and worse, his fearsome reputation. They decided some preventative measures had to be taken to keep both volunteers apart and active. They were needed. O'Mahony spoke first.

"It might be an idea now Martin if you were to gain some further experience outside the city." He sat and paused, chin resting on clasped hands, eyes looking above Marty, nodding sagely like an intelligent ostrich. "You've proved yourself a brave and skilled volunteer and a spell in Dundalk could be arranged." He smiled. Gerry joined in genially, trying to sweeten the pill.

"That's right! There's a few Belfast lads down there right now on the run, not that you'll be of course, but so much the better. The boys in South Armagh are some of the best around, you can learn a lot from them. Fuck's sake Marty it won't be forever and I remember your Ma has family down there as well, just a wee while now till things calm down." He put an avuncular and very hairy hand on Marty's arm. "I'll back up whatever you want to tell your Ma."

Marty knew it had already been decided. It wasn't his family he was thinking about right now but Tinks. He knew she was unlikely to go with him having recently started a teaching job, so she was happy enough. He grunted, dissatisfied with the idea but resigned. He would go.

Sergeant Grant Robson stood on the parade ground and examined his new recruits with studied sourness. He was an evil looking man and knew it, indeed liked it and cultivated the image. Large, square built and immensely fit, his head was round and bumpy like a badly cast cannon ball, the reddish stubble concealed under his adored maroon beret. His chipped leathery face seemed to have a permanent look of hatred, as if a smile was an alien and unwelcome event on his features. His eyes were an amber colour, almost yellow, beautiful in a woman, but on him they took on a frightening demonic appearance.

They stood before him in uneven lines, uniformed with freshly shaven heads, but that was the only military thing about them at the moment. He ran his tongue over the back of his teeth, feeling the gaps in their crooked line, knowing before training finished there would be also huge gaps in the line facing him as the weak, slovenly, cowardly, unfit and unsuitable were weeded out. They wanted only certain types for their elite and it was his job to help ensure this. The rejected would be sent home or passed onto other less prestigious regiments and become 'Crap hats', fit only to wear a common army cap and not the coveted beret of his wonderful regiment. They would strengthen their bodies and minds, train them as thoroughly as was humanly possible and mould them into the best soldiers in the world bar none. As for the Marines. A bunch of wankers!

Sergeant Robson was a straight forward sort of person and liked things black or white, having scant patience with the tedious grey areas of life. His preferred method on first acquaintance was the 'shock 'em and scare 'em' tactic. Be abusive and outrageous and watch the reaction, it usually told him all he needed to know about a person and saved time too. The fact he was apt to do this in civilian life was probably why he was divorced now and wed instead to the regiment.

He started straight away. Walking rapidly and suddenly towards a pale lanky recruit with a beaky nose, thin lips and pointed ears in the front rank he stopped in front of him, screaming inches from his face.

"What's your fucking name?"

The recruit stepped back a pace, alarmed at the sudden outburst of anger and stale booze breath.

"Stand still you piece of shit! What's your name?"

"Private Patterson sergeant!" He said loudly, straightening and looking over Robson's shoulder.

"You're not a private yet dickhead. You look like a fucking vampire! I expect you shag kittens too don't you? I'll be locking my door tonight."

No one laughed. He moved on, the yellow eyes searching, stopping at the end front row and examining another man with a handsome but delicate looking face which immediately offended him.

"Name?" he barked.

"Flowers. Ian, Sergeant," he replied, pushing his chest out and trying to sound manly. Robson grew even more inflamed and indignant, shouting for Corporal Allenby.

"This recruit's name is Flowers, he bloody well looks like a pansy. What do you think Corporal?"

"Yes sergeant, a little effeminate."

"Effeminate my arse! Look at him. He's a fucking bender! Anyone in his room better sleep on their backs if they want to avoid a shit stabbing in the small hours."

Robson watched carefully, noticing the twitch of hurt, not anger, probably an over educated twat that thought he was on an adventure. He had little time for that sort. School was all well and good, but it didn't teach you anything really useful like keeping warm and dry in bad weather or where to stick a blade in to best effect. Further along the line some of the others had leaned a little forward to look, each head a tiny bit further out than its neighbours like a fan of three kings in a hand of cards. Robson turned and the heads snapped back into the pack. Then suddenly he had gone between two lines and stood before another figure, shouting loudly into the face from six inches, spraying fine droplets of spittle.

"I saw you looking. You think you can have me don't you, think you could kick my head in?"

Roy resisted the urge to wipe his face and kept his eyes fixed steadily to his front. "No Sergeant." His accent instantly betrayed his origins.

"What you doing here Paddy, wouldn't the IRA let you join?"

"No Sergeant, I hate those scum." Roy kept his face neutral, but couldn't keep an edge from his voice.

Robson smirked. Hate was a good emotion to have if properly channelled. The Parachute Regiment prized aggression and spirit as they would find out. He moved on to another victim. This was Roy's first real introduction to the Regiment and was roughly what he had expected. He stared ahead and marvelled on how drastically his life had changed.

Several years earlier it was all so different. Roy had done well with his 'O' levels, securing seven in total and decided with his mother's gentle push and his father's hard shove to continue his education, get his 'A' levels, go to university and obtain a degree in history, his best subject. His father had it all well in hand it seemed and for the moment Roy was content enough to go along with it. He took his studies seriously and avoided as much as possible getting involved with what was going on around them.

North Belfast had become as dangerous as any place in Northern Ireland and the Antrim Road that ran through it deserved its sinister reputation as 'Murder Mile'. By the mid seventies, savage sectarian killings were frequent and random; people planned their routes home with much care, the penalty for error or just bad luck could be horrible, bloody death. People carried on with life, got married, had children, went to work, paid bills, laughed and cried and loved, but at night especially there was fear.

It was around this time that George was arrested on a botched assassination job. George had moved out and lived a short distance away on the Shore Road, to have a bit more independence and be nearer his girlfriend Liz, so he said. Things hadn't really been the same since George had joined the UDA, and secretly their military wing the Ulster Freedom Fighters. Their father often criticised the Protestant paramilitaries who were responsible for some of the most gruesome slayings in the area, labelling them 'a bunch of thugs and murderers no better than the IRA', ignorant of his eldest son's growing involvement, not noticing how George would go silent or leave the room. The very notion that one of his own would join this lawlessness and so defy him was unthinkable. Roy noticed however, and had tried and failed to influence his brother, so when the arrest came he had to pretend to be as astonished as the rest of the family.

His parents were devastated and although he had half expected this and a wall had long ago come between them, now a real prison wall, Roy genuinely grieved for his brother and loathed the circumstances and people that had made it possible. The Republicans who had started it, and the likes of that bastard Eddie Frazer, driving around in his swanky black Zephyr, its colour matching his black jacket and rotten black soul. He just knew he was in some way responsible, had probably planned it and given George his orders to go and kill what he had been told was a leading Republican, but in all probability was a simple Catholic nobody. The whole thing had been ludicrously organized and amateurishly attempted, his brother riding pillion on a motorcycle, shooting and missing their intended victim as he walked along the Cliftonville Road and running straight into an army patrol. George had fallen backwards, head over heels as the bike suddenly accelerated away and been left to his fate, the patrol giving him a kicking and taking him away to Castlereagh centre where he received another beating before being charged. Shortly after, Roy had watched miserably as his brother was sentenced to a minimum of twenty years and led away with a defiant shout of "No surrender!" His parents had refused to come, casting their son out in shame for what he had done.

Then came the day when Roy was to leave home. He had a place at the university in Coleraine and as it was only a couple of hours on the train, in theory he would be able to come home at weekends. With a proud handshake from his Da and a tearful clinging hug from his Ma he set off with his girlfriend Susan to Central Station, full of hope, freedom and energy.

University had been fun but an undistinguished failure. His outstanding memory which had gotten him through his 'A' levels with a minimum of effort had not helped, as not reading or attending lectures meant he had nothing to remember. The new sense of freedom Roy had, all too soon developed into an attitude where he did what he liked, when he liked. A generous government grant fuelled his social life which quickly took precedence over any notions of study, but Roy didn't give a damn. He was making new friends, seeing new things, drinking like a fish and generally having a wild and hedonistic time in a never ending cycle of house parties and discos.

He enjoyed living in the seaside towns of Portstewart and Portrush and rarely went back to the city, citing his studies and costs to his family and old friends. Susan came once and went home again in a tearful mascara smeared rage, finding him at a Halloween fancy dress ball, with a drunken cat woman on his lap shoving her breasts into his face. She had doused him in orange juice wishing at that instant it was something more flammable. Roy hardly noticed she was there and hadn't cared much when he did; he was enjoying himself.

There were quite a few Catholics here from various parts of the province and he even started mixing tentatively with them socially, especially the girls, although on the whole he tended to hang about with his own crowd. As long as politics were avoided things were generally smooth, which was usually the case, both sides instinctively avoiding the taboo. The only time there were problems were usually when one of the few English students would unthinkingly bring it up at a gathering or party and crassly open up old wounds, or some drunken Fenian wanker couldn't fight the urge and started up with one of those shite sentimental rebel songs. This fortunately was a rare event and most people were more interested in having a good time. He had never had such fun in all his life and even experimented with LSD and dope, walking for miles on the beach, laughing hysterically with others in the same state, or drinking from bottles of cider, splashing about fully clothed, whooping like an

Apache in the freezing North Atlantic waves. He spent more money than he had, took a loan and then even tried tapping his parents to pay the long suffering landlord. The answer to that was short, classic William. "You said you can manage and manage you will. We don't have any money to spare and even if we did the answer is still no."

Roy became wild and irresponsible, appearing on a number of occasions before the disciplinary committee for various misdemeanours and of course the result was a total mess in his end of year exams. He went home that summer and waited for the inevitable. His parents sensed the change in him and there was increasing tension between a less respectful Roy and his father. His results came in July: failure with no chance of readmission. Roy had expected it but oddly still found himself upset and disappointed, then guilty at letting everybody down. They sat and digested his news along with their dinner. Betty was shamed, having bragged to all the neighbours at every chance, whilst William was typically furious. The sound of cutlery seemed to be a lot louder in the heavily pregnant silence as his anger swelled before being spouted out.

"What the hell has happened to you? One son throws his life away in jail and now this! "

"Nothing. I'm sorry O.K, I didn't do it on purpose."

"Don't cheek me now," said William his voice raised and face reddening dangerously. "I'm telling ye! What're you going to do? Now you've failed that is."

"Get a job I suppose, I've still got 'A' levels."

His father had then nodded bitterly. "Aye, with all the unemployment these days, you've thrown away a great chance in life son, I hope you know that. As for a job, you'll take whatever is available and be glad of it, learn the hard way. Is that clear?"

So Roy had taken whatever was going and was lucky to get it. He did some casual labouring, then a month in a canning company doing twelve hour shifts, which really did teach him what a horribly futile and boring existence some people led. A period in an office had followed and some part time bar work, but he found it all deeply unsatisfying, and living at home fraught and tense as he was increasingly at odds with his father.

Some time later Uncle Sam had finally died and the funeral had brought back sad memories, and a lot of renewed anger at the sight of his Ma suffering yet again at the sound of earth falling on the coffin, the gash of her grief again open as the newly dug grave. Roy's restless character eventually led him to a career decision. His father was for once satisfied, sitting in his chair after work he leaned forwards nodding his approval.

"That might be for the best Roy, you can still make something of yourself and with your qualifications maybe go far. If you join the navy but, you'll get to see the world, and get paid doing it." His father began to warm to his subject.

"Think Roy, all those places, much better than the army. Where do they get to go? Germany or back over here maybe!" He laughed harshly.

"I'm going to join the Paras."

William stopped laughing. "Don't be so bloody stupid," he said.

Roy wasn't annoyed. He knew what his father's reaction would be, especially as he was an ex marine and had often told him of the deep and not always friendly rivalry between the two elite forces. That was another reason he wanted to join the Parachute regiment, but more importantly because of 'Bloody Sunday' and other various incidents down the years they were hated and feared by the Nationalist community like no other unit. They had been known to shoot IRA members whether they were armed or not and didn't take shit from anyone. Roy also had something to prove, that he wasn't a failure, to his father and family but mostly to himself. His father's disapproval and then loudly voiced doubts that he wouldn't pass the training had given him the extra boost he needed. He would prove him wrong whatever it cost.

On arrival at the depot he and the others had been allocated rooms in rectangular drab three story buildings that held twelve men each. They were issued their kit, boots and clothing and spent the first days on basics, polishing, washing, ironing and wearing kit in the correct manner and putting everything away in regulation order. For Roy and some of the others it was no problem, having done it all his life. They began to get to know each other too.

On Roy's side of the room was Ian Flowers, who had difficulties adjusting from a nice middle class background where everything was done for him and he had his own room. His pent up excitement had gone flat from the first moment he sat on his bed with its dingy blankets and looked up to see Dave from Edinburgh picking his nose with rapt concentration. There was also Lawrence, who had arrived in a sleeveless union jack shirt exposing bulging biceps, Pete from Newcastle, and in the bed next to him a very ugly, wiry and tough, but surprisingly well spoken guy from London named Keith Shepheard. Roy hit it off with him from the start. He made Roy laugh with his dry and suave one liners, his voice sounding like a young but profane James Mason. Facially he resembled a rubbery gap toothed 'Punch'. As a whole they had little in common apart from the fact they were all aged between nineteen and twenty four and wanted to be Paratroopers. Over the coming weeks Roy learned a lot about his new comrades and discovered that their motives were generally the same. They were bored with the mundane civilian life and restless, looking for adventure and a new way, to test and prove themselves and see just how tough they really were. Only Keith remained something of a mystery.

Training began. Their section corporal was named Burton, a big bloke with a squint and bad temper. First came square bashing, and learning how to march and move in unison took a little time. Persistent offenders who cocked it up were dealt with harshly, shouted at, insulted and on occasion given a quick slap. This happened to Flowers, who was nervous, and his awkward, swinging armed incompetence finally bankrupted Burton's limited patience. They then saw that discipline here was informal but effective, as he simply dragged Flowers out and gave him a punch to the stomach that doubled him over. Flowers had only just held back the tears and left the next day, deciding a military career wasn't what he wanted after all. They were soon up to the required standard and 'passed off the square'. The real training only then began.

The next few months Roy passed in a blur of constant hard activity, the hours where there was nothing to do whilst awake he could count on one hand. He had thought he was fit, but learned very quickly along with everybody else they were just in the foothills of fitness with the peaks still far ahead. Every soldier, no matter what his regiment was expected to be fit, but with the Parachute regiment this took on extra significance. This was outlined to them by Lieutenant Stewart, his piercing bright blue eyes roving around them before they began a run.

"In a combat situation each soldier will be expected to drop behind lines carrying all the equipment he needs, without further transport or backup and still achieve his objective. This is why your standards must be so much higher. Anything less is for the 'Hats' and will not be tolerated here! You will maintain the long and proud tradition of this regiment."

This last was a bit of an exaggeration, the Paras were a recent addition to the army and Roy nearly laughed aloud as he had a bizarre image of men dressed in tricorn hats, knee britches and long red coats floating down with their muskets at the ready. He stopped himself just in time, all too aware of what the consequences of this flight of fantasy might be.

The training continued and the ranks began to thin at the increased tempo and demands. Dave was the next to be 'binned' when he just could not carry on with a five mile run in full gear. He was blistered and had webbing burns and just dropped out, finished. Others could not take the discipline. Corporal Allenby had a crude method of teaching them the components of the various weapons they had to handle, strip down and put back together again: if you failed twice, he hit you. He had been demonstrating with a general purpose machine gun or GPMG and Lawrence had not satisfied him. He slapped him around the back of the head and Lawrence was fed up, tired, and foolish enough to take a swing back at him. There were no formal charges. Lawrence was given a painful but judicious beating and was gone the next day. Roy paid extra attention.

The first time they were issued with the standard Self Loading Rifle they also received a somewhat corny homily from Robson.

"This gun is your wife, treat her well and she'll give you full satisfaction."

"Poor Mrs Robson," Keith had muttered. "Imagine having to give satisfaction to *him.*"

Only fear kept Roy from laughter as his imagination flashed ghastly images. Roy had seen guns aplenty of course, and carefully supervised had handled his Uncle Sam's service pistol, but taking hold of an SLR for the first time he had to admit still felt adolescently good. Powerful. On the firing range another lesson was learned when a recruit failed to follow the first and most important procedure of removing the magazine and checking the breech to see if there was still a bullet up the spout. Sergeant Robson spotted this, and the offender was cursed and as he was still in a prone position received a shouted "Arsehole!" and booted foot in the gut.

"No old cock, I believe that's his stomach," Keith drawled in his refined whispered voice.

One of the stranger parts of training was known as 'milling' and this simply involved the recruits going to the gym where they would form a circle. They would be selected in pairs, and putting on boxing gloves would hammer and flail away at one another for a couple of minutes. Although seemingly informal and unimportant technically, each recruit was being scrutinised not for skill, but for his level of aggression and guts. Keith had warned Roy that a premium was put on this aggression and it was important to do well by being determined and battering hell out of your opponent. Roy's was a guy called Bowers. The whistle blew and he went straight into him arms swinging as hard as he could. It was over in two exhausting minutes, leaving them both bloodied and breathless. Lieutenant Stewart was present and taking note. Shepheard's opponent was from their own room, a lad called Duffy who was much bigger, so when the whistle went and they set to, Keith punched viciously and managed after half a minute to swing a seemingly accidental uppercut into Duffy's groin, halting the bout there and then.

"Terribly sorry matey!" Keith said with feigned concern all over his rubbery leering face, leaning over the retching, buckled figure.

The hard slog continued and most of them were feeling super fit and capable, if exhausted at the end of each day, and it was with some relief when this period came to an end. Those left over were now to go to Pre parachute training, 'P Company' which would be the toughest test so far.

Before they started P Company, Roy, Keith and a few others went out for some recreation in the town. It was Friday night and time for a piss up. In fine regimental tradition this meant going to various pubs and discos, drinking large quantities, trying to bag anything in a skirt and finding a few 'crap hats' to beat up. The evening had followed in the usual raucous manner, and at the end of it Roy found himself sat with Keith in a smoke filled noisy pub, both the worse for wear, having enjoyed letting off steam in all directions with Tina Charles shouting to everyone from the jukebox how she 'loved to love'. Roy was inquisitive about Keith, who rarely spoke about his background.

"So why did you join the Paras? Like the uniform or is it a family tradition?" he jokingly asked.

Keith looked at him sharply with his flecked grey eyes and shrugged. "Not exactly tradition, my father was an officer in the Grenadier Guards actually."

"He'll be proud then," said Roy opening his eyes wider and blowing out his cheeks in exaggerated surprise. "You've never mentioned it before, were you worried you'd get the piss took?"

"I doubt if he'll be proud. I hope not, the bastard! He hates the Paras. In fact he hates all soldiering since he caught religion some years ago. Became a fucking Jehovah Witness." The bitterness was sharp as lemon in his voice; he said religion like he was talking about a painful sexual disease, and mouthed Jehovah Witness as if he was describing a mutant pervert.

"In fact, when I get my wings I'm going to gate crash one of his meetings and embarrass him. First of course I'll get monstrously drunk."

Keith told Roy a little of his life. He had been well off when younger and gone to a minor public school, which explained his smooth manners and accent. His father had then joined the Jehovahs and his mother had separated and suddenly he was poor and very angry, but with the same spirit of adventure the rest of them had. The Paras had appealed to him on different levels: to get back at his father and indulge his aggressive tendencies, but he was also fiercely competitive and hated failing or losing. Roy had sensed a cruelty in Keith, some of the practical jokes he played had him in stitches, but behind it all was real malevolence. Roy didn't think too much about it, laughing aloud and remembering instead the time Keith had lined another recruit's beret with jam. The recruit had had no time and no choice but to just put it on and go on parade, whilst they struggled with laughter at the buzzing of wasps around his head. Another occasion he had super glued somebody's boots to the floor and he was always on hand to join in shaving a drunken recruit's eyebrows off. He had no remorse at all and could be relied upon to go to the very limit in twisted jokes, including pissing in another guy's whiskey bottle that he had taken a dislike to, holding it up against the sunlit window as he shook to clear it, asking a convulsed Roy.

"What do you think? Half empty or half full, optimist or pissimist?"

The very worst though was his gloating description of what he had added to some poor bastard's egg mayonnaise sandwich at school. Roy hadn't entirely believed him, but had felt his gorge rise the next time he saw anyone with that particular lunchtime treat. Keith took real pleasure in his work. He was bad and Roy was aware of this, but his ability to make him laugh excused a lot, that and the fact he was loyal in his friendship and never took liberties.

Roy watched him as he returned from the toilet, stopping casually behind a customer sat at the bar with a fashionable fuzz of high afro hair. He delicately placed a lighted cigarette on top and came back to view the result. Roy watched fascinated as the guy sat oblivious, coolly scanning the bar, a mini Vesuvius, the smoke rising vertically from his bushy head before he sat bolt upright with an eruption of pain as the glowing ash reached his scalp, then ducking down and tearing at his hair. They left the pub holding their sides in laughter.

P Company had been harder than anything Roy had ever experienced. Assault courses, log races, steeplechases, stretcher carrying, most involving running and marching in any weather, ignoring sprains, minor cuts and bruises, burns and excruciating blisters to test their stamina, fitness and sheer willpower. There was not an ounce of fat left on anyone. The ten mile battle march in full gear had nearly finished Roy, only the dreadful fear of failing and returning home kept him going, near sobbing, within the set time to the finish line. They had helped each other and the bonding and comradeship was all the stronger, cemented as it was by common hardship. At the end of this period and a further three weeks in the wilds of the Brecon Beacons came the final step into thin air, the jump itself. This was done first from a tethered balloon and Roy was in the same batch as Keith. They were all highly nervous apart from the instructor, who whistled to himself as he checked their static lines and reminded them of what they had been taught. They made ready and the cage door was lifted. Keith was first and Roy watched his white face, interested despite his own nervousness as he shuffled forwards and the instructor shouted a single word.

"Go!"

Keith took a breath, closed his eyes and stepped out. Roy was next, a shot of adrenalin went through him as he moved to the opening on watery legs.

"Go!"

He jumped out into a momentary silence before his canopy opened with a loud flap. He hadn't shouted the required count and check canopy, being too absorbed in this fantastic new sensation. He faintly heard somebody bawling instructions through a megaphone and then he was nearing the ground, feet and knees together, chin on chest and he hit the ground with a thud and a roll, exhilarated beyond belief. Everyone was talking, animated with excitement and shining eyes filled with their own prowess, it was an unforgettable moment.

Eight jumps and a couple of weeks later he received his hard earned and highly coveted wings, and shortly after there had been a formal passing out parade. Only his father and Aunt Heather had come although he knew his Ma and brothers were over the moon for him. When he met up with them after the parade, Heather had given him a warm embrace, seemingly happy for the first in a long time.

"Your Uncle Sam would have been so glad to see this day Roy. Well done!"

Roy had felt his emotions welling up, stinging his eyes as he turned to his father. To his amazement William was swallowing with difficulty, and his voice cracked when he spoke. There were tears in his eyes. It was the first time he could remember such a thing. He shook Roy's hand awkwardly. He cleared his throat, struggling for words, his heart full.

"I can only say I wish you all the success you deserve, and when you marry, a son to make you as proud as I am today ..." He tailed off and the handshake became a fierce but brief embrace. Roy had felt close to tears himself and decided to introduce them to the other mingling sets of beaming chattering relatives. It had been a grand day.

Chapter 6

Intermission 1981

Corporal Roy Ferguson stared into the mirror and gave a lop sided grimace. His eyes were as bloodshot as Dracula's, the bottom lip had a scabbed split and the bruise on his right cheek was turning a deathly greenish blue. His head throbbed as he splashed cold water over his suffering face, his stomach gurgled and heaved, the result of a massive weekend binge.

The regiment had recently returned to Tidworth from a four month tour of Northern Ireland, mainly around the beautiful countryside of Fermanagh with its myriad lakes, gentle green hills and misty mornings. Roy had never visited this part of his homeland and its natural beauty had impressed him. It had been bloody cold and as a lot of other visitors discovered, that green splendour was only achieved with copious amounts of rain. They had spent four months patrolling, setting observation points, road checks and waiting and had achieved absolutely nothing; four months without incident. The Provos simply hadn't come out to play. So they had returned to Tidworth and continued an army life as unchanged as ever, the routine maintained even through Roy's recent marriage and quick separation.

Her name was Sally and he had met her typically at the *Stardust* disco in Munster. The attraction had been immediate, the language barrier nonexistent as she was English, aged nineteen and the daughter of a Captain in an artillery regiment based nearby. Sally was a pretty girl with brown eyes, her hair long, curly and dark, with a heart shaped face and slightly pointed chin. The thing Roy found most delightful though was her voice of all things, light and melodious and very sexy. Roy had introduced himself, leaving her German companion to the unwelcome attentions of Keith, dragged her onto the dance floor and given her his best lines in flattery and compliments along with as much charm as he could muster. She in turn had liked his direct and confident approach, a little arrogant perhaps, but she would soon tame that out of him.

They began to see each other on a regular basis and pretty soon Sally imagined she was in love, thought about it and realised she didn't care, which was probably the surest sign of all. They went well together and the sex was great. Within a few short months they had decided to marry. It was more Sally's wish than his own, he simply went along with it to keep her happy. He liked her happy.

It wasn't long before things changed. Their life together swiftly degenerated into a constant round of petty arguments and minor grievances which waxed larger than they should have. The silly things like her yakking on the phone, or him humming, or her putting things back untidily, or him laughing too loud, minor and stupid differences, small as grains of sand yet still large enough when cemented together to produce a huge imposing monument to a failed marriage. Even that silvery voice he had delighted in listening to had turned into a jarring brass gong, and he hated the nagging way she said his name at the end of every bloody sentence to get his attention like a child tugging at his sleeve. They discovered within a year that they didn't really like each other much after all. There were only two things they seemed to do well together but eventually, inevitably, the fighting began to dominate and the sex was relegated to an embittered second place, and on occasion used as a weapon. Roy simply carried on where he had left off, knowing he was also to blame, but understanding that the mistake was made and they just had to get on with life.

They separated. She had even gone with other men, which she had thought would wound him deeply but had in fact caused him no pain at all, perhaps because he hadn't been in love as she had. Roy was philosophical about it all and wouldn't be baited. Sally had lately started a relationship with Mark Smith, a private from a different company. He hadn't seen the attraction himself; he had worryingly long arms and his only claim to fame seemed to be a body covered in tattoos. He had approached Smithy as soon as he heard, amused at the way he had tensed, the eyes wary as if expecting a right hander. Roy had merely laughed and wished him good luck. She was as free to do what she liked as he was. He thought about this now as he looked in the mirror.

There was movement behind him and Keith slouched in, sitting on his bed before lowering his head into his hands as if seeking to crush his own skull.

"Not a bad way to celebrate I suppose," he groaned.

"Mmm."

Keith raised his head, peeping slyly through his fingers. "I saw Smithy on the way over here," he observed casually, trying to get a rise. Roy ignored him, knowing the game.

"Yes, I think he's got a new tattoo which he is *very* proud of."

"Had he room for another? You know Keith maybe you should have some tattoos to pretty you up a wee bit, or maybe even surgery." Keith went for the kill.

"Yes, I'm pretty sure the latest one was a scroll or something. With the word Sally written on it. Anyone you know?" There was no answer so he tried again, carefully measuring the distance to the door. "Maybe Irish pork wasn't to her taste. Probably fancied a change, you know, a bit of English beef instead."

"I'm not surprised your Da turned to religion. You probably drove him to it."

He looked across at Keith, sat there on the brown and grey blankets and laughed, thinking of the previous few days mayhem and the last couple of years. He had enjoyed Germany. It had been his first time overseas and this excitement along with their youthful arrogance had made it all a wonderful time. Every day had been good and the next even better than the last. Certainly they had their share of ups and downs, but there was always something new to look forward to and a constant feeling of movement and optimism.

Their life had been fun. They felt honoured to be part of an elite and took soldiering seriously, their loyalty to the regiment unquestioned. His fitness was a constant source of pleasure, knowing he could perform just about any task he was asked to do; in short he felt great. One difference he shared with Keith however, was that although they were both proud of their status as Paras, they hadn't absorbed the mythical ethos of the regiment to the extent that there was nothing else in their lives. Maybe this was why they remained corporals. They enjoyed the life style and what the regiment had given them, but hadn't been seduced by this myth, maintaining their own self belief and individuality; they simply didn't need the regiment as others did. Both were intelligent enough to know a day would come when they would return to civilian life and have to adjust back into this world. His father was a good example of the difficulties of readjusting to normal life. A lot of others had found it too much, the fact that the skills they had were of little count in an everyday existence, in the factory, driving a van or a fork lift. In fact, the attributes of quick aggression and a willingness to fight were a definite handicap in civilian life.

Keith had made the decision to try and transfer to 'special duties' which probably meant intelligence sometime in the near future, and had been trying to get Roy to do the same. They had gone down to Southampton which was the nearest large city and gone on a pub crawl, ending up in a spit and sawdust bar near the docks, oddly named the *Frog and Frigate.* The ale brewed on the premises had stupefied them, and he vaguely remembered a snatch of drunken conversation as Keith slurred at him.

"You know what I like about you mate?"

"Go on surprise me. My charm?"

"Fuck off. No, your innate..." He lost the thread a moment before refocusing. "Yeh, your innate honesty and integrity cock. I hate it too."

For some reason this had sent them both into peals of laughter and his next memory was of some hours later, giggling and talking to the tarmac outside. Looking at him now, Roy knew he would miss his friend and his wicked practical jokes if he didn't go with him. He had been a good comrade and always there to back him up, but he had noticed he had been increasingly restless and jaded and the last tour with no action had decided him to try something else. They had agreed to give it another year and then see.

Roy had missed the tour his battalion had done in 1978 to West Belfast as he was laid up with a broken leg prior to departure, the result of a car accident. He had been driving along in an old banger, had lost his concentration for a split second and ended up in a field picking cubes of glass from his head along with a fractured left leg. It taught him a valuable lesson though on how quickly his own life could change. He had been on the training course however, which he had found quite amusing and instructive to how the army saw his city.

Known as 'tin city', it consisted of a couple of rows of pre fabs, a garage and a few other slummy buildings purpose built for urban warfare training. One street even had a couple of burnt car wrecks.

"Which house is yours Roy?" Keith had immediately asked with malicious glee.

"Get to fuck!"

"Now Roy, such language! What will the neighbours think? I say, any chance of a cup of tea?"

"Maybe Catholic areas look like this, but my street doesn't."

Derek 'Nosferatu' Patterson stopped to look at Roy. "You mean you're from Belfast and have never been where we're going?" he asked.

"Nope! Wouldn't be seen dead there! Come to think of it I haven't been in some of the streets just across the way from us either."

"And there I was thinking you would be of some use!"

"Away and fuck! You can forget the tea too."

Roy hadn't been home that much lately, preferring to spend his leave seeing other places and doing other things, with the occasional quick weekend visit to his family in between. He still had to be careful. Even though there was now a barrier, a misnamed 'peace line' at the most vulnerable flash point at Duncairn Gardens, you never knew who might know what or be watching. Several soldiers had been killed over the years in just such circumstances and he didn't want to join their ranks.

It was great to see his family, they were always happy to see him and he still had that warm feeling even now on returning to what was still his home. He hadn't seen George in a long time though. John now lived in Bangor, was doing well and was also in the RUC reserve to his parent's equal pride and concern. Wee Billy was now a hulking lad of sixteen with a keen interest in rugby and football and played regularly. Roy had laughed on seeing his younger brother's latest hair cut, short enough to please his father, but following various punk styles it was yellow with black spots like a leopard. William had looked, looked again and then shaken his head before leaving the room, obviously mellowing the older he got. Roy had seen some of Billy's mates and wondered how his father would cope with them. One looked like a Roman centurion with a high and stiff gelled Mohican of lilac hue, whilst the others wore a variety of chains, pins and ripped T shirts. One of them, taking it to extremes, had even walked about for a couple of days with a small bag of vomit around his neck.

Roy sat now and watched the news. Even when he wasn't in Ulster there could be no getting away from the place. Another hunger striker had died, another massive funeral and riot, five soldiers had been blown up in South

Armagh, murdered without a chance, their vehicle blown to smithereens by a huge blast, the occupants vaporised. It was easy for the bastards to just sit behind a hedge and push a button, which is why Roy and most other Protestants had no other emotion but a sense of gladness when their enemy starved themselves to death. Roy had nodded approvingly and snorted his laughter when Billy had told him of a football match he had recently attended, where the Protestant supporters had started singing 'Food, glorious food.' He reluctantly and grudgingly acknowledged the misguided bravery of the hunger strikers, fanaticism some might say, but he still hated and wished them all dead.

Marty sat alert and stone cold sober near the top of a hill in South Armagh. The sun was well up, and smoky dark and fluffy white clouds mingled, drifting slowly against a backdrop of azure blue, now and again crossing the sun and causing shadows to flit across the landscape before him, a patchwork of undulating green fields divided by darker thin hedges with here and there a lighter dry stone wall. A few farms dotted this bucolic scene, completed by a group of cattle in one field, the singing of birds and buzzing of a few early bees. A single road was visible in the middle, forming a long lazy S shape as it disappeared into the distance and it was this that Marty was watching, patient as a mantis along with three other volunteers. It remained empty apart from a tractor chugging and puffing before it turned off onto one of the tracks leading to Donnelly's farm, its driver unaware he had just driven past several hundred pounds of explosives; not that he was in any danger. They were very careful not to injure their own and would abandon an operation if there was a chance of this, the people here were their eyes and ears and must never be jeopardised. It was another thing he liked here. It was a cleaner war with only them and the Brits, and unlike Belfast, little chance of civilians getting in the way.

Marty glanced over at Pat who lay stretched on the grass, an M 16 Armalite next to him and incongruously a bottle of orange juice and wrap of sandwiches, just like any other workman on a break. Joe lit a fag and threw the packet of Majors to Eugene who caught them deftly with one hand. Eugene was deft at a lot of things, but his speciality was bomb making, not so much the mixing of fertiliser and diesel that went into most home made mixes, but rather at the delicate wiring and circuitry for the finished product. This particular one was remote control, very sophisticated and very deadly. He had witnessed the spectacular results of a number of Eugene's products and had a healthy respect for him. A small scout helicopter clattered faintly across the sky in the distance, watched longingly, almost hungrily by Joe, like a child looking at a just unobtainable fat ripe pear on the top branch. Marty turned back to watching the road, thinking how his view of them had changed these last few years.

When Marty had been sent here he had not liked the idea, living out in the sticks with a lot of 'cultchie' farmers. He had complained about it to Tinks.

"I'm really pissed off with this carry on. I have to go down there and you know what country folk are like?" She didn't look up from her reading. "My Da used to say it about my Ma's folks, a right queer lot of bumpkins. Used to stare at anyone if they didn't have cow dung on their boots. Cattle prod country so it is."

She had accompanied him on the way to his new place in Dundalk, a small flat on a council estate which had been found for him, but at least he wouldn't have to share, which meant Martina could come down at weekends and holidays. She was active herself in a support role these days, her house now her mother had died used as a weapons store and herself fulfilling any other duties she could.

A meeting was arranged outside a town centre pub, where someone would brief him and discuss where he was to fit in. A man in his late twenties with short dark hair and freckles approached.

"You're Marty?"

He had an open wide smile, showing large square teeth and he led Marty around the corner and along the street. "How're you doing? I'm Pat and that's my car," he said pointing at a large grey Vauxhall Viva. Marty grunted acknowledgement, slightly gritting his teeth at the soft country accent and way he said 'car' making it sound like 'Cyar'.

He was later interviewed by another couple of locals, with that same gently delivered accent. One of them was Joe and the other a much older man, again called Pat, who unlike his namesake was bald as an egg with a leathery red face that had obviously been in a lot of bad weather. Marty noticed the pleased expressions when he confirmed what they had already been told, especially that he had no arrests apart from the mistake of years ago, and more importantly to them, that his family came from these parts originally. Indeed, they knew his mother's relations as staunch and active. Unlike most Belfast men here he was not on the run, unwanted and probably unsuspected by the security forces and therefore 'clean'; he could be of use to them. They explained carefully that he would be slowly integrated if he proved himself with a unit that operated around the border. Old Pat emphasised this was unusual practice, as they much preferred to use local people. For a long time volunteers on the run from Belfast had even been barred from the area due to the problems and embarrassment they had caused in Dundalk, getting drunk, fighting and generally making problems with the Gardai.

The IRA in South Armagh tended to run things their own way and use only trusted people, which is why they were rarely caught. Here they had advantages: they knew the land intimately, the local population was either actively behind them or silent, and best of all they had a safe haven over the border if things did go wrong. Marty liked the ironic idea of the hated border being used in such a way, they had put it there and now to British frustration it was being used against them.

First however, Marty was sent further south to a remote part of county Cork for proper training, where he and a few other recruits practiced with a variety of weapons, cleaning and taking them apart and eventually firing them, although this was limited. It was good fun. Marty wasn't too keen on the bomb making course though and let them know it. He had seen the results of what happened if things went wrong. Only time spent with the very capable volunteers in South Armagh reassured him, their bombs were very rarely faulty, but when he thought about it, that was logical as most of them had done little else these last years but sit around thinking up new and ever more ingenious ways of killing soldiers. This, coupled with their natural advantages of a safe haven and local support, had made South Armagh a most dangerous place for crown forces. Marty had immediately noticed the age of the volunteers here, much older on average than those in Belfast for the simple reason they didn't get caught. The longer they were active, the more experienced and better they became at their lethal work. He soon appreciated his move might well increase his life expectancy, so he decided to stay even when he heard Beatle had been saying conciliatory things and held no grudges, that they should just put it all behind them. He was better here for now.

As well as these practical experiences, Marty was subjected to a lecture on anti interrogation techniques if he was arrested, which could be reduced to one golden rule: silence. Not even an acknowledgement that your captors were there, not allowing them any opening. This right to silence was the best possible defence and was a right that was used. Over the years this had developed into what was called the 'Green Book' which as far as Marty was concerned was just a lot of rules and regulations to ensure discipline. Every volunteer was required to go through it so there could be no excuse of ignorance.

Finally he was ready to help his new unit, which he had now been doing for over four years. It had been a slow process, they had only gradually brought him into the heart of things a step at a time, providing back up, keeping watch, driving and then eventually on active operations. He had been involved in a number of shootings and bombings since then, proving himself to them by his willingness and commitment. All told, Marty was responsible partly or personally for a round dozen deaths. He didn't resent it, but even now he was always the last to be informed of details, as if the trust in him, although great, had a limit. He had ribbed them, asking if he had to be here twenty inbred generations before he was considered part of the family. Marty smiled. Bloody cultchies.

He looked across at them again, listening to Joe and Pat arguing gently about the relative footballing merits of Aston Villa and Liverpool, that soft accent that was so at odds with their utter ruthlessness. They could laugh and joke and down the beer, blow somebody's brains out on their doorstep, and then go to mass the next day as if it was the most natural thing in the world. Some of them could buy you a pint or kill you with equal alacrity. An exhausted bee landed next to Eugene who carefully picked it up by the wings and put it to one side where Joe's heavy fist came down obliterating it. Marty admired their ruthless professionalism.

"I think that's them," Eugene called lightly to him. "Marty, you've good eyes now, is that the car?"

Marty shielded his eyes, focusing on a dark red Sierra, still toy like at this distance. The only way the army travelled around these parts was by helicopter, the roads had become far too risky and the RUC only used unmarked cars. A source unknown to Marty had provided valuable information however that a couple of cops should be in the area this day, driving that particular make and colour of car. It was all they had but it was enough.

"Aye, that's them."

Eugene took a brick shaped black box with a button and two switches, and removing a piece of tape pressed the button. It was wired to another smaller box with an aerial and amber light which now began flashing. The bomb was now armed. They waited for the car to approach a road sign marker. When the car pulled level Eugene flicked both switches at once. They saw a small puff of smoke at the side of the road and moments later came a muted crack, but not the huge fountain of earth and flash as the car and its occupants disintegrated. The main charge had failed to detonate. Eugene flung the box down cursing savagely, the car had stopped and as Marty and the others opened fire, it reversed at comical speed, turned and within seconds was flying along the road in the opposite direction. They ceased fire, knowing it was useless at that range but it vented their anger. Such mishaps were extremely rare; those were two very, very lucky cops. They quickly collected their gear and even cigarette butts, hurried to their own car and were soon safe across the border.

That evening he sat with Martina curled up beside him watching an episode of M.A.S.H. He sipped from a consoling glass of neat Powers whiskey, enjoying the slight burn of the first warming sips. Tinks cuddled up onto his chest, her blond hair smelling strongly of apple shampoo, her hand gently stroking his side. She wore one of his shirts which for some strange reason always made him feel good, confirming her as a part of team Marty.

"Do you ever think much on the fellas you've killed?" she asked. He shifted slightly. "I mean, I know it's war. You do what you have to." Marty thought for a second, removing her head from his chest as he poured another drink.

"How do you mean?"

"Well, you know, what were they like, who were they. Did they maybe like a drink, or go dancing, or play football or rugby or whatever?"

Marty got up and changed channels. 'Hill Street Blues' was near starting, but first came an advert for the wonders of a new age, the 'Atari consol' complete with space invaders and asteroids.

"None of that makes any difference after we've stiffed them does it?"

Martina watched him for a second, blue eyes waiting for more. She took the drink from him and took a sip before nestling again.

"It's just a pity is all. I'll be happy when it's all over." She yawned. Marty grunted, kissing the top of her head.

"So will I. Don't hold your breath but."

She took his hand and without looking up whispered to him, "Please be careful Marty."

Later that night after they had made love and the rain lashed against the window he lay awake, Tinkerbell's still form snug against him and her dainty painted hand on his chest. He was thinking about what she had said. No, he didn't dwell on the people he had killed and whether they enjoyed a joke or did any of the human things he did himself. He consciously didn't think about it because he knew it would weaken his resolve, the only way of managing after all this time was to see them as targets and not as people at all. When they put on a uniform they knew the risks the same as he did and had to take the consequences. They might think they were defending their country, well so was he. Marty couldn't afford to start having doubts. That was dangerous. He put it from his mind and drifted off into sleep.

The following day Marty walked into the pub with its smoke laden air and blurred sounds of fifty people talking at different volumes, punctuated with the regular 'caching!' as the till opened. He went to the bar with its traditional white handled beer pumps and newer wares, a pint of amber coloured lager in a panelled glass made of plastic and a synthetic garish pineapple for ice cubes. He ordered a pint of Harp, giving the barmaid a wink as he handed over the crinkly brown note. He took his pint and change and walked around the L shaped bar to where Brendan would be sitting, and immediately wished he hadn't come. Brendan waved him over, standing to greet him with a radiant sunflower smile, and next to him, like a huge malignant weed was Beatle. Marty managed to keep his own smile from falling, deciding instantly that tact would be best, at least until he found out what was behind this unpleasant surprise.

"What about you Marty? I haven't seen you these years," said Beatle.

"Oh, I've been in the long grass. How're you keeping yourself?"

"Fine, fine. Good to see you!"

Beatle patted him on the arm as he sat. Brendan was obviously embarrassed. He had been in Dundalk himself for the last couple of years. Dixie had gone down for fifteen years along with another volunteer, only he and Danny escaping after a robbery for funds had turned into a fiasco. Danny had later been picked up and given a sentence for other offences. Brendan was wanted for questioning, and although it wasn't certain he would be convicted he had decided to come south. Marty was careful when meeting his old mate, never going anywhere over the border with him and even here keeping a wary eye open. He couldn't afford to be seen with somebody who was suspected of being in the Provisionals. His relative anonymity was the best thing he had going for him. He got to the point.

"Something's up right?"

Brendan nodded his head, mouth full of beer. Beatle answered.

"There was a wee problem, nothing serious, but it was felt I'd better come down here for a while until things cool off." He laughed. "Just like yourself Marty!"

"What do you mean, 'a wee problem', what kind of wee problem? Are you on the run?"

"I can't go into details, orders, you know." Beatle fidgeted, tearing at a matchbox. He wasn't used to being questioned and didn't like it. "Look, for the time being I'm going to be down here with Brendan and his unit, so you'll probably see me around from time to time."

Marty thought about this, knowing there was little he could do but make the best of it. *'Aye you'll see me about will you? But not if I see you first.'* He gave them both a glittering smile which he hoped only Brendan would see through.

"O.K, welcome to Dundalk." Then he threw the pig some scraps. "Like another drink?"

A day later he was able to see Brendan alone when he visited his flat. He switched the T.V on as his friend sat down.

"How do you think I feel?" said Brendan. "I'm having to work with the bastard, at least you can keep your distance."

"So what is he really doing down here? What have you heard?" Marty was intrigued, it might be important.

"Not much. Only the complaints were building up, you know what he's like. Well the last few years he's been helping out with security and discipline and all that, sometimes he went a bit too far even for them. The fucker was enjoying it too much is what I think, he's getting a reputation as a head the ball.

It doesn't look good." Brendan stopped, briefly contemplating the TV and an anti smoking cartoon character called 'Nick O'Teen'. They both lit up as Brendan continued.

"You heard he sings to people when they're being questioned?" Marty narrowed his eyes and inclined his head. Brendan went on. "Yeh, I heard he sings bits of different Abba songs, 'Dancing Queen' and 'Name of the Game' in this high pitched weird voice and all this whilst he's battering some kid for joy riding. I heard the one time he started singing "Chiquitita tell me the truth..." to someone suspected of touting, waving a gun under his nose!" Brendan managed to look disgusted and concerned at the same time. "He gives a lot of people the creeps, most won't work with him anymore. The only reason I think he was allowed to carry on so long was because he gets results, he really fuckin' scares people."

"Is he a good singer?" Marty asked tittering and very soon they were both giggling and then laughing uncontrollably, tears in their eyes, coughing and choking. Brendan caught his breath a moment.

"I'd better watch myself if I'm sat in the pub with him and he puts the juke box on," he said. Marty burst into more gales of laughter until it was almost like old times.

Chapter 7

Dear Hearts Across the Sea

It was a quiet Friday afternoon and Roy was reading on his bunk, a tape deck playing a medley of different songs badly recorded from the radio that Billy had sent him. At the moment it was 'Don't You Want Me Baby'. Roy flipped another page. He had been intermittently reading a biography of Cromwell now for several weeks. He had resisted the temptation to search immediately for the Irish campaign and read it through from the beginning. When he came to the massacres in Drogheda and Wexford he was mildly surprised; that explained a few things. Still, the rules of war then were brutal and bloody and if you didn't give in you had to take what was coming, especially with a wrath of God, sword swinging, psalm singing chap like Cromwell.

As the battalion was now on standby, or 'Spearhead' as it was known with typical military bombast, he had taken the chance to indulge himself with some reading. He had even bought a volume of Kipling's poems with their distinctive army flavour.

He and Keith had finally made the decision to leave the regiment, at least temporarily and try and sign up for special duties, probably covert operations and an eventual return to Ireland, doing something more useful than pointless patrols. Before this however they had to be approved by the C.O. After a half hour of questioning he had finally agreed to release them for detachment, but only after the regiment was no longer on standby. The Talking Heads came crackling on. Roy was now at the point of the dissolution of Parliament, Cromwell working himself into a fearsome rage when the door was flung open with a bang and Corporal Dillon entered, his face flushed and Brummie accent to the fore.

"Rumour has it we moight be goin' to the Falklands!"

"Why? What's going on?"

"It's bin on the news loike, Argentina has invaded 'em and way moight 'ave to go and tak' 'em back."

Roy thought about it and pulled a doubtful face. He had seen a little about some illegal scrap metal merchants down there but hadn't thought much about it. Nobody had.

"Nah! They'll sort it out round the table. D'you know how far it is down there?" Dillon shook his head. "No, nor do I but it's a fucking long way I can tell you."

A pale freckled head with exaggerated features poked around the door and 'Nossy' Patterson came in. "You've heard then? There's a real flap going on. I heard everybody on detail has been called back, it could be the real thing! The battalion will be put on 24 hours notice to move."

They reminded Roy of kids just about to open their presents, but he had to admit he was getting excited at the prospect of real action himself. Dillon picked up his book and quickly put it down again. The only thing he was known to read were company orders and *The Sun*.

The following days were spent in a flurry of activity as the battalion made ready, incredibly it seemed they might actually be going off to a pucker war. They had seen the reaction of the country and also the humiliating departure of the small Royal Marine garrison, hooting and jeering at them for giving in so easily. The preparations became intense as the paraphernalia of the battalion was assembled, not just personal weapons and grenades, but radios, GPMGs, mortars, MILAN anti tank weapons, WOMBAT recoilless rifles, and a mass of other equipment to be readied and organised.

Within a week they were on their way, most of the 'Toms' by now boisterous and impatient to be gone, most would be really disappointed if a diplomatic solution was found. Roy, although caught up in the electric atmosphere couldn't help thinking about those old black and white grainy films of cheering crowds and soldiers on their way to the First World War. He wondered what his Granny would have made of it and then remembered her words, "You couldn't not go."

Soon after Beatle had made his unwanted appearance, Marty was also on the move to different parts. His problems only really began well into the new year, the first Marty heard of anything going on was Brendan telling him that Bunny had been arrested. His first reaction had been slight indifference. People got arrested all the time, maybe he would get off.

"It's not so simple Marty. A lot of people he knows have been lifted since, he's giving up the names of people he knows. Maybe us too, he's done a deal, turned tout. Have you not read the papers lately about 'Super grasses?' Bunny can give them an awful lot of stuff, the bastard!"

Marty wasn't too concerned, he hadn't done anything in the Republic so he just shrugged as he could do nothing about it anyway. A quote from later school days crossed his mind.

"What is without remedy should be without regard. Aye, Shaky sure knew his stuff."

"Eh?"

"Nothing. How's it going with our friend?"

Brendan grimaced. "I won't tell you details, and I can't prove it but I'm pretty sure he kept some money for himself on a wee job we done recently."

"You'll just have to keep your eye on the thieving shite, not that I'm surprised. I'm just glad I don't have to deal with him," Marty said.

A couple of days later Marty was called to a meeting and received some news. Brendan was there as well as old Pat and a guy named Dennis whom he hadn't met before. Marty observed the newcomer carefully, black hair threaded with grey at the sides, dark eyes with a thin neat moustache, probably good looking when he was younger and very even white teeth. He was dressed all in black, shoes, trousers and heavy winter pullover that showed a ring of white shirt collar. At a distance he could be mistaken for a man of the cloth. In fact he was the bearer of bad news. Marty and Brendan would have to go away for a while, they had been implicated by Bunny in a number of incidents in the North and also a robbery here in the South, the last untrue. It didn't matter; they would both have to get away and lie low for a while, but it was possible they might be able to get Bunny to retract, making any confessions he had made worthless. For the time being though they had better make themselves scarce to avoid being lifted. There was more. Dennis stretched his mouth in sympathy.

"I know, it's bad. We might be able to get something positive out of all this though. We were thinking and came up with an idea, you can have a wee holiday into the bargain."

Marty sat up straight, instantly alert as always when he heard 'we' mentioned, knowing that meant people high up.

"We were thinking maybe you two could go on an arms buying mission, see some contacts we made, have a nose about for anything we could use. We can have passports made up soon enough," he said, finger scratching his nose. Brendan perked up.

"Sounds alright to me! I've never been to the States."

"No, no, no." Pat gave a short laugh. "He means the Lebanon, Beirut."

Brendan's mouth fell open in horror. Marty spoke angrily.

"I'll be damned if I'm going to Beirut! Haven't you heard there's a war on there? And youse want us to go in the middle of it asking, please mister, have you any spare guns at all?"

Dennis put his palms up, smiling reassuringly, his words pointed yet reasonable. "You'll be damned if you don't go, you'll be lifted for that robbery." He waved an impatient hand. "Yes I know that wasn't you but that doesn't matter. Any road, Lebanon is safe enough these days, has been for years now since the Syrians sorted it out. It's only the south near Israel that's dodgy and you'll be nowhere near there. It's quite civilised these days really, we know some people there who'll look after you and you'll have enough money. It'll not be the first time we've sent people abroad. As well as having a sunny break you'll be working too, there's loads of spare gear floating about from the civil war. We need to be able to buy it and ship it. You two can look into it. It'll be safe. You're privileged. You'll be helping the movement more than you know."

Marty gave a grim laugh. "Aye, that's like telling the pig he'd be helping everyone more as sausage."

"Really," said Dennis, shaking his head. "You'll be safer there than here. It's all sorted, you might even enjoy it! We'll be killing two birds with one stone if you like."

"Birds? Aye." He sighed in submission. "When do we go?"

Shortly before they left, Marty and Brendan were called for a briefing at a local safe house where they were given passports, tickets, money and information. The previous night Marty had enjoyed a passionate and tearful farewell from Martina, her body twisting and shuddering beneath him as she bit her lip, eyes screwed shut, her cheeks flushing as he watched entranced, bringing him to his own noisy climax. He was tired as he sat on a rickety wooden chair and examined the proffered documents.

"Amsterdam?" Marty asked. Dennis nodded.

"You'll be in a wee town not far from there for a bit. We've safe people there who'll see you OK and make arrangements."

"Why can't we just stay there?" Brendan inquired. Dennis took a breath, impatience showing.

"Because we want you to go to bloody Lebanon that's why!" he snapped, then added more reasonably, but slightly mocking, "Come on Brendan, do your duty."

Marty looked at the passports carefully, holding them up and flipping through; they even had a couple of stamps in them. They were now Martin Jackson and Brendan Donovan.

"These are really good but!"

"That's because they're real," said Dennis with a small laugh. "Only the stamps are false." Marty gave him an expectant look. He continued. "That's all you need to know. When you get to Beirut you have to go to an address in the west of the city and ask for Saleh Filhama. He'll be your contact, we've dealt with him before and he's sound. Knows a lot of people, has links. We want arms and more importantly a safe method of delivery. Find out what you can, like what there is and how much of it and the cost, keep an eye open for rockets, heavy machine guns, you know anything we can't produce ourselves. There must be a lot of surplus since the civil war stopped. If everything looks good, get in contact via a number I'll give you and use the code words, again it's written down. Memorise it and destroy the paper, grenades are apples, automatic rifles are celery and so on, we'll make further arrangements then concerning money and banks. Oh aye, don't bother with ordinary explosives, as you know we can always make that ourselves."

Marty did know. Homemade stuff using fertiliser was potent enough and readily available. The amount that was bought around these parts the countryside should be the most fertilised and productive in the world, but the main harvest here was gathered in by the Grim Reaper. He would have liked more specifics before they left, he didn't like being kept too much in the dark, it was too vague. He had read as much as he could in the limited time, and although it did seem safe enough at the moment there were still various militias and likely to be some nasty characters floating about, and the only prisoners those bastards took were likely to be found sliced up like mutton. Also, what you didn't know yourself you couldn't quickly divulge if a gang of inquisitive Arabs approached bearing large knives.

They flew to Schiphol the next day and made their way to a small seaside town where they were put up by a middle aged man named Paul, who welcomed them into his small attic flat with hearty handshakes. He had been told to look after them for a few days and get them sorted with tickets to Athens. That was all he wanted to know, although glad to help out. He told them to relax for a few days whilst he made the arrangements. They went back to Amsterdam the next day, had a few beers, looked around like any other tourist at the red light area, took in a live sex show that was like no other show they had ever imagined and generally took it easy. Another real eye opener were the drugs openly on sale, the sound of gentle hissing on the street from seedy looking characters, offering everything from hash to heroin.

"Psst! Hashish? Weed? Trips? Coke, pure stuff, no shit! No? Heroine, brown, white? OK! Special offer! Methadone," one had leered at them to their incredulous laughter. At home he'd have lost his kneecaps in no time.

Paul had purchased tickets to Athens and handed them over along with a large wad of money to see them through the next month or so, further payments would be made later. Looking at the tickets, both had been disappointed to see they were for the coach and not air. Brendan was particularly annoyed.

"What the fuck is this? Coach? Could you not have gotten us a flight instead, it's a long way you know."

"That's what I was told to do," said Paul apologetically. "You'll be just two backpackers on holiday, saving your money and taking it easy. Anyway there's no rush is there? "

During the long trip down they concentrated on their reading material, nearly all of it about the history and politics of Lebanon. There wasn't too much and most of that was bad enough. All in all it sounded like a mix of different groups controlling different parts of the country, differing religions and nationalities all mixed together, confused and sometimes deadly. To Marty it sounded something like home, but instead of Provisional IRA, INLA, Official IRA, UVF, UFF, UDA, and all the other associates there was the PLO, PFLP, Druze, Muslim, Christian, Maronite and all the splinters thereof but with the added spice of no strong central authority. Looking at the sheer number of groups and nationalities all jockeying for their slice, Marty thought it was little wonder the place had blown apart. The terrible civil war in 1975-6 had added an element of lawlessness that was very different to home however, even in the darkest days it had never gotten as bad as Beirut. He just hoped the place had improved as much as they had been led to believe.

As they travelled down through Yugoslavia, Marty and Brendan both read on, from time to time swapping books or pointing out some fact of note, both taking the job seriously. There was little else to do or see anyway, the landscape outside still a prisoner of winter, ugly and dull with a bleak sky the colour of dirty putty and brown drabness everywhere. It took another two days before they eventually arrived in Athens, its white splendour bathed in early spring sunshine. Their hotel was one of many that catered for backpackers, modest enough and cheap, which they paid for as soon as they could change some money into drachmae. Their double room was high ceilinged and airy and even had a balcony although the view wasn't much, facing the wall of another block. Marty chucked his rucksack on the bed, raising a cloud of dust that floated in the yellow sunlight.

"I always wanted to see the Acropolis."

Brendan grunted, not an enthusiast of the classics. At the moment he had something else on his mind, as something on the menu at one of the stops had given him a bad stomach. He wasn't as keen on foreign foods as Marty and wouldn't even eat a Chinese takeaway at home; he'd have been happier in America with a hot dog.

The following days were some of the nicest that Marty could remember. He had money in his pocket, it was warm and they had plenty to eat, drink and see with no great rush to proceed. They gave themselves a week in Athens, strolled around the sights including the Acropolis, where even Brendan was impressed by the thousands of whitened buildings spread out before them. They ate and drank well, Brendan to his surprise quite liking the ouzo and mousakka Marty had recommended as it had potatoes in it. Marty loved it all, the sound of different language, the noise, smells and customs of a foreign capital and wouldn't have minded staying longer. Brendan wanted to get on though, thinking that the sooner they did the business in Beirut the sooner they could get back to Holland which was much more to his taste. Besides, their funds were not unlimited and when Marty called and asked for more money to be wired, it had been given, but not without grumbling about a need to be careful of expenses. Tight bastards thought Marty.

The following day they bought ferry tickets to Limassol in Cyprus and spent the rest of the day relaxing in the city centre, drinking the thick strong coffee and sampling the food. Brendan stuck to chips and salad, taking a little feta with it until Marty told him it came from a goat, then sniffed suspiciously at anything he didn't immediately recognise. He also refused to touch the delicious fat purple olives that Marty was developing a passion for. Their last evening they sat drinking and talking about home, what lay ahead and when they might return. They could see the Acropolis dramatically lit up in the night sky high on the hill, both excited and apprehensive too, both old and experienced enough to know the dangers yet young enough to enjoy the thrill and adventure, the importance and trust placed in them, doing their duty. They went to sleep that night with a keen sense of pride and anticipation, knowing that the coming weeks might be some of the most memorable of their lives.

Next morning they boarded the ferry at Piraeus, their euphoric mood from the previous evening somewhat duller as a wicked Metaxa hangover accompanied them. It was only dispelled by the cleansing effect of a cool sea wind when they pulled out into open sea, bringing smiles and laughter as they shouted to each other on deck. Going below, Brendan nabbed an English Sunday newspaper that had been left on a table by a tourist. Marty had gone to get something to eat and came back with a plate of salad, chips and bread. The paper was from April 5th but as they hadn't listened to the radio on their tape deck since last week it was news to them. The Falklands, wherever they were, had been invaded and to their delight Britain had been humiliated, with their soldiers turfed out unceremoniously by Argentina. Brendan crowed with heartfelt delight.

"Oh Yes! It says here Thatcher is the first PM to lose British territory since the war, they're going to hold her and that poncy Lord Carrington responsible. That's great news, I hope they hang the bitch out to dry."

The hatred like the pleasure was genuine. Since the hunger strikes, when she had allowed their brave men to die, Thatcher was enemy number one.

They arrived in Limassol, and from there hopped on a bus to Larnaca and found a cheap hotel before hitting the town to look about. There wasn't much, a few churches, some Greek ruins, a mosque and a castle. Plenty of bars and pubs though with a definite English influence, but there would be, as the grasping colonialist bastards had occupied this place too.

They stopped in a square and stared at a memorial statue of a guerrilla, frozen in the late 1950's with his sten gun forever at the ready. Marty knew that back then Cyprus had its own 'Troubles' and how those fighting against British soldiers had been labelled murderers the same as they were now. Some of those same men, those that the Brits hadn't shot or strung up like this one, had gone on after independence to become respected members of government. It was the way of things and why he, Brendan and the other volunteers merely curled their lips in cynicism when they in turn were also branded as mere terrorists. That would change after they had won. Another thing they noticed was the fact there were still British bases on the island. He wondered where they went for recreation, making a mental note to remember this interesting fact. They didn't wait too long in Larnaca, a quick trip to Nicosia to get a visa for Lebanon which was issued with surprising efficiency the next day and they were ready to go.

Within days Roy found himself along with the rest of the battalion in Southampton docks, getting ready to embark on the cruise liner *S.S 'Canberra'*. He watched out of the window and thought about his visit to this city last year with Keith. As the coaches pulled up they got their first good look at the place that was to be their home for the next five weeks. It towered above them at the quayside, and for most of the troops who had never seen a ship so close, the sheer size made them look in awe upon its huge white bulk. When Roy saw it he puzzled for a moment before realising with a happy flash of recognition where he had seen it before, this white cruise ship, with its distinctive twin mustard coloured funnels. It was on some of the bank notes back home, the ship in the corner that he had mused about sailing on one day long ago.

"There she is lads, Belfast built and just as beautiful," said Roy.

Keith stopped by his side, arms akimbo, staring up. "So was the *'Titanic'*. It sailed from Southampton too," he said.

Corporal Eric 'Hovis' Janson frowned at him, superstitions aroused at this bad omen. He was a dour Yorkshireman and one for chucking salt over his shoulder and touching wood to ward off evil spirits.

"Aw, fookin' shoorup will you?"

"It's Good Friday today isn't it?" Keith began laughing, anticipating more sport with such an easy target. "We sail tonight. I don't think seamen like departing on a Friday do they, and as for Good Friday..."

He skipped away snickering as Hovis came towards him. Sergeant Daniels came over.

"O.K, we can begin embarkation, up the gangplank and you'll receive instructions aboard as to your accommodation. Right! Get moving."

They collected their gear and began boarding, accompanied by music from the bands of their own regiment and the Royal Marines, with whom they would be sharing the voyage amongst others. He and Dillon had been allocated a double berth which was more luxurious than what they had been expecting. There would be in excess of three thousand troops aboard, but it appeared the *'Canberra'* would be able to fit them all in without much of a problem, with no need to sling hammocks or whatever it was troops normally did at sea. They sorted their gear and went to explore the ship, in particular the bars and restaurants, finding out in quick time which was to be their own mess. The officers and senior NCO s would of course eat and drink separately from other ranks. There had been a little grumbling at this from the newer men, some of the 'crows' who had only just arrived at battalion, but Roy understood it was not a case of class distinction, but that those in charge could never become too familiar with those they would be giving orders to. It was common sense. A man might hesitate taking an order from someone he had seen pissed as a fart, making a total knob of himself. A certain distance had to be kept; it was just a pity that the officers always seemed to end up with the better accommodation and mess.

Roy went on deck and was surprised to see men from the nearby ship builders still working at turning an open air swimming pool into a landing pad for helicopters. There was an air of urgency, cutting, welding, hammering and they still weren't finished. In fact they would be sailing with them and only be lifted off at Gibraltar once the work was completed. Seeing this made Roy wonder, first at the huge cost, and then at the hurried ad hoc nature of it all. Unlike most of the guys, Roy now thought this might be serious. They weren't going to all this trouble for nothing. For the most part everyone else thought a diplomatic solution still probable before it got to actual fighting, it was all so sudden and unreal.

He looked over and down at the quayside where troops were still coming aboard to the blaring and pomping of the bands. People were gathering and waving, some holding banners and flags and it began to resemble something from long ago, the patriotic crowds seeing their boys off to war yet again; Kipling come to life. They watched from the rails as gradually the light dimmed, and the crowds ashore grew thicker, and lights appeared all along the waterfront as they untied and the tugs pulled them to open water. The cheering continued, the ship blowing a deep resonating farewell salute as Roy looked at other members of his battalion. Some were chatting and joking, others watching quietly, deep in thought. One or two were pointing now at the lights from the shore, at the houses and blocks of flats, the occupants blinking their lights off and on in farewell, letting them know everybody was thinking of them and wishing them safe return. Roy felt a warm glow at that small act and glancing left saw with a burst of laughter Nossy Patterson having difficulty swallowing his emotion, like a giraffe with an apple in its throat. Dillon came up behind him.

"Are you coming to the bar?"

Their allocated bar was the 'Alice Springs', appropriate considering the ship was more often than not heading towards Australia. Officially, they were allowed a ration of two beers per night being now on active service, but in practice nobody was going to be foolish enough to enforce this rule so early into the voyage. The real law was don't get too drunk and if you did, it had better not affect your performance the next day.

Roy, Dillon, Nossy, and Hovis took a table and sat down in the crowded lounge, their eyes roving, showing approval at their surroundings. It was plush but casual, a large bar, lots of comfy chairs and a great view as it was near the stern of the vessel with floor to ceiling windows. There were also groups of marines which provoked good natured jibes but no serious disputes, most realising they would be together now for some time so had better make the best of it. A few came and sat at the next table, to exchange a bit of banter and professional chat, as well as opinions on the situation. The unreality of sitting on a cruise ship drinking beer made for a lot of congenial stories and laughter.

Talk of the quayside band reminded Roy of a tale his father had once told him when he had been in the marines as part of a good will visit to a Caribbean island, and he related this now to much laughter. As his father's ship was due to leave there had taken place the usual 'beating of the retreat,' the marine band playing to local dignitaries sat there in their fineries by the dock side, the Governor complete with ceremonial uniform and feathered hat. Unfortunately one of the shore parties was delayed getting back. As the band played late into the evening to the assembled guests, the approaching noise of drunken singing was heard. A few heads began to turn, craning to see what the commotion was. The singing became louder, accompanied by the breaking of bottles as twenty rum sodden matelots came closer. There was a scurry down the only gangplank directly in front of the dais as an embarrassed and now panicked officer rushed off, watched by an interested crowd to intercept the mob. The band played on. The officer, now in a dreadful sweat and not wanting to create further spectacle, had the bright idea of putting the sailors in a huge net and winching them the short distance aboard, thus avoiding the gangplank in full view. The rowdy drunken sailors were put into the net and lifted by crane, becoming compacted and thrown together, laughter turning to curses and then to pushing, shoving and eventually fists. The net was swung the wrong way directly over the band, their music now accompanied from above by screams, shouts and the sound of vomiting that brought every head in the throng up as it pattered down like gull droppings, splashing some of the unfortunate musicians. The struggling mass was landed on deck and herded unceremoniously below to the stifled laughter of many guests and crimson fury of the Governor.

Roy's story brought laughs and a few jeers of disbelief from the marines as he knew it would, but it didn't matter. It was important to break the ice and put professional rivalry aside, the best way as always with a joke. He glanced around the bar when he finished and caught the eye of Sergeant Robson who had popped in for a minute and was rewarded by an approving nod. Praise indeed. So passed a strangely pleasant first evening on their way to war.

The following days were spent getting into some sort of order. Everything had been done in such a hurry, with equipment in wrong ships, stuff stowed in the wrong order and the workmen finishing off. In the meantime a punishing fitness programme began, and the *'Canberra'* reverberated to the thumping and drumming of hundreds of boots as they ran circuits around the ship. There were also exercises on the upper deck and weapons training with small arms, the MILAN crews practicing but not actually firing any live rounds. Hovis was shocked at the reason why.

"Ye've got to be fookin' joking? How much per missile? I knew they were dear like..."

Everybody had a go at the 'gash shoots' however. Large bags of rubbish would be dropped over the side and groups would take it in turns using a variety of weapons, ripping and shredding the bags with their rifles, General Purpose Machine Gun or 'Gimpy' and even a few Sterlings. Most evenings Roy and his mates would spend in the 'Alice Springs' after a good dinner in the Atlantic restaurant, the 'scoff' a lot better than what they normally had. Over beer and cards they discussed the novelty of their situation.

"Never thought I'd go on a cruise ship. Free of charge too! This is the life eh?" Keith said beaming as he sat down with a refill.

They faced the stern of the ship, staring out at the wake and distant horizon as the sun went down all vermillion fire to their left, gilding their glass tops with its last rays. They were fast approaching West Africa.

"What's the name of the place we're goin'?" Dillon asked.

"The Falklands," Keith replied innocently.

"Don't be bloody daft. I mean where's first, you know. Tomorrow isn't it? I heard we've a stop off for water or summat."

"Freetown Sierra Leone, Mr Dillon," said Roy taking a sip.

"Why's it called Freetown?" he asked, glaring briefly at Keith, daring him. Nossy answered.

"It's to do with slavery, it was the first free colony or something. Do you think they'll let us ashore?"

"I doubt it, not enough time," said Roy with a shake of his head.

It was growing dark, but it stayed agreeably warm and from somewhere The Pretenders 'I Go To Sleep' drifted past them on the warm and gentle night breeze. Keith spoke again.

"Not that I'm complaining, but why are we going all this way? From what I've heard the Falklands are just a lot of sheep covered rocks with some farmers on them."

Roy answered with a poignant heavy emphasis. "Because it's part of Britain. It's British, even if it's eight thousand miles away, those people are British and you can't let someone walk in and take them over, it doesn't matter how far or how many, it's the principle of it!"

"Alright, keep your hair on." Keith winked slyly at Dillon and chuckled. "Just a joke."

"I wonder how far they've actually planned ahead," said Nossy as he stared out of the window. "I mean, how do they go about it?"

"Well now," said Keith, putting on his most serious, knowing voice and nodding sagely. "It involves some very complicated and time consuming procedures involving the chiefs of staff and their people, with input from logistics and politicos sorting through different scenarios and potential problems. They talk it through with each other, and plan to the last detail and make their final decisions only after a huge amount of deliberation. The top brass then, and *only* then, give out final orders which usually results in a massacre for someone."

Dillon eyed him sourly and changed the subject to football as he was wont to do recently. Aston Villa were nearing the final of the European Cup.

"Do you think we'll be back in time for the final at the end of May? It'd be a right shame to miss it."

Keith and Nossy started laughing and Hovis gave a scowling response. "You never know, it's early days. We might turn round tomorrow, I hope not though. Don't want some bloody politician ruining my war. Or bloody cruise!"

"That's right!" Keith clicked his fingers, remembering something. "I was reading about the *'Titanic'* the other night, you know about the band playing on as it sank. Did you know, it sailed exactly seventy years to the day we did. Coincidence or what?"

"Shut the fook up will tha? You'll put jinx on us!" Hovis turned to the others, checking his watch. "Anyone for watching film? 'Raiders of the Lost Ark' tonight."

"Yeh, O.K," said Keith with a yawn. "Watching that twat taking on fifty armed Nazis with a whip should get me ready for sleep. A good shag would be better but that'll have to wait."

"You could always try one of the crew Keith," said Roy.

The rest of the evening they just sat talking as a half moon climbed in a beautiful, violet black African sky, with here and there a glimpse of the stars before turning in for the night, pleasantly tired and enjoying the new experience. It was quite a nice little holiday.

Roy was right about Freetown; they stopped off for less than a day and were kept on board. He saw Sergeant Robson at the rail with Smithy just as a ships steward came over and said something with a nervous laugh and flick of his wrist at something in the distance. Roy wasn't shocked at the typical Robson repost. He looked the man carefully up and down, his amber eyes narrowing as if taking aim, before delivering a verbal shot straight through the head.

"What do you want you queer cunt?"

There was a sharp intake of breath and the poor man walked quickly away with as much dignity as he could muster amidst the wilting laughter.

"That's it, piss off bonehead, and take your mincing walk with you." He glanced over at Roy, pointing a stubby accusing finger at the retreating figure, "Bummers the lot of them." Roy smiled prudently, then turned back to the shore. Dillon stood next to him, laughing softly.

"Think what'll happen when he gets down there. Have you ever seen him on the football pitch? Plays like he's got rabies. Makes a good ref though, no one argues with his decisions. He doesn't give red cards, he just lays you out."

"Imagine being his prisoner, I'd pity that poor bastard so I would," said Roy.

Dillon wrinkled his brow. "How do you say 'Hands up' in Argentinian anyway?"

Not for the first time Roy wondered how Dillon had made it to corporal, it certainly couldn't be his general knowledge.

On Ascension Island it was hot, but it felt good to be liberated from the confines of the ship and train properly; indeed at the end of a week the whole battalion was helicoptered to the other side of the island with full equipment and 'tabbed' back in the full glare of the midday sun. When they arrived at the shore line, there waiting to take them back to *'Canberra'* were several landing craft. Getting from the craft into the liner was in itself another exercise. A hatch was opened in the side of the ship, and one by one in time to the swells they jumped into the liner, straight into the Atlantic restaurant. It was a slow process and Roy hoped they came up with a different solution. Keith made his usual gleefully pessimistic remark to Hovis.

"This is shit. Just think, sat there unloading from this bloody great white ship and maybe under fire. They can't miss a vessel of this size."

"Shut tha face!"

More ships appeared. One day Roy counted fourteen in all, including fleet tankers, bulky cargo vessels and sharp nosed warships. It gave him a warm confidence seeing they were part of such a powerful armada. The first days of May brought news that made everyone pause and think seriously for the first time about exactly what they were here to do. There had been a raid on Stanley, and then the Argentine cruiser *Belgrano* was sunk with hundreds probably drowned. A day later came the response when one of their own ships was destroyed: HMS *Sheffield* was burnt out by an exocet missile.

There was a slightly different atmosphere that night, not despondent or gung ho, but a realisation that this was for real. They would be leaving within the next couple of days. Roy had picked up an old *Time* magazine, probably left by a tourist a few short weeks ago and sat thumbing through it. He sniffed at the front cover which showed some geeky looking specimen called Steven Jobs with an apple on his head. It was all pretty boring stuff about computers. One day we'd all own one apparently. Yeh right! Dillon was talking.

"It's funny really. I don't know anything about the Argies except what weapons they use, corned beef and that they play a dirty game of football. Here, what if we meet them in the World Cup next month, that'll be interesting."

Nossy shook his head. "Won't happen the way the draw's been made, at least not until the semi finals." He looked at Roy smiling. "You and the Scots don't have to worry, you won't get that far."

"I know all I need to," said Roy, flinging the Steve Jobs geek aside and sitting forwards. "Football, rugby, polo, bollocks. The bastards won't know what's hit them."

"I hope you're right cock," said Keith rubbing his chin and glancing at Hovis. "Chances are though we'll take a few casualties ourselves. You know what they say, if a bullet has your name on it."

Roy snorted. "They were probably saying that old shite at Agincourt!" He let out another laugh as he briefly imagined an English archer carving 'Dear Pierre' on his arrow.

Two days later they set sail for their final destination. Now during the evenings the order went round to darken ship, a sure sign of coming danger. The weather was sometimes rough and people staggered as if drunk to fitness rooms and the daily lectures. It became noticeably colder, and another reminder of what they would soon be doing came when everybody was ordered to give blood to keep up supplies. There was the usual unoriginal wisecracking and Nossy in particular came in for some abuse from Keith.

"Fuck sake don't let him near the blood bank! Hey, Nossy, rumour has it you won't need an intravenous if you get hit, you can just bite someone."

"I hope I don't get your blood Keith, I've never had V.D before."

Then came the day they had been waiting for. They would transfer at first light to HMS *Intrepid* for final preparations and would be landing on Friday morning. They were assembled in one of the luxurious lounges and given a speech by the colonel about the task ahead, which to Roy and everyone else meant one thing: to win.

The dawn was cold and grey, the sea a bleaker hue of the same colour and choppy, alive with flashes of white foam that contrasted starkly with the slate charcoal ocean. They filed into the restaurant, fully kitted out with everything they might need ashore. The heavier stuff would come by helicopter. The strange looking queue, all armed to the teeth and many with bandoliers of bullets clanking around their necks shuffled forwards towards the side door, everybody timing their jump into the landing craft that rose and descended against the side of their ship. Cold and clammy hands grabbed Roy as he stumbled awkwardly into the craft and then they were off, bouncing about as they ploughed towards HMS *Intrepid* which would be their last stop before landing. On arrival they found the ship already crammed. It wasn't quite chaos, but Roy realised there would be little in the way of comforts, the sooner they were off the better. There now began for them the most trying part so far: waiting. They were keyed up and ready to go; being stuck on board a cramped vessel led to shortened tempers and friction. Keith had overheard Private Holden talking calmly and placating Private Ives who was a little claustrophobic. He waited a few minutes for him to settle and then interrupted the quiet conversation.

"Jesus, we're like sardines in here don't you think?" he asked cheerily.

Roy found himself a space in a storage area, put his hands behind his head and drifted off to sleep with mixed feelings of apprehension and pride. Now it was his turn to do his duty, just as his father and grandfather had done theirs.

They queued onto the ferry, showing passports, smiling at the Cypriot policeman and customs officer, who vaguely resembled a thinner and even sleepier Sylvester Stallone in uniform. He stopped them.

"Good morning sirs, whys do you go to Lebanon?" he asked.

"To see around the north, you know Bible places, Byblos and the famous cedars," said Marty, flashing a grin as warm and bright as the Mediterranean sun, before he let concern cloud his face. "Why? There's been no trouble has there? We want to stay away from any of that officer."

"That's right, some guy was telling us we'd be O.K so long as we stayed away from Beirut, that is the case still?" added Brendan frowning worriedly.

"Yes," the officer nodded. "Yes. Please."

He indicated their bags as if to search them, put a cursory hand in Brendan's rucksack, crossed it with chalk and allowed them through. Lazy bastard thought Marty. Several hours later they neared the port of Junieh, both on deck, eager for a first glimpse of this tragic country which until recently had only figured in their minds as television pictures of war and bloody civil strife, a place gone mad. Now they looked and saw the small city across cobalt, calm, almost pond like water. Junieh rose out of the sea before them, the buildings like giants descending the hills, dozens of white and grey modern tower blocks peeping out past one another at their ship, and sprinkled all around, the older and lower red tiled houses typical of the rest of the Mediterranean. They scrutinised the town and were pleased. It looked lovely, even affluent in the sunshine and not at all what they had expected.

"I think I might like it here," said Brendan.

They docked and proceeded to customs, where the two scruffy backpackers were waved almost contemptuously through after they had shown visas and paid an 'entry tax' of a few dollars. The first thing they did was change money at a nearby bank, skipping nimbly to avoid a couple of shady street dealers who were offering the same service; there was no need to risk getting swindled.

They came out of the bank with large wads of Lebanese pounds which they distributed carefully about their persons. Marty examined the joint French and Arab script 'Banque du Liban', the larger hundred lira notes went with their passports around their necks.

Both were hungry and decided to head into the small centre and find something to eat, strolling and getting a first close encounter with a piece of the Levant. Marty was fascinated by it all, the Arabic writing that reminded him of snakes and squiggles, mixed with French and English, the beeping of car horns and racket as a fruit vendor shouted his wares. There was a smell of roasting coffee and cooked spicy mutton, mingling with an underlying whiff of exhaust fumes from the scooters that honked and bustled past them. They found a cafe and sat down, taking what the smiling gold toothed owner brought them as lunch, salad and a couple of delicious toasted cheese sandwich type things. They paid, asking the owner in pidgin French where they could find a taxi. He pointed towards a building at the end of the street that fronted onto a small square where a couple of mini buses and taxis were parked, the owners lounging and smoking. On approaching them there was an immediate dropping of cigarettes and a rush towards them. Arabic, French and a smattering of heavily accented English soon filled the air as five drivers pushed and shoved them and each other. They chose one who could speak English, a squat, hairy balding man with a huge gut and a wheeze. He hustled them towards his car, a big old grey Mercedes, grabbed their bags and flung them into the boot. He shook their hands.

"OK where you want to go? My brother has nice hotel in Byblos, nearby, very good to see yes? We go yes?"

Marty shook his head. "We want to see Beirut."

"Why for? Byblos is good, please." He winked. "I can get you a good rate." Brendan smiled at him.

"No, Beirut."

The man stopped and looked at them with renewed interest. They didn't look like journalists or businessmen either. "OK, but I charge more for there, OK?"

From Junieh to Beirut it was only ten miles and they sped along the highway at hair raising speed, music wailing in Arabic, the windows open to try and ease the stifling heat. Brendan noticed a tiny statue of the Madonna that swung to and fro with a dangling air freshener in the front of the car and nudged Marty; Maronite then, or maybe Greek orthodox or Armenian or some other denomination, but definitely Christian. When Marty offered him the address he had shaken his head and told them he would only take them as far as the port. Marty pictured a map in his head and where the port was. That was alright, the man probably didn't want to go into the Muslim part of the city. The driver practiced his limited English as he careered along, making them wish he would shut up and concentrate on the road.

"Where you from?"

"Ireland."

He thought for a second. "How is it there?"

"How d'ye mean?" Marty asked in turn.

"Rich? Poor? Good? Bad? Pretty?"

"Aye, our city is pretty ugly"

"Huh?"

"No actually, you might say it's terribly beautiful."

Brendan tittered in the back at the incomprehension crossing the driver's face. He gave up. Within half an hour they were in the city. They could see it long before however across the bay, the white high rise buildings strangely familiar from reports down the years that they had only half watched, ignorant that one day they would be here themselves. As they entered the outskirts they looked around, seeing that Junieh, although only half an hour away was another world; another parallel with parts of home. They came to a road block and were waved through, olive uniformed soldiers sat at the side of the road drinking tea, eating or smoking, bored and unkempt looking, rifles stacked carelessly. Brendan pointed at some of the buildings, chipped and scarred from the war. Although they didn't yet know it, this part of the city had escaped relatively lightly the recent ravages. Marty nodded at one building, bullet holed and shrapnel splashed, one corner nibbled away by gunfire.

"Big mice you have here."

The driver knitted his brows in concentration, then shrugged, understanding the words but not the meaning of the foreigner. He stopped, pulling up suddenly at the side of a broad and busy street, jumping out with startling alacrity for his bulk.

"O.K we here. You want other taxi, place to stay you ask here people, no problem." He smiled at them as he opened the boot and placed their rucksacks on the dusty pavement. "When you finish, you see me same place, I take you to Byblos, Baalbek and around yes, my name is Dany, you ask for me." He shook their hands and drove off, the tooting of his horn submerged by a hundred others.

Marty fished out a packet of Marlboros he had bought from a vendor in Junieh, offering one to Brendan, drawing carefully on it as he looked around the bustling street. He glanced at his watch. It was now past two p.m and very hot. As Brendan wiped sweat from his brow, he ran his fingers through his own damp hair.

"Shall we leave finding this Filhama fella for tomorrow Brendan?" he asked.

"Aye, sounds alright to me. We'd better find somewhere to stay, I don't fancy humping bags and searching in the dark."

"That's what I was after thinking too, it's late enough. Let's get settled first, dump the bags and take a wee walk about, we can see your man tomorrow, there's no rush like. Might be best to find a taxi driver, sure he'll know some places to stay." He laughed, "Then we can find out how the grub and drink are too in Costa del Beirut, just like the good little tourists we are."

They shouldered their bags and looked for someone to ask directions. Brendan stopped an obese and sweating middle aged man in a brown open necked shirt who caught his eye.

"Excuse me, could you tell me where we can find a taxi?"

The man gave a small smile like a shy hippo, nodding, not understanding any word except taxi. To Brendan's surprise and Marty's amusement, he took him gently by the hand and led him along the street, waddling and speaking softly in Arabic. Brendan glanced over his shoulder at his friend's grin.

"I think he's taken a fancy to you."

They turned a corner, their guide still talking and now putting his arm through Brendan's who stiffened, cocking a suspicious eye at him, listening to Marty wisecracking behind him.

"Youse make a lovely couple."

They turned another corner and the man stopped, pointing to a tiny plaza that was obviously a drop off point the same as in Junieh. They thanked him and carried on towards a guy leaning on his white Fiat, newspaper open, smoking and scowling at what he was reading. The man saw their shadow approaching and glanced up warily, his features softening into a friendly nodding recognition of welcome, teeth showing under his thick moustache. Marty beamed back at him.

"Good day. Do you speak any English?"

"Yes, a little."

"We're looking for somewhere to stay, a hotel, room, apartment even, if it's cheap enough, do you know anywhere?"

The man sucked thoughtfully at his cigarette before dropping it, scratching his moustache with his other hand.

"Yes, I know of some places." He examined them, noting their dress of faded jeans and t shirts. "How much you want to spend?"

"We don't know how long we'll be here, so cheap as possible."

"O.K, come. I will take you not far from here."

Within ten minutes they were outside what claimed to be a pension in a backstreet of the Rue Riad Solh and Emir Amine, which unknown to them was quite near the so called 'Green line' separating Christian East from Muslim West Beirut. The building was not unlike many others; dilapidated grey white and grubby beige, but without too much Beirut style scarring, the only concession to the war being a single plate sized hole with a ring of shrapnel pitting above the entrance. The street was shaded and the smells of cooked food, exhaust fumes, rubbish and stale urine mixed in a way that made Marty crinkle his nose and want to get inside. The taxi driver had explained that rooms were less easy to come by due to some trouble and tensions in the south. Some people had fled here, so there was some overcrowding and prices were higher than usual. This place was cheap and available. They went to what might have been reception, looking at the decrepit state of the place, flies droning and several cats napping in what passed for a lobby. While they waited, Brendan flipped open an old travel book from the sixties and laughed.

"Listen to this. Beirut is the Paris of the East... blah, blah, its restless mercurial people..."

He cut off as an ancient man appeared behind the desk dressed in shirt, tie and moth eaten green cardigan that hung on his skeletal coat hanger shoulders. The taxi driver was right. It was cheap and they paid there and then for two weeks, a double room, communal bathroom and toilet. He croaked at them in a mix of Arabic and what sounded like broken French, handed them a key with Arabic numerals and pointed to the stairs with one yellowed, nicotine stained talon, the other hand scrambling crablike to put their money away. They tramped up the musty, scabby walled stairs with antique wrought iron railings until they came to their own floor. A long corridor with doors either side wound its way around in a long circuit, with here and there, piles of dusty furniture and junk. They passed more cats and what must have been the toilet judging from the smell, relieved it wasn't too close to where they found their room. They turned the key, shouldered open the creaky door and immediately wished they were rich. There were two beds, one with a broken mirror on it, the other with sheets and blankets and a lot of dust, the bare floor littered with cigarette ends, desiccated orange peel and the tiny corpses of long dead flies. There was a rickety balcony however which faced out onto a darkened courtyard below. Opening the twin doors Marty let in the smell and noise.

"Home sweet home, what do you think?"

Brendan dumped his pack down on one of the beds and carefully removed the pieces of mirror. "Beggars can't be choosers," he said. "Fuck it, we may not be here that long anyway and if we are, we can maybe find something else. We just need somewhere to sleep so we do. It'll do for now."

Marty went to the toilet, shaking his head in amused disbelief at the state of the bathrooms. No hot water. He didn't mind, it was warm enough to actually enjoy a cold shower. The toilet was a simple fetid hole in the floor with foot places, a jug of water, and a shit encrusted metal stick to push down any stubborn turds. Marty swallowed hard. From the corner of his eye he glimpsed a cockroach scuttling under the door and he decided there and then he would try to take a dump elsewhere, maybe restaurants or something and use this place in emergencies only. Later they went out for something to eat, finding a shoarma and sandwich bar close by and ate well, drinking a local beer and taking home a bottle of arrack and bottled water to pass the night whilst listening to their radio.

Marty sipped at his arrack later on the balcony and reflected. All in all it wasn't too bad, and it didn't appear to be dangerous. The accommodation could be better, but they wouldn't spend too much time there, anyway tomorrow they would see this bloke, make enquiries and be on their way back to Holland in a few weeks perhaps. A nice little working holiday.

Marty awoke the next morning with a foul taste of stale aniseed in his dry mouth which he removed by brushing his teeth, careful to use a splash of bottled water to wet and rinse. He got up and went to his papers, looking for the address of one Saleh Filhama, wondering if it was an apartment or home or just an office of some sort.

They washed, dressed, and went to find a taxi, feeling good to be out in the novel warmth of a hot morning sun without baggage. The sky was a near perfect azure, unblemished apart from a single long white scratch as a jet left its trail far above. They had a typical Lebanese breakfast at the sandwich bar owner's insistence of what he called manakeesh, hot bread and thyme and a cheese sandwich or manouche, which with some greasy olives Marty found delicious. Brendan just had the manouche. The taxi driver took the address, indicating for them to climb in, and again Marty noticed a Mercedes, this one bottle green. Whatever else about Lebanon, there didn't seem to be a shortage of quality cars, which contrasted sharply with the streets they passed through on the way to their destination. They bumped about in the back from the pot holed roads, looking at the squalor of some of the worse streets which hadn't been repaired from the conflict. Vendors sat in front of half ruined, dank and drab buildings, selling their cigarettes, pots, bread, nuts, fruit and eggs, whilst listening to music, wailing and shouting amidst the constant honking of horns. Every now and then a whiff of spices, coffee and garbage wafted through to them. The poverty seemed to get worse the further south they went, until the buildings thinned out, becoming interspersed with mere breezeblock hovels with corrugated roofing. This must be where most of the Palestinian refugees lived. He noticed a small girl of about five who stopped to watch their car pass, her frail barefoot little legs grimy from play, hair tangled. Marty waved and was rewarded with a huge open smile of such radiance, it momentarily brightened the surroundings and banished the squalor.

They pulled up at a low, square three story block, where they paid the driver and got out into a dusty hot street with a small open channel dug along the middle. They went inside. To the left was what might have been an office, dingy pale yellow walls, a few grey metal filing cabinets and near a closed window, a simple wooden table, cluttered with two paper trays, loose pens, a photo frame and a plate with the remains of cheese, a few slippery olives and some kind of brown paste and pita crust. Flies buzzed lazily. Marty's attention was drawn to the occupant behind the desk who looked at them without interest. He hoped this wasn't the man they had come to meet. He sat there obviously having just eaten, unshaven with about two days beard growth, greenish grubby uniform open to the waist, exposing a dirty white string vest spotted with grease over his pot belly.

"Saleh Filhama?" Brendan asked hesitantly.

The brown eyes in the tanned flabby face didn't blink, the moustache still flecked with a crumb or two didn't move. Marty repeated the question and asked if he spoke English. He snorted at Brendan.

"D'you think this is one of those restless mercurial people the guidebook was talking about?"

The man gave an almost imperceptible shrug of indifference, mouth turned down and eyebrows now slightly raised. At last he spoke, flicking out his pudgy wrist slightly and shaking his head before speaking.

"Ma beef ham."

Marty turned to Brendan and said, "I didn't ask for the menu now did I?"

"Shu ismak?"

"Aha," said Brendan. "That sounded like a question." A voice spoke behind them, a female voice, in lightly accented English and obviously educated.

"He is asking your name, he doesn't understand you."

They both turned, pleasantly surprised at this welcome intervention. A young woman stood there smiling slyly at their discomfort, dressed militarily in greens the same as the man, but there the resemblance ended. She was very pretty, fine dark shoulder length hair pulled back into a severe knot, a straight small nose and square chin, her full lips now pursed in amusement, the wide spaced eyes watching, dark brown and merry. They noticed for the first time she was carrying a rifle, but not threateningly and there was no magazine in it anyway. She placed the gun in the corner with her slender graceful arms, bare to the elbows exposing on one a thin gold chain, which along with her gold earrings seemed strangely to fit with her uniform. She looked to be in her early twenties.

"I am Hala," she said.

It had been a disappointing day in terms of results as Marty and Brendan sat on their creaky balcony, sipping tepid red wine and discussing what to do next. Interesting though, and they had made contact of a sort, but were no closer to accomplishing what they were here to do.

The girl Hala had deftly ignored their enquiries about Filhama, giving them a friendly smile and taking them into another more comfortable room with chairs and a large framed photo of Yassir Arafat, crowned as usual with a black and white checked kuffiah. She was studiously polite, serving them chilled orange juice, all the while skilfully asking questions of her own, finding out who and what they were, and finally why did they want to see Filhama? They told her more or less everything but the last, only that their organisation had dealt with him before which seemed to satisfy her curiosity. Marty had done most of the answering but had noticed wryly that her attention was not fully on him, her eyes constantly wandering to Brendan who sat pink cheeked and smiling like a moonstruck cherub, jumping up to light her cigarette, and beaming as she thanked him.

"He left to go to Sidon yesterday afternoon," Hala told them. Marty could have kicked himself. Shit!

"When will he be back?"

"I cannot say, he will be in touch soon." She studied Brendan again. "Why don't you come again tomorrow?"

They looked at each other, Marty laughed.

"O.K we'll do that."

They didn't leave immediately, Hala seemed to like talking with them and practicing her English. They were served thick, hot, very strong coffee and found out something of her life. She came from an affluent Palestinian Christian family, was born here and educated at the American university in Beirut. It was a pleasant couple of hours but ultimately not what they had come for.

This is why they were sat now on the balcony talking options, deciding eventually to just wait and see what happened rather than start looking around elsewhere. They wouldn't know where to begin anyway, and Brendan was suddenly in no rush to move. Marty poked him playfully in the ribs.

"Well, well Mr Price. I saw the way you two were watching each other. I didn't know you were into uniforms, you weren't at home but."

"She's a peach. Do you think I would have a chance there?" he asked eagerly.

"Aye, I do. I don't know what the customs are here, but why not. Jesus, she was well into you Brendan. Love at first sight eh? Aye, I'd say she's got the hots for you my lad."

He laughed some more at his friend's happy expression. They drank more wine and listened to the BBC world service and the latest on the Falklands, where a task force was nearing the conflict zone. Interesting.

They went back the next day and found the same guy sat in the very same place, string vest and all. Marty was tempted to prod him to see if he moved. Hala was waiting but had no news, so they went back the next day and the day after that and every day for the whole week, but there was still no sign of Filhama, who it turned out was Halas's uncle and sometime guardian, her own parents having died some years before. She herself was in the PLO and had a number of duties, her education enabling her to do translations and other office functions. She was trained in the use of firearms and they didn't doubt she would be prepared to use a gun if necessary. When she spoke of her people and their struggle Marty noticed her whole demeanour changed, from her normal sunny and gentle self to anger and bitterness, the voice grew louder, the foot started tapping and the hand began to slap the table in emphasis and frustration. They discussed the conflict here and in Ireland, Brendan in particular showing an empathy with her. Marty, although sympathetic, consciously stayed aloof, remembering why they were here. She was useful however with information about the city and Lebanon in general, giving them tips about this, that and everything, all the small change of a nation's life, but still very helpful. She also kept Brendan content and occupied.

In between visits they became better orientated with the rest of West Beirut. They walked the entire length of the Corniche by the sea, stopping off for a coffee or fruit juice, buying bread or corn on the cob from the boisterous street vendors, and later sitting outside a cafe sipping ice cold beer as the sun went down. It wasn't a bad life so they didn't mind waiting, explaining to Dublin over a crackling hotel line the delay and lack of progress. The voice at the other end merely told them to hang around, but not to spend too much. Sometimes Brendan would go by himself to see Hala and would be gone all day, coming back full of enthusiasm and wonder for his new found love. Marty didn't mind this and actually began to like where he was and to relax, finding the city one of interesting contrasts. The poverty and wealth existed cheek by jowl: top hotels despite a dearth of tourists, and refugee camps, people water skiing in the bay past squalid slums a few hundred metres away, the smell of flowers and orange and lemon trees mingling with garbage dumps. They had all gone to a fun fair on the Corniche complete with big Ferris wheel, sitting high up in one of the gondolas, laughing together and bringing back happier memories of years past. Strange and fascinating Beirut, fun fairs, militias and occasional extreme violence. It was near three weeks and into May before they had word from Filhama. They were taking coffee with Hala and another Palestinian guy called Sayed when he rang. Hala spoke rapidly and happily before offering the phone. Marty took it.

"Hello?"

"Yes, I am Saleh. You have been waiting for me? I am sorry, it has been busy here, I will see you next week O.K? "

"O.K, Mr Filhama, no problem, see you then."

He handed the phone back to Hala, who took it, curling one slender finger through the wire loops, winking unexpectedly at Brendan. She spoke a little more then hung up.

"So, my uncle will see you next week. I must go away tomorrow too." She glanced at Brendan. "Only for a few days."

It was D Day. Friday May 21st 1982. The sun came up, but it was cold as Roy stumped forwards into the landing craft, weighed down with full pack bergen, loaded rifle, grenades, webbing and bandolier of bullets that glinted gold toothed. There was little chatter, everybody now fixed on what lay ahead as the craft started towards shore, bumping and crashing through the freezing water. They heard a single screamed word from the marine in charge.

"Beach!"

With that, the ramp lowered and they advanced into icy numbing water that came up to their knees, running now and spitting out curses in all directions. There was no opposition. The battalion got itself into order and the individual companies hived off to their objectives, Roy, Keith and Dillon leading their sections, forming one of the rifle platoons. In charge of them was Lieutenant Ward, a blue eyed, blond haired short but stocky man, who was well respected if not liked. In actual charge of them was platoon Sergeant Allenby who some of them knew from training days. Everybody was thankful that Robson was at battalion headquarters so they wouldn't see much of him, funny as he could be on occasion.

They began to tramp uphill, bowed by the weight of their burdens, sometimes slipping and falling and having to wait for help to stand upright. A bit of levity returned and from ahead came the noise of braying in fair imitation of pack mules. Roy was able to get his first look at the islands they had come so far to win. The first thing that struck him was how empty the landscape was, the hills and fields devoid of trees, with lots of rocky outcrops. There was a lack of colour; it was all weak mossy dull greens and khakis with the hills various shades of brown, bronze and burnt ochre, stippled by the white and grey of rocks. It was fortunate none of them knew this was the island at its best, in sunshine. The land on the opposite side of the inlet was lighter amber and honey, the water and sky giving a splash of blue relief, reminding Roy somewhat of Donegal or some of the remote parts of Scotland. The islands were constantly windy, and sometimes visited by weather that came from ice laden seas, bringing snow, sleet, rain and clammy cold mists. It could be extreme, howling and roaring on bad days and plain uncomfortable on others, tirelessly blowing but exhausting to man. It was a hard place where only the hardy things of nature could survive.

Without warning there was a scream of jet engines as two aircraft flashed over them, causing everybody to fall to the ground shouting futile warnings. Roy watched them go, as they dived like gulls towards the ships in the bay. There was a loud crackling of small arms with the underlying meatier thumping of cannon shells from all around as just about every ship let rip, tracer rounds and then a couple of missiles corkscrewing smoke trails towards the jets but failing to score. They stood up, spellbound by the spectacle as large bomb splashes appeared in the water by the sunlit ships. It was over in a matter of seconds with no apparent damage done. They moved on, trudging over the boggy tufted grass, every now and then ducking as another raid came over, but soon realising they weren't the targets for the moment as there was better sport in the bay.

They arrived at their hill top destination and Roy spread his section into pairs, getting them to dig in. Roy helped Private Dunne with his trench, and they soon discovered it was going to be a hard campaign. It was wet, and when they dug down the trench soon became waterlogged and there was nothing to indicate that the rest of the island would be any different. They set arcs of fire, erected makeshift parapets from the sods and settled in, hoping that they wouldn't be here too long. Roy had a great view of the ships and all that afternoon he could see the aircraft roaring in, cheering when a missile struck home and disintegrated an attacker. The raids continued but disturbed them little, their preoccupation now being to get some hot food inside them and a brew. Keith wandered over towards dusk just after the last assault.

"What did you think of the show?" he asked, nodding towards the darkening water.

"Good enough. I saw we got at least one. Fair play to them, those boys know how to fly."

"Yes. That's what's worrying me, they've got balls too. I just hope their army isn't as good. Not that it'll matter too much."

They stayed there an entire week, the only battle was with the constant cold and horrible biting wind that never seemed to ease. It was painful, sometimes moaning and howling as it passed through them irrespective of clothing, faces seemed to be always stretched and eyes narrowed. Their days were spent either patrolling or improving their trenches, with the random air raids allowing them an opportunity to fire off their weapons at any aircraft but with little effect. The conditions and lack of movement were getting to some of them, it was worse than any exercise Roy could remember and there was little good news. Argentine jets had been downed, but the ship losses increased on a daily basis, and it was with relief that they received orders to move. The problem was that it would have to be on foot and without the gear they had been expecting, as one of the ships lost had most of their helicopters aboard. It was going to be a hard slog.

They started out that afternoon under a pewter heavy sky in rain that was cold and stinging, for hour after hour, with a few short breaks. Looking back near dusk he could see the long line of soldiers fading to dots, snaking back into the distance, heads down, rifles cradled as they plodded on, and Kipling's poem 'Boots' flitted through Roy's head. It went on, testing many to their limits physically, and draining them mentally until they received the order to halt. Roy noticed a couple of his section already having trouble with their feet, and trying to dry their socks was futile when they had to put them back into freezing water almost straight away. This was misery. It showed clearly at first light; haggard, white exhausted faces painfully standing, pulling on webbing and picking up weapons with numb, trembling fingers, like an outfit of winos greeting the morning with the worst hangover in the world. They were soaked and likely to remain that way for the rest of the day. They carried on with very little being said, knowing this was what they had signed on for, all part of the test. Although torturous, Roy found it preferable to sitting still as he painfully adjusted his own webbing and began to move.

They arrived at their destination, a group of houses on an inlet some hours later. It was dark. Roy did a quick mental calculation and estimated they had tabbed about thirty odd miles in a day and a half, not bad in such conditions. The rain had stopped and it was turning frosty. There were scattered sheds here and there which soon filled with soldiers seeking warmth and rest, but some weren't so lucky and were immediately assigned first watch around the perimeter. Roy's section were fortunate enough to find room in a sheep shed which provided a roof and shelter against the awful wind and raw wet cold. They huddled together for warmth, taking the opportunity to try and dry socks and boots, some of them making a brew to go with their rations. Morning came too quickly, and with it the unwelcome order to get outside and dig defensive positions. There was a chorus of groans and gasped swearing as painful swollen feet were put back into damp boots. It had been a night of sleet and snow which left the earth hard and made for a few hours of sweaty back breaking excavations to get trenches deep enough. Looking about, he noticed sullen faces, but nothing united them more than shared misery. Warfare at the end of the twentieth century and it still consisted of digging, human strength and stamina, with soldiers griping and sometimes joking. It had probably been the same along Hadrian's Wall. Roy looked for Keith, spotting one of his section at work.

"Where's Corporal Shepheard?" he asked, as he tried to rub some warmth into his hands.

Private Bridle's face carried a permanent expression of suppressed mirth, like he was just getting to the punch line of a good joke.

"Still in the barn there corporal." Bridle hadn't stopped digging. "His feet are in a right old state," he added.

Keith was sat with his back against the flaking wall along with half a dozen others, all with the same problem of trench foot. Roy had experienced it once on exercise, only mildly but it had been bad enough, as if the feet were being crushed between jagged hot rocks. He could see Keith fidgeting with discomfort, eating a morose porridge ration from his mess tin.

"Is it the gout?" he asked.

"It's not the gout, it's bloody agony is what it is."

"Well now, did I not tell you to lay off eating pheasant and swan for breakfast?"

Keith nodded slowly, helpless to react but knowing Roy was just trying to keep his humour going. "I think we're going to be laid up here for a few days cock, the way the Major went on you'd think we'd all crippled ourselves to spite him," he said.

"Think yourself lucky, rumour has it we're to be moving soon. Tabbing, probably another thirty miles closer to Stanley." Roy looked around. "If you're lucky maybe they'll give you a lift with the rest of the baggage."

Keith stretched his rubbery lips in a gap toothed grimace. Roy gave him a clap on the shoulder and winked. As he went towards the door he called back, doffing an imaginary cap.

"I'll just shoot the young master a few grouse for his lunch." He felt a splat of porridge hit him in the centre of his back.

It was another cold night and they started off again in the morning, minus a number of men who were forced to rest their damaged feet. Good news made the rounds before they left of the first land battle at Goose Green; a big success for their sister battalion who had beaten a force larger than their own and captured their objectives. There were hundreds of prisoners, everybody was talking about it. Their own losses made everybody pause and reflect a moment, about fifty casualties and the C.O killed. Dillon had his own good news, told to him whilst he was digging the previous day. Aston Villa had won the European Cup, the greatest day in the club's history. Dillon had rarely missed a game at the 'Holt End' supporting them through thick and thin. He stopped for a couple of seconds, his face white and baggy eyed, gave a weak "Hooray," then carried on. Right now he had other priorities.

The march took on the same aspects as the last one, an unremitting slog over a barren landscape of boggy soil and awkward tufty wet grass that continually twisted ankles and made men stumble. It was very cold. Night came, but there was no respite until sufficient progress had been made. They were to wait until first light, trying to rest as best they could but sleep was impossible, as their sleeping bags were in their bergens which they had to leave behind. These would be sent on once their new objective was reached. They gathered in groups, packed together to extract body heat, penguin like, shivering and bone weary, listening to the chatter of teeth and the cutting wind. The dawn was grey and Roy was again reminded of a bunch of hobos rising tiredly from newspaper beds, unshaven and unwell. He remembered the saying about war being hell, but nobody had said hell was so fucking cold. They were allowed to make a brew and eat rations, the best piece of equipment they had being the tiny portable heaters and hexamine blocks for fuel, these things along with sleeping bags were just as vital overall as a rifle. They rested and then it was back to the undulating hillocks, and then, just to enliven matters, one of the

Falklands many 'Stone Runs', great heaps of stones and boulders that ran stream like across the terrain and had to be crossed with great concentration and huge annoyance. The march went on with another long exasperating delay as they approached another small settlement on the way to Stanley. They took no chances and waited for dark before entering. When they eventually got the go ahead Roy was nearly happy, the small group of houses, sheds and barns were all but deserted apart from a couple of civilians. At least they had shelter for the night. Another day came, but with it a bit of humour had returned. Roy heard someone flatly singing a snatch from 'Madness'.

"My arms, my legs, my body aches, the sky outside is wet and grey, and so begins another weary day..." the soloist who sounded like Barry Tucker was soon joined by a few others in a wailing refrain, cut short by the terrible voice of Sergeant Robson.

"Shut that fucking row or I'll shut your mouths permanent!"

Private Barry Tucker was known to all as 'Bison' because of his huge ungainly head and shoulders that looked out of all proportion to the rest of his body. He came into Roy's line of vision around the side of the shed, stamping his feet to keep warm. He began humming, but this time quietly. Roy recognised it as the Eurovision winner, 'A Little Peace'. Aye, very funny. A quick brew and bar of chocolate and they were off, but this time only as far as the nearby hill. Here they would dig in again and wait for the final move towards Stanley, now a bare thirty miles or so away; touching distance.

The following days were spent either in, or improving trenches, on patrol, or in one of the barns that served as a rest area, providing a welcome occasional comfort. The weather was now familiar, but not a friend, alternating between drizzle, rain, sleet and the occasional snow shower to bright hard sunshine, sometimes all in the space of a few hours. The one constant was the cold wind. Keith had arrived back fit again and sometimes they got together with some of the others for a brew or gossip. Some of the nights were bitter, the sky a solid black canvas perforated with a million pricks of brilliant white. One day Roy received a surprise package from home and that night decided to share his manna with Keith, walking around to where his trench was. He climbed down into the dark interior. Keith was busy with his primus stove, watched by an anxious Hovis who hovered over him like a concerned parent. Roy surrendered his godsend to the ecstasy of his mates. To those outside it sounded as if they had struck gold.

"Jesus, Roy! You beauty."

"Don't use it all, I want to save some for Dillon when he comes back."

Within minutes a delicious aroma filled the trench and wafted outside where it was picked up by Private Bridle who moaned softly. There were more exclamations of delight and satisfied chuckling and a voice came from the left.

"What the hell is going on in there?"

Roy, Keith and Hovis made no reply, squatting, beaming contentedly at each other, their tin mugged treasure warming their hands, their stomachs and just for an instant their very souls. It was only Bovril, but nothing could have been better. At this moment the very basics were of vital importance and it amazed them that something as simple as dry socks and a warming cup of beef broth was all that was necessary to make the day a good one. They chatted and got onto the subject of names. Roy remarked on the fact there was a Private Coffin in one of the other companies. Keith smirked appreciatively.

"I hear we are going to be teamed up with them. Maybe you'll get lucky Eric and share a trench with him, maybe he'll bring you good fortune."

Janson smiled, ignoring the bait, his Yorkshire accent more pronounced. "I can remember at school we 'ad a kid from India or summat in class an' he got piss took right bad. Name was Belbinda but all t'other kids used to fook 'is name up, 'Bell binder', 'Bull binder', we settled on 'Ball bender' eventually like. Used to drive 'im crackers!"

Roy and Keith began laughing, as much at the accent as the story's content. Keith continued.

"At my school we had the House twins, different sizes so they were named upper and lower."

"You just made that up!"

"No, swear to God. Cross my heart and...." He glanced at Eric. "We had a couple of Dutch brothers there too, their father was a banker or some such thing. Ruud and Aad, pronounced of course rude and ard. Guess their sir name?"

"Go on, I'm stumped."

"Same as the Dutch plane company. Fokker, Ruud and Aad Fokker. Straight up!"

"Was this the school you were at before your old man went funny?"

"Yeh, I knew something was up when he started with the Samaritans." Keith took on a faraway look as he mused. "He even wanted me to do it when I was older."

Roy and Hovis looked at each other and burst into laughter, the idea of Keith giving advice to potential suicides.

"No, no don't jump from the bridge. There's a much better chance under the train," said Roy.

"That's right, safety catch is on left hand side, glad to be of assistance," said Hovis.

Keith joined in the laughter, all of them temporarily warmed. Roy took a peek out of the slit, nothing but an eerie landscape and bit of moonlight. "Did you know what the name of this whole operation is called?" he asked. The others shook their heads.

"Operation sheep shit?" Hovis suggested. "No? Operation killer? How about Operation kill every bastard that moves?"

A voice called out to keep it quiet. Hovis took a turn at peering out of their slit, far into the dark at the mountain in the distance they all knew they would have to capture.

"If I..." He hesitated, watched by the other two. He cleared his throat, "If I get wounded, you know, bad like..."

Roy completed his sentence. "If you mean crippled or a total veg, aye, we'll finish you off."

"Me too, also if I lose my knob," said Keith tonelessly. Hovis took a last look into the dark ahead.

"Do you think they'll have mined it?" he asked.

Roy shrugged before answering. He thought about the expression 'sown with mines' and had one of those bizarre mental images he was prone to, of a giant farmer, pissed up on scrumpy cider, broadcasting mines like seed to the wind and singing lustily about combine harvesters. He didn't share this thought.

"Maybe. We'll find out soon enough."

It was another cloyingly hot night as Marty lay on his bed and listened to the BBC, drowsily taking sips from a tin of flat and warm Pepsi. They were by now getting used to the waiting and constant delays and unorganised somewhat ramshackle nature of things here. Maybe it was the heat thought Marty idly. He could hear Brendan coming along the corridor and watched as the door opened and he came in looking smug.

"Got something here to pass the evening Marty!" he said as he triumphantly held up what looked like a small Mars bar out of the wrapper. It was a lump of hash, brown and sticky and he detected its strong sweetish smell from where he lay. "Cheap as well."

Marty grunted unenthusiastically. It would be cheap too, it grew in enormous abundance all over the bloody country. Still, he wasn't averse to a wee toke and it might take the edge off the evening's boredom. He sat up as Brendan began rolling a joint, expertly licking a cigarette along the seam to take out the tobacco and placing it on a couple of papers, heating the hash with his lighter and crumbling it the length of the spliff. He lit up with a satisfied smirk and puffed contentedly for a moment, spitting out a shred of loose tobacco before handing the joint to Marty. Brendan laid back and sighed, his thoughts meandering.

"If you were going for a night out with the lads who would you take with you?" he asked.

"How d'ye mean?"

"Well, say you could take anyone, meet anyone like..."

"Anyone from the past do you mean?" Marty tossed the joint back making Brendan shift quickly and pick it up, now on one elbow, eyes crinkling.

"Aye."

Marty thought a moment. "Oscar Wilde for one, Errol Flynn maybe, he was a bit of a laugh so I'm told. John Lennon? Nah, he'd not be much fun. Napoleon... of course, Che Guevara!"

"Yeah! What about Hitler? Just for a laugh mind, you could sit him next to Moses or if you really wanted a wild time Caligula."

Marty coughed out a laugh, the joint getting to him. "O.K, what about Genghis Khan or Blackbeard, Ivan the Terrible..."

"...and arsenic Annie doing the cooking." Brendan added.

Their laughter became louder the more their imaginations got to work thinking of various combinations, the more ludicrous the better.

They finished another joint and Marty put a favourite 'London Calling' tape in the deck, and Joe Strummer came on half way through 'Spanish Bombs' ... "buses went up in flashes, the Irish tomb was drenched in blood. Spanish bombs shatter the hotels, my senorita's rose was nipped in the buhhhd..." Marty stopped, trying to concentrate a second on the lyrics, and then noticed an ugly brown cockroach by his empty glass. He upended the tumbler and trapped the insect underneath.

"Got you, you wee bugger!"

"Come on Marty," said Brendan, looking up. "Let it go out the window. He hasn't done you any harm."

"He might have, how do you know?"

"Well like what?"

"Stealing food for one thing."

Brendan burst into laughter, the joint taking a firm hold and said, "Oh Aye, prove it then!"

"O.K, we'll give him a fair trial," said Marty, warming to the absurd discussion. "You can be council for the defence."

The result was that Colin Cockroach was put on trial for half an hour, both laughing uncontrollably and painfully the sillier the charges Marty brought and the preposterous defence ploys Brendan attempted. The defendant was eventually found guilty with malice aforethought, of theft, spreading disease, fouling the pavement, indecent exposure, possession of too many legs, and finally and undeniably being a cockroach. The charges of harbouring indecent thoughts, lewd behaviour likely to corrupt morals, being drunk and disorderly, fraud and lastly sorcery were thrown out by a stout Brendan council as unproven. Just as Marty woozily got to his feet to formally pass sentence of death by Pepsi there was a knock on the door. They looked at each other surprised as no one had ever disturbed them before now, despite the fact that a lot of the other rooms were becoming occupied by a variety of Lebanese and

Palestinians, temporarily taking a stay in Beirut from the south of the country where renewed violence had flared. Marty opened the door a crack and was shocked to see Hala standing there in a light green summer dress and headscarf. Brendan jumped off the bed with a whoop and gave her a hug and kiss whilst Marty tactfully looked the other way. He wondered if her uncle would be OK about this relationship even if his niece was of age, liberal and very independently modern. She disengaged herself, patting down the wrinkles in the dress.

"I cannot stay, I have a car waiting. My Uncle Saleh is back, he will see you tomorrow. Stay here in the morning and we will pick you up, he has a surprise for you."

Saleh Filhama enjoyed driving, the faster the better, taking sly amusement when he flicked the occasional glance in the mirror at the nervous faces of his passengers. Not Hala though, she had faith and chattered gaily to them over her shoulder, sometimes touching the man called Brendan of whom she had told him so much. Saleh didn't mind. Who could tell, maybe he would take her away from this place, and anyway he had other things to think about now, but he was glad to see her so happy.

Marty sat in the back of the black BMW and gripped the door to hold himself steady, watching with concentration tinged equally with concern and admiration as Saleh raced along the winding road. He hammered the car's gear shift from second, to third, to second as he flew around the bends, struggling and smashing at the stick with a large meaty hand, one expensively leathered foot skilfully easing the clutch up and down. That was the first thing Marty had noticed about him: he was evidently not one of Palestine's many poor. The car, whose details he had poured out with obvious pride, the well tailored light jacket and slacks covering his ample frame, watch and black leather shoes all pointed to somebody of means. Marty looked at him again; German car, French jacket, Italian shoes and flaring his nostrils a fraction, local sweat. He was prepared to be cynical but gave him the benefit of the doubt. Maybe he was just a good salesman. There was a vague facial resemblance to Hala, the same well spaced eyes and strong chin, but Saleh had a well groomed greying moustache and thick eyebrows, balding with the dome of his head completely uncovered, the nose was large and prominent. When he welcomed them this morning Marty was reminded of an intelligent budgie. His grey ring of hair was plastered sweatily now to his head like a withered Greek laurel wreath.

The surprise turned out to be a picnic. Saleh had the idea they could talk in nicer surroundings, a sort of business lunch. It would do them good to take a break from the city and he secretly hoped, relax them and put them in a generous frame of mind. After all he was a businessman whatever the circumstances. Before leaving, Saleh had first told them he had to see someone on the way, and Marty became apprehensive, not of danger, but that judging by what he had seen so far with their long formal politeness it might take hours. They drove through the usual grimy slum area until they arrived at a distinctive block of what once might have been offices. What made it distinctive was the fact it had been sliced down the middle as if by a gigantic blade, the rooms exposed like a frontless doll's house. Saleh got out and went through a blue door on the untouched side. Brendan and Hala stayed in the car talking. Marty decided to take a look and followed Saleh, hoping his presence might hurry him up. He went through the door and heard talking in a room to one side, knocked on the half open door and entered. Marty noticed the smell of the room, sweat and smoke and something he couldn't quite place. A couple of grubby chintz settees on either side of the wall, some red plastic backed chairs, a cupboard and what looked like an electric cooker next to an iron mattress frame. Curiously there was some kind of matting lining the walls. With a shock Marty realised it was sound proofing, and as this was definitely not a recording studio it must be a place of interrogation and torture, confirmed by the sight of steel hand cuffs on the iron frame. There were two others in the room besides Saleh, who turned, looking hesitant, nervous even. They stared at him for a moment before Saleh started speaking to them in a reassuring and smooth manner.

"I am telling them who you are. It would have been better to wait in the car."

One of the men picked up a magazine and returned to his reading, another sipped his glass of tea but came for a closer look and Marty felt a real butterfly of fear. He was probably in his early twenties, roughly dressed in check shirt and combat trousers. He had a cloud of dark thick hair and an ugly pock marked face, with small round ears that stuck out too high on his head. The eye brows were a thick, black, seemingly single Neanderthal line meeting above his nose, but it was the eyes that told all there was to know. Muddy greenish and blankly staring, roving around Marty's face like a blind man or someone watching a fly: insane. Marty felt if he could see into this man's head he would find only a ball of writhing maggots. The one sitting was slightly older and normal looking, mouth open in a gaping yawn. Marty spoke.

"Nice to meet you, I'm Marty." He held his hand out. The guy took it and smiled, not letting go for an uncomfortable half minute as he spoke in Arabic, Saleh translating.

"This is Samir, and that is Hamid. They are pleased to meet you. I have told them we must go soon, please wait in the car now Martin."

Marty was glad to comply, waving and giving them his best glittering grin, exhaling deeply as he left the building. He went back to the car, bummed a cigarette from Brendan and lit up.

"What's the matter?"

"I'll tell you later," Marty replied, shaking his head.

They drove out of the city, now accompanied by another car containing two other men, not that it wasn't safe Saleh was quick to emphasise, but he was always careful. Marty asked Saleh about what he had just seen.

"They are not people I see often but they have uses. I think you have guessed," he smiled grimly. Marty thought about where he had heard that before. Reflecting his own thoughts Hala gave a snort of disgust as Saleh continued.

"I know, it is not to my taste. We know them but they are not of our people, not PLO. Hamid and Samir have bad hearts, but they make results yes? You know what they told me once? That it was hard work, but they never fail, everyone breaks in the end and tells all. I ask them what they mean by 'hard work' and Samir says to me 'You try pulling nails and teeth all morning, it is loud, it hurts the ears when they are plugged in.' " Saleh shook his head grimacing, "The worst is the privates, you know? Hamid told me he used pliers on a man and I ask him how long and he says until they break."

The car was silent except for the shifting of legs being crossed as they realised exactly what it was that would break, before Saleh added, half giggling.

"Don't worry Martin, Samir likes you. Likes you much, you understand?"

"Shit, that's all I need," said Marty looking out the window. "Young Sammy there taking a shine to me and his mate Hammy."

Brendan began snickering. "You'd better hope Hammy doesn't get jealous."

He was now joined by Saleh and Hala who found the new names hilarious and kept repeating them, Saleh slapping the wheel and laughing. Hala rummaged in the glove compartment, found a tape and put it on. 'Blondie'. Again Marty was jolted by the coincidence of unfortunate lyrics. It was enough to make you superstitious as Debbie Harry sang out, "Die young, stay pretty...live fast, 'cos it won't last..." Frowning now Hala must have thought so too, as she turned it over and rewound. A drum roll and 'Union City Blues' blared out. Much better.

They settled back and began to enjoy the scenery, which in the first half hour didn't amount to much as they shot along the road that Marty noted wryly led eventually to Damascus, ascending and descending again gently, until they reached their turn off where Saleh headed north. Here it was truly beautiful, the hills were bathed in sunshine with everywhere splashes and whole fields of colour. They passed olive groves and ancient walled orange orchards, the scent of millions of flowers and blossoms filling the car with an exotic perfume, interrupted fleetingly when they sped through one of the picturesque villages by the less welcome human smell of hot refuse. They passed through a cloud of butterflies, an unfortunate few smacking violently against the windscreen, a field of violet and creamy white flowers passed by to the left of them, to the right a rash of scarlet vermillion. Seeing this Marty scratched absent minded at a neat line of dots of the same colour on his arm, probably from a bed bug. Saleh slalomed the car around a couple of bends as they approached their destination, the ancient Roman temple ruins of Baalbek.

They parked in the cool of some trees a little way from the site. Saleh and one of the men from the other car went to the entrance and spoke with a couple of guards and money changed hands. Saleh came back wreathed in smiles.

"O.K, we take the food and go in now."

The guards stayed by the cars. They had come prepared, a plastic cooling tub and a lot of food which they laid out on a rug in the lee of an ancient wall, a huge six pillared piece of temple towering over them. There was wrapped and still cold tabouleh salad, cheese, various breads and delicious dips which Hala teased Brendan into trying, cold lamb and mutton cuts, chicken legs and finally cold bottles of imported beer. The only sounds were their own voices and laughter, the rustling of the few trees in the welcome breeze and the ever present rasped whispering of cicadas.

They spoke at first of lighter things, fashion and music now and in Saleh's time, sport and home life but inevitably came back to their own struggles. They swapped tales, their hosts listening with polite respect, but Marty picked up the definite feeling they felt their own suffering was so much greater. Marty suspected their sympathy had an edge of indifference; his own certainly did. Saleh told them of the times in the civil war when it was absolute chaos, of the massacres that took place, the uncontrolled militias led by savage commanders that the violence stirring the waters had brought like monsters to the surface. Some Christians had been killed and what followed was known as 'Black Saturday' when 365 Muslims were stopped at roadblocks in the city and butchered in reprisal, selected simply because of their religion. Marty helped himself to some more olives and couldn't help thinking facetiously that was one for every day of the year and lucky for someone it wasn't a leap year. They finished their food and walked around the ancient ruins that were splendidly preserved, the sculpturing weathered but still beautiful in the beige and pale pink stone. As they entered the showpiece temple of Bacchus, Saleh drew Marty gently to one side, letting Brendan and Hala go in alone. Marty gave the nod to Brendan who had stopped, torn between business and the pleasure of being alone with Hala. Saleh walked with him and sat on a shaded fallen column, patting the place next to him for Marty to sit. He got down to business.

"O.K my friend, what exactly do you want from us?"

Marty repeated almost word for word what he had been told in Dundalk by Dennis. Saleh nodded, hand stroking his chin, eyes to one side concentrating, taking mental notes, interrupting only with occasional specifics. The price was also to be determined but Marty indicated they would pay a premium for anything special, marking the way Saleh gave a small approving grunt at the word premium.

"I think we can help. Small arms, not a problem. We have Kalashnikovs, a few other automatic types, pistols and ammunition as I am sure you know. Heavier things, machine guns. It is possible, I see. RPG? This we can get, no problem. Other as you say special?" he lifted his hands palm upwards. "I will enquire. It may take a little time but please be patient."

Marty agreed, already thinking of the effect loads of fresh modern arms might have. Brilliant. He would have to ring the Dublin contact with the good news that 'fruit' and 'veg' were for sale. A month of waiting and then a quick half hour discussion and it was underway; if this was how business was done he was all for it. He felt good, relieved too, and so enjoyed the rest of the day with an easy mind.

Another week had passed and Marty was becoming impatient again. He had called Dublin and to his annoyance been told to ring back in a few days. No reason was given, probably something silly or mundane as their contact having a weekend break Marty thought scathingly. It didn't matter though as Saleh had also been out of touch, back down south so Hala had said. He put his frustration to one side and made the best of things as it could be worse. He didn't mind the heat, and the periodic diarrhoea they had suffered from was now gone as they adjusted to their new diet. He enjoyed wandering alone in the city or going along with whatever Hala had arranged. He thought about how happy Brendan was, the satisfaction on his face yesterday as Hala clapped her hands in delight at his small present, a delicate blue glass eagle he had bought in a market.

"I shall call him Yassir and he will live on my desk," she told him solemnly.

She went to her bag and brought back something hidden in her closed fist, she opened it and they saw two silver rings, simple bands with Arabic script on the inside.

"A gift for a gift. I was saving them, but you may have them now. They will be lucky for you." They put them on, Marty only managing to fit his on a pinkie.

Listening to the radio in the evenings had the added bonus of hearing about the pasting the British ships were getting in the freezing South Atlantic. He chuckled lightly, glad he was here in sunny Lebanon.

More days passed and they took another picnic, passing the fields and hills, again like so many bright multi coloured rugs, to Baalbek where Saleh met them. He apologised for his absence and then gave them bad news. There would be a delay. He was quick to assure them, sweating sincerity, he had made enquiries and could get most of what they wanted on their shopping list, but things were a little tense at the moment. Patience, relax, take it easy and it would be fine. As there was little choice they agreed. Marty thought he'd give it a few more weeks, say until the middle of June and then ask if they could return. Looking now at Brendan he wondered what the situation there would be, hoping his friend wasn't getting too attached.

They spent the rest of the day amidst the ruins, which now turned from palest pink to splendid rose, then to almost blood red as the sun went down. They stayed for the stars which came out and it was as Hala had promised, a magnificent sight unlike anything they had ever seen in the city, laying on their backs in silent awe as they contemplated the splendour of a glittering billion flung carelessly onto indigo black velvet. They were driven back and dropped close to their street, strangely content despite the renewed delay. Pleasantly tired, they climbed the stairs. They passed a door on their landing and both froze at the same time, turning to look at each other with mouths agape, for undeniably what they had just heard was singing. In English. Bad, tuneless, curiously high pitched, 'Thank You For The Music'. Abba. No, it couldn't be. There it was again and then the door opened, the bad penny in a small world, Chris McCormick. Beatle. Fuck!

Chapter 8

Days with Socrates

Orders came through and by noon every man knew where and what he was supposed to do that evening. This time there would be fighting. Roy and his fellow NCOs had been briefed in a group, and it had reminded him of being back at school in the changing room at half time. They passed the instructions on to their men. The Major had addressed them and told them the situation in a typically no nonsense manner that had amounted to 'We are here. Stanley is there. To get to Stanley we must first take the mountain opposite. When that is done we have succeeded. Any questions?' The tactics were of course more complex and worked out in fine detail, but that was the sum of it. The advance was also to be made without any initial fire support from aircraft, warships or artillery, the aim being to surprise the enemy instead. Casualties would be quickly and efficiently evacuated by helicopter to hospital ship. This last was meant as a reassurance, but most understood the true meaning, as stark as the weather: some who were here now, whole hale human beings, would this evening be killed or horribly maimed.

They spent the afternoon making ready. Roy methodically checked his section, making sure they had enough spare magazines and two grenades apiece, water bottles full, biscuits and chocolate distributed about their webbing. Lastly he made certain that everybody had field dressings and the shot of morphine hung around their necks with their dog tags. Over to his right he could see Keith and Dillon doing the same. There were tight smiles from some and laughter from the newer soldiers, confident with all the courage of ignorant youth, sure they were too young and full of life to die. Roy was keen to get moving, and although he wasn't much of a smoker, he puffed away impatiently whenever he could.

"Will you be taking prayers before you go?" he shouted over to Keith.

The reply was two fingers. He didn't feel overly nervous. Whilst not exactly cheerful, he felt confident enough that they would get through this night and win the fight. Apart from a slight constriction in his throat, and heartbeat that was a little faster he felt fine. He stiffened his spine and mentally girded himself. At home he knew there were cynics who laughed at people like himself, fighting for Queen and country, but personally he had no doubts, doing no less than his forbears had done. He believed what he was doing was right, that this was as British as home, and he wanted them to be proud of him. He also wanted to live to see tomorrow.

They waited until it was fully dark and then began the steady tramp towards the Argentine positions on the mountain. The terrain was bad and men stumbled in the murk, keeping the vague silhouette of the craggy rock formation before them. Somewhere to the front Roy heard Tennyson being muttered and mangled, the few verses that most knew, "Ours not to make reply, ours not to reason why..." which was silenced by a hissed order further to his left. It was hard going for several hours before they halted and regrouped as best they could, the darkness alleviated only slightly by a rising half moon.

Roy could just make out the darker crest of the mount against the skyline with boulders and slabs of sharp jutting rock. To the side he made out shadowy figures and heard the breathing and sound of rubbing fabrics. Adrenalin coursed through his veins, keeping out the cold more effectively than anything he had tried so far. There was a sudden sharp bang and flash to his right, followed by a shout and an instant of quiet. They immediately hit the ground and took what cover they could find. Everything started happening at once. A machine gun opened up and then more automatic fire stuttered and a couple of flares were fired into the sky, briefly illuminating a scene of figures moving, crouching and shooting. Their own rifles and machine guns opened up, hosing red arcs of tracer at incredible speed towards the Argentine positions, the rounds ricocheting scarlet in all directions as they bounced off hard stone. Lines of white and green split the blackness as fire was returned and at any other time it would have been pretty. Roy fired his own rifle just twice, saving his fire for a more definite target. He became aware of somebody crawling forwards next to him, he could hear the harsh breathing and for an instant saw the camouflage creamed face under the helmet, finger smears of black on white with teeth gritted. Mixed with the gunfire were explosions, big and small that flashed white and bright fiery yellow, as grenades were thrown and rockets launched. Human noises were clearly audible amidst the clatter and blasts, shouts and orders to keep moving and feral screams, and shockingly close voices yelling in Spanish. It was chaos. The figure next to him moved forwards and Roy followed in a crouching monkey like stoop to a ledge of covering rock. The firing was nonstop, building to crescendos at different points in the dark before tailing off and beginning somewhere else. Occasionally there would be a brief pause apart from a crack or two, and the human sounds became horribly distinct, the cries of people in distress and long animal howls of pain. Directly ahead there appeared to be a dugout, but it was hard to tell as all he could see were flashes as guns were fired in their general direction, the rounds tearing and banging for the most part overhead. Roy tapped his companion and they raised themselves up, firing rapidly at the flashes before ducking down as fire was returned higher up, the bullets striking the ledge in front of them and much to Roy's surprise whanging away into the night, sounding like something out of an old Western. From behind they heard movement and then the sound of a rocket being launched. To his horror Roy thought it was directly at them and heard himself screaming a pointless "No!" as he flattened himself on the hard ground. The missile rushed overhead, followed by a searing brilliant white flash as the dugout in front was blown apart, fragments of rock and soil pattering down on them. The missiles had originally been earmarked for an anti tank role but were now proving very effective at bunker busting; Roy wasn't complaining. The firing carried on all about them, other figures could be discerned moving up, some of the dark shapes carrying more tubes. Good. Roy was able to make out the form of Bison in the gloom, no mistaking him. He was breathing heavily, his voice shaky.

"Fuck me! Is that you? Fucking hell! I just saw Bridle get hit, at least I think it was."

He crouched, clicking in a fresh magazine. Roy did the same and in a suddenly quiet few seconds noticed a new sound coming from a few feet away, a bubbling, rasping noise that made the hairs on his neck stand to attention. He felt his way over and discovered Private Crossan, the youngest member of his section, a nice lad with an easy going attitude and lazy grin. From what he could see he had been shot in the chest and throat and was struggling to breathe. Roy quickly got his field dressing out and with fumbling hands did his best to plug the wound in the neck, and feeling for the chest wound, found it just under the nipple. Bison was kneeling next to him, thrusting his own dressings forward as he injected morphine. The shooting resumed close by but to Roy it was a relief, better than listening to the sound of Crossan rasping for air like someone sawing at a stubborn piece of wood. He bound the hole in the chest and his fingers went to Crossan's back for the exit wound. His combat smock felt like a sopping wet warm cloth, and to Roy's horror he felt a massive ragged tear the size of a tea plate. He felt spongy, messy tissue with hard chips in it and quickly jerked his hand away. It didn't matter; the awful sawing noise had stopped. Roy wiped his hand and shook his head. They moved on, but not before first searching and taking Crossan's spare magazines with them.

To the din of battle came fresh sounds as artillery joined in from both sides, screeching and roaring, accompanied by the thudding and crumping of mortars. The conflict had degenerated into a melee of individual groups, pushing forwards in their own mini battles for a rock here and a trench there. It was bloody, savage and nerve racking. Roy and Bison found themselves part of a group of about twenty men, most of them from their own platoon. Roy was relieved to see Dillon and Nossy, but there was no sign of Keith. They were told to get moving by Sergeant Robson who had somehow managed to get himself involved. The mount was taking on the appearance of a rocky maze the further they went, with small dead end gullies and ledges jutting out everywhere, but slowly they were making progress. Roy was near the head of the line and found he was thinking an old school rhyme over and over again in a rapid mantra.

"Round the rugged rocks the rugged rascal ran! Round the..."

A nearby voice told him to give it a rest and he realised he had been nervously thinking aloud. They crept around a group of boulders into a tiny clearing where they were greeted by the rattle of several automatic weapons and the leaden drumming of a heavy machine gun. It sent tracer whizzing about them, tearing up the ground and blinding one of them with stone fragments, causing him to shriek and flail wildly. A grenade was tossed at them, the bang and flash sending them scurrying back into cover. Roy searched for a firing point behind two large rocks and loosed off six aimed shots where he thought they were. Others were doing the same, and within minutes the volume became deafening as heavier stuff focused on this new sore point on the mountain and weighed in with shell and bomb.

The fire died down again. Roy pulled up a sticky sleeve and glanced at his watch in wonder at the luminous dial, incredulous that so much time had passed so quickly. It was now one in the morning, meaning they had been at it for over four hours. Word was passed to start fixing bayonets to those who hadn't already, so Roy took his own and attached it, noticing the glint of bare metal and the uniquely ominous sound as it rasped and clicked into place. From above and to the right a heavy machine gun was still punching out its staccato tune, Roy could see it through a crevice and as he watched he heard the hollow 'Choooooshhhaww!' sound of a MILAN being launched, followed by a massive blast and intense white flash that left spots in front of his eyes. The gun silenced, they ran and stumbled towards it, rounds from elsewhere cracking past and into them, thumping sickeningly into one of the group who dropped with a winded grunt. Roy and Nossy reached the machine gun position and slid into what had been a sangar with a roof, but was now a stinking stony pit strewn with the detritus of war. Another flare drifted down and they got a look in the flickering white light at the comically twisted remains of a machine gun, ration tins, bits of olive green uniform, bits of equipment and what might have been bits of a person. It was hard to tell. Roy remembered how they had carped about the expense of a single missile, but realised now just how cheap death was. A soldier dived in nearly on top of them. It was Keith. He wrinkled his nose at the mixed stench of acrid explosive and burnt meat, with the still pervasive Parmesan smell of unwashed bodies. He had a gash under one eye like a bloodied prize fighter. The sounds of battle seemed to be moving over to the left so they took a breather. For the first time they now heard the regular shells of a warship firing from well out to sea, but still close enough to mallet the Argentine positions ahead of them. Unlike the artillery that came in salvos, these were single shells that followed one another with a monotonous but satisfying regularity.

"I'll be glad to get out of this bloody maze," said Nossy now standing next to Roy as he watched other soldiers going past their position.

Just then he noticed more soldiers approaching from the side and caught a glimpse of a helmet in silhouette, not indistinct and web covered like their own, but American GI style: Argentine.

"Argies!"

He opened up on the group, quickly followed by Nossy and Keith who had sprung up and joined in. Roy felt a thrill of elation as he fired into the nearest of them again and again. It took all of five seconds and the group of soldiers had become sprawled dark humps. One of them had gotten off a burst from an automatic, and one of the bullets that snapped around them had hit Keith, grooving a line where his cheek and jaw met, nicking his left ear lobe but not penetrating further. It bled but otherwise wasn't serious. He climbed out of the sangar shaking, watched fascinated by the others as he began to kick the bodies, berating them.

"You stupid, stupid bastards! Couldn't stay home eating steak and tangoing you dago twats! Making me come all this way. You near fucking killed me." He stuck the boot again and again into the inert yielding forms until exhausted, he slumped down.

"That'll teach them," a laconic voice called out. Roy went out and put an arm tenderly around Keith.

"Come on, you have to get that seen to."

"Never mind Keith," said Nossy who was busy with a dressing. "It might leave a handsome scar, make all the girls bat their lids at you." Keith gave him a bleak glance like an unhappy frog. "Well it won't ruin your looks now will it?"

Roy burst into laughter and soon all three of them were cackling uncontrollably, releasing themselves, surrounded by corpses, blood on the ground and still the noise of guns and explosions a little distance away. A sharper shriek and crash brought their laughter to an abrupt halt. A machine gun clattered away and flashed a childhood memory to Roy and the stories of the Somme, of lady death on her sewing machine with every stitch a life. They gathered spare ammunition and picked their way forwards.

The fight continued with varying ferocity the whole night, but gradually, yard by yard, the Argentines were pushed off their mountain redoubt. It wasn't that they had fought badly or even unskilfully. The simple harsh truth was that they were up against people who were not conscripts as they were. Their opponents were trained men, whose chosen profession was organised, efficient killing, with the means and will. Before dawn the battle was lost and the mountain with it, and those that could retreated whilst there was still darkness to conceal their flight.

Daylight came with painful slowness and a thin misty blanket, nature doing its best to shroud the corpses in silvery grey. The first thing Roy noticed was just what a messy shambles a battlefield is. All about the dugout he could see cartons, scattered papers, items of discarded clothing and abandoned weapons, used grubby bandages, the blood crusted fingerprints still visible, empty tins and boxes with ammunition sprinkled everywhere. His eye caught an Argentine helmet, this one was empty, but still with an inch long tear in it which was bad luck for someone. Then there were the bodies, which lay about in a variety of poses, fixed in place by cold death. There was still shelling from time to time, but Roy was hungry and went with Nossy and Keith in search of food and maybe the odd souvenir, picking carefully between the dead and other litter. Here was a shortened corpse with nothing below the knees, the mustachioed pock faced owner seemingly looking down in quiet contemplation. There was another with Indian features that reminded Nossy of a hamster he once had that had been 'unzipped' by the cat from throat to groin. There was another body, this one appeared to be hinged, neatly bisected from the waist down, the two parts at an impossible angle as if a sawing in half illusion had been botched by an incompetent magician. Others were in a better state, shot only once or twice but just as dead. Some had clearly been in agony before they died, mouths contorted and hands clawing frantically at wounds before mortality had frozen their movements. This had been a real battle in a real war and although they had trained and prepared long and hard for this, the actual experience was the difference between seeing a picture of a hill and climbing it. They came to a small clearing surrounded by rocks and it was more of the same, as if somebody had been chucking balloons of blood around. There was debris everywhere, and for the first time they got a look at living enemy soldiers, prisoners in the process of being searched and sent to the rear. Most looked scared or were simply still in wide eyed shock. A few were sullen and defiant. Keith nudged him, his voice a low whisper.

"I don't believe it."

There besides a great grey boulder was Sergeant Robson, with a wounded Argentine who didn't look more than a boy. He was speaking to him softly and cradling his head as he gave him a sip of water and lit a cigarette for him, puffing it alight before gently placing it between cold chapped lips. The yellow amber eyes turned on them with the grim mouth below and they all quickly found something else to look at. Sneaking another quick glance before they moved away Roy realised with a flash of insight that for Robson this was merely business, doing his job. He hated the Argentines as much as a butcher hated cows or a lion did a zebra.

As the morning progressed, the intermittent shelling continued. Now they had lost the mountain the Argentines could fire freely all over it and did so. It was generally safe as long as they had cover in the bunkers and crevices, but being caught in the open when a salvo came over had Roy and the others near soiling themselves, the thought of being killed now by a random shell, would as Keith remarked, be the absolute bloody limit. They found a nice little haven under an enormous rock shelf and stayed here for most of the day, being careful to first remove a small pile of grenades that had been stored in one corner, looking like an orgy of squat ugly toads. Amongst the other discarded refuse, Keith picked up a picture torn from a magazine of the new pope John Paul with his crinkle eyed, vinegar smile. He handed it to Roy with a smirk, who balled it gently between filthy hands and tossed it to one side without comment. Searching further they brewed up, making a stew using anything they could find. It was hot and tasted surprisingly good. Others came occasionally to swap stories and souvenirs. Nossy had a pistol and some Argentine money, he held up a couple of large denomination notes.

"How much is fifty thousand pesos worth?"

"Couple of quid maybe," Roy answered. Nossy quickly traded the notes. Private 'Jack' Frost walked past, absorbed with something in his hand. It was a gold ring; better he had it than it got buried, there had been enough waste for one day. Roy called out to him.

"Did you see Corporal Janson at all, Jack?"

He looked up at them sat there in their grotto sipping at their mugs and shook his head. Roy became impatient.

"What does that mean? Have you seen him or not?"

"Yeh, I saw him." He pointed to another gully opening, "He's over there. He's dead."

They sat and stared through their little fire in silence. Lieutenant Ward clumped up to their hideout with another soldier in tow.

"Sorry to break things up lads but we've got to consolidate and clear up. There are still a few Argies around waiting to surrender or hiding, so be careful. We won't be staying here too long, we might be going into Stanley in the next few days." He stopped a moment, stretching his mouth in sympathy before continuing, the words coming painfully slow with exhaustion. "We've had quite a few casualties, so we'll just have to fill the gaps and reorganise as best we can. I'm sorry to hear about the loss of Corporal Janson. Watch out for the bloody shells. That's all."

As if to emphasize this, another salvo screamed over but crashed some distance away as he left. They finished their tea and wearily got to their feet. They all wanted to go and find Hovis before they did anything else.

They went into the gully and came to another much smaller open patch where there had obviously been another of those mini battles of the previous evening. It was the same rubbish strewn arena, and it was here they found Eric Janson, his rifle stuck into the ground with his helmet on top to mark where he lay, the ritual marking as old as soldiering itself. He lay under a blanket with his boots poking out. Roy thought about what Lieutenant Ward had said. The expression had always irritated him, 'He lost his life' or 'the loss of Corporal so and so'. Just where the fuck exactly had he been lost, and was there a chance of him being found again like a pen or a favourite hat? Roy didn't look. He didn't want to, preferring to remember him alive, not now as he was, more than likely a shattered ugly lump of red and white flesh.

Private Brookes had come with them and his young face, still spotted with acne was staring open mouthed. He then saw he had one boot in what appeared to be a shallow rock pool, filled with blackish red, congealed blood. He stepped back in disgust, lost his footing and slipped, sliding into the awful muck, now shouting wildly as he writhed and spread it, putting out a hand to push himself up and feeling the slippery cold of it. He got to his feet and vomited, spewing wetly against a solid stony wall. Seemingly from nowhere an Argentine soldier popped up, no gun and no helmet, he came to them with hands raised, talking excitedly in Spanish. Nossy got up to check him out and suddenly there was an explosion as a round came over without warning, landing perhaps thirty feet away. They all ducked far too late, but only the Argentine was hit. He crumpled like an empty sack. Roy winced as he distinctly heard the dreadful noise as a large chunk of shrapnel hit him in the back, a rapid chirr and a gritty thump like a baseball bat hitting a bag of sand. The Argentine lay on his front, still very much alive and screaming into the hard ground, his neck tendons standing out with the force of his bellowing. Keith went to take a look, kneeling over him with the usual lies that "It would be alright mate." They could all see his spine was chopped through as if with an axe, the torn back clearly visible in the grey light; it even gave a wisp of fine blue smoke. He stopped screaming, much to their relief and his body seemed to subside even though it was flat to the ground like the last air from a sack. Brookes had stopped being sick and was now sat on a rock staring at the fresh body. He had taken his beret from inside his helmet and held it, twisting and wadding it tightly in his hands as if drawing comfort from it. They left, dragging Hovis with them as gently as possible.

It was just before dusk when Dillon turned up, his face splitting into a grin of pleasure on finding them alive. He already knew about Eric.

They set out together to pick over one of the less accessible parts of the hill before dark came, and it was here they made a final nasty discovery. They had climbed over a small stone ridge and came to a flattened area with the gouge and scorch mark of a landed mortar or shell. There were remains scattered all over the place but surprisingly little blood. From the rags of uniform and rifle they could tell at once it was one of their own. Dillon approached a naked torso without head or limbs, and there were no dog tags either. Keith found an arm further away and gingerly picked it up. He turned it around and examined it. Roy asked him without humour, suspecting but hoping it wasn't.

"What does it say?"

Keith put the tattooed arm softly down and answered without looking up.

"Sally."

They gathered up the remains in silence.

There was little to do that evening but get as much rest as possible. Sleep didn't come easy despite the fact they were all monstrously tired. Roy managed to find a couple of Argentine blankets and rolled himself into these, ignoring the pungent unwashed human smell that arose from them. He probably didn't smell too good himself, and at least he wasn't covered in somebody else's gore like Private Brookes.

He was left alone until first light, when he was awakened with a start by shell fire and then Dillon bearing coffee. He rubbed his eyes, fingering out hard grains of yellow mucus from the corners.

"Coffee! Where did you get it?"

"Found it. The owner didn't need it anymore. Say thank you to nice Mr Dillon then."

"Thanks nice Mr Dillon. I love being woken by coffee and shells in the morning."

Dillon got the allusion straight away and stood, clowning now, hands on hips in mock imitation of Colonel Kilgore from "Apocalypse Now," his Brummie accent deliberately thicker than ever.

"Yeh! I love the smell of coffee in the morning. Smells like... victory." He broke into laughter. "Which is more than you smell like mate. Where did you get those fucking blankets?"

All day long they spent in various dugouts and sangars waiting for orders. There had been more rumours, but the only definite was that tonight there would be more fighting. This time it would be the turn of others. The Scots Guards would be going onto Tumbledown Mountain in tandem with other assaults on the last defensive positions in front of Stanley. Roy didn't stay around to watch the show as the attacks went in across the valley and to the hill in front of them, he was weary and drained by having seven or eight bouts of diarrhoea. He wrapped himself in his foul blankets and went to sleep.

He was awake before the sun came up and watched it grow lighter, with Keith and a few others swaddled in blankets like a group of early morning Sioux.

"Rosy fingered dawn..." he muttered to no one in particular, not remembering where he had seen or heard this expression, but now knowing what it meant.

A few grey faces turned to peer at him curiously. To the left there was a clatter as someone dropped a mess tin, but apart from that it was unusually still. A thin layer of snow lay all about, and as they sat hunched in their little group Roy caught the first chemical whiff of hexamine as someone got a brew on. He became aware of just how hungry he was and rummaging, found a Mars bar which he wolfed ferociously, grunting satisfaction as the last bite went down.

There was a ripple of commotion behind them and Lieutenant Ward scurried over, followed warily by many swivelling eyes, and ears alert to hear what news the harbinger was bringing. He squatted in front of them, but to their relief he was smiling excitedly, although his eyes were ringed dark pits of exhaustion. Roy noticed his torn, stained smock and cut gloves revealing raw dirty fingers, Fagan like in stark contrast to his usual immaculate appearance. He half expected him to announce they had to pick a pocket or two.

"Rumour has it the Argies are collapsing. I've heard they're pouring back into Stanley as fast as their little legs will carry them!"

"Sir?" Keith replied, his voice neutral, all of them hoping and wondering.

"Well, it looks like they've had enough. We keep the pressure on they're finished." He grinned heroically, the effect somewhat diminished by the clear drop hanging from the end of his nose. "O.K. we have to be ready to move in half an hour so start forming up, we're going to finish it today." He scampered off to the next position, for once the happy bearer of happy news.

By the afternoon, rumours were flying up and down their extended snaking line that the Argentines had surrendered. Most of the troops had found a new energy and here and there were a few cheers and the appearance of maroon berets. They passed more war litter, a crashed helicopter, the body work pierced like a colander, abandoned artillery pieces, their barrels pointing uselessly now to their former positions, strewn shell casings gleaming. When they came to a real tarmac road Roy knew for sure it was nearly over. Final confirmation came later when he saw the first military police, and for once they were a welcome sight.

A couple of weeks later and both Para battalions found themselves on a former North Sea ferry to take them back to Ascension Island. It was early July and they were having a massive and rowdy party that started to take on the noise level of another battle as hundreds of soldiers became steadily drunker in release. A few drank with little joy, looking as if it was little more than a stoic duty to get themselves into a state of oblivion. Some had a strange feeling of guilt that they had survived whilst others had been written into the wrong side of the battle ledger, part of the age old butcher's bill. Keith wasn't one of them; he waved his arms expansively, a tin of lager in one hand when somebody foolishly aired this view.

"Bollocks! Would you rather swap places?"

"No," said Roy. "Personally I'm happy to be here in one piece thanks. Do you know how many casualties we have though?"

The hugely muscled Lance corporal Harris answered, his boyish freckled face taking on a curiously glum expression that didn't suit it. "About seventy all told, not including frost bite and trench foot, but they won't be out too long."

Keith rolled his eyes. "Is this supposed to be a party or what?" he said, pointing the now empty tin at Roy. "Lighten up old cock, and let's talk of happy things like leave and how I'm going to spend a couple of months fucking!"

"Aye you ugly bastard, you'll be spending alright if you want your hole. Anyway dummy, the reason I asked was that with all the missing we might not be able to transfer so easily."

"Nah, it's all arranged now mate, don't worry about it," said Keith, belching gently.

Harris brightened suddenly as he remembered something. "I'll be off to Paris with the missus."

"Ever seen the Eiffel Tower Harris?" said Keith standing up. "Maybe you should get your wife to show you." Swaying, his legs apart and arms high above his head, hands clasped prayer like, his rubbery face now guffawing and showing his spaced teeth, he lewdly bent his knees several times in parody of the tower over an imaginary penis. "She did the tower with me once!"

Harris lunged at him and missed as Keith skipped drunkenly away like a magpie teasing a cat, straight into another table that went over with a loud crash and many shouts. It was a wild night.

From Ascension they were airlifted back to Brize Norton in Oxfordshire where families waited anxiously, nobody was there for either Keith or Roy and both were relieved to have a little time to readjust before seeing them. They couldn't complain about their reception, they were treated as heroes for a while before everybody got back to their normal lives, working, eating, drinking and watching what the T.V had to offer. The stupid and prurient questions were mercifully few, the most common one of course after a slight pause.

"Did you kill any Argies?"

Some dealt with this aggressively, others ignored it. Roy simply asked them back, amused at the uncomfortable seat squirming his own question provoked.

"Why do you want to know?"

He spent a relaxing leave, pleased at his father's obvious pride and everyone's joy at seeing him, mentally preparing himself for the coming course of duties he had signed up for, glad that the footslogging part of his career was over and that he had not failed in this ultimate game of soldiers.

Beatle was singing more out of habit now than joy. He had been in this shithole less than a day and hated everything about it and everyone in it. He hadn't been keen in the first place and wished he hadn't been talked into it by that smarmy fucker Dennis. He'd been given a wedge of money, a plane ticket to Amsterdam and an address in Beirut where those other two were staying, with instructions to 'see what was going on, and maybe help out,' but suspected the real reason was somebody just wanted him out of the way for now. Bastards.

His temper hadn't been helped by the trip here; he had been humiliated and then ripped off in quick succession. He reddened again, thinking about this morning's scene in that port up the road when the customs guy noticed his reluctance to open his bag. Not that he had anything illegal, but the fact was he hadn't done any washing since Holland, and his sweaty clothes and old socks were minging and had somewhere gotten damp, adding to the smell. The officer's interest was aroused and he grabbed the bag, upending it, pulling the contents out with the other hand. The stench was appalling, a pungent mix something like what a dead body might smell like mixed with shit and cheese. There were peals of laughter as passengers backed off babbling in different languages. The two uniforms in front of him stood away, grasping their noses and indicating for him, now crimson faced to repack his stuff and get the hell away, cursing thickly in Arabic or whatever it was. He had frantically shoved the stinking mess back in fuming. Guts churning, he had dashed off looking for a toilet, his fourth attack of the day so far with one a little follow through and subsequent slight soiling. He had eventually got to this dump of a town, hating it at first sight, hot, stinking and the flaky buildings here looked like they had leprosy. He had been diddled by the taxi driver and then to his total shame, swindled by some little shit of a money changer, ripped off on the street by a mere teenager. He gritted his teeth thinking about it. He had thought he was so clever too. He had counted the money carefully, noticing it was short and asked for the rest and it was only *then* a switch happened. The thieving wee bastard took the wad back and somehow slipped out the large denomination notes from under whilst adding a few small notes on top. He had gone before he knew what had happened. Beatle clenched his fists impotently. Who did he think he was doing? He'd go back there and find that little fucker, stalk him and do him for that. He heard familiar voices and opened the door with a smile of yellowed tooth decay.

"Marty! Brendan! Am I glad to see youse." He shook them by their limp stunned hands. Brendan reacted first.

"Jesus, Be... Chris! Christ, I mean no one said you were coming, what's the crack?"

"Same as yourselves, maybe help out if I can, you know. Get away until that bastard Bunny does a retraction."

Marty looked at him, doubting if that was the truth, wondering why he was really here. He examined him, amazingly still in boots, jeans and a sweater despite the oppressive heat, his hair matted with sweat, damp patches under the arms, the flat pug face red from the sun. He really didn't want to be stuck with him for too long and prayed they could get business done quickly, before

Beatle went and pulled some stunt that got them all in the shit. For the moment he decided to keep him sweet, give him a chance even.

"What do you reckon then Chris, nice weather eh?"

"This place stinks, so does the food and so do the fucking people."

Brendan stiffened. "It's not bad once you get used to it and the people are fine, you have to remember this isn't Belfast Chris."

Beatle glowered at him, remembering this morning but unwilling to share his humiliation. "Aye, right." He brightened, "Fancy a drink? I collared a bottle of Pernod in that wee market down the street." Hesitant, but trying to hide their reluctance they agreed.

It was worse than Marty had feared. Beatle began throwing his considerable weight about within hours, getting drunk and haranguing them about "getting the job done" and how they ought to "deal with these lazy fuckers," and pompously slurring about the needs and hopes of the Republican movement. Marty realised it was this as much as anything that pissed him off about Beatle. He knew Beatle didn't really care, wasn't a true nationalist and used the conflict to satisfy his own needs, it was simply convenience; he wore Republican colours like a handy jacket to cover himself and in the process dirtied it and all of them. The other side probably had their own versions of Beatle. He hoped so.

The next few days they spent getting him orientated with the surroundings. He seemed keen on one area in particular where he had arrived. They listened to the constant stream of complaints as patiently as they could: the food was shit, the city crap, the weather too hot, everyone was stupid or lazy. Listening to the news it was the same on every subject: Reagan was a dickhead, Thatcher a bitch, Galtieri a cretin, Brezhnev an old twat, Michael Jackson a skinny poof, Diego Maradona a spastic. The deluge of negativity went on and on and worse, he now wanted to go and meet this 'Filhama prick'. They were both reluctant for obvious reasons, wondering how they would take to a Beatle opinion on that 'wog' Arafat. Unfortunately, when they went to meet Hala he insisted on coming, and within minutes he had her in a towering, tearful rage so they left in a hurry, only Brendan staying to calm her and find out the latest news. Marty kept his temper and by the time they got back it was late afternoon, but to Marty's surprise Beatle didn't go and get drunk in his room, but went out again. He had done this several times before, leaving Marty intrigued, and on a whim he decided to follow surreptitiously. He approached the taxi area where they had arrived and Marty observed Beatle slowing down, peeping around a corner, apparently at a thin kid leaning against a wall in the now quiet square. Beatle then moved with surprising speed, circling shark like and coming up on the kid from behind and grabbing him, one hand behind his back, the other over his mouth. He whispered something into his ear and rapidly frog marched him out of sight into a crumbling derelict building. Marty followed. Cautiously poking his head around the corner he saw the kid pinned against a cracked peeling wall, eyes darting from side to side in panic. Beatle jammed a wad of notes into his pocket and then head butted the frightened youth, having to duck down to do it right. There was a distinct crunch as he connected with his nose and the kid was squealing, blood dripping. A sudden memory of the school yard came rushing back to Marty.

"That's enough!" he half shouted, half whispered as he stepped out, angry not only at what Beatle was doing but at the horrendous risk he was taking. This wasn't home, people could shoot you here very quickly.

"This little shit ripped me off, I'm just getting my money back," said a surprised Beatle.

Before Marty could say anything else, he took the scrawny kid with his mop of brown hair and bloody nose by one thin arm, twisting it cruelly and deliberately until there was an audible pop and scream. He let go, his face now flushed with excitement as the boy ran past, one arm flopping uselessly. Marty could see he was no more than a child as he disappeared. Beatle sauntered past a disbelieving Marty who began to fill with a cold fury. He took a long deep breath, he *had* to hold it in, keep calm, but vowing he would get this evil bastard, he was a menace and fast becoming a danger to them all. He mentally stamped on his rage, tamping out the flame before it took hold. Beatle smacked his lips contentedly.

"I think I might have made a wee profit there. We'll call it compensation." He followed Beatle quickly away from his crime.

That evening Marty and Brendan talked in hushed voices, having left Beatle snoring in a drunken, sweaty near coma. It was tricky. They couldn't leave the city yet, that was certain. Brendan considered different accommodation, but that was difficult with even more people arriving from the south, where things seemed to be getting tenser every day. There had even been talk of an Israeli invasion of the border region, not that it would be any danger to them here. They were lucky to have rooms and they didn't know how Beatle would react, he knew where the office was and it might be better to keep him where they could see him as who knew what crass new boner he might pull if left to his own devices. He was an embarrassing liability, but one associated with them for now whether they liked it or not. He didn't fit in here, his very presence a huge ungainly mistake, as if a drunken Caliban had entered the wrong stage and made a sudden blundering appearance leering and grunting under Juliette's balcony. Marty had half jokingly suggested doing him in but Brendan had shaken his head vehemently.

"Don't even think about it. Anyway, what would we tell home?"

Marty dropped it. Brendan wasn't ready for such a drastic step as he hadn't actually seen what Beatle had done, and it was a fair point; getting rid of him might create fresh problems. They decided to keep an eye on him and just hope he wised up or was recalled, both of them still wondering why the hell he had been sent here at all.

Hot frustrating days passed without news of weaponry, made worse by having to tolerate Beatle, listening to him moaning during the day and drinking heavily in the sticky, hot clammy evenings. One particular night Brendan was with Hala, and Marty went to get his radio from Beatle, who typically had taken it without asking. He sat there now, toad like on his rumpled sweat stained bed, dressed only in a grubby T Shirt and huge, filthy off white underpants. He slurped noisily from a plastic beaker full of cheap booze and scratched his crotch with the other hand. He had somehow even managed to pick up a case of 'crabs'. Marty looked at him coldly, but roaring with laughter inside. What an ambassador for his country, sat there filthy, pissy drunk and jiving with bugs. Beatle was just one of those people, damned by their personality, crude, clumsy, cruel and brutal, unable and unwilling to change or adapt, he would stay this way his whole life, making misery wherever he went. You couldn't feel any sympathy for him, he was someone you could only be against.

"I need the radio back."

"Take it." He focused with difficulty, sneering, "Where's Brendan? Off seeing that fucking wee hoor of his I suppose?"

Marty ignored him, ejecting a cassette and chucking it on the small dusty wooden table that was the only furnishing, all the time wondering if pubic lice could walk.

"Not that she's so bad mind, I'd give her one myself," he continued. He let out a deep resonating belch, then laid back on the bed coughing and laughing. Marty left him to sleep. The following day everything changed at once and for ever.

The 6th of June started as most other days, Brendan and Marty leaving early to get some breakfast and to avoid seeing Beatle. They went into the centre where they rang Dublin and then after lunch took a taxi to see Hala, who unbeknown to them was on her way to find them. She had important news: there would be no arms deal. Israel had invaded this morning and they would need every gun themselves. She also wanted to see Brendan and warn him not to come to the Palestinian areas anymore. It might be dangerous as Israeli jets liked to bomb them now. She told her driver Daoud to wait, she wouldn't be long. She didn't find Brendan but did find Chris McCormick, who already half drunk, poked his head out and waved her to his room. She was wary despite his apparent joviality. Brendan had told her about him, including what he had done the other day. She went in.

"Where is Brendan?" she asked, feeling uncomfortable at the way he stared at her, up and down, the piggy eyes hungrily lingering on her breasts. She crossed her arms. He smiled slackly.

"Out." He licked his flaky dry lips as she went to leave, and then grabbed her by the arm. "What's the rush now?"

Her face flashed on and off between disbelief and outrage, then astonished and wide eyed she began to struggle as he pressed against her, actually trying to kiss her.

"Come now, good enough for Brendan..." He rasped as he clinched hold. She felt a moment of physical nausea as his hands grasped her buttocks and pushed her into his hardness. She screamed and squirmed free, getting him with a full slap as his hands went to her shirt, buttons flying as she tore away.

"Bitch!"

He swung a fist that luckily didn't quite connect, glancing off her left cheek. As he stumbled she made it to the door and ran straight into Marty and Brendan who had arrived back earlier than planned. Brendan instantly took it all in and advanced into the room. Without hesitation he swiftly grabbed a half full bottle of Pernod by the neck and swung it at Beatle, who saw the movement but had no time to duck as it smashed it into the side of his head, crumpling him to the floor. There was a sweetish stink of aniseed but a surprisingly small cut that bled little. Hala covered herself, shaking with shock at the suddenness of it, not believing what he had tried to do as Brendan turned to hold her. Marty looked at the inert figure on the ground, sickened and angry at the same time, hating the animal at his feet. He looked at Brendan and a wordless conversation passed between them.

Beatle came to with a throbbing head and had difficulty thinking. At first he thought he was hung over and in his shitty room, but then realised this place was different, darker, quieter and smelled funny. He focused slowly on a matted ceiling. Still confused he went to get up and with a bolt of fear realised he was chained down, and then, that he was not alone. Saleh Filhama stood over him. Expressionless, he pointed to a couple of men sat at what looked like a cooker. His voice was toneless, flat and dead.

"You wanted to meet me? Now you have. My friends here wish also to make your acquaintance. This is Hamid and Samir."

He turned and left, leaving Beatle sweating and sick to the stomach with fear as Samir came closer, looking down at him with mad eyes below the warlock thick black brows, giggling and saying something to the other one who shrugged. They had asked Filhama what he wanted, and Samir especially had been thrilled at the answer. Saleh wanted nothing, only that they took their time with this beast.

Samir was a simple enough man, he never questioned why the pain of others gave him such pleasure, he just knew it did so he sought it out and enjoyed it. This was a present. Beatle was babbling at them now, begging and gibbering.

Samir stood beside him, sampling his terror and finding it wonderfully intoxicating. Beatle tried a last fawning grin, but was answered with a dark fathomless stare. They let him sweat overnight and then worked on him for the next three days; there was no information to be had so they experimented on the shrieking, crying figure with cold savagery. The only thing they wanted to know was how long he could last, now and then gagging him when it became too noisy or they became tired of the squeaking and whimpering, only being careful he didn't choke on his vomit. Hamid had a smattering of English but couldn't make out why this fool seemed to be crying about birds, frogs and other such creatures. They got back to work and sent electric current through him, watching enthralled as he rose up from the iron bedstead, ripped out finger nails and toenails, rammed a thin stick into one ear, crisped his nostrils and nipples with cigarettes, scalded, blistered and burned grooves into him with hot irons and boiling water. Finally they slowly crushed his testicles with pliers, and turning him over in a final obscene parody, inserted with some difficulty, a boiling hot egg into his anus. The end came fortunately for Beatle soon after, not from his torturers, but from above. With a terrifying loud whooshing rush of welcome blackness, a thousand pound bomb came crashing down from an Israeli jet, random and merciful.

As soon as he heard news of the invasion Marty knew their mission was over. He had done his best, followed instructions and could leave with a clear conscience, in fact it was a benefit in one respect. There would be no awkward questions to be answered. *"Chris? Why I've no idea what became of him, he just disappeared one day in the bombing."* There was no need to mention his unfortunate introduction to Hammy and Sammy, only Saleh knew the truth and he wouldn't say anything. He didn't understand how Beatle could have been so stupid, the guy must have had a death wish, now horribly fulfilled. Marty shed no tears though. The Israelis had surprised everyone by the scale of their attack. This was no border reprisal. Within a couple of days it was clear they were coming all the way to Beirut to destroy the PLO entirely. The sound of shelling and bombing got closer. It was no place to be.

On the evening of June 11th as Roy was advancing towards a battle in freezing cold, Marty sat thousands of miles away in sweltering heat. Beirut was rapidly becoming a centre of chaos, refugees filled the buildings including their own, food had vanished from supermarket shelves, there had been power cuts and large numbers of armed men were roaming about. Marty had managed to buy some candles at about three times their normal price and went to light one. He wanted to get going first thing in the morning, there were confused reports the Israelis had now totally surrounded them, and he had seen with his own eyes their Christian militia allies searching and questioning people trying to cross into the east of the city. Brendan spoke from the darkness.

"I'm staying." It was what Marty had feared.

"Brendan, this isn't our fight. We've done our best, we'll be needed back. This is no place for us. Holy fuck! Wise up would you?" He could see his friend in the flickering soft light, the features waxy and yellow looking, sad but determined.

"I won't go and leave her, she can't leave here or her people. She stays, I stay. I'm sorry mate, you'il have to go back without me."

Marty rubbed his forehead, breathing out heavily. He knew Brendan long enough to see it was pointless and knew himself too, so he didn't waste time in futile argument.

"O.K, we've enough money I reckon to last another month or so if we're careful."

"Thanks." He detected a hint of a smile.

He knew Brendan would have done exactly the same. It was a simple yet undefinable love. He had known some women to be jealous of it, knowing it wasn't in any way sexual, but a stronger, closer bond, based on shared laughter and pain, likes and dislikes over many years that couldn't be understood by anyone other than themselves. Marty knew this without even thinking, annoyed at the situation rather than his friend. Hala couldn't go, Brendan was attached to her and he was bound to him, the last link in a human chain connected to the good ship Beirut. It would be alright, it couldn't last that long before the big powers intervened and there was a ceasefire and some sort of normality, they would see it through.

The next month they lived a somewhat bizarre existence as the siege of West Beirut intensified. The major powers to their surprise did nothing to halt the violence, the heat grew worse and the smell too, as rubbish piled up and electricity and sometimes water was cut off. The Israelis began to intermittently bombard them, first raining leaflets in clouds of fluttering yellow and green, telling the people to flee and then with shells and bombs over the whole western half of the city, trying to pressure the PLO into leaving. There were hundreds, then thousands of civilian casualties. It fast became a place of terrible danger. They had seen nothing like this. Belfast even at its worst bore no comparison. Hala worked at the hospital but sometimes helped out in what was left of their offices, which had been one of the first places struck. Marty found it all a bit surreal. They were in a war zone, under frightening bombardment with shortages of food, stumbling about in the dark most nights with torches and candles, yet still able when electricity permitted to watch the World Cup in the lobby. They also listened with mounting disappointment to the BBC where they heard of the fighting around Stanley, then of the bitter victory.

The days ran together and became a series of events rather than dates, like the first time they experienced serious shelling. Marty had been out searching for food when it began, a quick series of harsh explosions and puffs of innocent looking white smoke at one end of the street. He ran into the nearest building for shelter, beckoned by a man in the doorway. Incredibly, he went inside and found about a dozen people all sat around an old TV watching the Brazilian football team. A few glanced up at him, but most were determinedly absorbed in the game, gratefully mesmerised by the skill of Zico, Falcao, mid field genius Socrates and the team in gold. After the match it was safe and Marty ventured out. Others had emerged earlier and were picking through some rubble. A man shouted and carried a teenage girl to a waiting ambulance, her blood turning his blue shirt a dark burgundy. A small boy lay on the road, a half time casualty, seemingly uninjured, but eyes closed in eternal sleep.

Shelling was bad but bombing was far more destructive and terrifying, seeing the fear on faces as they sheltered in basements hoping their block wouldn't be the one to be collapsed and turned into an obscene concrete sandwich with human filling. One day he had seen it from a distance sitting on a roof and been awed at the spectacular scene as a bomb dropped. A monstrous yellow flame, shot through with black and orange bloomed a mile away, before turning into a dirty mushroom of smoke, like flora turning to fungi, quickly followed by the noise and vibration of the blast. The aftermath was appalling and he had witnessed that too, helping pull people from the ruins, their domestic privacy exposed in a flash to the world like a huge, full sized diorama as he climbed over cookers, fridges, baths and beds. Gunmen emerged, firing angrily into the air, showing their machismo but ultimately a total impotence. Sometimes there were international news crews come to report the carnage and squalor. He avoided them but laughed aloud at one short conversation as an American stuck his microphone up a rescuer's nose.

"Hello, I'm from ABC News, do you speak English?"

"Yes. Fuck you! Fuck America!"

"Cut!"

Another time they had strayed close to the 'Green line' just as a full scale battle erupted, breaking yet another ceasefire. Marty thought it might be time to get moving when he saw a group of heavily armed guerrillas suddenly emerge from a side street, one of them with a quiver of rockets on his back like a modern day Robin Hood. They had left as the shooting began. By July the violence became almost casual. Marty stopped one day at some desultory sniping, reminding him of the bad days years ago back home. It was safe enough from his vantage point. He watched as a gunman sipped his tea, carefully putting the glass to one side in between taking pot shots from behind his sand bagged emplacement. In the distance he heard a dull, almost lazy bapping as another AK47 joined in.

Ever present was the heat, which sapped energy and increased the stink and led to an incident that made them really, physically ill. It was a Monday afternoon and they had just watched Brazil and Socrates being knocked out by Italy. They had gone outside and walked for some time, glad to be in the open air even if it was still hot and sweaty, but it was also quiet for a change. They had come to a patch of waste ground littered with old boxes, a rusting fridge, broken odds and ends of furniture and other twisted metal items now unrecognizable. They found a wreck of a sofa, and avoiding the sharp jutting springs sat down for a smoke. It was still and they enjoyed the moment. Brendan was looking at something half buried under some gritty soil a few metres away, unsure what it was. Puzzled, they got up for a better view. It appeared to be a brown tailor's dummy covered in rice, but then there was a slight breeze and they got a sickly high sweet whiff of utter rot and corruption that made them cover their noses and retch. Backing off, Marty noticed the rice was moving as the maggots gorged themselves on the bloated corpse, which under the decaying skin was in a state close to liquefaction. Marty now began thinking more seriously about getting away, he'd had enough. The problem was how to persuade Brendan and maybe Hala too. The solution proved terribly simple.

Another burning hot day and Mohamed, aged twelve, fidgeted impatiently in the queue, wanting to get away back to his friends and play football, where he would take on the identity of the great Paulo Rossi, top scorer and world champion. To his irritation he had to stand here waiting to be served, but it was something that had to be done as if he didn't, they wouldn't eat. A few cars honked impatiently in the next street mirroring his own feelings. In front of him Nezar drew heavily and nervously on a Marlboro looking upwards, his view of the sky limited to a strip of blue that ran the length of the canyon like street of high buildings. He saw nothing and hoped it stayed that way. He had a family to feed and here was a rare opportunity of vegetables and bread that had gotten through. They wouldn't be fresh and would certainly be overpriced, but they would see it out despite their dwindling savings. Behind Mohamed stood eight year old Leyla clutching a colouring book along with her grandmother. Hala stood behind the little girl, and as they all shuffled forwards a few paces she asked gently if she could see her nice drawings. Leyla was pleased and handed her book over proudly. Hala smiled and leafed through the drawings, now trying hard to keep her smile from wavering as her eyes made sense of what she was looking at. Page after page of drawings, the dominant colour being made by a thick red crayon that appeared everywhere on people, and yellow fire on what were obviously ruined buildings and rudely drawn soldiers and aircraft. Hala noticed the figures were mainly horizontal, resembling a modern day Bayeux tapestry of limbs and sometimes heads unattached to their trunks, apart from one that appeared to be cartwheeling through the air like a reddened and terminal acrobat. She handed back the book with a fixed grin and looked for Brendan and Martin who had stopped to talk with someone at the end of the street.

They never heard the plane or saw the bombs that hurtled down without warning from the cloudless sky, crashing into the street and building opposite with a thunderous roar and a flame of yellow brighter than any crayon could ever produce. Marty and Brendan had been speaking haltingly to a Palestinian leaning next to his parked jeep about the situation, when it seemed the surrounding buildings and walls and even the air itself shook. They were physically picked up by the blast and thrown into him, landing in a heap. Stunned, they got to their feet. Marty was winded, the feeling of breathless painful nausea reminding him of a long ago football kicked directly into his stomach. Turning now, he saw a brown cloud billowing into the air and grey dust swirling before their eyes where the food queue had been. As they went forwards another building front seemed to sway before their horrified eyes before tumbling in a thunder of falling masonry. Within a minute what was left of the street began to fill with people and the noise of pain and distress. Marty tried to clear his eyes, rubbing them and seeing a couple of women walk and weave unsteadily past him in headscarves and bright print flowered dresses, waving their arms and crying in high pitched grief filled voices. Another stood howling next to a large concrete slab, hugging herself and then slapping at her own face as she looked down at a sandaled leg protruding from underneath. The dust was everywhere. Marty felt it on his clothes, on his face and clogging his hair, it was up his nose and in his mouth, making his teeth feel gritty as he spat on the ground. Very quickly Red Crescent workers were there, carrying stretchers to ambulances, the whole area now resembling a disturbed ant hill with people rushing in all directions in a cauldron of noise. He watched as a stretcher came past, the arms of a woman swinging loosely, brushing the rubble. Another went past and one of the carriers stumbled. The lump of carcass they were carrying flopped off. Marty stooped to help them as they retrieved their cargo and rushed away. He carried on, tripping over a pair of smouldering trousered legs bisected at the waist, averting his gaze when he saw a young man being lifted causing his entire face to simply fall off, just like a piece of sliced apple. Brendan came towards him and stood mutely, hands hanging at his sides. Marty didn't want to ask but had to, dreading the answer.

"Where's Hala?"

He sat down on a grey honeycombed breezeblock, staring at a wrecked car, its blue colour showing through only vaguely under a film of fine grey dust and small stones.

"She's dead, they're all dead." Marty looked at his powdered white face, a tear worming a wet path to his chin where it curled round and dropped. "She was next to a little girl and some others, they were all dead. All dead, all dead." His mouth was working now and more tears formed, he wiped them away angrily.

"Come on Brendan, we're getting away from here," said Marty putting his arm around him. There was nothing else to do.

Leaving was surprisingly easy. With the money they had left they were back in Cyprus within a day, using yet another ceasefire to cross through a porous Green Line in the dark, take a taxi to Junieh and wait for the boat. They were briefly stopped and searched, most of the guards indifferent and bored except for one who got up and asked them for their papers. He looked at the passports, a thin smile half forming, and then he did something completely unexpected, putting his hand on Marty's chest by the heart, his eyes searching his face. Marty winked at him. The guard took his hand away, indicating with a jerk of his head for them to move. They had nothing with them, a few clothes, some dollars and one souvenir, a single dirty brown bank note showing the ruins of Baalbek and a reminder of a happier day.

Chapter 9

My Place or Yours?

Roy stood on the Sealink ferry and looked towards land as the ship churned through the water. He felt the throb of the engines beneath him, and listened to the gulls that scudded and screamed their welcome above. The journey between Scotland and Northern Ireland was only twenty odd miles, the landscape he was leaving remarkably similar to that which was approaching. Roy always felt good coming home. The beautiful rugged patchwork of green Antrim fields, neatly divided by hedgerows, with small white blobs that moved and grazed peacefully, the farmhouses of whiter stone, all seemed to be tilted for his inspection. He smiled, and then whooped out loud, the wind blowing his long hair, the feeling unfamiliar. This was his country, his home.

He had been back during his subsequent leave, but once the initial joyous reception had passed he had found it increasingly difficult to relax, and after barely a week of doing nothing his impatience was returning. His Ma of course noticed he was ready to go before he did himself, watching as he scoffed his breakfast, flipped rapidly through the newspaper and finished a mug of tea, the fingers of one hand drumming on the table before he got up to pace the room. She cleared the table, a fond knowing smile on her face.

"You'll be going back soon?"

"I've still a couple of weeks to go Ma."

"Come on Roy," she stood beside him and gently laid a hand on his shoulder. "You're beginning to look like one of the lions in the zoo."

That had been eight months ago, and since then Roy had embarked on a fresh programme of courses that had strained him to the limit. When he and Keith had applied for special duties they had known the pass rate was low, and suspected the course would be tougher than anything they had ever experienced. Keith had not made it. Roy had, and was now a fledgling member of the 14th intelligence company, the vital undercover surveillance unit in Northern Ireland, known within the army as the 'Detachment' or simply the 'Det'. Without them the security forces would be near blind and deaf. Their role was gathering intelligence, tracking bad boys, watching and listening, bugging, photographing and filming. They obtained evidence to be used in a court of law, and when possible set up IRA members for arrest, or if there was no alternative, more severe 'executive action' involving the SAS. It was a dangerous job, as being spotted would at the very least ruin a lot of hard work and at worst could be a quick road to the cemetery. Indeed, operators had been involved in a number of deadly shoot outs over the years when compromised. Any ideas about James Bond style thrills were immediately quashed however; this was a professional, cold and effective method of fighting the enemy. Roy approved and was proud to be a part of this elite, getting to grips with the terrorists blighting his land.

It had started gently enough with an interview, IQ test and one day fitness evaluation before arrival at an old army base in the wilds of Herefordshire. Roy was now as fit as he ever would be, which was a real bonus as the bodily strength needed to pass was of the highest, toughest standard. This was to weed out the doubtful and half hearted.

The following weeks had seen the tempo and range of tests intensify as they were subjected to vigorous physical training, weapons handling, map reading interspersed with various mental exercises with generous helpings of verbal abuse. The mental tests, which appeared usually when they were already exhausted, also helped in the winnowing out process. They would be roused from bed at midnight following a gruelling day, and presented with a table of various objects which they would later have to remember and list. Everything was designed to evaluate performance under pressure, and the instructors never let anyone know how they were progressing. Other tests included being sent into a village and told to make notes with which they were to draw a detailed map. They were dropped off in Leominster and given instructions from phone boxes at specific times and told to proceed here and there, sleeping rough and eventually make their own way back and report what they had done. By the time this selection period was over, Roy and Keith were in the remaining third deemed suitable for the next stage.

Roy thought they might be able to relax a little when they were told they would now learn photography. Obviously this would play a vital part of any surveillance, so it was important they became adept and as expert as possible, using the very latest equipment and technology. Any thoughts of an easy couple of weeks were dispelled the first day. The sheer range and depth of knowledge they had to acquire gave them headaches, and technical spiel about apertures, wide angles, light metres, converters, infra red, PNG, 28mm, 200mm, 400mm, had another two candidates packing their bags.

The driving course was like nothing any of them had experienced and completing it compulsory. Roy had always been a competent driver bar his little accident in Germany, and he passed with the help of the expert instructors although it had been touch and go. It was thrilling and dangerous, speeding around country roads and performing handbrake and J turns that made engines scream and left a stench of burnt rubber. It was at this point Keith had been returned to unit, not due to failure but injury, which made it all the more bitter for him, a stupid and unnecessary accident during an impromptu kick about. He and Roy jostled and he had stumbled and to their mutual shock he found his ankle swelling with a fracture. Roy was gutted for him, he had hoped to have him as his operating partner when they passed. They had been through a lot together and importantly knew each other so well, a most useful trait when operating as a team. Keith had cursed and thumped the ground in a frustrated temper before subsiding into glum contemplation, unmoved by the assurance he could try again on recovery. He was gone before dark.

For the next few months they endured intense further training and honed their new skills of driving, close quarter combat, photography and learning how to track a target both on foot and in a vehicle until their skills were second nature. Now he was ready.

A gull swooped, flashing white past his face. He turned to go back down to the car deck and glanced briefly at a tall young woman in a dark green jacket and stone washed jeans, her long reddish hair flying like a pennant in the stiff breeze. She gave him a warm and inviting smile, making him hesitate a second before he smiled back and walked on. He reflected on the one part of his life that wasn't fully satisfactory. His Ma of course had asked him about when he was going to settle down and 'make roots' as she put it, but he couldn't tell her he had little time for anything but the briefest of encounters at the moment. His life for the next two years was not one he could share, the requirements of the 'Det' dominated. Certainly there had been a few women on the course who he had found attractive, but Roy admitted to himself he liked his women a little more traditional. Not the sort that when you looked into their eyes it was as if they were calculating the best way of killing you if you stepped out of line. It made him think of mating spiders.

He carried on, reaching the metal stairs, descending into the spacious diesel smelling car deck, and peering around as he got into his car. For a fleeting moment he caught the eye of a man four vehicles along, getting into the passenger seat of an old Renault. The face was vaguely familiar, but the last thing Roy wanted now was an old acquaintance popping up and sniffing around what he was doing back in the province. He ducked into his own car and became invisible. He drummed on the wheel slowly, thinking, place the face. It would come to him eventually.

The passenger deck that doubled as a dining area shifted slightly under his feet, causing people walking with trays of food to adjust their grip as they hurried to find unoccupied tables. Marty stood to one side and carefully scanned the area, here and there lingering on a person before moving on.

He was coming back from a trip to London. He had boarded here as a foot passenger after helping a single woman and her two children with their baggage, chatting with her and practicing his charm as he hefted her suitcase, all the while smoothly conversing and wisecracking with her two daughters as they passed the security desk. The policeman looked bored, his plain clothed colleague was watching somebody further back in the queue and got ready to stop and ask routine questions. There was no passport control here of course. As far as they were concerned he was merely travelling from Scotland to Northern Ireland and was therefore merely going from one part of the United Kingdom to another. Not that Marty was overly worried if he was stopped. Although Bunny had implicated him in various incidents, he had since retracted, making his evidence worthless and all those that had been arrested on his word free men again. The 'Super Grasses' had ultimately failed and were being rapidly discredited. Without hard evidence they couldn't hold them for any longer than seven days before either charging or releasing them. The trouble was, the Brits now knew quite a lot of people who were involved but had not previously come to their attention. It opened up a lot of new leads and potential informers too. There were a number of active volunteers who had been totally unsuspected, 'clean skins' who were now known to the security forces. Marty was one of them, and although he wasn't yet a 'Red Light', he had lost his anonymity. It hadn't stopped them however, it just meant they had to adapt and become even more wary and circumspect and as cunning as their enemy. It was a different sort of conflict now. Large scale mob clashes and drawn out gunfights were a thing of the past, it was now much more cat and mouse with here and there an explosion of violence. Or just an explosion.

Marty didn't want to draw attention and be stopped and questioned so he carried on with his passenger survey, having dumped the woman and her kids who had someone meeting them on the other side. His eyes stopped at a table near one of the windows, the lone occupant biting into some kind of glazed bun. Marty ran his eyes over him. Perfect. A priest returning home and odds on to have a car and give a poor man a lift, and good cover into the bargain. Marty introduced himself as he sat down, noticing the friendly clear blue eyes and red, crack veined nose that suggested he drank more of the blood of Christ than was good for him. Half an hour later, using a nice blend of lies, wit, sincerity and charm Marty had his promise of a lift to Belfast. He then went up on deck, ostensibly to get some fresh air, but actually to avoid any probing questions; priests were no fools at spotting lies if their curiosity was aroused, it went with the job.

Marty stood on the portside and enjoyed the sea breeze. It wasn't his first time back since the Lebanon. He and Brendan had not lingered on their journey home, a few days in Athens and a short stay in Holland where they had received the glad tidings of Bunny's retraction. They got a flight to Dublin and were back in Dundalk by evening with no problems at all and a sense of real relief. The only worry as far as Marty was concerned was Brendan, who had stayed morose and withdrawn the whole time. He hoped the old one about time being a great healer was true for his friend. He remembered his own pain, which although leaving scars had to a large extent healed. He had regained his sense of humour even if he had also developed a hardened carapace. Marty felt he probably had no tears left for the world. That emotional account had been cleared out some time ago, spent in a rapid and involuntary splurge in his teens. Brendan was probably going through the same thing, he just needed time, his pain and anguish were the price of his love which had been short, sweet and terribly expensive.

They were given a couple of days to relax before being told to report, money had been spent and ultimately their mission was a failure. There was also the more serious matter of what had become of Christopher McCormick. They had been summoned to a small farmhouse near the town of Omeath for their debriefing. It had a disused and neglected look, the walls peeling and some slates missing, the low stone wall unkempt and near invisible under straggly growth, the trees about it dark with ivy. They had discussed what line to take in Athens and decided to say they believed he had been killed by shellfire, but hadn't found his body in all the chaos. To their surprise Frank Saunders greeted them at the door, giving them both a handshake and clap on the back. Dennis was there too, dressed exactly the same as when they left, and sat at a table was a spiky haired woman who resembled Siouxie Sioux. She looked up from a notepad, pen in hand. They went through their odyssey from day one, interrupted a few times for more clarity or if they were going too fast. Tea was produced, and although it had been an unsuccessful mission the atmosphere was relaxed and there were no recriminations. They had all seen Beirut being blitzed nightly on the news; their exoneration was a foregone conclusion, circumstances beyond their control and so forth and thank you for your efforts. True enough, but Marty had trouble remaining straight faced when Dennis had commiserated with them on the loss of their close comrade, thinking he had lost closer friends the last time he visited the toilet. They were probably relieved to be rid of an embarrassment, so the mission hadn't been a total failure; according to Frankie only O'Mahony had apparently shown much concern about Beatle. They were told to take some time off and then driven back to Marty's place, after which they had gone their separate ways for a while, Brendan managing an understanding wistful smile as he went to leave.

"You won't want me around for a bit when you see the missus. When she gets here tell her hello."

"I'll do that. We might head to Belfast ourselves next week, visit the family, test the water too. See if any peelers want a word."

"All right Marty. All the best now, see you soon kiddo!"

Martina arrived early the next morning whilst Marty was still asleep. Letting herself in she quietly put her bag in the living room and tip toed to the bedroom door, carefully avoiding the creaky floorboard. Opening the door she could hear his regular deep breathing. She started to undress, her eyes adjusting to the half light of the room, the heavy belt from her jeans clunked on the floor and he was instantly awake, sitting bolt upright, understanding coming in a delighted flash as he took in the familiar shape of her coming closer to the bed. Her hair was slightly longer, but everything else the same as he had pictured over and over again these last months. She opened one curtain, giving him a better view of her nakedness, the small but perfect shaped breasts, body tapering to a slim waist with wider hips and soft rounded rump. He looked down at her triangle of hair, entranced by her beauty that made him ache, as she put a single finger to his lips and drew back the covers revealing his own browned body. She looked at his erect penis, smiling mischievously, wondering again how such an ugly looking thing could do such marvellous things as she climbed in beside him. They stayed in bed for a whole and very happy day, only getting out to eat and drink before returning to enjoy each other some more. They stayed a few short days and then Tinks, who now had her own little red Opel Ascona, drove them back to her place in Belfast despite his initial reluctance.

Standing now on board and seeing his homeland again he sighed as he looked at the land with its uniquely Irish shades of broody green and grey shadowed skies. He turned and headed back to find his temporary travelling companion. The priest chatted amiably as they went below, enquiring casually about Marty's home life and what he had been doing away. He lied glibly and changed the subject, asking questions himself and flattering the priest by showing the utmost interest in his answers to avoid any further nosey parkering. As he got into the car he glanced back and caught the eye of a face that seemed to scrutinise him for a half second before ducking out of view, the face somehow familiar. The last thing he needed now was to bump into an old acquaintance after all the lies he'd told the priest, so he got in quickly. He sat and tried unsuccessfully to place the face before finally dismissing it with a shrug.

The 14th Intelligence Company was divided into regional detachments covering all six counties of Northern Ireland. Before he arrived for duty, Roy was informed he was to join the East 'Det' which was the Belfast area. This suited Roy and seemed to be a logical choice, although to his surprise there had been reservations from one of his commanding officers, who thought it better to send him to Londonderry. Major John Pierce thought otherwise and discussed it with his colleague Guy Molyneaux, also a Major.

"I think it would be a positive advantage to have him in Belfast, he doesn't have to learn the accent, knows his way about some parts already and just has that intimate knowledge of the million and one things that makes him *local*."

Molyneaux grimaced and gave his large aristocratic nose a slow tug before answering in his perfect drawl. "Yes, that's all true but he could work just as well in another urban environment, and as you well know I have my doubts about native Belfast operators, they can still be too bloody tribal and..."

"As highly motivated as possible." Pierce cut him off, knowing Guy's dislike of 'certain types' and their being potentially unprofessional.

"Is there any chance of him being recognised? Unlikely perhaps, but we have to consider everything."

"Hardly," Pierce snorted derisively. "He's been away a long time and being tribal as you put it, he's unlikely to have casual acquaintances on the other side that might recognise him."

"You know he has a brother in the Maze?"

"Yes, that was an oversight somewhere along the line. I thought myself about that and normally it might have disqualified him, but he hasn't seen him for a long time and political views don't run in the blood. Anyway, I'm convinced Ferguson will prove a great asset to us. Besides, since you're little misfortune last month we're short an operator there at the moment, we need someone now."

Molyneaux pouted, not liking to be reminded of an operational cock up that had meant two of his team compromised and forced to relocate. As for Ferguson's brother, well, he had a few relatives himself that were better kept out of sight.

"Very well, but if anything unsavoury happens, like information being passed to the wrong people, such as his brother's paramilitary chums, don't say I didn't warn you."

Pierce nodded slightly in acknowledgement, knowing Guy's main concern was simply covering his own arse if it didn't work out. He knew Ferguson better than Guy and was a fine judge of men; he was straight and could be trusted. There had indeed been isolated cases of police collusion with Protestant paramilitaries, but that was something else as far as he was concerned. As Molyneaux would soon be moving to a different part of intelligence it wasn't his decision anyway.

There was a knock on the door which opened on his barked "Enter!" Sergeant Roy Ferguson late of the Parachute regiment came to attention before them, sensing the different feelings coming towards him despite their composed neutral faces. Molyneaux had a long and horsy countenance with cool blue eyes. Pierce was square chinned, his gaze steady and unwinking from eyes the colour of teak. Roy thought to himself that between them these two represented the best and worst of the British Army. Pierce was highly professional, fair but hard, at times ruthless but dedicated to the service. He had a wry sense of humour which showed as small deep crow's feet at the sides of his eyes. He would selflessly protect his men if he thought they had done right. He sensed a mild hostility from Molyneaux, and although respecting his rank he made Roy uneasy. He came across as career driven first and foremost and had a snobby air about him, with his aquiline features and haughty manner, as if he was slumming it here temporarily. The bastard walked about like he had a pole up his hole. He wondered briefly why he had been summoned.

Pierce pursed his lips and nodded approvingly at Roy's less than military appearance, his ordinary trainers, jeans and slightly rumpled grey sweat shirt that adequately disguised a super fit torso. His hair had been allowed to grow and now had fashionable blond highlights, his overall figure hidden from what he knew personally and what the reports before him confirmed. He should make a good team member. He told Roy to stand easy and came to the point, making clear to him the slight doubt that had been raised as to his suitability. Molyneaux broke in sharply.

"What about your brother, the UFF terrorist in the Maze?"

Roy looked at his pompous stare and imagined how he would look on the toilet, sweating and straining a constipated stool.

"Nothing to do with me sir, he did wrong and that's all there is to it. I think you'll find he left the organization some time ago and no longer associates with other members."

"Well of course we have to take everything into consideration Ferguson, we wouldn't want any divided loyalties," he smirked.

Roy now imagined him on the job, eyes bulging and teeth clenched. Pierce interrupted his amusing thoughts.

"O.K, you will be going to East Det Roy. You have a spot of leave coming up and then you report for duties. Congratulations." He gave a crinkly grin and said, "Oh by the way, love the hair! Dismissed."

Chapter 10

Home to Roost

Hugh Smith loped along the Andersontown Road, passing the pub, shops and take away. Crossing over, he looked around him searching for any evidence of surveillance, then doubled back, heading quickly and unexpectedly into the tobacconists he had just passed. He pretended to think about which cigarettes to buy whilst peeking out of the window at anything that might be out of place, such as the same car or face appearing more than once. Satisfied, he paid for a packet of ten John Players and went into the hot sunshine again. Most volunteers were extra careful these days, it prolonged their shelf life.

Although he knew the area well he hadn't lived here all his life, coming originally from a predominantly Protestant area in East Belfast. His family had always got on with the neighbours or so they thought, but when the violence started and a local man had been killed, this had changed. The first indication came from the next door neighbour's four year old daughter who had cheerily addressed his parents one morning with an innocent, "Hello Mr Taig, Hello Mrs Taig." Her mother had reddened and quickly shooed her on. Obviously someone had been talking indiscreetly about "the taigs next door". This had proved to be just the start. The worse the violence became, the more isolated they felt, so prudently moved here after several threats of arson to their house. Although there had been no actual physical damage, Hugh was at times a very angry and bitter man whose volatile temper had worsened the older he got. When drinking he could be affable and boisterous, but if aroused his rage was terrifying and near uncontrollable, eventually earning him the name 'Taz' which was short for Tasmanian Devil. Just like the cartoon character, his fury after a session with his friends Mr Smirnoff or Captain Morgan and Johnny Walker could result in a destructive whirlwind of broken tables, smashed crockery, flattened noses and altered faces. Messing with him after a few drinks was like teasing a starving bear with fresh meat, and those who did provoke his ire were truly to be pitied. The fact that not many people did annoy him deliberately was pleasing, as he didn't go out of his way to do violence. He was kind to his wife and friends, was generally good natured and adored his two year old son. His nickname he didn't mind at all, acknowledging the truth in it and secretly finding it hilarious. His looks also played a factor: medium height but thick set, heavily muscled with virtually no neck, his bright blue eyes stared out from his massive close cropped bulging head, his overall appearance radiating a warning bell to all but the most obtuse of people.

A teenager limped passed him and nodded a shy greeting. Another petty miscreant who had recently strolled along to 'knee cap alley', been judged and would never stroll the same way again. 'Taz' didn't go in for that type of discipline. Calmly blowing a hole through one of your own people's knees didn't appeal to him, even if it did keep order. As to anything in a uniform, that was a different matter; the more holes the better.

He turned into the estate, the houses here quite comfortable, larger semi detached jobs with some nicely maintained gardens, some of them now in full bloom. He liked flowers and loved the blaze of fuchsias in his own garden every summer. He eventually came to 'Mutsy' John May's house, which wasn't one of the better ones and could have used a lick of paint. Taz noted with a tut of disapproval the wild hedge and the small garden with shrivelled dandelions and weeds, the one redeeming factor some pretty baby blue hortensias tucked away in the corner, but badly in need of attention. There was no movement in the small bay window or behind the door. He used the side entrance and entered via the kitchen.

Roy drove carefully along the Andersontown Road in a brown Vauxhall Cavalier, glad of the busy traffic that kept them to a slow pace. It enabled them to keep a visual on Smith, known as Bravo One a little longer. Helen sat next to him and kept a running commentary on the figure some distance ahead that turned now for a quick scan. The car looked as ordinary as its occupants, but was in fact strategically armoured and carried the most sophisticated cameras and recording equipment available. Speaking quietly, their voices could be heard clearly by other team members in their various positions as well as the operations room. They were both heavily armed: a pump action shot gun was under her seat, Helen was carrying a Walther pistol in her bag, Roy had the same model, the smallness of it enabling him to have it concealed and strapped on the inside of his left ankle under his loose fitting light trousers. He was also sat on a Browning, with a compact and deadly Heckler and Koch submachine gun under the seat within easy reach. Hot days such as this were unwelcome as they made hiding weapons around the body much more difficult. Wearing anything but the lightest of clothes in this heat looked odd. The glove compartment contained another Browning. Not that they were expecting trouble today.

"Tango, Bravo One still Foxtrot on right towards Green One Five."

"Zero, roger."

One of Belfast's omnipresent black taxis came to a stop in front of them, waiting for the lights to turn.

"Tango, Bravo One...wait. Entered shop nearing Green One Seven." Helen held a news paper and looked as if she was reading from it.

"Zero."

"Kilo, Foxtrot approaching Red Two Seven." That was Carl walking his way down. Ben came on.

"Lima, mobile approaching Blue Two Nine, acknowledge." Roy thought for a second. That meant he would be driving down from the opposite Glen Road direction.

"Zero, roger."

"Kilo roger."

"Tango, roger." Smith left the shop. "Tango, Bravo One now intending Red One Three, Kilo should have soon. Tango towards Green Two Eight."

"Zero, roger. Kilo, do you have Bravo One yet?"

There was a low hissing of the net and then a quick confirming double click, indicating other people within ear shot. Roy drove further and turned right at the next junction, listening as the others called in, terse and economical, describing their various locations and where Smith was now. Helen continued the commentary as they drove past Smith in the opposite direction, carefully avoiding any eye contact. The call came through that he was now at a known location, others would cover it from here.

"Tango, roger."

As they left the area, Roy reflected on his arrival four months ago and how he had initially hated the orientation period. There had been so much to learn and so little time to cram it all in, but now he was glad of it. Their commanding officer was surnamed Jack, a largish man with receding hair and a trace of West Country in his accent. He had a curious habit of emphasizing certain words as he spoke. He had greeted Roy with a firm handshake, indicating him to take a seat, outlining what was expected of him.

"Let me fill you *in*." Roy blinked, half expecting a physical assault before realising what he meant.

"You've already *been* made aware that we are not here to shoot terrorists. That is not our job. *We* are the eyes and ears, *that* is our role. You've probably heard about the various shoot outs we have had over the years, but these were purely the results of *accident*, co incidence and a couple of times *mistakes* on our part. We're the best but we're not infallible, and if you *are* involved in a shooting, the operation will have been compromised, you will be *known*, which means a lot of time, energy and valuable knowledge gone when you are *moved* to a different part of the province. We leave the arrests or *executive* action to others where possible. We don't want to see any dramatic headlines in the paper about shoot outs involving us. Now, you can get yourself *billeted* and join us for a drink later. Welcome aboard!"

So it had begun. He had to learn everything they had on all the known players in their area, where they lived, what they had done, with who and where they socialised. He had studied their photos until he could pick them out of a crowd at thirty paces. Also, there was the necessity of getting to know the area intimately, not just main roads, but every street, cul de sac and short cut, which roads led where and which routes were best at any particular time. This he was assured came with time and plenty of practice, but in the meantime it was essential he had a good working knowledge. He also had to learn the spot and colour codes of the area that were essential for speed and accuracy in covert communications until it became more natural than the street and location names themselves.

He had liked the other members of the team straight away. Ben was his usual partner and teacher too and had been here nearly a year, short and stocky with a mop of yellow hair that made Roy think of 'Barney Rubble'. He had a ready wit and had been of immense help to Roy. At one point he had raised his eyes at having to know about a piece of local trivia piled already on top of what his head was trying to remember and complained jokingly to him.

"I feel like my head will explode if it takes in any more today Ben." There had been no rebuke, only an understanding laugh and riposte.

"If you don't take it all in, your head might really explode!"

He appreciated the more informal atmosphere, and the humour and subtle reminder that everything he was learning might be one day of critical value. Carl was an intense man, dark and sometimes bearded. Then there was Bryan, a merry sort from Cardiff who typically had a passion for rugby, borne out by his squat build and lack of neck. Helen was one of their female operators, at the moment having plain brown shoulder length hair, greyish blue eyes and a slim, super fit build. She was of immense value, enabling them to drive about the worst places and even sit for short periods without arousing too much suspicion, whereas a man alone, or two men in a car would be more thoroughly scrutinised. What could be more ordinary than a man and his wife, sitting, talking, driving perhaps to visit the in laws, when what they were actually doing was photographing and filming out of their modified cars and her handbag, watching, waiting and reporting. She had a proud and sometimes imperious manner about her, and when she tilted her head and looked down her nose, Roy couldn't help imagining her walking about Versailles with a high wig and silk dress. He had discovered that beneath this haughty crust she had a very healthy sexual appetite, and they had sex a couple of times off duty. It hadn't been great. Roy had felt used by her as she coldly pushed him out immediately the act was over and she had what she wanted. He wasn't complaining however, she was quite honest, and it sort of kept everything on a professional basis. He thought again about spiders. It had been an intense and taxing period, but Roy felt he was now fitting in and becoming of use. He wouldn't have swapped his position for anything.

"Alright there Mutsy? Hey Danny! So you're our new helper? Good man yourself! How long have you been out but?" Taz asked. He was surprised to see Danny Gardner sat in an overstuffed armchair and glad too. He knew him, knew he'd done some time and must be quite recently home and there he was rejoining the struggle. Danny got up and shook his hand, feeling awkward as always.

"Good to see you Taz... er, I got out a couple of months ago. How're you doing yourself?"

"Grand."

He glanced over at Kevin, another new boy with only a few operations under his belt, waved a greeting and received a raised hand in return, his eyes focused on the TV.

"What time is Siobhan due?"

Mutsy scratched black two day old stubble and pulled the ring on a can of lager before answering, "Soon." He went into the kitchen, with the unwashed plates stacked high. Opening the fridge he shouted through.

"Fancy one yourself?"

Taz shook his head, half in refusal and half in disgust at the way Mutsy kept house. He wasn't known for his personal hygiene or vigour with the domestic chores. The house was a tip and had a pungent smell of old food, sweat, dog, and stale beer farts.

Siobhan walked in neatly dressed as always, her jean clad buttocks catching a few sly glances. It was widely conceded this was her best feature as when it came to looks she hadn't been blessed. She had a thin body from too much smoking, a flat chest, long mousy hair that never sat right, dull hazel eyes and worse, the face was flat with a mouth that stuck out like that of a baboon. She had been taunted from an early age and learned to live with it and even utilise it, growing a thick skin over the years which was a plus in the life she had chosen. Now she had a little more respect too. She looked around, wrinkling her pug nose.

Siobhan McErlean was an intelligence officer and worked at gathering information, collating it and helping to plan operations, whether it was a robbery, bombing or even a 'stiffing'. She was clever, never having had the distractions of boys she was usually top of the class at school and carried this on until leaving university with a good degree and volunteering. Joining the movement had been an easy decision, she believed deeply in the rightness of their struggle and it had given her something to commit her life to. She was as dedicated as a nun.

Today she had something for them. If all the information she had put together from various sources was correct, then there would shortly be one less policeman alive. It had taken a lot of time for this particular target, from an initial sighting, watching, waiting and following until they knew what car he drove and then best of all, a gold nugget of information had come along: where he lived. The target's movements, times and routes in and out of the station were carefully random, but they now had the one thing that made him vulnerable, his home address. She and a couple of other volunteers had patiently observed his house in passing, both on foot and by car, once actually seeing the target as he was about to drive away, noting how he looked under his car before getting in. Sometimes they had sat in an adjoining main road watching for movements, and eventually discovered that there was one routine the target followed most Saturday afternoons if he wasn't on duty. His car, a maroon Ford Escort was to be seen heading away at lunchtime, sometimes it would arrive back within an hour with an elderly passenger that Siobhan guessed was either his or his wife's mother. They knew he was married and had at least one teenage boy. She decided it would be best to hit him as he left his house one Saturday. A white van had already been earmarked, and this Saturday there would be a dry run. That was the plan she was to tell them, leaving out one small difference that only Taz was aware of. She believed in being security conscious, and like their enemy worked on a need to know basis. She summed up.

"This boyo has been living just a mile away, almost under our noses. It's a straight run down the Finaghy Road." She indicated on the street map. Taz noted how far along this particular road her finger traced, the whole of Finaghy North, safe enough but then over the Lisburn Road intersection and into Finaghy South, not so friendly anymore.

"He lives in this estate. There are two exits, traffic lights here by the shop with a wee forecourt and that's where we'll get him, then straight back the same way. Dump the cars when you get to the meet point from where you go on foot. Johnno will be waiting in another van, just dump the guns in the back door and go. Danny you'll be driving the scout car, Taz you'll do the hit and Mutsy will drive and provide back up. We do a practice run this weekend. Kevin will be reserve on this one."

"Why don't we just do him on his doorstep?" asked Mutsy.

"We think he has a good security door, and you don't know who might answer the knock, or even if he'll open up. Then he knows. This way is surer and safer."

"Can we not just leave him a little surprise package under the car?" Danny asked.

"No, too open and too risky. Besides, he always looks underneath, so no up and under this job."

"Why not this weekend?"

Her eyes gave a small flicker. "Questions, questions, Oh ye of little faith! We've info he might not be there, a little while from now will be soon enough. Did no one ever tell you patience is a virtue Danny?"

Taz looked at her and nodded his assent. She reminded him of an intelligent chimp. He grudgingly admitted she seemed to know her stuff, although he wasn't keen on too many women in the ranks, and this was reflected in the paucity of females in the leadership. Women volunteers hiding weapons, concealing small incendiaries, carrying messages and spying did their revolutionary image a power of good, but Taz was old fashioned about them doing anything else. Shooting was for the men.

Roy sat off duty drinking tea, hearing the click of balls behind him as Bryan potted one on the pool table. He was tired. Since arriving it had been all go, the volume of work had shocked him but he was satisfied. They had been successful and prevented or pre empted several attacks without loss to themselves or being compromised. He sat back and got a faint whiff of shit again. It seemed to cling to him, although he had showered long and hot an hour before, the result of lying in an attic the whole day in stifling heat with only a single tile cracked open for observation on the street below. He needed a crap and had to do it in a plastic bag, but somehow the smell still lingered, even when he sealed and tied it off. A hand clapped onto his shoulder.

"Prayers."

He followed Carl along the corridor and into the 'prayer room' used for briefings. He took a seat next to Helen and noticed for the first time a familiar face which mirrored his own recognition and nodded to him. Captain Jack stood up.

"Robert, as you *may* already know is from Special Branch and will be *liaising* with us on this one."

Rob didn't look all that much older than when Roy had last seen him at his uncle's funeral, a little heavier and thicker in the middle but otherwise the same dark hair, rosy cheeks and everyday features he remembered. He wondered how long he had been with the Branch. Rob took a mock bow and gave them carefully pruned information, as usual on a need to know basis.

"Thank you Captain. We have reason to believe that a reserve police officer, Constable Geoffrey Carson, living in the Finaghy area has been targeted by PIRA, and that the attack will take place within the next month. Our understanding is that the ASU will perform a practice run tomorrow. You know some of the players and have I believe had them already under surveillance for some time. If all goes according to plan, we may be able to catch them all red handed and put them away for a long, long time. Captain?"

"Thanks. Tomorrow we will simply keep tabs at a distance and with a bit of luck spot some *new* faces." Files were passed around, maps, information and mug shots, all of them by now as familiar as old friends.

"Hugh Smith, John May, Daniel Gardener, Brenda McErlean. From what we already know Smith or possibly May will be the *shooter*, Gardner probably driving backup or scouting. McErlean of course *won't* be there, she's an IO. We'll find out more tomorrow hopefully." He then gave them their individual instructions, start times and locations in more detail, reading from his own file in that strange inflected voice.

"Any questions?"

Helen raised a hand. "We aren't using a full crew tomorrow, what other back up will there be?"

"As you well *know,* we have other fish to fry and the others have been assigned elsewhere. We are not expecting an attack *tomorrow.* Usual back up resources will be available."

"Is the police officer in question aware he is under threat?"

Robert answered this one. "Yes and wishes to carry on as normal as possible until next week, a brave man Mr Carson. He was keen to help if it meant putting away some terrorists, although he is going to re locate as soon as this is over."

Roy had been surprised at the question. Surely they always told the intended target what was happening without revealing exact details, even if it meant lessening their own chances of a successful interception.

"Very good ladies and gentlemen, I *know* I say it all the time, but extra care please, do not initiate a confrontation unless there is absolutely *no* other course. You've all seen their profiles and Smith is one who has been loose *too* long. Dismissed."

The next morning as Roy checked his weapons a third and final time, Marty was on his way to do the same thing. Far across the border in safe County Monaghan, he and young Pat went to retrieve some guns from a cache.

It was a beautiful end of summer morning, already warm in what had been a long hot season. Another golden bright day was promised as Pat drove easily along winding lanes and tracks, singing along to the radio, 'Club Tropicana' before turning it down and reverting to a jolly and appropriate rendition of 'The One Road' as the car vibrated and bumped about. Marty rubbed his nose and gave a relaxed laugh at George Michael and rebellion all before breakfast. He looked out of the window at passing dew drenched fields of lush green, the sun gaining strength and doing its best to banish the ghostly mist that covered the ground. Ireland in all its romantic splendour, the sight of it never failing to stir Marty and strengthen his purpose. Lately he had needed it. Since coming back from Beirut he had felt a real anti climax. He couldn't put his finger on what exactly was amiss, but knew something within in him had changed, as if all he had experienced in a few short months had somehow altered how he looked at things. It was strange. Anyway, there was work to be done so he spared little time for deep analysis; it would only get in the way.

They turned onto a dirt track, high hedged and slightly sunken which petered out into a farm complex of barns and cattle sheds, with a bright red tractor parked outside. It belonged to one of Pat's numerous cousins. He stopped just outside, and immediately the farm stink hit Marty, the dung smell almost making his eyes water. He could never get used to it. Pat didn't seem to notice, as going around to the boot he opened it and took out a long canvas holdall, handing it to Marty.

"O.K." He led off, passing the farm gate and going through a hole in the hedge at the end of the track.

A few black and white heads lifted themselves slowly in curiosity as they passed through a field of cows, the grass still moist, darkening their jeans above the ankles. The only sounds were their footsteps swishing and the bird song as they advanced towards a small wooded copse. They followed a little used path, the undergrowth either side stretching tentacles of thorn, the brambles here and there snaking out and seeking to block their way before gradually thinning out as they approached the trees. Wood pigeons cooed and quite close the staccato burst of a woodpecker made them both glance up to the right, searching amongst the branches that rustled continuously in a light breeze, the sunlight penetrating to the floor of the wood with golden shafts. Pat led on, slowing slightly before getting his bearings and heading to the left, tramping over some brambles before they came to a stop before a large tree. He gave the smooth grey bark a friendly slap as he angled his head up, examining one side. Marty gave a short laugh as he saw what Pat was looking at. Carved into the wood, smeared with soil was a heart with the initials AK and below it RA. Pat began rooting about behind the trunk, shifting leaves and a fallen branch. Marty turned away and examined the wood, listening as Pat rustled and hummed behind him before giving a small chuckle.

"Ah, you beauties. As good as new." Pat stood before him brushing moss and soil from the clear plastic sheeting that covered an AK 47. "Give us the holdall then."

Marty opened the bag and Pat unwrapped the rifle and placed it tenderly inside before retrieving another gun of the same type, a pistol, a closed square Tupperware box and finally half a dozen banana shaped magazines. Pat gave a contented sigh as he put the last magazine in and began tidying up at the foot of the tree. Marty closed the holdall and hoisted it onto his shoulder, thinking momentarily of what he was carrying, that the bullets that now sat snugly in those magazines would in all probability be resting in flesh this very evening, turning the warm to cold. It was an unusual thought and annoyed he dismissed it with a flick of his head. Pat had resumed his singing, as together they went back to their car and drove away.

A Stone's Throw

Thomas Bailey was tired but pleasantly so. It had been a long, hot day of hard work, but well worth the effort, starting at seven he had gotten a brave bit done about the farm and was looking forwards to a shower and hot meal. He thought about maybe driving into the village later for a pint or two but then thought about his Ma, in her seventies and not in the best of health and to his distress rapidly going senile. Her brain seemed to have floated away to another place and time, and now he truly understood when people spoke of a mind 'wandering'. Maybe he would stay and keep her company; maybe she would actually notice.

He climbed down from the cab of the digger he had borrowed from his neighbour, removed his old cloth cap a moment, wiped his brow and looked about proudly at the rolling landscape and fields, one day to be his fields and property. He had grown up here and so had his father and generations of Baileys before him, and when his father had died five years before, he and his wife came home to look after both his Ma and the place itself which had needed a good deal of restoration. Thomas had spent a lot of money and effort since, the money saved up from a long career as a police officer. He had left the force completely on the death of his father, not even taking a reserve role and devoted himself entirely to his new life.

He was fifty now, still had a good crop of thick brown hair, portly perhaps but the fat on him was firm and didn't bounce. His face was stern, with small somewhat porcine eyes and a large bulbous nose that reddened in cold weather, but despite his appearance he was at heart a jolly sort of man and liked a drink and a laugh. He missed the comradeship of the force, and although he bumped into former colleagues from time to time it wasn't quite the same. It didn't matter though too much as when he looked around him it was more than compensated for. He loved this place and would leave it to his son in turn.

He began walking towards the house, the sun lowering and turning red, the only road which led to the nearby border going past his property was empty. That was another reason he had left the force and made sure everyone was aware of the fact too; it would be extremely dangerous to have any role at all with the security forces and live where he did. He was too vulnerable. Now he was content to be a civilian. His ample stomach rumbled and he wondered what was for dinner, now tramping a little faster in his wellingtons like an eager Paddington Bear on his way to marmalade. His thoughts were interrupted by the sound of an approaching car.

Young Pat was driving. Marty sat next to him and in the back along with the guns sat a relative novice Damien, whom they had been using gradually for various jobs, building him up and testing his aptitude at the same time. Pat knew his family of course and had done a little cross border smuggling with his elder brother as lots of people did around these parts. Marty had once enquired casually about how much money they made from smuggling and customs avoidance and been brusquely told to mind his own business. Not that he had any time for the tax man, as his father had long ago complained, if all you had was a bag of shit they'd still want half. Pat had made smuggling sound like a patriotic duty, an act of rebellion in itself denying the crown money that could be used against it in the struggle. Marty could see the logic, but had an uncomfortable suspicion that perhaps some funds got lost on the way, some of the bigger smugglers seemed to be pretty affluent, although carefully unostentatious. He looked behind him and gave Damien a reassuring wink, noticing he was keen and ready for the big one. There was no scout car tonight or any elaborate planning. This was a relatively easy job and just the thing to blood their new boy. Also there was a certain urgency as old Pat had explained to them the night before.

"We have to hit them back straight away, they'll not be getting away with pulling that kind of shit around here!" The previous day a UVF hit team had dared to venture a little into the area and tried to murder a local Nationalist, shooting and leaving him paralysed across his doorstep.

"Who?" asked young Pat quietly.

"His name's Thomas Bailey, a right bastard of an Orangeman, used to be RUC."

Marty raised his head slightly. "Used to be?"

"Still in the reserve but, still spying on his neighbours and passing it on to his wee friends. He's been seen about, talking to serving officers. The man is a threat, he'll have to go."

"Aye, I know of him." Young Pat nodded, his interest clear. "He has that big farm along the Tullygally Road."

"Easy, less than a mile across the line," said Old Pat nodding emphatically. "We can use Damien on this one I'm thinking." He gave a harsh and ugly laugh. "Alright then, you and Marty can pick up some gear in the morning and give Bailey the good news later!"

Marty had felt a rare twinge of unease, not doubting it would be easy enough but was it necessary? If this man was such a threat why had he been allowed to live so long? He knew all about tit for tat in Belfast and didn't like it. This sounded like simple revenge, but rushed, and not where it should be.

Pat drove along the narrow grass verged ribbon of road, past an isolated farmhouse and large brown barn, its rounded roof giving it the appearance of a huge loaf of bread. On the left was a low wide shed, dozens of logs stacked outside beneath a crude shelter. They slowed as they came level with the bungalow before turning up the path towards it. Marty saw for the first time a JCB digger in the field to the left.

A big man, sleeves rolled up, baggy trousers soiled green at the knees was walking from the digger in the direction of the bungalow. His step faltered as he peered, trying to see into the car against the back drop of the slowly disappearing sun. The car lurched to a stop, the doors flung open and his nightmare jumped out, awful and real, hats rolled down into black balaclavas, hands whitened by the surgical gloves they wore, armed and moving with terrifying speed. His face froze as his mind raced and Thomas realised in an instant he was going to die, here on his own beautiful land with the late birdsong and hum of a warm summer evening in his ears. They advanced towards him and Marty could clearly see the horror bright in his widened eyes, the ruddy face had bleached and turned the same pale grey as his shirt, mouth open before he snapped and turned to run in futile desperation. Marty and new kid Damien quickly raised their rifles and fired at the figure stumbling awkwardly in his boots. A burst caught him squarely in the back and lifted him bodily into the air as if hurrying his flight before crashing him down with a thud. He was still alive and crawled slowly, coughing wetly out of leaking lungs, the blood on his chin red against the chalk of his face as he rolled over gasping and exhausted. A shrill scream like an excited gull sounded behind them, as turning, Marty saw a woman rushing towards their little group. He froze. For a moment he had thought it was his own mother, the resemblance was uncanny until she stopped a few metres away, tearing at her hair as she took in the scene. There was another loud Whack! Whack! As Pat shot the top of Bailey's head off with the pistol, then a rapid burst as Damien emptied the rest of the magazine into the figure on the ground, making it jump and dance in a bloody horizontal samba. The woman screamed again and fell to her knees. They moved off quickly, Marty hesitating and taking in the scene a last time, still in shock at the likeness to his mother, remembering her grief and the sameness of it. He looked again at the prone figure, transfixed by the way a rivulet of blood seemed to shiver and pulse weakly from a rip in the neck before stopping. He wrenched himself away and rushed after the others who were sprinting to the car, watched by an old woman in the window who smiled and waved at them as they got in. Pat paused and stared at the bizarre sight before they screeched away to nearby sanctuary, the sun now fully down, darkening and bleeding the fields of life and colour, the bird song dying away to nothing.

Roy was on his way to pick up James and Helen using the same car they had used the previous week, although this time it was dark green and had a different number plate. They had it worked out in detail, who was to be where and when, but were always ready to improvise if planning went wrong or there was a breakdown in communication. Roy chuckled to himself, remembering suddenly the baldy old monk on T.V in his orange robe from 'Kung Fu' and his words of wisdom. "Remember, Grasshopper. Always expect the unexpected."

"Zero. Didn't catch that Whiskey, repeat."

Shit! He'd said it out loud, and with a funny Chinese accent.

"Whiskey, nothing Zero, picking up James and Tango now."

"Zero, roger."

Aye, that baldy auld git was right in one respect, you never knew when somebody would slip up, or a joy rider would come tearing along out of the blue, or some drunk would blunder into you at a critical moment and screw up the entire operation. He wondered how baldy would react to a joy rider in a stolen Capri bearing down on him at seventy miles an hour. Yes, you could prepare but not foresee. He pulled over as he saw Helen and James standing waiting for him. She was checking her watch and gave a tiny nod as she opened the rear passenger door and climbed in with James. He liked James, apart from his habit of trying to hump everything in sight. He looked at him slavering in the back seat with his cock out again. James was a collie, the pet of Bryan and very useful as cover when out walking and spying, which is why he was here today, the idea being to drop off Helen, then park and walk the dog around the target area. Other operators were already in position or waiting to follow as soon as the ASU moved. She spoke tersely.

"Tango, Whiskey mobile towards Alpha One."

She fiddled around in her leather shoulder bag, adjusting a camera and checking her weapon. Roy noted her hair drawn back in a short pony tail, no makeup, sensible flat black shoes that she could run in, jeans, baggy loose blouse, but not showing any cleavage. She didn't want to attract attention to herself or what else was concealed under that blouse. Today she was a blond. So was Roy, with false thick framed national health glasses, casual jacket with hidden microphone for communication sewn into the collar completing his attempt at appearing like a respectable pen pusher type just out walking the dog. He carried a Browning, a spare magazine loose in the jacket pocket. Others began their call signs.

"Kilo, going complete now towards Alpha Two."

"Zero."

"Juliet, mobile past Alpha Two. No movement yet. Towards Green Two One."

"Zero."

"Lima, in position Orange Three Two."

They listened carefully as James panted, tongue lolling. They had driven past the terrorist house at Alpha Two on the way to their places and Carl would be doing the same, Bryan was heading towards the junction and would wait nearby to report activity whilst Ben was already in position and ready to follow. There was no static observation point at Alpha Two so they were positioned about their intended route. He dropped Helen off and drove back, parking in the next road to the intended victim's house, reporting his movements and listening. He checked his communications and earpiece one last time. Ready.

Mutsy lounged in his soft chair and waited, his eyes flicking across to the window where he could just about see through the grimy netting. He lit another fag, crushing the empty pack and tossing it into the copper bin by his chair where it rested on paper wrappings, ash, cigarette butts and orange peel. Taz lifted his head and watched him. Mutsy wasn't a bad lad he thought, just a slob who needed a woman to look after him. The place stank, but not from cooking which Mutsy avoided; he would eat anything that was easy and was the only person Taz had seen who could eat the cheapest supermarket Irish stew cold from the can. The man was a human rubbish bin. He had, to his utter disgust once seen baked beans there and although actually on a plate, the damn things had grown a fine fuzz of bluish green hair. Taz popped another stick of gum into his mouth and chewed aggressively, wanting to get out of here, get the job done and go home. His temper hadn't been improved this morning when he discovered his son had shoved a thick slice of toast into the new video recorder, not everybody had one and now his was fucked. He kept his temper in check, leaving earlier than planned, his annoyance now fermenting nicely and putting him in the right mood for murder. He had told Mutsy as he entered about the deviance from the plan, that the job was on for today and that he had already made a dry run, getting an indifferent look in response that denoted a very cool or very lazy attitude. There was movement at the window and Danny approached, hands in denim jacket pockets, loping in through the door and managing to bash an elbow as he did so.

"Youse ready?" he asked.

"There's been a wee change Danny," said Taz, watching as Danny's eyes narrowed slightly.

"How changed?"

"It's on for today, I've the dry run done already, no problems and as the woman says it's a straight run."

"Aye," said Danny, giving a lopsided rueful smile like a man hearing something funny on the way to the gallows. "The last straight run I done took a turn into the Maze, do not pass go, do not collect two hundred."

Mutsy gave a smoky, phlegm choked laugh and Taz was pleased he was taking it without argument.

A little later and having nervously checked watches every five minutes they were on their way, Danny leading in a blue Mini, the other two following in the promised work a day white van. Mutsy carried an old pistol, but it was Taz who had the real fire power, a folded Armalite rifle. It was another nice day as they drove past rows of beige semi detached houses. They turned left, heading downhill before taking a right into Finaghy Road North, Mutsy careful to keep Danny in sight. They came to the lights at the junction and waited, a couple of army vehicles went past, but nothing unusual so far. They crossed over and began to see the alien red, white and blue painted kerbs and hanging union flags, the sight of this colour scheme making them unconsciously quicken speed. Their man should be coming along the road within the next half hour. Taz's stomach gave a grumble. He hadn't eaten at Mutsy's place, life being dangerous enough without the risk of food poisoning. They parked and waited whilst Danny drove on for one final check to see if the maroon car was where it should be.

Kenneth Carson stared into the mirror, lips pursed in annoyance, eyes watering as he put his forefingers together like a pair of thick flesh tweezers and squeezed the disgusting large spot at the side of his nostril. He grunted as it erupted with a tiny custard spurt onto the mirror, quickly wiping it away as a tiny disc of red appeared. Shit, he didn't want a scab. He turned his head in slow examination, tried a smile and nodded at himself, overall not bad, no major zits anywhere else and nothing worthy of a squeeze. Good, nothing worse than trying to look cool with a crater face.

Kenny yawned, it was late in the morning and his parents had let him sleep in. He couldn't go out until much later though, not until his granny had arrived and settled for a few hours. It was something his father insisted on even if he did find it unfair. Aged fifteen Kenny was finding a lot in life that was unfair. He didn't want to go along to any more prayer meetings either; he hated them and tried to keep his parent's embarrassingly square beliefs from his friends, but was forced to attend by them. He loved his parents of course and was grateful they were a little more relaxed than some of the others who Kenny thought were always on the lookout for evil and usually finding it too. He had even been more or less accused of having sinful thoughts by one of the elders and urged to cast out his wickedness with the purging power of prayer. Of course he had such thoughts, the old pillock, he was nearly sixteen and couldn't wait for a shag. He also disliked all that singing, most of the congregation with their arms raised to heaven, eyes closed in rapt concentration as if they were shitting glass shards.

He dressed and dragged himself downstairs, mumbled a surly good morning and drifted into the living room to watch Saturday morning TV. His Ma went into the garden and he heard her exchange a few pleasantries with the neighbour. His father came into the room, tall and bearing a strange resemblance to gangster Ronnie Kray, especially the thick eyebrows, which was ironic considering he was a policeman, even if only a part time one. He sat and crossed his long legs.

"I'll be picking your Gran up in a bit," he said.

Kenny nodded without answering, his eyes fixed on the screen.

"We're out of tea."

Again no answer. His father got up and brandished one of the shiny new pound coins in front of his nose, waving it slowly in front of his eyes between thumb and finger like an amateur hypnotist.

"Hello? Contact?" Kenny finally looked at him frowning. "Ah! Would you be good enough to pop along to the shop and get some?"

Kenny took the coin with a petulant swipe and futile, unspoken complaint. His father breathed out heavily, keeping his patience, then laughed as his son got to his feet, arms already swinging at the obvious and terrible injustice of the request. He had been a teenager himself once.

"Can you give me a lift on your way?"

"No, don't be so lazy."

He had told his wife of the threat to his life but not his son, and although they were both deeply religious and believed in predestination, he still didn't feel comfortable with his son in the car until this was over, despite the reassurances that everything was under control. He had never worried overly about his own safety, taking the necessary precautions, but believed if it was your time, the Lord would take you no matter what. Kenny went out slamming the door. He passed his mother, on her knees as usual but now busy pruning instead of praying. Closing the gate he began walking towards the shop, hardly noticing the blue Mini that passed slowly before it accelerated away.

Roy was on the other side of the road, having conveniently stopped by a street lamp as James cocked a leg with perfect timing and left a small puddle. He spoke quietly, head to one side and jaw resting briefly on his shoulder, as if scratching an itchy chin without using his hands, lips hardly moving.

"Whiskey, Bravo Three mobile past Alpha One, towards Orange One Four, am foxtrot towards same."

"Zero, roger."

He listened to the others calling in their positions. Ben was delayed in traffic, the others slowly nearing their destinations, Helen on foot coming in the other direction and Carl now circling the vicinity. He gave James a quick tug and received a reproachful stare as he stopped his snuffling and joined Roy, now walking slowly the same way as the boy he had just seen leaving the house.

Danny drove on, having confirmed he had the right house with its easily identifiable car, the only one of that colour and make in the street parked on a tiny area at the side of an end house. He glanced in his mirror and caught sight of Carson shutting his door and talking to his wife before he was out of vision. Danny approached the crossroads, slowed and gave the occupants of the white van a quick nod of confirmation before turning left as the lights changed. Taz had returned the briefest of nods before leaning down to get his weapon ready. Danny had missed the boy leaving by a few seconds.

A few minutes later Helen approached the shop, not paying the van parked in the forecourt any attention as she walked past, the camera hidden in her shoulder bag filming the scene, a letter in her hand which she dropped into the red post box a few metres away. She thought about returning and going into the shop but saw Roy and James coming and decided to just keep going, speaking softly, letting everyone know her next stop which would be their parked car and a drive past a little later. Roy could take over now and keep up the continual observation. They passed each other without looking. His earpiece burst into life.

"Zero, Whiskey do you have Charlie One yet?"

Roy put a hand in his pocket as if searching for a sweet and gave a quick double click 'yes' on the radio transmit button as he was now too close to talk. Withdrawing his hand which now held a packet of Polos, he stopped to tear at the wrapping, keeping the van in the corner of his eye, not enough to see directly, but sufficient to spot movement. Again the voices in his head.

"Kilo, approaching Yellow Two One, will pass Orange One Four in about five minutes." Then to his alarm the operations officer came on again.

"Zero, Whiskey repeat, do you have Charlie One yet?"

This could only mean that his communication was down, and at a crucial moment. Charlie One was the van the terrorists now known as Bravo One and Two were sat in, he had already confirmed they were in sight, but this obviously hadn't registered. Roy cursed inwardly, fucking technology, fucking code talk, fucking traffic and delays. Everything had worked perfectly for ages and then right when you needed it most it cut out. Damn! The calm dispassionate voice came on again.

"Zero, Lima can you make Orange One Four ASAP, we seem to have a comms problem."

"Lima, Zero be there in five."

Roy walked past the van intending to go into the shop and dawdle until fresh eyes arrived. As he passed he glanced casually in, no weapons, but he did notice something that sent a current vibrating through him as he saw what they were wearing, the boiler suits were inconclusive, but he also had the briefest glimpse of a white surgical glove. Why would anyone on a mere dry run take such forensic precautions? They had missed them as they left and nobody had spotted their attire on the short distance here, if they had it would have made all the difference. Roy became sure within seconds this was no dry run but the real thing. To make matters worse he noticed the boy coming out of the shop with a packet of tea and an acid expression as he looked up the road at an oncoming maroon Escort that was slowing for the lights and providing an easy target. The van's ignition gave a cough and a slight rev as Mutsy got ready to put his foot down. Roy didn't have to think about what to do next. He dropped the dog lead, his right hand went to his jacket and drew his Browning at the exact moment the unmistakable short barrel of an Armalite poked out of the side window, aimed straight at the white staring face of reserve constable Carson. Taz was taking aim just as there was a shout and the van lurched forwards spoiling his first shots that cracked past Carson's nose, making him drop flat out of sight as if the car had a trap door. Taz was instantly ablaze with fury and turned his crazed eyes on his partner who had chickened out at the last second, unaware of what Mutsy had seen, the man with the dog who had suddenly shouted and pulled a gun.

"You bloody coward ..." was all he could get out before the dashboard in front of Mutsy seemed to jump and then glass cubes from the window sprinkled on them from the side as Mutsy swerved the van frantically into the road, engine screaming. Taz twisted around and immediately registered the window gone and a man in a crouched position with a hand gun, but to his relief not firing as they veered and swerved crazily putting some distance between them. Taz was unhurt but looking at Mutsy he could see he had been hit, one bullet must have creased his head which was bleeding all down his face on the right side. As he turned his head to look behind he flicked scarlet drops around him, his eyes wide and open mouth breathing harshly. Taz saw straight away he had also been shot high in the right shoulder, the stain expanding as he watched.

Roy had fired half a clip, the sudden violent movement of the van had thrown him momentarily, spoiling his own aim as well as that of the gunman. Then Carson's vehicle was in his line of fire and as the van raced away he was again thwarted by the presence of other civilian cars, too near for him to shoot without risking his bullets finding a wrong mark. He ran back to check Carson who was unhurt, now out of the car with his arm around his son's shoulder who was staring in shock, trembling, the box of tea still clutched in his hand. There was a screech of brakes and the people who had come out of the shop to look, comically turned and fought each other to get back inside as Carl pulled up, the passenger door open. Roy jumped in, quickly replacing the half clip with a fresh one as Carl put his driving skills to good use whilst giving a running commentary. The van was obviously still on the road and going fast judging by the reactions of other drivers who were swerving and pulling up on kerbs ahead of them, the noise of horns sounding angrily.

"Kilo, contact, have Charlie One mobile towards Orange Two Four hot pursuit."

"Zero, roger."

Ben was coming the opposite way and would intercept them on their current course and if necessary ram and shoot them if they didn't stop. Carl eased past other cars at high speed, the back of the van now visible as it mounted the pavement and crashed straight into a street lamp. One man staggered out and began a weaving clumsy run, head down, he vanished into an adjoining road, a few bystanders stopping to stare or quickly crossing over, putting distance between themselves and what was obviously trouble. Carl pulled up and they sprang out. The driver of the van was slumped over the wheel, coughing weakly, he'd live but was no threat. Carl reached in and fished out a hand gun and the dropped Armalite. Roy carried on, the ground sprinkled with blood, indicating the passenger was also injured. He simply followed the spots which went a short distance before petering out into a front garden where Hugh Smith lay face up, waiting on the weedy lawn and blowing like a whale. In the window a group of children stared out at the unexpected visitor. Roy covered him and looking into his eyes clearly saw a gamut of emotions pass on his face: hate, rage, fear, relief and finally resignation. More people were now coming out of their houses, and then there was the sound of police Land Rovers. Ben appeared and put a hand on his shoulder.

"Nice work mate, soon as the RUC get here hand your gun and everything else over to them for forensics, then out of here, the less people see your face the better. Special prayers at seven."

It was getting dark as Martina let herself into the flat, stopping as she heard voices before recognising them and continuing. Brendan was on a visit and already laughing loudly as she entered, dropping her bunch of keys with a rattle onto the small table by the door. Marty was sprawled lazily, slowly shuffling a pack of cards, laughing lightly and relaxed as she stooped to give him a quick kiss on the lips before going over to give Brendan a peck on the cheek. He was pouring vodka into glass tumblers, the twisting silvery rope of liquid joining the Coke already there. They were not small measures, and when he had finished the colour in his own glass was barely tinged brown.

"We were just having a blather there about old days, you remember when we all first met but?"

Martina looked at Marty and smirked. "How could I forget?"

Brendan took a long pull on his glass and then shook his head suddenly, all apologetic, shaking the bottle at her. "Sorry, d'you want one yourself?" he asked. He was already beginning to slur and she noticed the bottle was half empty and Marty still looked pretty sober.

"Aye, I will. Plenty of Coke now."

He poured and she took the drink and sat down, pushing Marty's legs to one side, who gave her a wink before resuming his slow shuffling. She reached to take the cards from him.

"What are you playing for big man?"

"To see if I get yodelling up your canyon tonight."

There was a coughing yelp of laughter from Brendan as she snatched the cards and playfully threw them at his face, then punched him lightly.

"You've one filthy tongue in your head so you have," she said.

Brendan glanced at his watch, narrowing his eyes to focus before chugging the drink back, arm stiff as it poured down his throat before heaving himself up out of his chair.

"That's right Martina, he never was much of a sweet talker. I'd better be putting my skates on. I'll pop round before I head back to the city tomorrow, O.K?" Marty nodded, picking up the cards in reach, chin on chest as he answered.

"Aye, right. See you then."

Brendan gave him an affectionate pat on the cheek as he went past. They heard the door close behind him before Martina spoke again.

"How is he? Really?"

"About the same," said Marty with a resigned shrug. "I can't stop him drinking, just slow him down a bit is all. He'll get over it in time. Believe me, I've been here before Tinks."

She looked at him doubtfully. Brendan was worrying her. "It's been over a year and if anything he seems worse. What's he going to be like on ops, he's of no use like he is and he's determined to get back into things," she said.

"He'll be fine, just a wee bit longer. Anyway what's the rush?" He became alert as she took a breath before speaking again,

"You obviously haven't heard?" He stared blankly. "One of our operations went wrong and two were lifted on a job. You know Taz Smith? Him and some guy Mutsy got caught, Danny got picked up later but they won't have enough to put him away so he'll probably get off. That's according to Siobhan anyway, you know her?"

Marty was saddened at the news but hardened; anyway it could have been worse. He frowned a second before he realised whom she meant. He gave a guffaw and said, "King Louis?"

It was Tinks turn to look blank. Marty sat up, arms loosely outstretched simian style. "You know King Louis out of the 'Jungle Book'."

Martina tried not to laugh, thinking about the resemblance, trying to banish it from her mind and concentrate on the serious subject at hand. "For God's sake don't be saying that in front of her!" she exclaimed.

He knew Siobhan only by sight and what Brendan had told him. According to him she was alright, but a bit of a revolutionary zealot, which he suspected masked some deeply sectarian feelings. Marty knew there were some on his own side every bit as vicious as the worst Orange bigot. He briefly thought of Thomas Bailey, who it turned out hadn't been a cop for a long time. He had pushed this to the back of his mind, but deep down knew that his comrades had known his true status but had decided to kill him anyway. And he had helped them do it.

"Anyway," Martina continued. "They want to put another team together using experienced people." She stopped as Marty studied her, waiting. "Somebody thinks you and Brendan might fit the bill. You can live with me." Marty rolled his eyes in exasperation before answering.

"Why do you think we've lasted so long down here when near everybody I've done jobs with in the city has been lifted at one time or another?" She didn't answer. "I'll tell you, because here there are damn few touts about and if there is he doesn't last long. Belfast is crawling with people willing to sell us out for a few quid or because someone's been heavy on them or whatever. O.K, they've nothing on me yet but don't they realise we'll be watched, everything we do, or don't they care?"

"Marty, I know it, you know it and so do they," Martina acknowledged with a sad smile. "I'm just telling you what they told me, everybody is in the same boat, if we think like that we may as well give up. Sure, a lot of plans get scrapped and people get caught, but there are still some successes, it just means we have to be very, very careful."

She could see he remained unconvinced, reluctance beginning to harden into resolve and she thought perhaps maybe he wouldn't go and this made her secretly happy, torn between wanting him by her all the time, but knowing he was safer here. Then she saw a thoughtful expression and his eyes seemed to cloud as he spoke.

"Brendan's going up tomorrow." He ran his fingers through his hair and massaged his head, letting out a deep breath. "I think we'd better be going with him."

Brendan awoke with a strangled yell and heavy breathing, tangled in bed clothes, his whole body lathered in a slick of sweat like a horse that had run itself lame. It was the dream again. He swung his legs onto the ground and put his head into his hands. Hala had come to him many times over the last year, always fresh and smiling, her gentle moaning as they made love in stolen hot moments before everything changed, the moan turning to a shriek of terrified agony as the huge block of cement crushed the life out of her. Her eyes bulged and then quickly filmed over as he frantically pushed at the enormous weight, as hopeless as an ant with a pebble.

Brendan got up and walked unsteadily to the window, looking out but not seeing. A few short months of complete happiness was all they had, even discussing an exciting future together that would last forever. Their forever had lasted just weeks. His shoulders sagged. He had felt so alive with her, his senses tingling at being with someone that so understood everything, when they thought the same things at the same time, on another planet in fact from those around them. Now he felt constantly tired, everything looked dull and drained of colour. On occasion he actually thought he was cracking up. He needed to be doing something, getting back on track in some way and cut down his drinking which he used as a daily anaesthetic. He tottered back to his damp bed and sat, groping for a cigarette.

He thought about his family and friends and the movement, then came back to thinking about Marty. He had been a good mate, looking out for him as he had himself done many years ago. He felt guilt too at how he had caught himself once resenting his friend, watching him with Martina he had felt a hot rush of jealousy as they kissed, this fleeting envy not really aimed at his friend, but rather at the fact he had something to live for. The moment had passed and the jealousy had been immediately replaced by love and shame. He couldn't really explain how he felt. He had tried but got the impression that Marty didn't understand, but then again how could he? Just the other day they had been in the pub playing on the 'Draw Poker 1000' machine and having a bit of luck. It was his turn and he drew a pair of kings, an eight, and a pair of tens which meant they were winning already, with the possibility of more if the eight was ditched and they got another king or ten for the full house. Marty took a sip of his beer, and watched in disbelief as Brendan discarded all but the ten and king of hearts and drew three new cards. He lost.

"For fuck sake Brendan, what are you at?"

"How else would I get a royal flush?" Marty had sat down in disgust.

He didn't understand, it just wasn't important. What difference did it make if he won or lost, what difference did it make if he got so pissed he couldn't stand. None of it mattered. Sitting on his bed in the growing light he stubbed his cigarette out, and rubbing his temples he realised with a new clarity he didn't care enough about anything anymore to make him want to live.

Chapter 11

A Shadow on the Shoulder

They arrived at a house off the Shaws Road, where they were to be briefed on the set up and structure of their unit and future role. Martina had a key and entered, watched only by a couple of kids kicking a ball unenthusiastically against a wall opposite who kept a look out, a primitive yet effective early warning system. When they entered the front room he was only mildly surprised to see Gerry Fox sat at a linen covered table by the window, pouring tea from a pot and passing it to Siobhan. Frank Saunders was there too, formally and neatly attired in shirt and tie. Two other men sat opposite Gerry, sipping from their own cups and eating from a plate of sandwiches. He didn't recognise them. One looked to be in his late twenties, medium height, prematurely bald and dressed casually in faded jeans and white T shirt. He rose to shake their hands with an easy smile, his accent had a touch of American, sounding as if he had only recently returned.

"Pleased to meetcha, I'm Terry, Terry Corr but everybody calls me 'Tin-Tin'. God knows why but, one of them things that kinda stuck."

The other man half raised himself as Gerry made an introduction. "This is Declan Owens. He'll be in charge of the squad. Tin-Tin there is explosives."

Declan shook hands and muttered a soft greeting. Marty had half hoped he would be leading, but knew he wasn't enough of a yes man. Declan was tall, dark haired, with a moustache, probably in his mid thirties, and to be fair didn't look a yes man either. A little older than Marty, he pursed his lips together and nodded, satisfied so it seemed at what he had got. Frankie cleared his throat, taking off and polishing his glasses as he addressed them, his head tilted up in a slightly arrogant manner, suggesting to Marty he must be going up in the world. He had a sudden flashback of Frankie as a child, his face peeping through a letterbox.

"Now then, as you know we lost a major part of the unit when Taz and Mutsy were taken. Danny is now in custody but he'll probably be out soon enough though when we'll thoroughly debrief him. The other two members of the squad are stood down temporarily until we have investigated and seen what went wrong. And why."

There was an uncomfortable silence, broken only by the tinkling of Siobhan stirring her tea, as head down she stared glumly at the table. They all knew what investigation and 'debriefing' meant: a visit from internal security to see if they had a leak. The finger of suspicion was moving slowly through the air but hadn't pointed at anyone yet, but it could potentially be very bad news for somebody, unless of course they deduced that the failure was due solely to surveillance, and some good work by the Brits. Lucky coincidence sometimes figured, but not in this case. Frankie continued.

"The new unit will consist of Declan as officer, Marty and Brendan small arms, Terry explosives and if all goes well, Danny and Johnno will rejoin as support. Until then, Martina will take part and liaise directly with me or Gerry there who will be in contact with intelligence and finance as needs be. We'll be keeping it tight."

"Why'd you choose us?" Brendan enquired.

"I didn't, higher up did," Frankie answered, smiling and showing teeth. "Someone thinks you're special, and you do have plenty of experience."

Marty knew who that probably was. O' Mahoney, shifting them about like they were so many pieces in his own private chess game. He wondered what he was. A rook? A bishop? No, more likely a simple pawn. Gerry interrupted his thoughts.

"C'mon now Brendan, I thought you'd jump at the chance."

Brendan raised his hands and said, "No I didn't mean it like that, I just wanted to know is all."

Gerry looked across to Marty. "Surely you're happy to be back? You didn't want to leave here but, as I remember." Marty nodded once and gave Frankie a mocking grin, unable to resist giving his tail a wee twist.

"So if it was up to you we wouldn't be here?" he asked.

Frankie went pink and tried to be humorous in turn. "Och, no, no it's not like that at all. Marty, I sometimes think you never liked me, even when we were kids," he tittered uncertainly.

"C'mon Frankie," Marty laughed. "I was probably the only one who actually did like you."

There was a ripple of mirth at the barbed joke, the grin fixed tight on a now reddened Frankie, the comment all the more painful because of the truth in it. He wrapped the meeting up, looking around the table with an imperious lifting of the chin. It had lasted less than ten minutes.

"Good. There's nothing planned for now, so get yourselves comfortable and I'll leave you to get acquainted."

He got up from the table, taking his tweed jacket from the back of the chair. Gerry got up with him, giving them a clap on the back as he passed and Siobhan followed them out. They sat in the vacated chairs.

"Whose house is this anyway? Nice sandwiches so they are," said Tin-Tin helping himself from the plate.

"It's a new one, I've not been here before either," said Declan, sitting back. "They must be worried about bugs."

"Aye, that's right." Tin-Tin sputtered suddenly through a mouthful of tuna and onion. "I was at one meeting where no one spoke, we all had pens and notepads and passed messages, I couldn't stop laughing it was so fucking ridiculous."

Brendan licked his lips and took the last sandwich. "Did they leave any beer in the fridge?" he asked. "Well he did say take it easy for the moment."

"I'll go see, we don't need to leave for an hour or so," Tin-Tin answered with a grin. He went out and was back in seconds, putting a six pack on the table. "Sliante!"

Major Guy Molyneaux tipped his nose using his left index finger, the nostrils now pointing double barrelled, he squinted into the polished mirror as he deftly shaved those last few hairs away on his upper lip. He splashed water on his visage and felt the satisfying smooth result with his hand. Dressing unhurriedly in casual trousers, shirt and black blazer, he slipped polished glossy black shoes on and went downstairs for breakfast.

He made toast, thinly spreading good English butter on one piece and Robertson's marmalade on the other, and went out into the walled garden of his temporary home, here on Northern Ireland's so called 'Gold Coast'. It was a nice house in a well to do area in a small village just past Holywood, where everybody was respectable and kept themselves at a respectful distance. The house was large and red brick, having a Tudor feel with ivy climbing up one wall as far as the overhanging bedroom window. The garden wall was trellised with more climbing roses and an arched doorway in the middle. A garage stood next to the yellow gravelled front of the house so he didn't have to leave his car outside, not that there was any risk here; despite being only ten miles from Belfast it was quite safe. The IRA wouldn't dare come even if they knew where to look, as there was but one main road in and out. It was just too risky.

Although he didn't show it Major Molyneaux was bothered. He was still only a Major and this irked him. There had been that cock up last year, and another more recently that had been unfairly laid at his door. This brought a flush to his face when he thought about it, to be berated by that lower class sod even if his rank was higher, and in such terms too! It wasn't his fault, and no real damage had been done. Some of his agents had to be moved temporarily and a source had been lost, but what was one informer when you looked at the overall picture? He was intelligent enough to know that some colleagues thought him a bit of an anachronism in this age of classless professionalism, in army slang he was a 'Rupert'. What he needed was a success or two, that would do the trick, promotion and kudos could only be attained by getting results. He wanted to further his career and eventually enter politics. He ought to be good at that, as he already knew when to pull the trigger, grease a palm or slip an unseen knife home and he could dissemble with the best of them. It came with the job he had at this moment which he neither liked nor disliked; it was simply a means to an end. He certainly disliked some of the odious people they had to deal with however, informers and petty crooks and he abhorred the way some of his handlers treated their sources, looking out for them and mollycoddling them like some kind of agony aunt. Personally he felt no obligation to be open or honest with such human rubbish. He said nothing however as long as they gave what he was looking for: information. As for the Irish in general, well, what could one say? A brutish lot, the whole damn lot of them, both sides of the same coin concerned only with their centuries long grudges. It was all he could do to keep the contempt from his voice when he had to deal with them. He looked at his watch, a lovely old Omega left to him by his father and unbolted the back gate, sitting down again at the white metal garden table to finish his coffee. There was the sound of scrunching gravel and Keith Shepheard entered, a smile of greeting on his face as he approached and stood patiently.

"Good morning sir, a fine day don't you think?"

Molyneaux took a last sip, putting his cup down with a drawled reply, Winchester and Sandhurst in every syllable.

"Ye- e-s. Yes indeed."

He stood and began a slow walk around the edge of the well trimmed and watered lawn. It had been a scorching summer but he had ignored that bloody silly ban on sprinklers, having no intention of letting his plants and flowers perish, he enjoyed them too much. Keith kept step beside him. He found him pleasantly agreeable, indeed had studied his file approvingly. He had done well on the course before injury had disrupted his progress, but had then gone into intelligence and passed the source handling tests with flying colours, proving himself skilful, intelligent, resourceful and ruthless. Besides, anyone whose father was a Guards officer couldn't be bad. Molyneaux was pleased to have him as a handler, helping him run informers and agents. He now wished to have a chat and find out just how committed his new protégé would be.

"You've settled in well Keith, how did the meeting go yesterday?"

"Fine sir, he didn't have much high grade stuff to pass on but every little bit counts doesn't it?"

"Hope you didn't pay him too much."

"No sir, as you said, keep this one hungry."

"Yes. Good." He curled his lip and flared his nostrils as if he was sampling a particularly bad Burgundy. "Yes, Shepheard you know the old saying that if you roast an Irishman you'll always find another one to turn the spit. It's so simple really to catch a man; all you need is the right bait. I think your talents would have been wasted on the streets Keith, with mere surveillance. With our little unit you have more room to manoeuvre and use your initiative. You do appreciate the honour?"

"Yes indeed sir!" Keith replied enthusiastically. He meant it too, even if they were short of skilled handlers and the work load was tremendous. He was really enjoying the job, free to work outside normal structures in a privileged unit with seemingly unlimited resources, handling informers and agents. The thrill of being in a top branch of the intelligence tree was fantastic. Molyneaux continued.

"Excellent. I shall have an important task for you in the near future. Peter is off to Hong Kong so you'll have a new partner and some important sources to take care of. You will also step up one rank."

"Yes sir, thank you."

Molyneaux stopped and toed a small terracotta pot, then stooped to pick it up revealing a large white grub wriggling slowly underneath. He picked it up and put it on the palm of his hand, continuing his slow walk.

"You know sometimes Keith we have to use somewhat unorthodox methods to attain our ends?"

"Sir?"

"Our ends being the defeat of the terrorists of course."

"Yes sir."

"You have no aversion to these ways, there are so many grey areas aren't there?" His eyes swivelled and Keith nodded. "Yes, we have to remain within the law of course but even the law has grey bits, you understand?"

He stopped again and examined the ground where a tangle of ivy roots grew upwards, clinging to the wall, dark and shadowed at the bottom. A silken web extended down to the earth from the dark leaves and roots.

"We have to be as ruthless as they are, more so on occasion. Sometimes we even have to give a little to get something big in return." He bent down and gently coaxed and nudged the grub from his palm onto the web where it lay immobile for a few seconds. It moved and a large house spider shot out, seized the grub and dragged it writhing back to its hole. He straightened and turned to Keith, his eyes focused in an icy judging stare.

"We always have to see things in wider terms, the bigger picture, we have to get results to win. You understand?" Keith understood. He met his eyes and nodded grimly.

"Absolutely sir."

Molyneaux gave a satisfied noise of approval like a golfer watching his putt dropping as expected. Not much chance of Keith mollycoddling anyone or becoming too attached to a source; he knew Shepheard would do whatever was needed, as he was someone that hated losing.

"Good. I know you'll do your utmost to succeed, a lack of results will... disappoint me." Keith noted the current of smooth understated menace in his voice.

"I won't let you down you sir."

"When I heard you had just done the course I asked if I could have you as my assistant. I explained we knew each other for ages and worked well together, they approved so here you are. Welcome to the unit. Here, allow me to fill your glass dear boy."

Roy rubbed his chin as Keith finished speaking and headed to the bar, wondering at the coincidence and fate that had brought them together again. Immediately after the successful interception of Constable Carson's would be assassins, Roy was feeling pretty damn pleased with himself. He had acted swiftly and with initiative, a fact not unnoticed by Ben and Carl who had enthusiastically lauded him in the bar that night. Helen had sat across the table from him, her face resting in cupped hands as she appraised him and gave cool compliments. The RUC had arrived in minutes and cleared up, an open and shut case with the bad guys caught and certain to be jailed for a long many a day. All in all a cause for celebration. To Roy's chagrin this wasn't how some others saw things. They had been commended for their good work at the debriefing, and then Roy had been summoned for an interview with Captain Jack and another civilian dressed officer he remembered seeing once in training. Rob was just leaving and gave him a clap on the shoulder and handshake. Jack looked up from a file.

"Sit down Roy, we'd like to go over *again* a few details of what *happened* today." He didn't introduce the new figure who sat calmly watching him.

"It's all as you know sir, I've nothing new to add," said Roy.

"We may have a problem." said the other in a quiet, clipped voice. "You may have a problem. You were seen."

"Aye, true enough, but I can always change appearance and those who saw me are hardly likely to be on the street identifying me are they?"

Jack and the officer exchanged glances before Jack continued. "What if you were *spotted* by someone who isn't going down and will be walking around?"

"Sir?" asked Roy, tilting his head.

Again Jack looked at the new officer, who didn't answer the question directly. "You understand the position? It's the same for all operators. If you're face is known, you can't be used for surveillance work, at least not for some time and not in this area."

"I'd rather not transfer elsewhere sir..."

He was cut off sharply by the mild voice. "You will do as you are told or resign and return to unit!"

Roy shut up, concealing his resentment. Captain Jack gave a small reasonable smile. "You did well today Roy, nobody is *criticising* your operating skills but under the circumstances we feel some sort of temporary move may be best."

The other officer suddenly gave a grim laugh which he cut short like a man hearing a good joke, but remembering he was at a funeral.

"It's not bad news, not for you at any rate. I think you have the potential to join our unit and run informers and agents and if you pass selection you will be promoted and return here immediately for duties. You'll be gone a couple of months, time for memories to fade but you won't be too much on the street anyway. You have to look at this as an opportunity. Now, what do you say?"

"When do I begin?"

He had gone to advanced training and had spent yet more weeks on a course much subtler than any previous he had done. Certainly there was the usual weapons handling, fitness and technical detail, but now more emphasis was put on learning how to communicate, in effect how to *talk* to people. Not long ago, the very idea of speaking with those connected or actively involved with the Provisionals would have revolted him; it went against everything in his upbringing. The last year though he had learned a lot, and this distaste was now tempered by a realisation that the only way they were going to stop the IRA was by use of intelligence. This thought, and the fact that by using informers and agents he would be helping save lives enabled Roy to submerge his initial reluctance and dedicate himself fully to the tasks involved in passing the course. He learned not only the ways of targeting and making initial contacts with potential sources, but how to maintain existing source handler relations, to build up trust and extract as much information as possible. It was complicated and involved a lot of psychology, the source having to be carefully handled and in effect, bonded with. An experienced handler had answered his own unspoken question.

"Some of you may be wondering how you can maintain amiability with a source who may well be a complete prick. My own experience is that they come in different shapes and sizes, from loveable rogue looking for thrills and a bit of cash, to dedicated man or woman out solely to save lives even at the risk to their own. Some of them are decent people. You may find it easier than you think, but never forget, lives are on the line; theirs and yours." He had been passed and here he was waiting for Keith to return with a fresh pint.

"Penny for them?" Keith asked as he placed the glass in front of him.

"Oh I was just wondering, you know, about the personal side of things."

"Sorry matey, not with you there. Personal?" His voice took on an inquiring tone and he mouthed the last word as if it was foreign and meaningless. He took a sip and continued. "As far as I'm concerned I like them as far as they're useful. It pisses me off royally seeing some of these bastards walking around, knowing full well what they've done but we don't have enough to convict, or there's some technicality where they get off. I want to beat them and if using informers helps then so be it." He gave a wicked vulpine grin. "It'll be fun Roy.

Get that drink down your neck and we'll have another. Tomorrow I'll show you around. Cheers!"

Tin-Tin bent to his task at the table next to the window where the light was best. He sucked on his teeth in concentration, watched by Marty and Danny who kept glancing out of the sixth floor window at the Monday morning scene below. It was another grey windy day, the dim sun all but invisible as it hid, showing briefly and intermittently like a weak pen light moving behind thick, dirty white paper. Nothing of interest was going on, mothers with prams and toddlers, a few of the unemployed men up early with nowhere to go. Marty took a quick look himself. A couple of teenagers, finished with school and fresh to the unemployed ranks sat on a low wall, bored and smoking roll ups, scrutinising any faces not known to them. They weren't totally unemployed; in fact it could be argued they were serving their apprenticeship as so many had before them: lookout, errand running, driving, storing weapons before full graduation to active service, a balaclava taking the place of a mortar board hat. It was all mildly depressing. Danny continued to twitch the netting, drawing deeply on his cigarette before he also stepped back from the window.

Tin-Tin was still busy, the paraphernalia of his task lay scattered over the table but all within reach: two watches, super glue, bits of plastic tubing, a deep and large rectangular plastic tub, batteries, wiring, a small bulb and lastly a soldering iron which Tin-Tin now delicately used on a piece of board connecting wires and a glued battery. It looked complicated but it was perfectly safe, the detonator would only be attached at the last stage. Danny casually picked up the tube, his fingers nicotine orange against the white of the plastic and tilted it from side to side, feeling the gratifyingly heavy weight of the mercury inside flow from end to end. It brought an immediate and sharp rebuke from Tin-Tin.

"For fucks sake put it down! You've no gloves on even, what's the matter with you?"

Danny flushed and put it carefully back where it was instantly seized by Tin-Tin's surgically gloved hand and carefully wiped. He frowned, gently reproving like a mother with an errant child.

"You should know better Danny."

That was true enough Marty thought. After an explosion the Brits went over the area with a fine tooth comb and with some success. People had been convicted after their finger prints had been found on the smallest fragments of material. Tin-Tin worked on, absorbed in his task. He finally stopped soldering and tested his circuitry. The light bulb flashed and he gave a satisfied smack of his lips as if finishing a good meal, his voice now in sales mode.

"The art of bomb making. Another fine creation from the exclusive Terry Corr range, guaranteed to give your life a real boost."

"Ever had one go wrong?" Danny asked.

Tin-Tin raised his eyebrows and then his hands, the fingers spread. "How many fingers do you see Danny? Any road, if this fucker went wrong I'd be scattered far and wide, not that there's any chance of that but. It ain't like the old days."

That was a fact too. Over the years their bomb making had become more sophisticated through desperate necessity. Dozens of volunteers had died horribly mutilated deaths in the first years due to incompetence, primitive equipment and dodgy timers. Gone were the days of clothes pegs, tin tacks, fishing wire for booby traps, rubber bands and unstable explosives. Now their volunteers were taught carefully by experts in electronics. Marty eyed the tube containing the mercury with distaste, it was obvious that this particular device was going to be used as an under car booby trap. Once in place using a strong magnet, the timer would be set for twenty minutes at the end of which the bomb would be armed, the mercury would shift when the car moved and a circuit completed detonating the bomb. It had been used before with deadly results. The advantage was they didn't have to stick around and increase their chances of getting caught, but on the other hand and this was what made Marty uneasy, the risk of someone innocent getting done also increased. That had happened too. The wife or friend borrowing the vehicle, or even a child getting in for a lift. Marty had discussed it with Tinks who had the same misgivings, but Saunders had insisted they had a safe target yet to be revealed.

The orange street lamps glowed without warmth, the streets empty and glistening as more cold rain fell in a blustery uncertain wind that chased people away to their homes. A filthy night but good for checking the target, as being so quiet it made any attempt to follow them that much easier to spot. Any hint of surveillance and they would abort and wait for another opportunity. Martina was driving a borrowed Datsun, the owner having been asked politely with reassurances that it would be returned undamaged within a few hours. He had handed over the keys without fuss. Like everybody else in the district he knew the score and was not averse to helping, especially when there was no personal risk. He also understood that to complain or refuse was not a viable option. The Provos had more control and power in these particular streets than the security forces ever would; although the army passed through all the time, the IRA lived here.

She had seen Saunders earlier. He had quickly and efficiently given her the details to memorise, nothing was to be written down. The only other person present had been Gerry, his only contribution reminding her to be careful and not to be worried about abandoning the operation if she felt it was at all compromised. The safety of the volunteers always came first. So here she was, on this dark and dirty night on her way to the alien eastern outskirts to check out the target area.

Their intelligence had discovered a hotel bar where a few servicemen were known to drink, where they thought they were safe when off duty; to the IRA 'off duty' was a nonsense of naivety. A gun attack had been ruled out as too risky so far from base, so a booby trap was the logical solution. It would limit the destruction to the target and enable them to be well away in time. Tinks drove carefully, the windshield wipers squeaking and swishing, the noise competing with Downtown Radio. She turned it up as Pete Wylie sang 'The Story of the Blues'. Next to her Brendan hummed along as they passed over the Ormeau Road Bridge, the waters of the Lagan spitting and jumping in the downpour, deliberately taking a less direct route and so lessening the chance of a check point. Marty would not be involved, only Tin-Tin, Brendan and maybe Danny. Declan had been left with the operational details and this was his decision. They drove further along the Ormeau Road, Martina frequently checking the mirror, Brendan turning to watch as she turned into Jameson Street and stopped a minute, before resuming her roundabout drive and returning to the Ormeau Road. Brendan spoke, turning in his seat.

"You're all right, nothing following. Yourself?"

Martina didn't look at him, merely giving her blond fringe a quick shake, pursing her pretty lips and concentrating on the road. She had smelled drink on his breath. As if reading her mind Brendan rolled his eyes.

"All right, I had a wee one a little earlier there, just a six o'clock smile. I'm not stupid, I won't touch any tomorrow. Promise."

"I hope you're paying attention, it'll be just you and Terry with maybe Danny driving scout."

They drove on in near silence, Martina muting the radio as she peered through the now slackening rain at passing houses, streets and then avenues which soon became lanes as the suburbs were left behind. Eventually she switched the wipers off as they entered the hotel car park, passing a board announcing 'Disco every Friday'. She stopped close to one of the low white walls that enclosed the place, under rustling trees that dripped and pattered rain water onto the car as she switched off the engine. They studied the place carefully. The car park was large and seemed to be divided, one part for guests nearer the hotel and the other where they were, for visitors. The hotel was a large white Georgian style mansion, with chimney structures at both ends, potted trees at the entrance, with modern wings attached to increase the accommodation. The foyer and several of the windows gave off a welcoming yellow glow, the bar was in the left wing and showed dull orange through thick glass windows. Martina spoke without turning her head.

"O.K, Brendan. You saw the board on the way in about the disco?" He nodded, now hard faced and alert. "Right, according to Frankie they have this to drum up a bit of extra money and quite a few people come from round the area, and from what we've learned it's becoming a bit of a pickup place for bored soldiers, mainly engineers, catering corps and that type. Because it's way out here they think it's a safe bet, it hasn't ever been out of bounds, never an incident which means they're become a wee bit complacent. We've been watching for weeks now and it's not always the same people come, apart from two soldiers who have been here nearly every Friday we have. They drive a yellow Audi 80 with a black roof, you can't miss it. They usually park this side, about eight o'clock or so, stay for a few pints and then leave. That's the target."

"So they're just there for a beer? No pickups?"

"Men! No, Frankie says these two have wedding rings and actually are here just for a Friday night social drink, besides they never stay long enough to chat anyone up and they've never been seen even trying."

"O.K, tomorrow." Brendan tapped his front teeth with his finger nail, thinking. "What's the weather forecast?"

"Same as now."

"Grand. The less people outside the better." He looked at the hotel again. "I'm surprised this place hasn't been done before, a car bomb could do a lot of damage and no civilians need get in the way."

"No, you can't park the car near enough and broken windows don't amount to much damage. Besides, no one wants another La Mon."

Brendan agreed, thinking about the gruesome posters of incinerated bodies that had appeared after that balls up of an operation. Twelve ordinary innocent husbands and wives, just out for a meal in a hotel had been burnt to death by a massive fire bomb. It had been disaster for the IRA.

"O.K, Martina lets go."

The transit van was parked at the edge of a playing field next to some road repairs, the driver seemingly bored, smoking with one arm leaning out of the open window, just another worker taking a sneaky break. The place had been carefully chosen to give a good view all around, the road works providing good cover. The van was white or had been once upon a time, but now it was so filthy it seemed even generous Irish rainfall couldn't wash away the grime. Actually, the dirt was carefully contrived. Inside, Keith sat waiting impatiently. Gerald McKee, otherwise known as 'Big Gee' to all and sundry was always bloody late. He stopped tapping his fingers and called to Roy in the driver's seat.

"See anything?"

"Aye, Maggie Thatcher's taking a dump behind the bushes there, Gerry Adams is passing her some paper, Elton John is still standing... picking his nose, and Ronnie Reagan's making a speech."

Keith didn't even smile. He was annoyed, this was costing time and they had someone else to see today so the bastard better have some useful information. Right now he was paying money for little return and his patience was thinning. Molyneaux had been on his back again, looking at him with those chilly appraising eyes, despite the fact they had caused the aborting of two attacks in as many weeks. He wanted more. He was like a hungry chick in the nest, his beak always open for another morsel, never satiated. Just then Roy spotted 'Big Gee' coming towards them with his usual swaying sailor's gait as he ambled towards the van, the happy ever present grin on his big face. With his six foot two bulk and longish curled black hair, Roy thought he resembled a cross between Peter the Great and a merry citizen from a Jan Steen painting.

Forty two and a living advert for the old one about life beginning at forty. He had certainly begun a whole new life at forty, that of an informer, his natural jolly demeanour now hiding his second secret life. He was married with a girl and a boy and owed allegiance to nobody but them and his wife Martha. She knew what he was, but her only care was he didn't get caught. She had never had much time for the Provisionals since they had shaved the head of her best friend and tied her to a lamp post some years ago, a public humiliation for the heinous crime of going out with a soldier. Since then she had tried her best to ignore it all, mouthing a few Republican sentiments where appropriate, but she had never forgotten or forgiven. Gerald had at first been all for the IRA, seeing them as defenders of the people against their British and Protestant oppressors. Although not a member, he had helped out, driving people and letting them use his house for meetings, and even storing some weapons now and again. His change of heart had been a gradual process of disillusionment and doubts as he noticed the dreadful results of 'mistakes' and abuses by certain volunteers. Then one day that little runt of a man Donal had too much to drink in the club and started swearing at Gerald for no particular reason. He had ignored the wee shite until to his utter humiliation he had been half turned in his stool and slapped back handed across the face, the noise of it turning every head to witness his shame. Donal was a volunteer and friends with some very tough people and therefore inviolate. Gerald had sat dumb with shock, the hot fury welling inside him, unable to retaliate. There was a silence and then a girlish laugh before one of Donal's mates came over to lead him away, another putting a placating hand on Gerald's shoulder.

"Sorry about that Gee, the wee man's had one too many. No hard feelings eh?"

He went out with Donal. Laughing. He saw the others, avoiding his red faced glare, talking behind their hands, the whispers deafening. The next day he complained but nothing was done, not even an apology from that toe rag midget. He had walked about the rest of that evening and the next day with little else on his mind, burning with rage, his head buzzing and his hand constantly rubbing at his cheek, as if to wipe away a smudge of dirt or stain, the physical injury tiny, but the insult and disgrace massive and ever present. It was then his disillusionment with the movement turned to a real hatred and need to do something about these people, to get even and he genuinely believed help his community at the same time. He drove to the other side of the city and walked into a joint RUC Army base and offered his services. Once committed, he started to enjoy life once more with his usual gusto, now spiced with an extra thrill and the added cold desert of revenge.

Watching him walking towards the van, whistling and swinging his arms like he hadn't a care in the world, Roy couldn't help smiling. To his amazement he had discovered that he actually liked the man, despite his background, despite his politics and religion, despite everything; the man was a great character with the typical Belfast wit he had grown up with himself. He also respected him and his reasons for helping them, knowing it wasn't simply revenge and although he took money he wasn't greedy. Indeed on one occasion he hadn't asked for anything and had left once he had passed on some information where a couple of grenades were hidden. Money was not his motivation and Roy liked that. Keith didn't give a shit, regarding them all as traitors, scum and just a resource to be squeezed. He despised them as much as the IRA although his acting ability was top class and it never showed.

"What about ye?"

"Alright, how's the missus Gee?"

"Fine. See the game the other night..." Keith's head poked out past Roy, like angry Mr Punch at the show.

"In the back. Now! You're fucking late. Again!" He disappeared and they heard him muttering in the back as Roy and Gee shared smirks before he ambled to the back and climbed in. Keith called to Roy, giving Gee a withering look. "You can drive while we speak, we've lost enough time as it is."

Roy waved to their back up and pulled away, followed immediately by another car. They never went alone to a meeting, the source could have been turned or discovered and followed.

"Okay, what do you have?" asked Keith.

Gee couldn't help winding him up, deliberately taking his time as he rolled a cigarette and lit it before answering, amused at the obvious impatience on Keith's features. His own face took on a look of exaggerated puzzlement.

"What do you mean?"

Keith's fist clenched on his thigh before relaxing. He nodded slowly and said, "Very funny, now seriously, you called this meeting, what's up?"

"Oh Aye, that's it. I'm going fishing this weekend, d'ye fancy coming?"

Roy glanced around and burst into laughter at the look on Keith's face, who was struggling to keep calm.

"Only joking you," said Gee, giving him a playful tap on the shoulder. "Seriously now, I overheard something the other day about a hit being planned on a prison officer living in Newtownabbey. That's all I know, no name but that should be enough eh?"

"Anything else?" Keith asked, resuming his impassive gaze.

"Only rumours," said Gee. He rubbed his chin thoughtfully. "Tittle tattle, nothing sure like. They don't always talk in the back of the cab you know, and I've to be careful as well so don't be expecting me to ask questions, right?"

Keith concentrated on getting as much background information as possible in place of operational news. It was all of value, who was seen where and just as importantly who hadn't been seen around for a while, who was getting married or seeing someone else, how was morale and what were the main fears and concerns of the moment. All of it went into their security mosaic. The smallest particle of information seemingly unimportant and unconnected could be that missing piece revealing the picture. A half hour later and they were finished. They dropped Gee off, Roy handing him an envelope containing a hundred pounds.

"Take it easy big man."

"I will that, see ya!"

Keith managed a fairly warm smile as he waved him on his way then glared at his back, his grin vanishing as he murmured his own farewell. "Arsehole."

It began drizzling as it grew dark and they headed for their last rendezvous, the lights from the transit cutting through the fine mist like rain. This time a pub, back up was already in position, inside and out, waiting and watching. It was a gloomy place, the lighting poor, probably to hide the stains and grime of years. It wasn't busy, a few early drinkers, an unshaven old man sat alone with his cloth cap, grubby rain coat and pint of mild. Roy bought a couple of pints of Bass and they sat near the juke box to mask conversation, listening to The Smiths 'What Difference Does it Make'. The toilet door to their left opened and a waft of stale piss emerged along with a figure that shuffled nearer to them, Roy registering the unsavoury presence from the corner of his eye before looking up and greeting Daly.

Roy looked at him, careful to keep his face blank before going to order a pint of Guinness and a Powers chaser to lubricate his tongue. Daly was a truly unpleasant man, his appearance matching his character. He was nearing fifty, with receding sandy hair, a long nose, blotchy pock marked face, dry flaky skin and bad teeth to compliment his pungent halitosis. His dress was comparably shabby, old and functional and nothing fitted or matched. Roy looked at his scuffed boots, frayed brown corduroys, a custard yellow shirt and dark green v neck sweater all covered by a raincoat of pale but uncertain colour; it looked as if he had robbed a charity shop in the dark.

He had never had a job in his life or even looked for one, a petty criminal from Cork he had moved here some time ago since terrible rumours had took hold that he had interfered with a young lad on the estate. He hadn't waited to be questioned personally by the father, but had prudently packed his meagre belongings and got the train as far away as possible up to Belfast. He stayed with his one remaining cousin in Ballymurphy before moving into a derelict when his cousin became rapidly fed up with his filthy habits, such as never flushing the toilet, leaving dirty clothes and used tissues all over the place and hardly ever bathing. The small room he had been allocated was soon a stinking midden of bad feet, soiled clothing and semen stained bed, but the real reason his cousin told him to go was the uneasy feeling he gave him. He had seen how Daly leered out of the window at passing women and girls, and felt queasy at some of his tasteless jokes. Having no desire to be associated with such a character, family or not, he told him to go.

Daly wasn't stupid, and although he couldn't spell intellectual he had a rat like street cunning. He drew his dole and stayed aloof, not wanting anyone to know of his past, not that anyone showed much interest anyway in the smelly tramp like figure that drifted about at all hours. That cunning he had been putting to good use for several years to supplement his dole, as with all that walking about he started to notice things, suspicious movements and people hiding things. Such tit bits of information might have a value to certain others so he began watching and passing everything on to the RUC. To his annoyance they had not taken him seriously, had contemptuously paid him a few quid now and then and passed him on to the army, which they would never have done had they thought him of value, the snobby bastards. Since then he had been informing for the odd tenner and couple of pints on a regular basis. He got on well with his latest handlers although the Belfast lad was a bit narky. He had no remorse about what he was doing and never had. He was both physically and morally of no fixed abode.

Keith took a sip as Daly sat next to him, opening a bag of Tayto cheese and onion crisps, trying to keep his head back as far as possible when Daly spoke, and the repellence he felt from his features. He studied him again, marvelling at the state of the guy, trying not to laugh as he noticed a tiny bit of skin flake off onto the table joining some crumbs from the packet as he scratched one hand with the other. For the most part his information was very low grade and he had contemplated dropping him, but he didn't take much time and he was cheap, so he kept him on board. For the time being that was and you never knew when he might come up with something important. Keith eyed him now like a crocodile before submerging to get closer to its prey, thinking, yes, he might have other uses. Daly spoke, his voice low with conspiracy.

"I was having a wander about the other day..."

Keith interrupted as he wanted to keep it short. "Yes, and?"

Daly pouted and knocked back the whiskey. "Stewartstown Road, by the sweet shop at the start, two men messing about behind a lamp post, acting rare. Might be nothing..." Keith took it in; it probably was nothing, a couple of workmen fixing it perhaps, still he'd check it out.

"Took a stroll along the Falls too a couple of days ago, you know Leeson Street..."

Keith let him ramble a few minutes, both he and Roy trying to breathe through their mouths as Daly gave them house numbers and cars parked with suspicious characters carrying suspicious items. Again nothing to write home about but he'd cross check. At last Daly was finished.

"You could have phoned on the special number with all this you know," said Keith.

Roy nodded his agreement. He certainly could have, and saved them a journey, with the bonus that halitosis couldn't travel down the phone line, but then Daly was obviously in need of a little cash. They wished he had a bank account. He gave a quick glance around the bar, checking to see if anyone was watching, then thrust his hand out. Keith put a ten and then a five pound note onto the table taking care not to touch the scabby long nailed hand that seized the money. Getting a scratch from those black rimmed nails would probably mean a tetanus injection or Detol swabbing at the very least. Fucking tramp. He got up and slid out through the door.

"So, that's us for the day. No one else is there?" Roy asked.

Keith exhaled deeply before answering. "No, that's it. Back to base and do a little checking in the files, see what we've got. Incidentally did you read *his* file in full? It doesn't make pleasant reading I can tell you, even some gossip he's a bit of a nonce."

Roy's face scrunched up in disgust although it didn't really surprise him. He thought about the extensive files, some of them the containing details of suspects he had seen before in other surveillance material with the Det. He even recognised a recently taken photograph as one he had surreptitiously taken himself at a funeral, zooming in for a close up on the well known Republican face, like so many others he had examined, with a grim expression as he helped carry a coffin. He wondered briefly about this latest distasteful revelation.

"How'd you find that out?"

"I know lots of things cock."

"Well we got something of value today with Gee."

Keith peered at him over his glass before putting it down and wiping his mouth. "Waste of a hundred notes matey, I already knew it."

"How?"

Keith paused before making a decision. "We bugged his car and his flat, that's how. He talks a lot with the missus and I didn't want him leaving out anything of importance. He doesn't know so I wouldn't mention it if I was you."

Roy was shocked, not at the hesitance from Keith and the 'need to know' bollocks, but at the fact they were breaking trust and as he saw it needlessly putting a source's life at risk. If that bug was ever found...

"He knows the risks Roy, you know the saying. 'Big boy's games, big boy's rules'. I much prefer my own saying though, 'use 'em and lose 'em." He gave a short yipping laugh and Roy got a peep into his dark side again, seeing that Keith's ugliness was anything but just skin deep.

"Sorry Keith, but it's a mistake. Short term gains maybe, but if we lose too many sources who's going to trust us in the future if they think we don't give a shit. Who's going to risk a bullet through the face on those terms? We have to look after them, even the likes of auld fart breath Daly."

Keith looked at him now with real irritation, a slight contempt even. Perhaps he had been wrong about his friend who was right about one thing; it was short term gains but neither he nor Molyneaux were bothered about that. They wanted success now, and not merely spoiling tactics and foiling of operations, but infiltration and real disruption with arrests and if necessary executive action. He spoke slowly and coldly.

"You just concentrate on your job without all the moral shit, and try to remember who's running this show, O.K?"

That evening after the short drive to their operations room in Lisburn, Keith and Roy sat, chairs tilted, going through files for the umpteenth time, cross checking information before writing out a Military Intelligence Source Report to Major Molyneaux, warning of a probable attack on the prison officer. All the jargon and acronyms sometimes provoked Roy to wearily close his eyes and yawn: MISR, SITREPs, SOPs, UCP,TCG, OOB, that was a good one meaning Out Of Bounds and one that always made him grimace UCBT or to put it another way, under car booby trap. Their office was strictly members only. No one outside their small unit had access, the information they held was shared only with other divisions of the intelligence community such as Special Branch, MI5 and other senior RUC and army officers with high enough clearance. On paper their unit was still attached to the 14th Intelligence company and officially they didn't exist, but in practice they had their own seemingly limitless budget and resources and own voice on the Co Ordination Group. This sharing and co operation was fine in theory and worked most of the time, but as in anything where human personalities were involved, frailties were exposed by rivalries, jealousy, personal antagonisms and private ambitions. The one thing they never shared were sources. Their informers and agents were ran and handled only by themselves. Neither Roy nor Keith knew the identities of all these sources; some were very, very special and were handled only by the top people, using kid gloves and lavish bribes.

Their office was Spartan and bare of anything but the functional, with several large grey combination locked filing cabinets, a very expensive computer with a massive 128 kb RAM , white walls with a huge street map of Belfast, and another smaller one of the whole province with a clock ticking silently in between. There was a paper shredder and three phones of differing colours, black and red and white that waited under the bright light. The white phone was for everyday use, the black for internal official use and the red, confidential and secure for incoming calls from their sources, carefully filtered and the numbers changed frequently. The short sometimes whispered conversations that passed on this line could change a life forever. It was manned night and day.

The extent of their intelligence had been a surprise to Roy, the web of informers much broader than he believed possible, enabling them to stop many attacks before they happened, which frustrated the terrorists and satisfied him personally. Some attacks still got through however, less here than in places like South Armagh, but overall in Belfast they seemed to be getting on top. He had been reading a dossier yesterday about a terrorist based in Dundalk who had recently come to their attention and was, so a source now told them, back in Belfast. Annoyingly there was no accompanying photo yet, but the name looked vaguely familiar. This boy had some track record if the source codenamed 'Hermes' was to be believed. He had been going for years without a single arrest leaving a trail of destruction. It was reported he'd even been to the Lebanon. Roy mused on how he hadn't come to their attention before now.

Roy tipped his chair further until he was leaning against the wall, now reading through a different personality card of a known sympathiser living in Ballymurphy that they believed might be on the cusp of becoming a little bit more active. As well as name, address, national insurance and phone number, the file had his car type, registration and a myriad of other information concerning his extended family, friends, girlfriends, acquaintances, where he went to drink , hobbies, membership of clubs, in fact just about everything bar his favourite colour. The photo clipped to one corner was only a couple of months old, taken at another funeral, the subject taking his turn as pall bearer, the shadow on his shoulder. Roy looked at it briefly wondering who had taken it. He still socialised with some of his old crew from time to time, occasionally sharing a drink with Rob too and discussing the overall situation, but neither of them were specific. He was amused at Keith's palpable distrust as he came and sat with them once, all good natured cheer and waving ears.

Keith was busy typing as Roy lowered the file and peeked over the top of it at his colleague and friend, examining him in a new light. He had always known Keith as someone with a cruel sense of humour and a ruthless streak, but this had never bothered him, indeed that part of him had provided a lot of fun over the years, bad people unfortunately being usually a sight more fascinating than the good. Since teaming up again he had noticed a change in Keith that made him feel less comfortable however; he had become harder, more ambitious, his humour darker and even bitter. There was a time when they would have shared everything without question, the bond between them cemented by common experience, fear and bloody risk, but this had subtly changed, as if they were no longer travelling the same direction anymore on life's highway. Keith had taken a turn into selfish avenue, another left into ego street and was currently driving along ambition road with Roy now wondering if he was little more than a passenger in the same car. Keith looked up from his typing, not at Roy but at the white phone, then at the clock, then at the phone again.

"Are you expecting a call?" asked Roy.

"Yes." The dark flecked grey eyes watched him, contemplating. "Yes," he repeated, "from home. My mother rang last week to tell me to expect a call from my father. I promised I would take the call. He's got cancer, it's terminal."

"God! I'm so sorry."

Keith shrugged and resumed typing, mentioning a two hundred pounds payment. A minute later the white phone rang, very loud in the strained silence. Roy got up to leave, Keith waved for him to sit, lighting a cigarette.

"It won't take a minute..." He typed another unhurried line, letting the phone ring some more before picking it up. Roy resumed reading, intrigued and uneasy at being present. Maybe Keith just needed some friendly support.

"Hello." He listened for a few seconds. "Yes, I know, mother told me. What's that?" His voice was smooth and emotionless, "Whatever do you mean, *Why me?* Why not you? Good night."

He casually replaced the receiver and carried on with his typing. Roy sat, unable to believe what he had just heard. He had always known of the deep resentment Keith had against his Da, but this was something else. He stopped reading, unable to concentrate. Keith read through the MISR, smiled and got up to go.

It was another evening of lashing rain and swerving winds as Sergeant Pete Walls pulled up outside the hotel, happy as it was Friday and they were finished until Sunday evening when they would be back on duty. It was getting a bit routine just like any other job, even to the point of having a Friday evening after work drink. Sat next to him was his mate Ian, who also liked a pint. He was a Sergeant too, both of them in the Signals Corps. The Friday night drink was the only relaxation they had, both of them now well into their third tour of Northern Ireland and thoroughly bored with it. They had never seen action and that was the way they liked it. There was no danger, they stayed most of the time in barracks, but all the same they couldn't wait to finish and get back to Germany as here they were merely marking time.

"Couldn't you have parked a bit nearer the door?" Ian said. "Wouldn't want to get my hair wet,"

"Poof!" Pete snorted as they exited and made the short dash to the warm welcoming glow of the hotel.

They ordered a couple of pints and took a seat, noticing it was still quiet at this hour, a few scattered couples around the tables with two women nearer the bar in animated conversation. Pete studied them and with a start recognised one of them from his last tour a couple of years ago, the same shoulder length curly dark hair, oval tanned looking face with a cute dimple. She'd put on a bit of weight but looked good enough all the same. He noted her dress, white with a black belt and shoulder pads and legs that ended in white high heels. He unconsciously patted and smoothed his hair as he thought about the last time he had seen her under similar circumstances, he and a mate out for a drink and she and her mate out on the razzle and what the wife didn't know wouldn't hurt her. He nudged Ian just as she turned to look at him with the same surprised recognition, before flashing him a nice open smile. With Ian he wouldn't normally have bothered as he was happily married whatever that meant, but he knew an invitation when he saw one and wasn't going to refuse this unexpected opportunity. Ian was looking at the other woman. Not bad he thought, dressed the same but in darker blue, about the same age, but fatter and blonder. She smiled.

"Do you know them?"

"Yeh, I seem to remember her name was Jane, don't know the other one but they're up for it. Come on and I'll introduce you."

"What about..." Ian hesitated, doubt in his eyes.

"Don't worry about it," said Pete, laughing and patting his cheeks. "No one will ever know. Relax." Then he got up, pint in hand and glancing down at his groin he muttered, "Lead on Dick, you're in charge."

A man reading his paper at the bar slid off his stool unnoticed, gave his glass to the barmaid for washing and went into the lobby where a large grey pay phone hung on the wall. He pulled out a coin and dialled a local number, carefully handling it by the edges and inserting the ten pence piece as the person waiting at the other end immediately answered. He spoke a few terse words and putting the phone down carefully on its cradle, looked around before giving it a surreptitious wipe, then picked up his paper and left.

Martina put the phone down and gave a quick nod to Brendan, Tin-Tin and Danny who yawned nervously as they rose from the couch and quickly went to their cars, Danny leading with the others following close behind. This was the nearest safe house to the hotel, but it was still a twenty minute drive, time enough unless the target left early. There was tension in the car and not just from nerves. Terry glanced at Brendan tight lipped, the bomb at his feet under a blanket, perfectly safe until he armed it. He had arrived earlier to discover a worried Martina and Danny already there, but no sign of Brendan who had turned up with less than half an hour to spare, dishevelled and sleepy, unshaven with bloodshot eyes. He had obviously been on the piss the night before. Tin-Tin had exploded.

"Look at the cut of you! I hope you've not taken any drink today?"

"Nope! Not a drop, just a carry out last night. Or was it early this morning?" he waved a dismissive hand as if swatting a fly and broke into song tunelessly. "I didn't wake up this morning 'cos I didn't go to bed, I was watching the whites of my eyes turn red...anyway I'm sober."

"The fucking eyes on you, Jesus!"

"You should see them from my side."

They drove in near silence, the only noise the swish of wipers and beat of rain. They approached the hotel and Danny drove on, his job done as Brendan turned in, his reddened eyes now alert and searching. He immediately spotted the distinctive yellow Audi and parked expertly next to it. There were as yet few other cars. Tin-Tin was already bent down as Brendan scanned about them. Now came the real risk.

"O.K, go!"

Terry was out of the car and scrabbling under the Audi by the driver's door within seconds. Brendan shifted over and gingerly passed the weighty plastic box, now covered in tape to his outstretched hands. There was a sound of scratching, grunting and a splash as Tin-Tin worked, setting the timer that would arm it in ten minutes, then a dull metallic clunk as the heavy duty magnets on the top attached it to the underside of the chassis. Brendan tapped anxiously on the steering wheel as Tin-Tin heaved himself from under, panting with excitement and effort as he got in, the back of his coat now sodden black.

"O.K, done, let's go."

An hour later Pete, Ian and their new friends Jane and Gillian were preparing to leave. Jane had convinced them she knew of a place that was much better crack and that the night was young, with a wink that had Pete licking his lips in anticipation. They got up, Pete taking a quick look out of the window at the rain that had started up again. Ian finished his last drops, now a little more relaxed.

"Hang on, I'm just going for a tinkle." Gillian nodded her agreement. "Me too."

Pete was already on his way out, now arm in arm with a slightly tipsy Jane. He shouted over his shoulder, "Alright, I'll bring the car over. I wouldn't want you to get your hair wet!"

They left the hotel running, Jane giggling as she tottered on her high heels. Pete was there first and got in, leaning over to open the passenger door. Jane got in. He started up and moved off, meaning to halt just in front of the doorway where he could see Ian waiting for Gillian to reappear. He felt a thump under his seat and then it was instantly bright hot daylight and for a fraction of a second he saw the hotel wobble before he felt himself flying painlessly with a roaring whoosh in his ears. The flash and tremendous bang made Ian duck his head. He turned to see the car had become a flaming ripped tin, a last bit of metal hitting the ground with a hollow clank as he stood transfixed. There was a scream behind him and shouting as he took in the whole infernal tableaux. The roof of the car seemed to have been punched upwards by a giant fist from the inside, the bonnet was gone, one door blown five metres away, the other hanging by a thread of twisted metal, and two figures either side, one of them crawling and trying feebly to beat out a small flame on the leg before falling back. The other was Jane and she was still and smouldering. Ian came out of shock and rushed to where they lay, now joined by Gillian. Amazingly Pete was still alive although he had drifted into unconsciousness, his body and clothes burnt, shredded and torn, the legs were a twisted mess of angles and his face was bloody and streaked black. Gillian was crying as she held on to Jane, who had also by freak chance been blown out alive. At first she had felt nothing, but now she awakened to a gnawing pain that rapidly became excruciating, staring down at where her legs had been removed at the knees, her feet still in the burning, hissing car. There was little blood, the heat having cauterised the wounds, the same searing heat having done the same to where her nose had been. Ian looked at her and tried not to vomit, that shocked marble white staring face, stupid looking without a nose, like an ancient Roman statue that had been wantonly vandalised. Somebody brought blankets and they waited crying in the rain.

Frank Saunders was hungry this morning and decided to really treat himself and have a cooked breakfast. He patted his concave stomach and thoughtfully ran a hand over his skinny ribs. He was rarely alone, there was always work to be done, plans to make, orders to give or pass down through the chain of command. This Saturday though he would take it easy, he only had O'Mahony to see tomorrow and Martina on Monday.

He finished reading through Republican News and looked up at Gary sat in the stuffed armchair watching TV, legs flung carelessly over one side, ashtray balanced precariously, smoke rising in a straight line to the ceiling. He liked Gary and allowed him privileges he wouldn't with others, such as puffing roll ups in his living room and being a little untidier than he would tolerate in himself even. Gary was only twenty one, a big fresh faced lad from Whiterock who had been in the movement one way or another his whole life. Right now he was a sort of unofficial body guard cum messenger, who often slept over like a faithful watch dog. Although it was relatively safe here Frankie believed in taking precautions, and having Gary there might buy him valuable minutes in an emergency. He had determined long ago that the idiom of the revolutionary being a doomed man need not apply to him.

"Hey Gary, how about doing us a good hearty breakfast? There's bacon and sausage and a couple of chops in the fridge." Gary turned, interested, crushed out the roll up and swung off the chair heading for the kitchen.

"Good man," said Frankie, his eyes following him out. He would have to have a word with him about wearing what he scathingly thought of as the 'Provo uniform' of boots, stone washed jeans and that bomber jacket. He had intelligence, his watchful eyes rarely missed anything; he could do better than to emulate a common volunteer.

Half an hour later and Frank sat at the table with three pork chops and a nice pot of tea, Gary had the bacon and sausages, noisily consuming them with bread and lots of ketchup sat in the armchair again. There was a knock on the front door that made them both stop, four knocks and then two. Gary looked at Frankie, who shrugged before speaking.

"I wasn't expecting anyone. Go see who it is there's a good lad." He started in on the last chop with knife and fork.

Gary came back in and sat down followed by Martina and Marty who stood in front of the dining table. Frankie continued eating, scraping on the plate as he cut. Martina spoke first, her voice cracking slightly.

"Where the hell did you get your intelligence for that carry on last night? You told me there would be no innocent people hurt!"

Frankie swallowed. "There were none," he said, and resumed his precise cutting before popping in another mouthful.

"Haven't you heard the news then? From what they said that poor woman might not survive!"

He chewed some more and carefully downed his cutlery before answering. He could see she was angry as well as upset. "I repeat, there were no *innocent* people hurt. Well done. You helped in a successful attack on the forces of occupation without loss to ourselves."

He picked up a bone, napkin at the ready as he nibbled the last flesh. Marty looked at Tinks and put a hand on her shoulder, seeing she was near tears. She had taken the news silently this morning and remained tight lipped all the way here. He knew exactly how she felt, he had been thinking a lot recently about his own participation in the killing of Thomas Bailey, feeling lied to and ill used. He had experienced a new and unwelcome sensation. He had felt bad about it, guilty even. He looked at Frankie, sat there all prim; nibble nibble, and then dabbing his mouth with the damned cloth like he was in a fucking restaurant or something. Tinks voice went up in pitch, sounding like a child lied to at Christmas.

"You told me they couldn't pick anyone up, no chance of it you said. You didn't tell it straight!"

Frankie dropped the bone onto the plate with a final definitive clack. He spoke calmly as he cleaned his fingers one by one. "You know the risks. Don't be standing there and saying you didn't know things like this could happen, if anyone deceived you it was you yourself." His slow thin smile stretched outwards. "Anyway, one soldier and one soldier's whore, you should be pleased to have been involved in such a success."

Martina took a quick step forwards intending to slap him. Marty pulled her back. She brushed away an angry tear, head slumped at his words. The noisy eating of Gary had stopped as he watched with an alert but neutral expression. Frankie stood up. Newly cleaned hands resting lightly on the linen he moved away from the table to indicate he expected them to leave.

"Martina, you must put this behind you. I'll see you on Monday. As arranged," he said.

"C'mon, let's go," Marty whispered to her and turned her towards the door. He gave her a tissue and threw a last, feeble but satisfying Parthian shot over his shoulder, knowing Frankie to be sensitive about his scrawny figure.

"You should watch how much you're eating there Frankie, my Da always said a good feed might kill you."

Twin blotches of anger coloured Frankie's cheeks as he noted Gary's smirk and listened to that disrespectful laughter all the way to the door.

They drove as far as Carrickfergus some distance along the coast, Martina needing to get out of the city and breathe some clean fresh air away from the urban sprawl. They drove past the old castle, parked the car and walked along the sea front, descending steps to get to the shore line. She was still angry, as much at her own naive stupidity as anything, it galled her that maybe that skinny misogynistic wee bastard was right. She had *allowed* herself to be deceived, had known all along what might happen, had known deep down that people like Frankie didn't really give a damn who got in the way. Before though, it had been other people doing it. She loathed herself and with a new clarity realised she wasn't up to doing anything like this ever again. She looked at Marty with a new understanding. He in turn looked at her and recognised her emotions. Now she knew. They stopped and looked at the sea, grey as city concrete, the weather uncertain.

"Did you feel this way after your first time?" she asked.

"No. That was different but, a different place and time. A different me maybe."

"What about now?"

"I don't know."

"What about after Bailey was..."

"I don't know!" He hardly ever raised his voice at her, this last was shouted in her face. She fell back a step. Continued walking.

"Marty, let's just go away. You've done your bit and more, let the likes of O'Mahony and Saunders do their own dirty work."

"It's not as simple as that..."

"Yes it is! Volunteers come and go all the time, they just walk away, sometimes for a wee while and sometimes for good."

"That's not what I meant." He stopped again, looking out at the sea as if he might find the answers bobbing about there. "Has it all been for nothing? Do I stop believing, give up? Have we been wrong to fight?"

He turned as she touched his face, tears again brimming blue. She shook her head slowly, dislodging the first drop as salty as the sea breeze that blew at them.

"No, it wasn't wrong, there had to be change. There has been change, we haven't been beaten, we have a voice now. Marty, there was a lot of injustice, there still is, but I don't want to be making new ones... like I helped do the other night. I won't ever feel this way again, there has to be another way."

He was thinking, remembering his brother Thomas in jail for sitting in a car with the wrong people, his father and the mark they had left on him, also the conversation last year with his Da after another mistake that had left an innocent bystander dead. "There's been an apology for that Da," he had half heartedly said, remembering again the scorn on his father's face as he answered. "Oh that's alright then, I'm sure his wee daughters will be right as rain knowing that." A more recent scene popped into his head of a woman screaming as she saw the body of her husband Thomas Bailey. He ran his fingers through his hair and breathed out hard, nothing seemed to be clear anymore. He wanted to see his brother and talk to Brendan.

"I don't know... We'll see."

One person who had no doubts whatsoever about what he was doing was at that moment entering the garden of Major Molyneaux for a second meeting in as many days. The major seemed to spend more time here than at base, liking to work from home. Keith momentarily thought he might want to query expenses, but seeing him now, sat at the metal table with another man, his fleeting concern was wiped away. Molyneaux waved him over with an affable smile.

"Good morning Shepheard, take a seat. Davis was just leaving."

Davis, although dressed in civilian clothing had military written all over him from the top of his close cropped head to the polished shine of his shoes. He gathered up a manila folder, nodded at Keith and exited. Molyneaux waited until they could hear his shoes scrunching on the gravel outside the gate and a car door slamming shut. Molyneaux tried to put some sympathy into his voice.

"Sorry to hear about your father, terrible news."

"Yes sir."

Keith waited, wondering how he knew about this so soon. Not that it mattered, and at least it wasn't a complaint about how much money was being spent, but now he thought about it properly, that wasn't likely. From what Keith had seen of Molyneaux he had a typically Patrician contempt for cash, despising it as vulgar, just like others who had always had it and never had to worry or even think about it. Keith thought for a second how Molyneaux would cope with no money, see how vulgar he found it then, on the bones of his arse.

"Any problems Keith?"

"No sir, everything is going fine."

"Yes." He rubbed his nose. "We certainly are getting a good volume of information. TCG is pleased I might add. So am I, we have done well in recruiting, in fact you might say we have sources to spare." He gave Keith a sidelong glance. "Yes. There is nothing wrong with the quantity of information on a tactical level, but we could use more quality stuff. It's a shame we don't have more sources in their higher positions. What do you think?"

Keith paused before answering, waiting to see if he would come straight out and say what he wanted. "Yes sir, I agree."

Molyneaux continued. "When the terrorists adopted the cell structure it limited the damage, an informer could only really tell us specifics about his particular cell, the infection was localised so to speak. I thought perhaps we should be concentrating more on the higher echelons. We might be able to help a couple of our sources, those with potential such as Hermes for example to penetrate further up. You know, give a helping hand."

"What exactly do you mean sir?"

"To get our source better insulated within their organization he needs to be successful and trusted absolutely," said Molyneaux. He was silent a moment, staring pensively at the lawn. "The question is how does one manage this? How does he prove his worth to them?" He dropped another hint. "That small arms 'find' recently, a nice success but it did make them ask questions, some of them close to our man. It would be better if any suspicion was cast elsewhere." He added some bait. "Funding would need to be generous but money well spent."

"Well sir, I think the best way would be to give our source valuable information he can use to protect himself. Nothing too valuable of course, perhaps a minor tout or two. It would certainly look good if he was to 'expose' a couple of informers within the ranks and pin a few things on them."

"Excellent Keith, naturally we would have to let our minor informers know they had been compromised even if they are mere dross." He gave Keith another meaningful look. "If there was a slip up and we couldn't tell them in time... well, it would make our man all the more plausible. Of course that won't happen, the consequences for them could be grave."

Keith nearly laughed at all this circumspection; the consequences would not be grave, but *the* grave, a slight but important distinction. Still, he would be alright, plenty of cash to play with and some more success and Molyneaux would have something to boast about to his chiefs, shut up any talk of short term thinking too, even if a little unorthodox. It was time they took the gloves off anyway.

"You understand Keith?"

"Yes sir."

"Good. I have faith in your judgement which is why I am going to allow you to run things without the bother of having to go through me for every little thing. You know what I want."

"Yes sir, leave it with me."

Roy listened stone faced as Keith expounded the plan with an unfeigned eagerness, his grin shark like as he rubbed his hands together in anticipation.

"I love the idea, it's so dirty and devious it can't fail. Feed the Provos scraps via our man and up the tree he goes, providing us with a damn sight more useful intelligence than we're getting now. Also, once there he's ours to control, a top asset for a regular fee. We're in charge of that side of things too, Molyneaux more or less gave us carte blanche."

"He has that. Have you thought about what will happen if it goes wrong? Is this even legal? "

"Oh for fuck sake stop being so negative! We're being given a chance to run things here including the budget and you're getting all namby pamby. Granted, you might not find it in Queens Regulations but we're not a regular unit are we? Don't you think Special Branch play games, you've heard of participation status haven't you? Are you telling me you'll shed tears if that dirty old pervert Daly has to go into hiding or leave the country? We'd be doing everyone a favour and you know it." Keith brooded a moment in contemplation. "If I had my way that filthy pervert would be dildoed to death." Roy's imagination conjured up a scene that he quickly dismissed with a laugh and a shudder.

"Right enough, but participation status is allowing a small crime to prevent a bigger crime, it doesn't allow murder. I'm after wondering if we're the first to do this. We have some pretty well positioned people as it is, rumour has it quite high up indeed."

"Yeah, maybe. Anyway this will be our project, our man and there's no question of murder." He stretched his thick lips in a satisfied smile. "You never know, we give enough little tips in the right places we might even get them so paranoid they'll start a witch hunt and start burning the wrong people." He gave a cackle of laughter.

Roy was studying him again, thinking about the words carte blanche and Molyneaux in the same sentence, but decided to keep his suspicions to himself for the moment. As for the bit about witch hunts, well it had been known. Some years ago bodies had started turning up in alleyways, as the Provos sought out the traitors in their ranks and dispensed brutal justice. Several of the victims had in fact been dedicated and skilled terrorists who had been implicated by a real informer under torture, who in turn had told their interrogators what they wanted to hear, after being promised mercy and the result was a terrible and bloody domino effect. Roy wondered if this was also part of Molyneaux's thinking. He thought of something else.

"Who else will we be using?" he asked.

"I think 'Sonny' James might fit the bill, no great loss and we can fit him up with the small arms find and that info about the bomb we were given. What do you think? Should 'Sonny' boy take a long vacation abroad?"

Roy nodded a mix of concern and relief. "Molyneaux might think we've sources enough, but does he know how much work went into getting them in the first place?"

Keith acknowledged the truth of this with a slow nod. A lot of effort was spent recruiting agents; first came the initial examination of reports and weighing up if an individual might be approachable. Then approval was needed from HQ to make sure they weren't encroaching on somebody else's territory, then the 14th watched, collating habits and movement, they waited for the right moment, sometimes for weeks before they moved in with whatever inducement was suitable. Even then the success rate was a miserable ten per cent or less. Sonny James had been one of their easier ones, having expensive tastes, no job and a lot of debts he had become immediately pliable, his ferrety eyes shining greedily at the sight hard cash.

"He thinks it's worth it."

"When will you be giving them the good news?"

"Soon enough, in the meantime we'll just jolly them along."

"Bullshit them you mean," said Roy with a snort.

"Lie? Deceive? Me?" Keith shrank back putting his hand theatrically to his mouth in mock horror. "Wash my mouth out with soap, the very idea." He really was enjoying this. Roy could still marvel at his performance.

"I've a wee bit of leave starting tomorrow. Can it wait until I'm back next week, I'd like to see the auld minger's face when we tell him he has to be a tramp elsewhere." Keith thought a moment, then nodded assent.

They drove from the Maze in near silence, not a tense or awkward quiet but rather the comfortable stillness that only long and old friends could share, both deep in thought. They had just visited Thomas. Only Marty had gone in, Brendan had a dread horror of jail and had remained in the car, the mere sight of the fences, security gates and razor wire had put him into a pale sweat.

Thomas had been fine, joking and laughing and it suddenly hit Marty that his brother was incongruously trying to cheer him up as if their roles had somehow become reversed. There was the usual bantering news of family and friends until it was time to go. Marty tried to leave on a positive note.

"Keep the chin up Thomas, it won't be long now."

"The worst is behind me. I won't be back for another stretch I can tell you." He stared at Marty and whispered, "Make sure you don't end up here either."

"Has it been bad?"

"Not so much now, I never said but that first night..." he shook his head. "The first night here when that door slams shut it's like your whole life has just been shut off and you've nothing ahead but years to think on it." He brightened suddenly. "Anyway, not long now and that's me. Take it easy Marty."

They left the motorway and entered their own streets, Brendan automatically looking behind as he spoke. "You alright? He'll be out soon with remission won't he?" He gave a shudder. "Bloody jails. How's Martina?" There was a pause before Marty answered.

"She really has taken it bad."

"What about yourself?"

"I don't know, maybe I'm just tired."

"I know what you mean. There's times when I get sick of it myself, dick heads like Saunders and that. When was the last time he did an op? When was the last time he fired a shot or has he ever? That's half the trouble, the likes of them are better at reading and talking. You should have seen the look on his face the other day when he was spouting off some revolutionary shite, quoting Lenin on something when your man Gary there all confused like says 'John Lennon?'" Brendan laughed briefly before scowling. "Looks to me like they're more interested in getting votes for Sinn Fein nowadays."

"Is that it?" Marty suddenly blurted out a doubt that he wouldn't to anyone else. "Is the struggle finished? Votes? Are we risking our lives for nothing, I don't want to be some loose change in a game of three card brag."

"It'll drag on for a while yet," said Brendan becoming serious. "People like Saunders and O'Mahony, well what would they be without the war? Nobodies." He chuckled emptily, "Unemployed nobodies."

They passed a mural of a smiling, benevolent Bobby Sands. They both looked at it, a more recent addition to the cause, a newer hero, but just as dead as Connolly, their arguments and words immortalised and unimpeachable. He admired them enormously, but being dead they had a huge advantage in that they couldn't be questioned or argued with. Marty watched, thinking about what Brendan had said as other familiar murals passed by. His uncertainty began to vanish and with it he felt a great lightening. He might be unsure what the future held but was certain of one thing. He didn't want to kill again.

Keith put the red phone down and went to the bottom of the filing cabinet, withdrawing a bubble wrap brown envelope. He counted out a hundred pounds, stopped a second and then pocketed another five notes before putting the rest back and shutting the drawer with a click. He glanced at his expensive new Tissot before picking up the black phone and calling Alex.

"Hi, Keith here. Could you do me a favour? I've got a bit of a flap on, Roy's away and I need another partner for a meeting. Yes, no problem I've already got back up and route sorted."

The van was dark blue this time, with a different registration and different driver. They waited on the edge of some waste ground in the much safer east of the city. It was dark, the street lights out of action as eyes using the latest technology were stationed strategically at other points to observe anyone coming or going. Keith sat in the unlit interior and waited. The door swung open, momentarily revealing a slightly darker form in the gloom before it was closed with a dull clunk. A slightly cheesy smell wafted through the confined space as Daly spoke softly.

"Could you not turn the light on, it's as black as Satan's arse in here!"

"No. Listen. We want you to watch an address and let us know if you see anything going in or out."

There was a second of silence before Keith heard the sound of Daly scratching his stubbly chin followed by the 'psst' of a tin opening. A glug and another rasp as a mouth was wiped. The yeasty smell of beer now blended with the other odours.

"How much, where and when?"

"A hundred pounds for a couple of days starting Wednesday, the address is inside," said Keith passing him an envelope. "Ring if you spot something, anything good you get a bonus."

The envelope was tugged from his grasp and to his irritation he heard more glugging and the sound of an empty tin being dropped, followed by a belch. The door opened and Daly was gone.

An hour later and the van was parked safely in a garage on the outskirts of the city. Keith waited, slightly tense, the stakes so much higher. He heard footsteps and a greeting as Hermes came in.

"This garage hasn't been used in a while that's for sure."

"Nah, the last car in here was a model T."

The door opened and Hermes got in, sniffing the air sulkily. Not for the first time this evening Keith cursed Daly. The visitor didn't waste time.

"What is it?"

"We think you might be under suspicion, not serious at the moment but we have a plan to help you." The eyes watching Keith now gleamed.

"Everyone is sometimes. Go on."

"We think by giving you some names to pass on it will get security looking elsewhere and help your own standing in the movement."

The lips curled in scorn. "Fuck the movement."

"I thought you wanted to get on?" asked Keith.

"I do." A sly smile escaped from the face opposite. "What else do you have?"

"That's about it for now. You will be well... renumerated for your troubles. Of course the more valuable your information the better it will be." Keith tried sincerity, the way a man might try a different sized pair of gloves in search of a better fit. "You mustn't think you'll be working *for* us on this one, that's not how we see it. No, you are working *with* us, together." The effort was wasted on this cold fish.

"Right. Sure." The voice was heavy with a mix of sarcasm, irony and honesty. "Now let me say something about my *remuneration.* We both know without people like me you'd be screwed. Without touts you've nothing. I know a lot of people, sure there is a cell system which is fine in theory, but someone like me knows a lot of volunteers and listens to a lot of talk. You know how it is in tight knit little communities like ours, people blab. I know my value you see so don't be trying to pay me off in sweeties." Keith remained silent as Hermes went on.

"You know yourself how people like me are hated, tout, informer, grass, Judas, the amount of names shows you just how much we are hated. And feared. That's why I want a lot of money and a guarantee that if I'm exposed I get properly relocated, not like the ones I'll be giving up. I'm taking the risks here not you, I'm the one under pressure not being able to talk to anyone but the likes of you, one wrong word and I'm finished, so you'd better make it worth my while."

Keith watched, carefully concealing his surprise at this good sense, he handed over a piece of paper which was quickly read and passed back.

"Well now, I wouldn't have thought he was a tout, but there you go. As for this bum Daly, you may as well have wrapped him in a ribbon, thanks for the gift."

"We will leave the details to you how you expose them. Payment will be direct to your account, standard procedures."

"Right, and I'll leave the details to you of how and when you warn them. One last thing. I can tell you who was responsible for that up and under booby trap the other week." A piece of scrap paper was handed over. "That must be worth a couple of quid. Good night now."

Daly sat in the middle of a room bare of all furniture bar the wooden chair he was tied to, the cord cutting into his sweating wrists as he vibrated in terror. A voice spoke behind him, gentle and understanding, watching Daly wriggle like a worm frantically trying to avoid the inevitable hook.

"You've been hanging around outside that house the whole day. Do you think we're stupid? Now, I know you were probably pressured to spy on us, it's alright, we're not the mad dogs the Brits make us out to be. Has anyone hit you or even threatened to? No, we can be lenient but only if you come clean."

"Please, I swear on my mother's life, I was just ... I was looking for places to doss. That's the truth, I've no home."

"So where did you get the money we found in your pocket? A nice role of crispy new notes too!"

"I found it, please I'm not lying."

Listening to himself Daly realised just how lame he sounded. The voice came closer and let out an exaggerated sigh of regret. Daly turned his head and found he was staring into the black hole of a gun muzzle. He felt suddenly very hot and tears came to his eyes. He didn't have that great a life, but it was better than this alternative. The voice seemed to be coming out of that horrible tube, his eyes fixed on it.

"I am losing patience so just tell us about how and who approached you. I promise no harm will come to you if you tell us, you'll have to leave the country but that's it. O.K? We can use you better alive as an example of what bastards the Brits are, low enough to exploit a homeless man even."

A friendly hand rested on his shoulder and Daly at last believed, relief that he was going to live coursing through his body. He told them everything, which wasn't much and even volunteered to ring the special number he had memorised to arrange a meeting. Turning his head as far as he could he saw there were three men, they moved off to one side speaking in low whispers.

"What d'you reckon?"

"Let him ring, but you know as well as I do they'll take no chances. More likely one of our lads gets spotted. That's if they turn up at all." Daly craned his neck further as one of them turned to him.

"We're talking about you, not to you! Now face the wall!"

They finished their conference and he began to breathe easier as they cut his ties and a phone was uncoiled and brought to him. He looked up at them, an uncertain ingratiating smile trying to form as they surrounded the chair like three hungry cats with a shabby played out mouse. He began dialling, fumbled and tried again with shaking fingers, waiting, waiting, waiting for an answer.

Roy had decided to spend his leave in the province with Helen. He had seen her intermittently, and gradually she had unwound and once she had dropped her reserve and let him in he discovered he liked her for more than just sex.

They spent a few days in Portrush, Roy pointing out various places he knew, wasting money in the crowded arcades, eating ice cream and walking along the strand. Appetites huge from the sea air, they bought fish and chips from the place at the end of Main Street, run by the same friendly little Italian he remembered from student days. It was great to just get away from it all and relax. In their hotel room he had just finished showering and was drying himself, padding into the lounge as Helen sat on the bed pouring two measures of Bushmills. She handed one to Roy and put the TV on in the middle of the regional news. Immediately the Troubles invaded their room and destroyed the mood.

"The bodies of two men found yesterday in the West of the city have been identified as Michael Daly and Gerald McKee. The Provisional IRA has said they carried out the killing of Mr McKee claiming he was working for British intelligence as an informer. They further warned that anyone else who knowingly passed information would be dealt with accordingly. The body of Michael Daly was discovered in a derelict house in the Ballymurphy area, police have disclosed that Mr Daly who was believed to be homeless was battered to death in a brutal assault. No organisation has claimed responsibility. In other news today..."

He marched to the TV and switched it off, banging down his glass and slopping some whiskey over his hand. Helen eyed him, curious.

"Anyone you know?"

She took a sip as Roy stood glaring out of the window at a gorgeous sunset, the sky a hazy burnished bronze and the sea briefly golden before darkening to inky blue. He watched in silence for a minute quietly fuming.

"The fucking bastard! The callous treacherous bastard! Why McKee?" he asked himself.

"I take it this is something to do with Keith Shepheard?" He spun around in surprise.

"What makes you say that?"

"Oh, nothing really. Just the words bastard, callous and treacherous in the same sentence perhaps." Roy stared. She put her own glass down. "Roy, your dear friend does have a bit of a reputation you know, nothing specific but he's not exactly loved by all."

Roy stared some more, lost for a few seconds in further thought before he shook his head as if clearing it, he dressed in record speed, picking up his car keys as he went to the door.

"Sorry Helen I've to go, you don't know him like I do, there must be some explanation."

Then he was gone. Helen took another sip, addressing the door in resignation.

"There is an explanation. You already gave it."

Roy drove as fast as he could, knowing it was too late but the speed acted as a balm, he wanted to find out what had gone wrong. He arrived and went straight in, rudely ignoring Dave and another colleague as he slammed the door shut behind him. Keith was sat with his feet up on the desk, papers scattered carelessly, a single slim file in his hands. His face showed neither emotion nor surprise at Roy's noisy entrance or at his rapid fire questions, the voice strained with his suppressed anger.

"Why didn't you wait? What went wrong? Why didn't you get them out?"

Keith languidly put his feet back on the floor before answering. "I was going to ring you when I heard, but what was the point, it wasn't Lazarus and I'm no Jesus, it was just too late."

"So what happened?"

"Circumstances changed. We had to move faster than originally planned and they got to McKee before we did. We managed to find Sonny though." He put his hands out palms up in an appeal for understanding. "I'm as pissed off as you are mate, Molyneaux has already been on the blower," Keith said, looking as crestfallen as Roy could remember, but then he knew his acting skills could be academy award standard. He was listening very carefully now to his voice, noting the cadence and every little nuance.

"What about Daly?"

"What about him? Look, we couldn't find him. He was supposed to check in that very day but didn't." Keith stopped a second thinking of yesterday when he had seen the body. McKee lay covered apart from a pair of huge bare yellow feet sticking out of trousers under the blanket somebody had put on him to hide the dreadful damage to his head. He hadn't bothered to see Daly. "It's a pity," he continued. "One nil to them you might say, we thought we'd have more time."

"One nil? Is this what it is to you, a game of football?"

Keith looked down at the file in what might have been a gesture of apology. "Roy. Look. We have to trust each other if we're to work efficiently. I am sorry, really. Wrong words, it was just a simple and tragic balls up, I give you my word."

He held his hand out. Roy hesitated, unsure but not wanting to believe the friend he had shared so much with could betray people so easily. Not accepting that the betrayal was of him too, not yet, they had been through so much together, it couldn't be so. He owed him the benefit of doubt. He shook the proffered hand but at full stretch, a new distance between them. Keith appeared relieved.

"Bad business all round but every cloud has a silver lining. At least our man is safe, his bona fides will be a hundred per cent now."

Roy was silent as he distractedly picked one of the loose papers up from the desk. The photo in the corner was of Gerald McKee. It wasn't the jolly face he remembered, but it was the same man that had put his life in their hands. A brave man and one whom Roy would have hated and despised not so long ago, a man that he had come to like however and even respect, a man trying to do what he thought was right and finally a man he had helped to a mean and sordid death in an alley. He felt a new and unwelcome stab of guilt and shame. He put the file down where it was gathered up by Keith for removal to the archives.

"Come on matey, we're still winning. Still work to do, come for a late drink and I'll tell you what's on this week."

Chapter 12

Whatever You Say, Say Nothing

They sat in Martina's house watching the lunchtime news, sipping from cups of hot sweet tea as they viewed another funeral. This one was small and virtually unattended except for family, weeping children and a stoop shouldered, hollow eyed wife leaning on an older man for support; the funeral of an informer was never going to be well attended. It was as Marty had thought, Belfast was riddled with touts and he was lucky not to have been lifted yet himself, a fact commented upon by Frank recently. A 'charmed life' was how the weasel bastard had put it, in a voice that was almost insinuating, and not for the first time he thought how Saunders might benefit from a quick elbow to the throat.

Tinks got up to go, bending and kissing Marty lightly on the head as she went, leaving the faintest scent of violets. The toilet flushed and Declan came out, going to the kitchen to wash his hands and make a sandwich. He had let Declan know yesterday about his decision to quit. Declan had been disappointed and tried to get him to reconsider, but had finally gone to see their superiors. He had come back this morning and as expected told him to wait a few days, take a holiday if he needed but not to be too hasty. They didn't want to lose someone as valuable as himself. Tinks had been quietly delighted and immediately started making plans for a move to Dublin which was where she was headed now, looking for a place to rent using her savings. Marty was broke as usual, the twenty pounds a week he was provided with by the organization's finance officer and his dole barely covered everyday expenses. Declan came in, plate in one hand, walked to the window and peered out. He dropped the plate and sandwich onto the carpet,

"Shit! Peelers!"

He was out the back door in seconds, propelled by well honed instincts, stopped the first car he saw, threatened the driver and was away. Marty went to the window too, but not in panic. Maybe it was something else, the house was clean if they wanted to search and he was certain they had nothing on him. There were two army vehicles outside and a police Landrover with its two little blue lights on the roof like the horns on a grey squat beast. The doorbell rang and Marty thought how different it was to the old days. He opened up and was pushed back inside by a large mustachioed cop, a soldier stood by the doorway as others came inside along with two more policemen. He was arrested, but to his surprise led uncuffed to the Landrover. Marty looked at his travelling companions. Some things hadn't changed. Although they remained silent, he could feel the hatred coming from them as if he was sat opposite the glowing bars of an electric fire.

He had indeed led a charmed life as far as arrests and jail were concerned, but knew they had seven days to question him, after which he would be released unless charged with a specific crime. Seven days. Marty was relieved Tinks had gone when she had. All volunteers were trained in anti interrogation techniques, the best defence against sophisticated and well tried methods that was drummed into them over and over was to remain silent, not to even acknowledge their existence, focus on the wall or do whatever it took to keep the interrogator out of your mind. Marty was confident he could do this, but even so, seven days was a long time.

They arrived at Castlereagh holding centre, a place of infamy to Republicans, with its barbed wire topped fences and numerous holding cells, where both they and some Loyalists were 'processed'. Constable William Snow sat opposite the terrorist, thinking the bastard was lucky he had been arrested now and not sooner. In earlier years the methods had been quite brutal, involving a lot of psychological pressure and physical beatings as a matter of course; some of them had been well and truly battered. It had produced results and lots of convictions, but this so called systematic ill treatment couldn't go forever unnoticed, and eventually led to investigation by some nosey liberal lawyers and accusations of torture. A report had followed which had backed up some of the allegations. Prisoners were given better access to lawyers and doctors and interrogations were monitored on close circuit cameras with only two officers at any one time. Snow curled his lip at the thought. Didn't they realise what they were up against here? Having to go soft on people who had murdered colleagues and friends, and if let out would do the same to him given a chance. He stared again at the prisoner as he opened the door. Yes, he was lucky it wasn't him who was conducting the interviews. He brightened somewhat at the thought of this bastard being pressured for seven days. With luck he might even break and end up doing a long, long stretch.

Marty was led into the reception area where his details were taken and his fingers printed. His belt was removed, along with the contents of his pockets and his watch before he was walked to another room. A doctor gave him a cursory examination and asked questions concerning his health. Ten minutes later he was in a cell with a single fixed bed and a steel framed light, the brightness intensified by the white walls. Marty lay on the bed, put his hands behind his head, closed his eyes and waited.

Unable to sleep he opened his eyes. He could hear people coming along the corridor, boots, voices, silence as an eye was put to the peep hole and then the heavy door swung open. Two officers stood outside, one of them stretched his hand out indicating the corridor, bowing slightly in exaggerated sarcastic courtesy.

"Time for your first interview Mr McKenna. Be so kind as to accompany us."

Marty came slowly off the bed, saying nothing and not looking at them as they escorted him to the interview room. They put him inside and closed the door. There was a table in the middle of the room and behind it two chairs with another in front. The only other item on the table was a red tinfoil tray that had once contained a mince pie, but was now humbled as an ashtray. A short middle aged man sat, going through some papers. He glanced up at Marty with mild azure blue eyes and indicated for him to sit in a friendly way, as if this was nothing more than a simple job interview. Leaning against the wall was another man, slim build with curly hair and a large nose, both wore shirts and ties despite the warmth. Marty sat, noticing the box shaped camera in one top corner. The standing officer sat down, now emphasising the smallness of the other and the fact he was a bit overweight. He opened a drawer on his side of the desk.

"Would you like a cigarette Marty? You don't mind me using your first name?" Marty looked at a fixed point just above his shoulder.

"No? Very well, let's get started." He rummaged again in the drawer and produced a file, watching to see if Marty was following his movements. He wasn't.

"We know all about you." He winced and sighed loudly, like a man feeling a preliminary stab of gout before the inevitable full attack. He began reading. "Terrible Martin, terrible. Your past had to catch up with you one day, you must have known that surely. I see you've been in the Provisionals for a long while. You've been lucky, but now it's over. I see you were based down in Dundalk for a long period? Yes? Marty you have to talk eventually, why don't you save us all a lot of bother and come clean now? Get it all off your chest, all those bad things. Wipe the slate clean." He waited, the soft blue eyes full of sympathetic understanding.

"What about all those wrecked lives, look at this." He slid a black and white photograph across the desk, then picked it up and held it in front of Marty's face, who couldn't help but see the image for a brief second of a body, or rather a limbless, headless torso that had been flung into a field by an explosion.

"You helped do this to another human being Marty. Don't you regret it?" Another photo came across. "What about this, he was just nineteen years old Marty. Yes, just old enough to be in uniform and you might think that's justification, but you can't blow up a uniform Marty, a uniform doesn't scream in pain. People do. Think of his mother."

"Surely you see what you've done is very, very wrong," the other man said, oblivious to the lack of any reaction. "It's not too late. I'm a Catholic myself, you know it's wrong what you've done. Help us and help yourself, you'll feel better for confessing and coming clean."

Marty tried not to listen. It was difficult at first, but the longer it went on the easier it became, and it did go on and on in the same droning vein with cigarettes smoked until that little cake tin was full of butts and the air was blue. Eventually they fell silent, exchanged a quick glance and then a sly peep at their watches.

"Alright Marty, we tried to help you. There's still time, this is just the start. You can go back to your cell and think about it. All those deaths Martin, lives destroyed, children orphaned. How could you do that?"

He was escorted back, their words worthless seeds scattered again and again on stony ground. He knew their game. He felt it was an insult to his intelligence, any repentance he might do would be private and not done in jail.

Food was brought: a pork chop, mash and carrots. He ate it all, knowing he would need to keep strong physically and mentally. It was time for another interview, this time in a different room with a different pair and a different attitude. The room was furnished exactly like the last, but without an ashtray and only two plastic orange chairs. He quickly examined the two cops, both with sleeves rolled up and ties off, the one sat down, tall with very deep set eyes and a bald, almost skull like head. The only thing noticeable about the other was his large frame and the redness of his face. Marty checked to see if the camera was in the top corner, immediately noticed by red face who smiled nastily.

"Aye, check all you like son. Strange, we've been having problems with that camera, it goes on the blink so it does."

Marty fixed his gaze and readied himself. Red face came up to him and stared, so close Marty could feel his heavy breath tickle his nostrils. He walked slowly behind him, watched by the skull sat opposite. There was a sudden deafening shout in his ear.

"We're going to put you away you murdering Fenian cunt!" screamed red face. He was shoved, pulled and pushed. "We know what you done. Now you'll talk to us! Understand!"

Again there was a shove. The skull spoke, his voice harsh but not at the same deafening pitch as red face. "You think you're going to just walk out of here? Think again boy, you're going down for thirty years you dirty papish bastard." He addressed red face. "This turd would probably be happy living in his own shit. Dirty protest? I thought that was how all you Fenians lived."

There was a slap to the back of his head as red face circled, still bawling insults. "If I had my way that rubbish you'll be joining soon would all be on hunger strike again, this time enforced. I'll bet the fastest thing in hell right now is Sands chasing a chicken!"

Marty felt his fists balling in fury. So this was it, not exactly good cop, bad cop, but more good pair, bad pair. He stared at the wall, his blank refusal to acknowledge their presence sending them both into a seeming rage, the skull boy's face getting as red as the other guy's had been; his was now turning crimson. Marty managed to blank out the insults, but then felt a blinding pain as two cupped hands smashed onto his ears. He screamed and fell, feeling like his eardrums had burst. He was hauled to his feet, covering his ears. The shouting continued, interspersed with threats of violence and hurled questions and demands he tell them what they wanted to know. There was more shoving and pulling, red face grabbed him by the arm, and tugging down with excruciating violence left Marty curled on the floor. His tormentors stood over him screaming hate, but he also noticed through his pain, they were careful not to leave any marks on him.

"We know! Your mate was brought in just after you. He's yellow as a canary and singing. He's told us all about you. You're fucked so you are, you Provo bastard!"

Marty thought a second and realised that was probably bullshit. He held firm and waited for the session to end.

Food was brought: a curled up corned beef sandwich. He ate it and swilled down the tepid tea with angry determination. They wouldn't break him. He was taken to yet a different room, where the 'nice' cops waited. Marty was tired, but able to completely drown out their spiel about guilt and unburdening himself. Two more hours of photographs and haranguing him with the inevitability of his conviction followed. They even tried to convince him he needed to confess for the good of his soul. Finally they let him back to the security of his cell.

Food was brought: bacon, eggs, white bread and weak tea. He ate it as if it was his last, scraping and wiping the last yolk up with the crust. The 'bad' cops were back, looking fresh and eager. They started in straight away, this time a single clap over the ears, but always the threat of more as they circled, making Marty flinch involuntarily and curse himself. He tried not to listen but couldn't help it, when to his concealed shock their roared accusations revealed how much they knew of his past operations, meaning some gobshite somewhere had been blabbing. He blanked his mind again, saving his analysis for later.

"You think you're going to be released? If I had my way you would be, but first I'd tattoo 'Provo' on your forehead and drop you in the middle of the Shankill you evil bastard!" Marty knew from the gloating way his tormentor caressed the words with a dreamy look he probably fantasized about it.

Another session ended. Food came and another interrogation, then more food and more questions and accusations and so it went on and on, Marty having difficulty keeping track of time. After another gruelling session he reasoned as best he could that they were making educated guesses about his activities on the border. They sounded much vaguer, the only touts in those parts were the ones left at the side of the road. No, the stuff they really knew about only concerned here in the city, which logically meant that was where they had the leak. He sat up as the door opened, uncertain if it was time for interrogation or nutrition. A uniformed cop stood in the doorway with a plate and let a dribble of spittle fall onto it. He put the plate on the floor as if feeding a dog and watched crooked mouthed as Marty picked it up. Marty took the plastic fork and with great deliberation squashed the spit further into the mashed potato. He bored his eyes into the cop and willed himself to take a mouthful, then another. The cop said something under his breath and shut the door with a bang. He ate it all, gagging at one point, but more determined than ever, seeing by what was on the plate it was dinner and so only one more interview for this, the fifth day. Only a couple more and he was free, they had nothing yet to charge him with and that was the law.

They took him out again, collecting his plate at the same time. Marty saw with silent satisfaction the look of annoyance on the peeler's face at having to play waiter as he bent down to clear up. Again he was led to an interview room, another new one and even smaller with the usual table and chairs. He thought it was bad cop time. He took a seat. Two men came in he hadn't met before and sat opposite, casually dressed and relaxed looking as if they would be going out on the town later for a few beers. The first was tall, muscular and very ordinary, brown hair and eyes he sat back now with an almost friendly smile, putting his hands behind his head as he examined Marty. The other, who bore an uncanny resemblance to Paul Weller, unlocked the table drawer and searched about. Marty liked 'The Jam' but doubted he was going to like this prick. An ashtray was produced and then with a conjuror's flourish, a half full bottle of Glenlivet and some white plastic cups. He poured three generous measures and took out a packet of cigarettes, offering one to Marty with a cheery expression.

"Congratulations Martin, you've done very well," he said, turning to his colleague. "Hasn't he?"

"He has that, not a single word so I've been told." He nodded approvingly and sat forwards winking as he took a cup and sipped appreciatively. "Go on man, take a sip. You deserve it. No water, but then it is a single malt." Marty resisted the temptation he suddenly felt.

"I did tell them you wouldn't talk. I read your file, took me ages. You have been busy! You'll have to forgive our colleagues who may have been a bit too keen, I expect they made you a little uncomfortable." The eyes crinkled sympathetically.

"You won't be seeing them again Martin, we don't approve of all that shouting," said the other. He laughed and lit a cigarette.

"Do you like fishing Martin?"

The question caught him off guard for a second and he almost answered. There was an instant flash of interest from them.

"Aha! Nearly had you there didn't we?"

"Look, we're not going to mess about, your mate Declan has broken. The poor man did his best but he's saying all sorts of things now."

"Yes, he wasn't very good at making a getaway either. After he made a run for it he took someone's car..." Paul Weller broke off and started laughing, as the other guy finished the story for him.

"Aye, took a car, not any car mind, but a clapped out old Citroen 2 CV. I heard he made an astonishing thirty miles per hour as far as the next street before he was caught." He began laughing again, shaking his head in rueful mockery. "Imagine that, the colour too. Poor bastard tried to make a discreet getaway in a brightly coloured orange dustbin!"

They were both giggling now, and in his surprise and tiredness Marty almost joined in as he imagined the scene. He reminded himself of the gravity of the situation and kept his lips tight. For all their seeming good humour Marty wasn't fooled, these two were clever and dangerous. They became serious too.

"Martin, we don't have anything personal against you. For us it's a job. If you don't cooperate with us we'll use the testimony Declan has spilled and put you away. He has implicated you in that bombing. We know you never meant the woman to get hurt but you'll still go down for murder. There is another alternative. You can work with us and you'll have immunity, you'll be out of here a free man."

Marty felt a surge of relief. He knew now they had no real evidence, they were bluffing and lying because he hadn't been involved in that particular attack and could prove his whereabouts if necessary. They were either guessing or someone had fed them faulty information as well as some good stuff. He would walk out of here a free man anyway, free from them and anyone else. He closed his mind and focused on the wall, the voices trailing off and eventually they gave up and returned him to his cell.

"Bastard! I thought we almost had him then," said the first interrogator, chucking a pen against the wall in frustration. The Paul Weller lookalike shrugged in a resigned way.

"That's the way the cookie crumbles. We can't do him for anything and he won't be bluffed." He put his feet up on the table and leafed through the papers he held. "The report here though says he is... quote 'lately increasingly disenchanted with the Republican movement and leadership.' In other words ripe for an approach."

"I know, he'd have made a great source for us. Does Molyneaux want a crack at him too?"

"Yes, Shepheard is due in later. They're pissed off we haven't let them see him sooner."

"Huh! They should be thankful. We've softened him up for them. Come on, I've had enough for today."

Roy drove the freshly painted green Ford Escort as fast and skilfully as he could to Castlereagh, according to Keith time was of the essence. They were familiar with the layout of the place, having made visits to the building on a regular basis. It was an ideal environment for the recruitment of agents and informers and some of their best successes had begun here. Keith was keen to get on, and fiddled with the small slim briefcase in his lap.

"This guy would be invaluable to us," he said. "Very experienced, but has managed to stay out of our way until very recently. That's probably because he spent so much time down on the border rather than up here. That's also another reason he'd be of immense value, we have a real lack of intelligence in that area, a 'paucity of information' as Molyneaux says and he's right. This bloke is apparently still trusted by them down there and could be our first real shoe in the door. Even if he stays here he can still tell us bags of stuff."

Roy grunted, non committed. "True enough, but he's probably trusted for the simple reason that no matter how pissed off he is, and we don't know that for sure, he won't come over to us."

Keith tutted, mocking in a slow, stoned hippy drawl, "Those are like, such negative vibes man." He slapped the case on his lap, his voice returning to normal. "There's a couple of thousand good reasons why he should help us right here pal."

Roy said nothing as he pulled up to the front gate and passed his ID for inspection. He was right about one thing: such a man would be of use to them. Interesting, but he doubted if they would have any luck, Keith was putting too much faith in hard cash. They entered and signed themselves in, going straight to their allocated room. Everything was prepared for them as they sat and got comfortable, Keith leaning the case next to a table leg and pulling out their file on the subject, then opening the drawer for the latest stuff on him. He read through quickly, noting who had already interviewed him and when, frowning and lighting up a cigarette at the same time.

"We'll only have a few sessions so there won't be much time to get into his head. Damn! I see here they had Greaves in with him. That won't help us much the bloody fools, we want him with us, not harbouring fresh grudges."

Roy took the file from him. Keith was right, he knew Greaves as a hard bastard with a bad temper who absolutely enjoyed knocking people about. He also knew Greaves had barely survived an attempt on his life by the Provos some years ago, so understood his viewpoint entirely, but this didn't help them now. He looked at the new file and the mug shot taken a bare few days ago and stared at that face knowing he had seen it somewhere before, annoyed at himself for not being able to place it. Then it came to him all at once, the years rolled away and he saw the face slightly thinner and happier, grinning. Then he saw the name again. It couldn't be! Keith was watching him, interested.

"Are you alright? You look like you've seen a ghost."

"Jesus! I think I know this fella from years ago. Marty. That's right, he used to live at the other end of our street."

"What do you mean, he's a friend?" Keith asked incredulously.

"No, no, don't be bloody daft, nothing like that. He won't know my name even, we were only there a few years, I just remember him is all." Roy had a flashback of the street, then the chip shop. Fuck! That's right. Then of the night when everything was burning.

"Listen Roy, if he has any bad feeling it might be best if you pissed off..."

The door opened and it was too late. Martin McKenna stood in the doorway flanked by his escorting officers, glancing first at Keith and then Roy, his face frowning in concentration before his eyes opened wide in shock. He recovered and took a seat. They stared at each other a full ten seconds, steady green unwavering eyes held by unblinking dark blue. Keith looked from one to the other. It didn't look like there was any love lost here, but then again there didn't seem to be that much animosity yet either and he might even find a way to exploit this unexpected situation. He cleared his throat and spoke.

"Allow me to introduce ourselves. I'm Kevin and this is Alan. I won't lie to you or beat about the bush, we think you might be able to help out. I'm sure Special Branch has already made an approach and frankly I don't blame you for not responding. We are not Special Branch however, if you were to work for... with us you would be well taken care of, you'd be with the best. You would also be well paid. All we want is information, we want to prevent any more needless suffering. I'm sure you do too."

Marty remained silent, studying the man opposite him, the shock of recognition slowly receding as the other guy talked on. He was remembering now, all those years ago. Yes it was definitely him, he pursed his lips in concentration for a couple of seconds and it came to him. Roy. That was it. He couldn't remember his last name, only that he had lived on his street. He looked at the other guy still making his offers, his grey eyes wide with sincerity and almost laughed in contempt, Alan was it? Lying bastard. He turned back to those green eyes that were scrutinising him the same way. More memories came of black night, yellows, oranges and whooshing crackling flames as they stood and watched their home burn with the stink of smoke and whole families on the move, some still in their pyjamas. He had seen that face again a couple of years later. He must have moved house too, on the dividing line where they had their regular riots. They had both come a long way from throwing stones, yet here they were again facing each other, this time across a table. Marty looked at him and frustration welled up with his anger, he wanted so badly to tell this bastard just what he thought of him, ask him if he had been watching that night.

Roy's stare remained fixed as he strained his memory, taking in every feature, the clothing and even the curious small silver ring on his little finger. A snapshot flashed in his head of this guy getting into a car on the ferry, why, that couldn't have been more than a couple of years ago at most. How the hell had he missed him then? It was hard to equate the happy lad from long ago with this hardened and dangerous terrorist. He wanted to ask him why he had done the things he had, what had gone wrong with him to join such murdering cowardly scum that killed innocent people. Years ago he would have dismissed such thoughts as a waste of effort, he was what he was and the best and simplest solution was a bullet or jail cell. And most of the people he had grown up with would just love to burn the bastard alive. These last years and months though had brought a subtle change in him. He had witnessed and experienced things that took some people a lifetime, as if decades had been compressed into days and hours and minutes. He felt an overwhelming urge to know, to talk to this man and find out what made him tick. Keith had stopped his sales pitch; he wasn't buying it. He looked at Roy, silently giving him the go ahead to see what he could do. They had nothing to lose. Keith sat back and lit another fag.

"It's you isn't it? You know me from before all this," said Roy.

For a moment it looked as if Marty was going to reply, he sat slightly forwards but then subsided again. He was listening.

"What happened? You moved and then joined that lot. Became one of them."

The words were flat, a cold accusation, provoking. Marty was breathing heavier and thinking. Why shouldn't he talk? He didn't have to help them, he could do whatever the hell he wanted. So it was forbidden for volunteers to talk, well he wasn't a volunteer anymore. No one was going to tell him anymore what he could or couldn't do. He was sick of orders.

"We were burnt out by a Protestant mob you recall. Or don't you want to remember that part of it?" he said, his voice scratchy from a lack of use.

"I remember. A lot of people had to move then. We moved too eventually."

"You weren't burned out in the middle of the night though were you?"

"No. Others were but. That gives you the excuse to go and murder people does it?"

"Murder like Bloody Sunday?"

"No, murder like Bloody Friday! I was there that day so don't be sitting there telling me you have an excuse to kill."

"I didn't say that. In war sometimes people get hurt."

"War?" Roy's voice went up an octave.

"Aye, war! Youse people try and make criminals of Republicans and say it's just a handful of evil terrorists out for their own ends. So why are there thousands of soldiers and thousands more police and helicopters, bases and armoured cars and all the rest of it if it isn't a war?"

"This is no war, I've seen real war. Your trouble is you want to have your cake and eat it, say you're soldiers then whinge when you get shot and go on about human rights and all that. Blowing up innocent people going about their business, oh aye and claim your benefits every week from the system you hate so much!"

"Every penny helps." Marty sat back with an acid smile. "Do you know there's something always baffled me about loyalists. Why is it there must be a hundred million around the world claim Irish descent, are proud of it and you alone, what a million or so? You people shun it."

"So you're a nationalist? So what, so am I. I'm British first, and proud of it."

"Proud of what? Not that old empire shite surely? In history class when I saw all that red on the map I thought the world had a rash."

"I'm proud to be part of a nation that has given so much to..."

"Such as?"

"Wise up, look at all the inventions for one thing, TV, telephones, radar, penicillin, trains, Darwin, football, rugby." Roy warmed to the subject, ticking off the achievements on his fingers. Keith joined in half amused, his tongue in cheek at the same time trying to keep them talking. Any dialogue was better than nothing.

"Don't forget the boy scouts, then you've got all those explorers, Captain Cook, Livingstone and all the artists and writers, Turner, Constable, Dickens, Hardy and where would the world be without dear old Shakespeare eh?"

"Aye!" Roy continued. "What about standing up to Hitler and Napoleon. Another thing, what music do you listen to? Think of the Stones and the Beatles..."

"Oh!" Marty interrupted. "Don't be forgetting what else *your* country has given. Hooligans, the first concentration camps, Dresden, Cromwell murdering thousands of innocents and all the countries like this one you fucking well occupied and looted for centuries!"

Keith gave a short hoot of laughter; the man was speaking even if they were arguing. He wanted to keep it going and discreetly gave Roy a gentle shoe under the table. Roy changed tack slightly, remembering why they were here.

"Why does it have to be this way? Do you think we go about arresting people for fun?"

"No, but let's not be naive. Are you assuming you have to do something to get arrested? Well...Alan, I can tell you from experience that's a load of shit." Roy raised a hand in acknowledgement.

"I'll admit, errors were made, but at least we've been trying to sort it out and not repeat those mistakes. Sure there are Protestants who are bigoted bastards through and through." He gave a small cynical laugh as he continued, "Haven't you the same on your side? What's the flag again? Green, white and gold. Why gold? There's me thinking it was orange like Wolfe Tone originally intended or is it we don't really have a place in Ireland?" Marty raised his eyebrows at this knowledge even if it was basic stuff.

"If you knew your history you'll know true Republicans make no religious distinctions, Protestants are treated the same as everyone else. In my family any bigotry was always frowned upon, but we'll never give up the idea of a united Ireland. You people left us with no choice but to fight." Marty sat back, tired now and wanting to stop. He had made his point without giving them anything they could use.

Roy slowly nodded. It had been interesting but ultimately futile. He had one last thing to say. "O.K Martin, you want a united Ireland, I know you're not going to confess to anything but think about this. What have you gotten out of it personally? More to the point, what have you and the movement gained or achieved besides a lot of death and bitterness? Are you any nearer to a united Ireland or have you pushed it further away? Do you think you're going to bomb and shoot us into it? Catch yourselves on!"

Marty glared at him, angry at being confronted with the self same thoughts he had tried to submerge himself. He answered wearily.

"Every people has a right to defend themselves, I will never betray my people. Would you? You are wasting your time. Anyway I'm going to live in Dublin in a week or so, permanently, you get my drift? One day, and I want to see it peacefully now, this country will be one again." He yawned, "Who knows, maybe I'll buy you a pint one day. Now let me back to my cell, I've nothing more to say."

They stared at each other again, both unflinching, both of them didn't just think they were right, they knew it. Keith hurriedly put his cigarette out, off balance by the sudden termination of the discussion.

"Hang on, you haven't heard us out!"

He ducked down and picked up the small black case, putting it gently on the table and opening it with some panache. Marty's eyes widened as he rapidly calculated how much was sat in front of him, for a split second seeing a new life. The feeling passed, quickly replaced by embarrassed anger at his moment of weakness, the anger redirected at the ugly rotten bastard sat opposite with his temptation.

"Stick your pieces of silver up your arse," he glowered. "Sideways."

Five minutes later Keith was still fuming, his pique tinged with disbelief that he had been balked when so much money had been offered, more than had ever been authorised before and the self righteous fool had refused. He paced as he spoke, fists clenched in his pockets.

"What the hell is the matter with him? Once in a lifetime opportunity like that and he spurns it." He looked at Roy who sat impassively watching.

"Another thing, you could have helped more, been a little less argumentative, shown a bit more..." He searched for words, his hands coming out of his pockets, fingers outstretched and raised to the ceiling in frustration. "Yes, a bit more understanding. You were supposed to make him amenable, not bloody well put his back up. I knew this was a mistake having you here, Molyneaux was very keen to have this one."

Roy knew immediately that Keith was already trying to pass the blame, just as the Major would too, knowing where the finger would be pointed and realising he didn't care anymore.

Marty had been released after seven days, the officers covering their chagrin with a cheery, "See you soon" as he signed for his belongings. He came home to an empty house and waited to hear from Tinks. He already knew she was safe in Dublin, as word had been quietly passed via his lawyer during his brief visit. The phone rang and he rushed to answer it, disappointed when a man curtly told him to wait for a visit and further instructions. He knew the score, they would want to thoroughly debrief him, it was standard procedure to find out what had gone on, check to make sure he hadn't let anything slip, to see what questions had been asked and try and work out from this anything they could use themselves. They would go over everything in minute detail like men panning for gold. It would be a pain in the arse, especially when he told them he had spoken at the end, knowing this would lead to yet more questions and a tongue lashing about keeping his discipline. The phone rang again and this time, happily it was her.

Early next morning Marty was woken by the persistent ringing of his doorbell. He got up and walked to the window to check who was outside, his irritation at being woken so early replaced by a glad feeling that the sooner it was over the sooner he could get away. He rubbed his eyes and rapped on the window, mood lightening even more as he saw Brendan outside, arms now crossed as he waited. He went downstairs and let him in.

"What time do you call this?" he asked.

"Ours not to reason why mate, I expect they want to get you whilst everything is still fresh in your mind. How was it?" Brendan asked.

"You've been through it yourself. Bad enough. Do I have time for breakfast?"

He nodded. "I'll join you."

"Scrounging bastard, is that the only reason you're here?" He looked at his friend properly and noticed how rough he appeared: at least two days beard growth, red sore looking eyes with dark rings. "Anyone would think you'd done a seven dayer yourself Brendan, you alright?"

"Grand. Get the eggs on then."

Marty got dressed first before making them both breakfast from what wasn't out of date in the fridge. He took out some bacon, a couple of dried out mushrooms, and some Special offer 68p Thick Irish Sausages. He looked in on the milk and rejected it, made two mugs of instant black coffee instead and brought it all in.

"I've to bring you to a place in Turf Lodge in an hour or so. Usual stuff."

Marty watched as he ate, trying not to notice how Brendan's hand trembled as he speared a sausage and lifted it to his mouth. Maybe it was time Brendan took a break. He chewed as he thought and came to a decision.

"How do you fancy coming down to Dublin for a bit Brendan, stay with me and Tinks for a couple of weeks?"

"Nah, I'd just cramp your style. In a bit maybe, let you get settled first." Brendan smiled in a tired knowing way. Marty gave him an affectionate slap on the shoulder, thinking again about how close they were, in some ways more than brothers; they had shared their lives and all the things therein.

"I'll hold you to that, finish up and let's go."

They drove to Turf Lodge, parking some way from their designated house and walked the rest of the way, constantly looking over shoulders, going through the front door of a house without stopping, exiting by the back and continuing before arriving at their address. Only Marty went in.

"I'll see you tonight Marty, have a few beers maybe. Take it easy."

"Alright Marty?" an unseen but friendly voice shouted from the top of the stairs. "Come on up. Nothing to worry about, you know the drill."

He went upstairs and entered the only open bedroom door. The heavy curtains were closed and he could just make out two seated figures in the gloom and the orange heat of a cigarette that rose to an unseen mouth and glowed brighter. There was no bed, just the stools and linoleum and what looked like a small table at the side. One of the stools faced the closed curtains. He could just make out the shape of their masked faces.

"Sit in the stool and face the curtains, it's just for security and it'll help you concentrate too. We can take the bloody masks off then as well."

Marty did as he was told and waited, hearing the sound of a zip opening and rustle of paper, then the click of a desk lamp that did little to lighten the room.

"That's better. Sorry for all the cloak and dagger shite but you know how it is. O.K, right from the start, right from the moment you were lifted. Tell us exactly what happened. There's no rush, if you miss something we can come back to it. Relax."

Marty took a breath and began. He told them everything, stopping occasionally as he tried to remember a certain phrase or the exact order of his interrogations, but it wasn't as easy as he thought it would be. The voices behind him coaxed gently, patiently, only interrupting if they needed to clarify a point before allowing him to continue. A pot of tea was brought up and he heard the dull chinking of heavy mugs. It went on for a couple of hours, sometimes they asked the same questions several times with pauses as they obviously checked his previous answers, but as he had nothing to hide there was no problem. As expected they were displeased at his breaking silence and concentrated minutely on what had been said.

"Why the hell did you say anything? You know very well the best defence is silence. It's a breach of discipline too, although I see the circumstances were a bit odd. Roy did you say his name was? We'll see if we can fit a last name to that, you never know." The voice behind him stopped and he made out whispering and low murmurs. "Alright Marty, what you've said seems to fit. We're satisfied for the moment, but you will have to come back here tomorrow for a final interview. You can go now. Oh, before you do there's someone downstairs wants a wee word first. Tell them we're finished here. See you tomorrow lad."

The light was flicked off and they faced the other way as Marty went downstairs, glad to get out, despite their apparent congeniality.

"In here Marty."

As expected, the voice of Frankie Saunders drifted through from the living room. He went and sat on the couch, raising his chin in recognition to Gary. Frankie was staring out of the window. He turned around.

"Did it go alright? No problems?"

Marty shook his head before answering, unsure whether that was disappointment or concern that flitted across the sneaky face. For some reason he had a mental image of those T shirts that were getting popular lately, the ones with 'Frankie Says' in big bold black lettering.

"They seemed to know an awful lot about me in Castlereagh, Frankie. No proof and a few things wrong but it's just as I thought, this place is riddled with touts."

"Is that why you want to give up?" said Frankie staring at him, and then looking away. "Or is it you're being nagged into such a decision?"

Marty flared. "Who are you to say anything, I don't see you taking any risks. When was the last time you fired a gun?"

He immediately saw he had struck a painful nerve. Frankie reddened and the lips became taut over those protruding teeth and he saw the boy from years ago, realising he hadn't changed that much. The taunts that Frankie endured as a kid he still carried, like a stain on cloth that faded but remained visible no matter how often it was washed. Brendan had once warned him the man was plain jealous of him and always had been. He was nearly stuttering with anger, trying to keep calm and controlled in front of Gary.

"Someone has to organise and plan. I have done ops too!" To Marty's quiet satisfaction he saw he was nearly stamping his foot. Gary murmured something about making a pot noodle and left the embarrassing scene. "As for informers in the ranks, that's for the people upstairs to sort out. Not you!" He seemed to think of something and taking a deep breath calmed himself. Marty watched his internal struggle, fascinated as he suddenly adopted a warmer, more accommodating tone.

"Let's not argue, I'm sure it'll all be sorted soon, we have our own intelligence too you know. Didn't we just recently execute a couple of traitors? What I'm saying is, don't be so hasty in leaving the movement Marty." He hesitated, his voice becoming thicker as he swallowed, almost gagging the last words out. "We need people like you."

Marty almost laughed out loud as he thought to himself that he wished he could say the same, and how much those last words must have cost Frankie. He thought it best to string them along for the moment.

"I have to come back tomorrow. After that I'm taking a break, but I'll think about it."

"I did warn you about using locals in such sensitive circumstances. I emphasised the same thing to HQ and they also refused to take heed. The hatred is too deep. That man could have provided invaluable information. I don't want to lose confidence in you..."

"It was too late sir!" Keith interrupted Major Molyneaux, his own anxiety and eagerness to exonerate himself overcoming his caution. "Anyway I don't think he would ..." he broke off as Molyneaux stared down his nose at him with cold Olympian scorn, his voice was clipped, precise and little above a whisper.

"Do not ever interrupt me. You do as you are ordered, and do not question my judgement again. Understood?" Keith bowed his head. "Very well, the damage is done, whatever the reason. Do you have anyone else lined up? I have to attend a meeting on Monday and would like to bring some positive news."

"Yes indeed sir," said Keith, nodding his lie vigorously. "I'll see to it first thing tomorrow."

Molyneaux seemed satisfied and gave an oblique glance. "One more thing Keith, I know the holding centre is a good place for gaining a source but it is a little too public sometimes. Everyone who is anyone knows about McKenna and your failed attempt, it reflects badly. Try a more unofficial approach tomorrow, something a little more discreet." He smiled thinly and it reminded Keith of a crack spreading across glass. "Save yourself some paper work too."

Brendan rolled out of bed half awake and confused, before focusing on the little white alarm clock that was beeping with an insistent racket fit to wake the dead. He grabbed at it clumsily, knocking it to the floor where it continued to annoy him before he managed to bend down and turn it off. He straightened up too quickly, feeling as if his head was a second or so behind the rest of his body. He collapsed back onto the bed, his palms at his temples and swallowing hard. He lay still and gathered his thoughts.

It wasn't surprising he felt so ill the amount of drink he had taken the previous night. He'd had a couple of pints before going to Marty's, where he had consumed more beer and vodka, exactly how much he couldn't remember. Then it was to the club for a couple of night caps and home where he had spied a bottle of Paddy with some nips in it that simply *had* to be disposed of. He didn't remember going to bed or virtually any of the previous evening, his memory wiped clean with alcohol. He was still quite drunk. Not that it mattered, he only had his meeting with Tin-Tin today and he wouldn't be driving, Johnno could do that. He struggled again to sit up, gingerly putting his feet on the floor and getting dressed with exaggerated care, trying not to cough as he knew he would retch.

He gripped the banister as he made his way downstairs, feeling a wave of nausea that brought sweat to his face and the first thumps of a new headache. He sat at the kitchen table and stared at the wall as he had a hundred times recently, usually with a glass in one hand, whiskey or vodka bottle in the other, trying to fight off the despair that came as regular black tides. He had even tried attending mass and gone as far as confession but it hadn't helped, the ritual and attempt at trying to find some meaning had been futile, leaving him feeling depressed, angry and as hopeless as ever. He felt like he was running on empty, his only fuel coming in those bottles of liquid silver and gold. After a bottle nothing was so terrible and all was seemingly possible, even happiness, at least for a little while, but then came the new day and old despair. What was the point of anything?

There was a knock at the door and he let Johnno in, oblivious to his wary and furtive looks. "You ready?" he asked Brendan, the voice edged with real doubt.

Brendan looked at Johnno blearily, taking in the blue eyes below the fringe of floppy dark hair. He wasn't a bad lad, although not the smartest and he had heard him boasting of being a volunteer with the more gullible women. He shrugged, rising slowly.

"Come on then."

"You haven't forgotten?" Johnno asked.

Brendan tried to concentrate, his thoughts slow and ponderous as elephants in a pool of mud. Johnno continued as he opened the door.

"Last night in the club, you said you could do a pick up on the way. I have to move a short, take a couple of minutes at most." Brendan rubbed his head; he couldn't remember a bloody thing about it.

"Oh, aye. Right! No probs. You're driving."

They got into Brendan's old Mazda and headed in the direction of Lenadoon where Tin-Tin had his flat, first stopping off at a house on the way where Johnno got out, his head turning from side to side as if crossing a busy road before going inside. Brendan decided to go in with him. He followed Johnno up the uncarpeted stairs where he stopped at a bedroom door, searching around before finding a small stool. Johnno got up on the stool and ran his fingers along the top of the door, stopping half way. His fingers went into the door frame and began pulling on a length of fishing wire, hauling out a pistol which he handed to Brendan. He had seen such clever hides before, this one inside the slightly thicker doorframe with padding to stop any knocking if the door was opened. The pistol was unfamiliar to him. He turned it over, feeling its nice weight and balance, black, slim and loaded.

"It's a Beretta, old model but good enough." Johnno explained helpfully. Brendan examined it, found and checked the safety before putting it in his waistband, carefully covering it with his jacket. They exited and Johnno pulled away. As they got back onto the main road a dirty white works van pulled out and began following them.

Dave started up immediately they saw the car coming out of the side street, Keith muttering under his breath and thinking furiously. He had to make a decision and quickly. They knew Price would be making his regular visit to one Terry Corr alias 'Tin-Tin' and it would provide a perfect opportunity for an initial tap up. Simply put up a quick VCP, stop him and make an offer. He had another large envelope of money already waiting, a couple of the crispy purple notes poking out seductively as a tempting little teaser. That coupled with heartfelt appeals to his humanity might do the trick, all in all it would only take a few minutes. The trouble was, Price wasn't travelling alone today, the little detour they had made probably an anti surveillance trick. Normally they would abort and simply wait for a more suitable opportunity, but Keith was in a hurry after fibbing the Major he had somebody else already lined up. The radio broke into life, wanting to know now whether to go or not. Damn! He was confident they could do it, stop them at a check point, get the driver out for questioning whilst he went for a quick chat with Price, job done, everyone happy. Ten minutes tops. He gave the go ahead, studiously ignoring the clear misgivings on Dave's face.

Now they were carrying a prison sentence in Brendan's belt, Johnno was unconsciously putting his foot down as much as possible. Brendan was experiencing another bout of nausea, his head not right at all, he was seriously thinking of cancelling his meeting. The traffic ahead seemed to have slowed down before a bend in the road and with growing unease they inched forwards, Johnno showing signs of distress.

"What do you think, heavy traffic at this hour? I don't remember any road works. An accident..." Brendan rubbed his head, using one hand as a visor against the painfully bright light and voiced what Johnno was really thinking,

"Or a snap check point. I'm not waiting to find out. Let me out then drive on, I'll start walking there."

To their left was a row of shops, an off license, mini market, chippy and a book makers with one parking space still free which Johnno now swung into. Brendan got out, giving a quick wave as if he was being dropped off like any other passenger given a lift. He crossed over to a small green with a couple of stunted, spindly saplings that moated the entrance to yet another housing estate. A couple of kids were arguing about the ownership of a ball, voices rising in shrill competition. It was then he noticed the white van, the door opening and his eyes fixed on the man coming towards him.

"What the hell..." Dave was a couple of vehicles behind, the sudden appearance of Brendan puzzling him for a moment. Keith saw in a flash what was happening.

"He's carrying! No time to wait for back up."

Keith made a snap decision and exited, taking his Browning with him and leaving Dave calling through the situation in rapid staccato as he reached under the seat for the Heckler and Koch. As Keith stepped out he realised the situation had changed in a second. If the guy was armed he could be arrested and possibly even blackmailed. There was also another alternative: either way it was win, win.

Their eyes locked and Brendan knew instantly what was happening as the man approached, one hand behind his back, a queer half smile on his thick lips and for that instant it felt as if time had frozen. Dreamlike, his own hand went so slowly to his waist to pull out the Beretta, half turning to break into a shambling bowed run. He felt something pluck at his collar and heard the first gunshot, then somebody gave him a hammer blow of a thump high up near the left shoulder that sent him sprawling onto the pavement just short of the green. More shots and one, two, three kicks to his ankle, calf and left buttock, the last one really hurting as it seemed to tear upwards into his spine. Now he could hear shouts, but none of them made any sense. It was so hard to think. He tried to sit up and was rewarded by a quick double punch to his chest either side, as two more bullets thudded into him and out the other side in twin gouts of red, crashing him brutally back into the ground, the pistol flying from his hand, his head bouncing and twisting to one side. Brendan tried to move his lips but couldn't make any sound. He knew he was dying and thought that if this was it maybe it wasn't all that bad after all. He focused on a tuft of grass directly in his line of vision, each individual blade so very, very bright and green. A shiny black ant was climbing to the top and others pulling at an intensely pink blob of chewed bubble gum at the base of the tuft. He gave an involuntary cough and saw a spray of tiny droplets of a rich and vivid scarlet. His eyes became very heavy and he closed them, a tiny smile forming as faces appeared. Where had they come from? Wasn't his whole life supposed to flash before him now? But no, it was just faces, snapshots of his dad, his mum, brother and sister, Tinks and Marty, then Hala and then dark.

Marty had just completed his second interview, which had been even more tedious than the first. At last it finished and he was allowed downstairs with a parting handshake. This time Gerry Fox was there to try and reason with him, suggesting he take as much time off as he needed to get himself sorted, but not to leave the movement entirely. There was also a veiled threat about not influencing anyone else, or using knowledge or equipment for his own ends. In a way Marty was flattered, but his mind was made up. He was sat relaxed now with Gerry talking about past events and operations, finishing a cup of coffee when somebody came to the door. Gerry got up and there was a whispered conversation before the visitor left and Gerry came slowly and thoughtfully back into the room. He stood in front of Marty and put his hand on his shoulder. Instantly Marty knew it was bad news and braced himself.

"What? What is it?"

"It's Brendan." He stopped at the grief that suddenly twisted the face before him, the tears that sprung into the eyes. "Jesus I'm sorry Marty. He's dead."

Roy waited in the car, window open. Keith had said he wouldn't be long, he just had to hand in his preliminary report on what had happened the other day, but Roy knew the real reason was he wanted to see Major Molyneaux, expecting praise and a pat on the back. Keith had been flushed and excited as he recounted several times what he had done, gloating over the final moments as he put shot after shot into the man. Roy didn't want to go in with him and have to listen to it all again. He was annoyed at the lack of trust, using another member of the unit in his place and lying to him about it.

Earlier this morning he had entered the office to find Keith on the red phone, jotting down something on a pad, pressing the pen down hard in annoyance. He had turned away, picking up the notepad as he did so. He finished listening and put the phone down, tearing off the top page and stuffing it into his pocket. He didn't volunteer anything and Roy didn't ask, guessing straight away the response would be the usual 'need to know' bullshit. It was typical of their relationship these days; he felt not so much a trusted colleague but more like a half trusted servant, driver and body guard. Roy had an option coming up soon to extend his detachment but was giving serious consideration to jacking it in, he was disappointed and disillusioned. In any case they might well decide he was too compromised to be of much further use. He would take the rest of his leave that had been interrupted and think about it.

"Good work Keith, you acted as I would have wished in a fluid situation. The man was armed and dangerous. Of course, such executive actions are out of our bailiwick, but with no immediate back up available you did the right thing. We didn't gain a source but it can still certainly be considered a success for us." Molyneaux chuckled now, looking at Keith in the mirror as he adjusted his tie. "Yes, one less terrorist and you certainly showed it isn't just the SAS that can take action if necessary. That'll raise a few eyebrows, well done!"

"Thank you sir." Keith hesitated a fraction. "There was something else sir."

"Go on."

"Hermes called in this morning. You may remember he told us of planning for an attack on a part time UDR man working in the city. It was all a bit vague to be of any use though." Molyneaux watched him expressionless. "They called it off as you also know sir, but our man Hermes says it's back on again. The trouble is he will be involved directly this time. The man in question works as a driver and they're going to kill him on his rounds this Saturday morning. Hermes said it might be a good idea if the target was to go sick and then change jobs. Apparently they don't have his home address yet, just where he works."

Molyneaux was still. Then seemingly irritated, as if an unwelcome guest had just appeared drunk at a formal dinner. He fiddled with his cuffs, shooting them out. It was as if he hadn't heard him. Keith waited a full ten seconds.

"Sir?"

"Does anyone else know about this?"

"No sir."

"Good. I suggest we keep it that way. Yes, getting high grade information in the future from Hermes is of the first importance, we really mustn't jeopardise our position with trivialities. Remember the overall picture Keith. We've invested a lot in this man and he will pay us off for a long time to come if we remain careful." Keith understood. And agreed.

"Yes sir."

The day of Brendan's funeral was the saddest of Marty's life. A mist like drizzle fell from ashen skies as he took his turn shouldering the coffin on its way to the final resting place in Milltown cemetery. He had sat through the church service deep in his own thoughts, the words and prayers an unheard mumbling background to his memory's private picture show. He closed his eyes and saw sunlit days, laughing and carrying on, Brendan as a kid, playing football on the street, the window he had broken that Brendan had taken the blame for, the seaside, first girlfriends and sticking together in school. Then their adult lives, the fighting, hardships they had shared, supporting each other unquestioningly through thick and thin. His friend. The flag was removed and the coffin lowered into the hole surrounded by a sombre wet throng, the only noise the subdued weeping and the clattering drone of a helicopter far above. Marty put the wreath from himself and absent Martina down and walked away, not staying for the speech from the leadership who had attended; he had heard it all before. He wasn't part of that war anymore, his own war was now a very personal one and would consist of a single last assault.

The days immediately after were a time of utter turmoil, his moods swinging from apathy, sadness and anguish to anger, and then hatred and back again. He was drunk at the wake, but after he stayed cold and sober, his only relief when talking to Martina on the phone, who quietly pushed him to come to Dublin, sensing something amiss in his conversation that wasn't just sorrow. There was a clipped undertone, a purpose in his voice that made her fear when he spoke of staying another week or so to tie up loose ends. Marty had been busy, the details surrounding Brendan's shooting vague and he wanted to know exactly what had happened. It was burning him up inside. He wanted to make whoever was responsible pay for it with their own life; revenge was personal cure and salvation.

There had been little enough to go on, it could have just been plain bad luck. A careless weapons pick up, that much they did know, a check point and some undercover soldiers on a surveillance job. Maybe Brendan should have stayed in the car, maybe they were being followed, probably, but who could be sure? Maybe a lot of things. He decided to go to the spot itself and just ask people what they had seen, not caring what internal security thought. He had to know. He persuaded a reluctant Tin-Tin to accompany him, as although some people in the area knew him, they knew Terry better and would therefore be less suspicious and more open. He asked first in the shops, but the girl serving in the mini market had only seen the aftermath. A few customers shook their heads in sympathy, yes a terrible business but they hadn't been there. Next came the chippy that had just opened for the day and no luck there either, the owner lived above the shop, had heard the shots but only seen the resulting flood of police and army after. They walked over the small green and tried a few of the houses that bordered it, knocking on doors, only two of which opened with anxious glares and nothing of use. It had all happened so quickly.

Tin-Tin gave him a commiserating clap on the shoulder and left. Marty stopped for a last look at the spot where Brendan had died. As he stared a small voice piped up behind him.

"That's where they shot yer man. I saw it all so I did," he added proudly. Marty turned and looked down at a kid holding a cheap plastic black and white football.

"Did you now? What happened then exactly?"

"I was just going to the shop 'cos Da said to go and get some Lucozade." The boy shifted onto his other foot, turning the ball tightly in his hands, making it squeak as he spoke. "My Da hasn't been so well, last night he..." Marty nodded impatiently and pulled out a fifty pence piece, the eyes on the boy swivelling down like a hungry chameleon.

"Oh, anyway. All the cars were going real slow like, you know there was a car check thing up ahead I heard. I seen the man get out of the car and sort of walk and then run. Then another man was chasing him and there was shooting and the man fell and there was more shooting and then people came out and then the peelers and soldiers came and I went home and Da was angry 'cos I didn't have the Lucozade..." He paused to get his breath and a sudden thought hit Marty.

"Did you see the other men who were shooting? What did they look like?"

"I didn't see the man in the van good but him with the gun, I saw him real close. He looked right at me after. He was really ugly looking, had a big nose and real rubbery face so he did..."

"Did he have grey eyes?"

"I think so. Aye, he did." Marty handed him the coin.

"Thanks son, you've been a big help, go and get yourself some crisps. Bye now."

The boy ambled off, happily putting the fifty pence piece in his pocket, bouncing the ball as he went. Marty knew enough. He knew enough to know who had shot his friend in cold blood and finished him off without pity. He had sat opposite them just recently, had even spoken to the murdering bastards. He felt the anger come hot and strong and then a warming sensation as he remembered he had a clue to go on, there was a slight chance he could find the one called Roy and show the Orange fucker the same mercy Brendan had been shown. He would do it alone so there was no chance of being compromised; his faith in their security had been considerably shaken these last months. He knew where he could get a pistol and crucially one that wasn't one under IRA control, a slight difference but of huge importance: taking a weapon from the IRA and using it for your own ends was a court martial offence that could result in a sentence of death. Not informing about the whereabouts of arms was merely dismissal 'with ignominy' as the rules stated. He could live with that, even with the thought of a smiling Frank Saunders announcing the verdict. Although it wasn't as if he was doing a robbery and keeping the money they still wouldn't like it. He swatted his doubts away. It would be alright.

The biggest problem of all was actually finding the target. All he had was a first name and the area where his family had once lived, if they were still there, if he still visited them, if he could find the address, if a lot of things. The only certainty was that he would need to be ruthless, determined and somehow get that one lucky break in finding him.

Chapter 13

Beyond Reasonable Doubt

Charlie Scott walked up to the security gates, unhurried and unworried on this fine Saturday morning, clicking through the turnstile, trying not to catch the eye of the civilian searchers or soldier that stood guard. He submitted to a quick frisk, he didn't have anything to hide. A sulky expression must have unwittingly made its way onto his face as the searcher repeated a well worn line in a bored tone.

"Just doing my job sir."

Charlie said nothing. True, the man was just doing his job, but that didn't make it right. Later he would also just be doing his job and with some pleasure. He had the details from the Intelligence Officer and completed a dry run yesterday. He had time to kill before he picked up his weapon, so he walked about, staring yet again at the pretentious City Hall with its massive green cupola and union flag waving in the breeze mockingly. He would get his gun from a by now taut and tense shop assistant, then he would be met by Donny on the motorbike and they would go and get their man. Charlie had watched him yesterday, swishing the spit through his teeth as he did so, as oblivious to the passers by as a lion to the grass around it as he focused on his prey, singled out from the herd. He hadn't stayed long, but long enough, the man whistling cheerfully as he took boxes from the back of his van was mentally filed and as good as dead already.

Charlie preferred it this way. He was a simple man and liked to keep the job simple too, this was so much better than all that complicated crap like the last effort he had been on. A bomb had been fashioned and shaped and cunningly put into a wall to catch a passing foot patrol, the command wire painstakingly concealed, running from the fire point, along the length of the wall, along a garden path, through a specially drilled hole in another wall and the end result was a big fat nothing. The patrol hadn't appeared, so they had to dismantle it all and start again. No, this was the way, a little public, but a couple of quick shots up close and away. A piece of cake.

Roy was just finishing a lunchtime apple when the black phone rang. He dropped the core into the waste bin with a hollow thunk before picking it up.

"Yes?"

"Hello Roy, how's it going?" a familiar voice answered him. He listened to the neutral tone before slotting a face to it. Robert, Special Branch.

"Fine. What about yourself Rob?" he asked in return.

"Ach, not so bad. Listen, d'you fancy coming for a beer and a blether sometime?"

"Sure, whenever you like, how about tomorrow night?"

"Good enough. I'll see you about seven. Oh, by the way did you hear about the UDR man shot dead near the city centre this morning?" There was a moments silence before Robert continued. "His name was Derek Oswald. You hadn't heard?"

"No I've heard nothing. Why?" Roy was alert now, listening carefully. The news was saddening, another good man murdered, but he was getting the distinct feeling the name should have meant something more. He became aware that Robert was listening to his answers with just as much attention. What was it he was after? The guarded careful voice assumed a more casual tone.

"Oh, I just thought you might have known of him is all." More silence, then Robert cleared his throat. "Well Roy, I'll be getting along now, see you tomorrow. Bye now."

"O.K Rob, see you tomorrow," said Roy rubbing his chin, deep in thought.

He put the phone down and sat back, finger now tapping impatiently as he played back the short conversation, trying to work out what exactly was being said, certain there was something hidden. Why would Robert ask if he knew him unless he thought he did, or had information about the man? It was far from a routine sort of call. More like fishing. There was something else he couldn't put his finger on, as if a coded message had been passed, a warning almost. Maybe he was reading too much into it, or just getting paranoid.

He picked up a pen and tapped it against his teeth, his narrowed eyes coming to rest on a writing pad, the one Keith used. He would be away until Monday. A meeting with Molyneaux this afternoon and Keith was free for the rest of the weekend. Suddenly he had a hunch and got up, reaching for the pad, noting the poor quality of the paper for the first time and its softness. Keith had torn off the top page, but now before he really thought about what he was doing, Roy held the pad up to the light at an angle. There were definite indentations from heavy ballpoint writing, not all of which were legible, but with rising certainty and sickness Roy was able to make out what looked like a U and two other letters, then a D and finally a whole name: OSWALD.

He dropped the pad and felt a wave of anger and shame. He had been a fool, used, lied to, betrayed; a stupid and blind accomplice to death. Again. What was he doing here? Why had he joined in the first place, surely to save lives, to prevent this sort of thing happening, not collude in it however unwittingly. This destroyed the whole ethos of being part of such a unit, the likes of Keith and that snooty bastard Molyneaux might be able to square their conscience with spurious and devious excuses, but he knew he never could. He felt sick, humiliated and dirty. He had a sudden flash back to sitting in a car with his Uncle Sam as he painstakingly tried to explain why laws had to be followed, even if sometimes they seemed less than perfect. What was it he had said? A fence or barrier. Which side of the fence was he on now?

Major Molyneaux was as pleased as he had ever been or probably ever would be in this God forsaken part of Her Majesty's realm, gratified with recent success and even more so with the praise that had come his way, but best of all the news that he would soon be leaving. Promotion and a new assignment called. He hummed a snatch of Strauss, 'Tales of the Vienna Woods' as he showered and changed. A single meeting with Shepheard and he was free until Tuesday. He would nip across to London this evening and spend a civilised couple of days in his real home.

He treated himself to a cup of Lapsang Souchong and settled in his tastefully decorated lounge, sipping carefully as he leafed through a MISR, a grimace of real disgust forming as he read. He glanced at his watch, putting the papers down with relief as he went to the conservatory to receive his visitor, noting with quiet satisfaction that Keith was punctual. Yes, he could congratulate himself on his choice of Shepheard; cunning, devious, ruthless and quite lacking in any false morality, he was just what was needed for this work. As Keith came through the gate he opened the door with a slight smile of welcome, he could afford to condescend a little now, the man had sworn fealty to his overlord and proved a good servant, one that knew his place. All he needed was a firm hand, a few kind pats and the occasional bone of reward and he was fine.

"Come in Keith, would you like a cup of tea perhaps?"

"Thank you very much sir," said Keith with an ingratiating smile. He followed the Major through to the sparkling kitchen, which after three previous cleaners was now reaching the required standard of cleanliness. Molyneaux busied himself with the pot before turning to Keith.

"So, everything alright? Anything unusual to report?"

"No sir, you may have already heard about the shooting this morning in the..." Molyneaux quickly cut him off.

"That isn't what I meant. Is everything else going well? Have you heard any *other* news from Hermes?"

"Not yet sir."

"Who is Hermes?"

They both turned in surprise. Roy stood in the doorway. They hadn't heard a thing. Molyneaux recovered first, the blood rushing to his face as much in indignation as shock.

"Who the hell do you think you're talking to Ferguson? How dare you come here unannounced and uninvited!"

He looked at Roy's face and felt a worm of unease at the grim set of the jaw and eyes that flashed green danger. Then he noticed he had one hand in his jacket pocket. Surely not. He couldn't be that out of control. He noticed Keith was looking nervous, as well as guilty and this increased his own discomfort. How much did he know? He thought about his own promotion potentially evaporating and tried a different approach.

"Look Roy, Hermes is a very valuable agent, very well placed and getting higher all the time. His identity and certain other things had to be kept strictly on a need to know basis. You understand?"

"I understand a man was murdered today in cold blood. I understand now what happened to McKee and Daly. I understand perfectly." Roy stood rock still and expressionless.

"Roy, you mustn't jump to conclusions," said Molyneaux licking his lips, now clearly rattled. "Don't forget the fundamentals of the game. They know we have informers and know some of their secrets. The key to winning is that they don't know *who* or *which* secrets we have until they can be put to maximum effect. Sometimes sacrifices have to be made, surely you can see that?" Roy was surprised at the tone, never having heard it before, it was almost kind as well as wheedling.

"What about the rule of law, the justice we're supposed to be upholding. What about plain old right and wrong and even morality, you might want to lose that but I don't!"

Moiyneaux shook his head sadly, speaking softly as if to a simple child. "I haven't lost any of those things, they're just on hold in the current circumstances. Stored if you like for a better place and time, those admirable sentiments are quite out of place here I'm afraid."

"Come on, everyone knows the rules," said Keith, now recovering from his shock.

"Rules? Oh, that's right, rules. I'm fucking *sick* of rules and games. You play God and change the rules when it suits and some poor bastard winds up with half his head shot away! You didn't just betray them, you betrayed me and everything I am!"

Keith moved his eyes slowly upwards in disbelieving exasperation as if watching a kite soar in the distance, mouth open. He smirked at Roy's futile anger.

"What a waste of a good passion. Just think of it as a game of poker matey, sometimes they win, sometimes we win. The beauty is that ultimately we're using their chips."

There was a heavy silence. Keith had badly misjudged him. Roy launched himself at that mocking face like a shot putter, his right fist balled tight, he landed a punch flush on his left cheekbone with all the strength he had, connecting perfectly at the end of his lunge, his full weight and all his pent up frustration and anger behind it. Keith flew backwards and crashed into the oven, head lolling slackly and out for the count. Molyneaux gaped but did nothing to help him. Roy looked at him contemptuously, his accent thickening as he spoke.

"If I thought I could get youse done for this I would you bastards. I quit, and I don't want any problems about it. No real proof, but if I was to tell certain people, well you know how rumours spread and the damage they do to reputations. We're quits."

He walked away, knowing he was finished with the army and this life but not caring, neither of them would say anything. That he did know; the likelihood of any comebacks was negligible, his path out would in all probability be smoothed, they had much more to lose than he did. He felt nothing but relief and an urge to return home to the people who would never betray him.

The lucky break that Marty was looking for came from a wholly unexpected quarter. He was sat upstairs in his old room, his parents and Rosemary out, the only noise a low murmuring from the radio as he pored over a street map. It was more for reference really, but of little use at the moment as he was stuck for a name. He lay on his bed, hands behind his head and eyes closed in concentration when suddenly the radio gave him what he sought. The sports news was on, Marty only half listening when the announcer started talking about Scottish football and a refreshing new scene, the new challenge to the dominance of Rangers and Celtic by Dundee Utd and Aberdeen whose manager Alex Ferguson had brought them success undreamed of... Marty's eyes snapped open. Ferguson! That was it! He was sure of it.

He jumped off the bed and ran downstairs to the telephone directory, thumbing rapidly through the pages, his index finger running down the F list. There, Ferguson. Shit. There were quite a few of them but he was only looking in certain streets which narrowed it considerably. More luck: only two potentials. He looked at the first but discounted it as not quite within the range. Yes, the second looked more promising. It wasn't a definite and he had thought that somebody with security force connections would probably be ex directory anyway. It was a start. He put the phone book down with a thump and returned upstairs, picking up the map and running his finger along the street, picturing where it came out onto the main road and the escape run back to his own area, on a motor bike perhaps. If he got his timing right he could do it and be back here in a bare couple of minutes before the hue and cry had started properly. It could be done, indeed had been done in the past by both the IRA and by the Protestant paramilitaries going the other way. Now all he had to do was find out if it was the right address and if and when the prodigal son ever visited.

The more he thought about it, the more unrealistic he saw his chances were, there were just so many variables. He smiled as he punned to himself, he would just have to give it his best shot. He spent the rest of the morning preparing, planning his route and 'borrowing' a motorbike from a neighbour. Marty had an old helmet bought some years ago from a second hand shop in Smithfield which he put on, before taking a quick passing look at the target house. No result. He waited until the afternoon before trying again, calling to his parents as he went.

"Just popping out."

His Ma came out of the living room as he put his jacket on and put her hand on his arm. "You'll be home for dinner?"

"Wouldn't miss it Ma." He gave her a wink and the grin.

He didn't use the motorbike this time, preferring to do his reconnaissance on foot. He made sure he had entirely different clothes on from the last two times he had been through the area as he searched for any sort of clue that might lead him to his target. He would only make one pass, if memory served him right there were even a few unoccupied houses on this street, the area like his own badly overdue a redevelopment.

He walked on, hands in pockets, careful not to make eye contact with anyone as he entered the alien red, white and blue paved world with here and there an occasional flag hanging limply in the still air. He turned to gaze at the sky which was heavily, darkly pregnant, with just a single lighter silver grey band silhouetting the distant cranes. There were few people about which was a relief to Marty as he silently counted the house numbers, paying special attention to cars, discounting any that were too old. His man would in all likelihood have one of the newer better cars on the street.

He approached the house, slowing ever so slightly then stopping to tie a lace. To his surprise somebody was coming out and he had a moment of panic. If it was Roy Ferguson the game was up, he wasn't armed and he would never get another chance. He took a quick look and missed a heartbeat as his first impression was that it was indeed him, but then he realised the man was far too old, but the brief look was enough. Those eyes were the same green and the set of the jaw although flabbier was the same as what he had stared across the table at so recently, that just had to be his Da. Even the upright stiff bearing was the same. A woman stood with an apron calling from the doorway and

Marty couldn't believe his incredible fortune at the words, it was almost too good to be true.

"Flour and eggs and butter mind, not margarine. I want everyone to enjoy this cake." The man walked on past him muttering and he just picked up the last words. "...bloody birthday."

It was all he needed, if there was a celebration tonight then he would just have to invite himself along. After dinner.

The rest of the day dragged as Marty sat waiting in his room, everything now ready. Outside it was raining. This was the worst part, the waiting with too much time to think. A new voice in his head seemingly coming from nowhere had asked him a single disquieting question.

Why don't I just go away now?

He crushed it immediately, ruthlessly as he would any others that tried to join it, knowing from experience, doubt or hesitation in such circumstances could be fatal. To his relief the phone rang downstairs and he listened to his Da bantering a moment before he shouted up to him.

"Marty! Somebody for you!" He went down, his father waiting to hand him the phone with a mischievous smile before adding deliberately loud, "Why don't you just marry the girl and settle down son, if you're not careful you'll be left on the shelf so you will." Marty took the phone.

"Hey Tinks! How's it going?"

"Good, just about everything sorted now. When will you be down?"

Marty felt a stab of guilt at his deceit, not just to Martina but to his family too. He had told them his plans for the future and his decision, but hadn't gone into details about why. They were so obviously happy.

"Eh, won't be long now. I was thinking tomorrow..." The inner voice came again completing the sentence, *just after I've shot an old acquaintance I met again recently.*

"That's brilliant, no problems about leaving from you know who?"

"Nah, I think they're O.K with it. I'll see you soon enough love." *Right after I've stiffed this man Roy Ferguson.*

"Alright then, see you soon." A soft and sexy chuckle came down the line. "I'll be waiting, be a good boy now and we can be bad together tomorrow." He cleared his throat as his imagination took fleeting hold.

"I will, Bye now." He heard the click and put the phone down. *Aye, I'll be good. Straight after I've shot him in the face.* Jesus! What was wrong with him? His Ma brushed past him with two bowls.

"Come and eat now before it gets cold," she said.

He sat at the table where Jimmy was already buttering bread, eyes bright and evidently hungry. "Fuck that's..." Rosemary shot him a look and he started again. "Now that's what I call a good meal on a night like this. What could be better on a cold wet evening than a good hearty feed of Irish stew?"

Rosemary smiled sweetly at him. "Yes Daddy, but only if there's nothing added."

Jimmy feigned wide eyed innocence, mouth full. Marty knew what she meant. His Da maintained it tasted better with a bottle of stout thrown into the pot and he had to be closely watched. The smell of mutton and vegetables with parsley hit Marty and his mouth watered despite his lack of hunger and hollow feel. He dipped a bit of bread and tried to eat. His Ma addressed him as she sat.

"So you'll be off tomorrow then. When do you think you'll be back to visit?" Marty chewed slowly before he answered.

"Soon enough Ma, I'll get settled in first and try and find a job." *That's right, I might be able to visit or perhaps you might visit me in jail after I've been put away for a thirty minimum.*

"A good thing too," said Jimmy. "Get away from it all." He waved his spoon expansively, the room temporarily substituting for the whole province. "Best thing you could do." There was a flash and low rumble of thunder as his Ma raised herself and pulled one curtain back and peered out into the dark, watching the rain.

"Are you going out tonight?"

"Aye." *Just popping out to kill someone, won't be long.*

"In this?"

"It's just rain Ma, it might stop later anyway." *It'll be good for washing the blood away too.* She eyed him uncertainly.

"Well, if you must. Wear the leather jacket, don't be taking that new one it's not waterproof."

"Yes Ma." *What about blood proof?* Marty got up abruptly from the table his head buzzing, having only had a few mouthfuls, he had to get away and get this over with. They looked up at him in unison so he pretended to examine his watch.

"Nice dinner Ma, thanks. I've to be going though. Don't wait up." *Have to rush, somebody is waiting to have their brains blown out.*

He left the table and closing the door behind him went to put his jacket on, not the leather though as everything he had on now would later be burned. He went upstairs to retrieve the hidden pistol, a 9mm Browning, the same as the army used. He noticed he was breathing heavily and cursed himself, thumping his thigh, thinking of his friend dead on the street, fortifying himself with that mental image like an alcoholic with a stiff whiskey. Everything was ready, the gun, the bike and the helmet to conceal his face and a little less conspicuous than a balaclava, a spare set of clothes in a vacated house in the next street. He went back down, taking the crash helmet from under the hall table and went out into the hissing rain.

The smell from the oven was absolutely delicious Betty thought as she peeked through the glass at the cake, now risen and yellow brown. Another hour on low would golden it. She turned the dial and started putting plates out, getting everything ready for later. She hummed as she worked, happy that her family would soon be together again to celebrate William's birthday. She corrected herself, almost all together. George would of course be absent, but even that couldn't dampen her joy, at least her eldest had renounced his evil connections, he had found God but remained in jail. She knew her son and believed his repentance genuine, unlike some of his fellow inmates; it was strange how many turned to religion only after they were incarcerated. Anyone would think God was locked up with them. If only George had searched for the Lord sooner. At least now there was hope. She saw William softening with age and was sure reconciliation must follow.

Her other boys were doing well and even Roy would be here tonight, a fact that cheered her husband and made him forget his grumpy attitude to birthdays. She was particularly glad Roy would be here, despite the fact he was based in the province his visits were infrequent and at all hours, usually at night, but she understood the reason for this. She had noticed a change in him the last few times he had called, he seemed to be moody, sometimes staring off into the distance preoccupied and deep in thought. The doorbell rang and she heard William welcoming John and his new wife into their home. She wiped her hands and went to greet the first guests.

The rain was lashing down in torrents as night came, the thunderous dark clouds revealed in occasional flashes as the storm grew stronger and nearer, making some of the older Victorian buildings real Gothic horrors as he passed. Roy almost expected bats to flap past his windscreen at any moment or somebody green and riding a broomstick to put in an appearance. He was driving his own car towards his father's birthday, not at all in the mood for small talk and merry making, but he had promised and he couldn't think of anywhere else he would like to be anyway. He drove carefully despite the fact there was little traffic and even fewer pedestrians. His right hand had started swelling almost as soon as he had left Molyneaux's house. He winced as he tried to move the fingers which were rapidly stiffening, with one or possibly two broken for sure, but he couldn't remember pain being so well paid for. The punch he had inflicted on his treacherous, conniving and just plain evil ex colleague had been the most satisfying thing he had done in a long many a day. His anger at himself would remain for some time. How could he have been so naive, to trust a bastard like that for so long? He had discovered far too late to what an extent Keith had changed, remembering now the drunken conversation years before about how he both admired and hated integrity and honesty. The hate had won and Shepheard had become a corrupt, corrupting influence. Men like Keith and Molyneaux saw everyone as mere stepping stones on the way to greater things. They were a matching pair of bastards.

He approached the turn off into the street he knew so well, slowing to avoid a careless motorcyclist who was too close going the same way, noticing briefly how drenched the man was. Bloody fool out in this weather. He pulled up outside his parent's house and took a closer look at his hand, gingerly pushing the fingers one by one with his other hand, flexing them and judging the extent of the damage. Ouch! The index and middle fingers seemed to be worst affected and were now puffed, the damage all too visible. He suddenly felt like a boy again as he remembered coming home and trying to think of excuses to explain away cuts and bruises to his eagle eyed parents. It was exactly the same now, and despite the throbbing of his knuckles he let out a small rueful laugh.

He looked in front of him through the teeming water and recognised John's Opel, its whiteness lit up by another flash of lightning. To the right he could just make out shadows moving behind the drawn curtains inside and wondered who else was coming tonight. On impulse he went to his wallet, carefully pulling it out and hissing slightly with the pain as he opened it. Inside was an old picture, it was the second time today he had looked at it. A family snapshot, black and white on a summer day long ago in Sam and Heather's garden, Sam with his arm around his shoulder, both beaming into the camera. He stared for another minute, remembering that happy day before putting it back and thinking about a cover story for his hand. His eye caught movement to his left and suddenly there was another flash of lightning, this time so close that the accompanying thunder was instantaneous. The window collapsed into crystal cubes and he felt a searing burn pass through his left shoulder. The thought that he had been struck by lightning passed in a split second and then he found himself staring at the dripping muzzle of a Browning pistol, fully extended in an outstretched double grip, the owner now darkly silhouetted against a dramatic backdrop of rolling thunder and flashes.

Marty was soaked to the skin as he went past the house a third time, noting the white Opel that had been there since his first round. It was a possible, but he didn't think Ferguson would be so soon or take the albeit small risk of putting in a daylight appearance. If he came at all.

More thunder and lightning lit up the streets, the rain hurtling down in sheets. He would give it another pass in ten minutes. He rode away, conscious of the weight in his pocket, the cold starting to seep past his skin into his flesh and very bones, making him shiver. He turned and was nearly hit by a car heading the same way that slowed to let him by. He moved his head slightly and peered through his visor as the driver was revealed like a movie star caught in a paparazzi flash as more thunder rumbled. It was him.

He accelerated to the top of the street and headed back, slowing down as he saw the headlights of the car disappear, the driver not moving, seemingly preoccupied, just sitting there looking at his hands. He didn't have a moment to lose, so almost jumping off his bike he walked quickly, his feet squelching at every step, pulling out the gun and releasing the safety, cocking it ready to go. More flashes, more noise. Good. He approached the car, hands extended and fired. The glass blew and he had an unobstructed view of the interior. He had him. Roy's eyes flicked from the gun to his own behind the helmet and they stared at each other for an hour long second.

Billy was late and driving his new car as fast as he could, hoping he didn't get pulled over, the half packet of mints he had crunched up was good enough for his parents, but wouldn't disguise the amount of beer he had in his system from a breathalyser. He didn't do it often, but with three pints he was over the limit.

Nearly there now. Jesus what kind of weather was this? He would rather be with his girlfriend or have stayed in the pub with his mates before heading off to Robinsons for a last one, but as Roy would be there tonight he decided to go. Life was just becoming really good for Billy. He had his first real job and money in his pocket, enough to go out with the lads, enjoy evenings with his girlfriend, and buy the car he was driving now, not really new, but good enough and none of his mates had a motor. Aye, he was having fun. Even tonight might be a laugh, his Da would unwind a little and his Ma was in much better form lately. As for John, well, they always liked to give each other a slagging. It would be even better now his wife was there, casually mentioning events from the past that he might find a wee bit embarrassing.

He sped along the road, slowing at the lights, but seeing no one around on this shitty wet night carried on through and picked up speed, gliding gracefully into his own street, slowing again as he neared home. His headlights made the wet asphalt shine and then picked out a figure in a crash helmet standing foolishly in the middle of the road in the driving rain. At first glance Billy thought he was talking to the driver of a car, parked in what he considered his own spot and this annoyed him. He considered winding down the window and shouting for him to get the fuck out of the road, but as he didn't want to get wet he simply inched his way forwards and gave his horn a long wailing beep. That would do the trick.

Betty came into the living room as she had spent her life doing, bearing food. First a huge plate of sandwiches, tuna, ham, cheese and onion, liver paste, all nicely cut into posh triangles which went onto the table, delivering a slap on the hand to John that was more playful than annoyed as he reached for one.

"Wait until it's all out and everyone is here."

His wife tutted her agreement. Next came a round of drinks and empty plates, two left standing for Billy and Roy and finally the cake was brought in, candle not yet lit. William insisted on everything done properly and at the right time, although pretty much relaxed he still managed to frown as he looked at his watch, but more out of habit than agitation. He looked around him now at the smiling faces of John and his wife Margaret, a good, decent hard working, level headed girl in the civil service, Heather who had put in an unexpected but very welcome appearance and finally his own wife. No, he couldn't complain. Together they had brought up a family in bad times in a rough area and he couldn't help a little self satisfaction that his boys, bar George of course, had turned out as well as they had; respectable decent people, despite the circumstances. He had to concede even George was now on the right road again, and he looked forwards to the day when he could welcome his eldest son back into his home. He was proud of them all.

He poured another congratulatory beer and sipped contentedly. From outside came more thunder with an underlying crack that sounded odd, followed by a long and very annoying car horn honking as if the driver had his damn hand stuck there. He got up to go to the window. If that was Billy showing off his bloody car again... He pulled the curtains apart and peered out at the deluge, before he was able to make out Roy's car and, yes Billy's behind it with the headlights on. He watched, knitting his eyebrows together, slightly perplexed as he saw his youngest son leave his own car and run over to Roy. What was the young fool doing now, he'd get soaked. Then for the first time he noticed another figure across the road climbing onto a motorbike, which roared away and for the first time felt a shaft of unease which turned to dread as he saw Billy now running towards the house, his face white and shouting incoherently through the torrent of raindrops. He moved quickly to the front door, past the faces now staring up at him, conversation stopped as the realisation came in a hot rush that something was badly wrong. He opened the door to another blast of thunder as Billy barged past him, pushing wetly through the gathering in the hallway and confirming their worst fears as he went to pick up the phone.

"Ambulance, he's shot!"

"What?"

"Who?"

Instant pandemonium and raised voices, shouted questions and women holding each other, hands covering cheeks in shock and fear. Billy shouting into the phone, William and John sprinting outside to the car, a door opening in a house opposite, spilling yellow light onto the wet kerb and jumping splashing puddles, a woman standing in the doorway with her man behind her. William felt his heart pounding as he ran the short distance, feeling neither rain nor wind before coming to an abrupt halt as he saw inside the car. Betty had broken free from Margaret's restraining grip, the terror of not knowing overcoming her fear of what she would find. She moved quickly, her slippers sodden within seconds as she stopped, wiping wet hair out of her face. William was now on the other side of the car, he was sat half in and had Roy's head cradled in his arms. She came around slowly, now noticing the small cubes of glass scattered on the seat, the road and on her son's lap. There was blood on her husband's hands, appearing more black than red as he gently stroked Roy's hair. Then he gave a low moan and a sharper intake of breath and when he spoke she felt every emotion flood through her.

"I'm alright Da. It's not as bad as it looks. Just the shoulder is all," said Roy.

Then he looked directly at her and straightened, giving a trace of a smile. John was striding back into the house to check on Billy's progress and reassure his own wife, also to call for assistance in trying to catch the bastard who had done this, although knowing it was probably too late. Roy was sitting again, hand pressed against his wounded shoulder to stem the blood which was still seeping out but much slower, it was a straight through flesh wound. His father still had his arm around him.

"God, son you've been lucky."

Roy nodded and then shook his head. No, it wasn't luck: he had seen the gun pointing right at him for that instant, one of the hands with a small silver pinkie ring and waited for the next shot and death, helpless as a baby. The gun had stayed pointed, then wavered, gleaming dully and dripping. A car horn had sounded and the gun had lowered a fraction and then been whipped away, the man simply walking off and getting on his bike. He was confused, as if he had been told the answer to four plus four was now seven.

"Can you walk Roy?" his father asked. He noticed his mother weeping and laughing gently at the same time.

"I think so."

He stood unaided, one arm holding the other and allowed himself to be led indoors, the whole street now with curtains opening and doorways showing rectangles of light.

Roy had his own room. White sterilised looking walls that didn't appear as if dust had ever dared land on them, a portable TV and a small bedside table with the *Belfast Telegraph* on it. He was in the paper although not named, and his condition was said to be comfortable. Well, he wouldn't go that far. He was sat up in his raised bed, stitched up and the shoulder swollen, black, blue, sickly yellow and very painful. Although just a flesh wound they were keeping him in a few days to make sure.

He would be released soon, but first somebody was coming to interview him and the thought of who this might be made him uneasy, the last person he wanted to see now was Keith Shepheard with his toad like false bonhomie, forgiveness and poisoned bitter grapes. He never wanted to see that bastard again; the man was an evil, dangerous, manipulative, walking body of corruption. He discounted Major Molyneaux, there was little chance of that polished turd appearing in such plebeian surroundings or wishing him well even by post. He had already had one visitor, but he was happy enough to see Helen come through the door, a little surprised too. She had been warm enough and gave him all the latest news and passed on the well wishes of his former colleagues. She also told him that a few arrests had been made, and one in particular from the New Lodge that looked like a good bet. They chatted and before she left gave him what for her was a warm lingering kiss and hug that made him yelp. Now he waited apprehensively for his next visitor, but was sure the course he was going to take was the right one. For himself. There was a polite knock and in walked Robert Allen, a broader than average smile creasing his face as he pulled up a chair and shook his hand.

"O.K Roy? How's the arm? Don't get up," he joked.

"Fine, nearly fine. I'll be out of here in a day or two. No lasting damage so I'll be as right as rain."

"Great! Now you know this isn't just a social visit." He tapped the folder he was clutching and opened it. "Standard stuff, what happened exactly and all that, any little details might come in handy. Look I don't have to go through all that, you know yourself how it goes. Let's just start from the beginning."

So Roy did, leaving out the earlier part of the day and how he had come to break a knuckle on somebody's head. It wasn't relevant, even if the distraction of it all had led to his being caught off guard. He went through how he had been shot, the arrival of Billy, and how he had seen the man riding away on his motorbike, keeping it short and to the point. He gave a physical description that could have fitted anyone between the ages of sixteen and seventy unless they were hunchbacked or crippled.

"Nothing else you can add?" Robert asked.

"No, sorry it all happened so fast but. He was wearing a helmet so no way I could be sure or pick out anyone on an ID parade." Robert was disappointed.

"That's a pity, we're holding who we think did it but the forensics just aren't there. It wouldn't hold up in court without a positive identification." He hesitated a second before throwing Roy the clue. "You remember a guy you interviewed named McKenna? Well we picked him up near his parent's home, strangely he was dry but with absolutely soaking wet footwear, almost as if he had forgotten to change everything. Or didn't have time. Not much more than a stone's throw from your house is it?"

Roy raised his eye brows and attempted to shrug which brought on a wince. Robert watched him, waiting like a cat at a mousehole before finally adding.

"You're sure you couldn't pick the culprit out of a line up?"

"No." Roy shook his head firmly. "In all honesty I couldn't." Robert wrote a last note in the file and closed it.

"I don't think you've the right man there Rob," he added as he went to leave. "As far as we could tell he was off to live in Dublin. I believe him. I don't think he's a threat whatever he might have in his past. You might tell him to stay down there though if he wants to keep healthy."

Robert put his head slightly to one side, lips pursed, knowing there was something he was missing here but unable to say what. Not unusual in this line of work. Although dissatisfied he wasn't going to be able to put McKenna away for a long Maze holiday he shook Roy's hand again before leaving.

"I'll tell him. After we've had him for the full seven days. Right, bye Roy. Take care now."

Keith was in a foul mood and was letting it show as he waited for Hermes. It was the same garage as last time, a nice safe environment that they could control and now at least he didn't have to put up with the likes of Daly filling the air with 'eau de turd.' He thought about the other week, and his face darkened even further as he touched his cheek. It was still a bit sore and a sticking plaster covered a graze where he had fallen. He had wanted some action taken, they were still in the army weren't they and subject to orders and discipline? This was the line he had taken with Molyneaux, but to his disgust the Major had merely looked down his nose at him and told him to forget it, in fact, had told him not to be such a bloody fool. Ferguson was out and that was as far as it was going, he would think of a convenient reason and no further action was to be taken, either officially or unofficially. Molyneaux had paused and given him a pointed long stare when he added that last bit, leaving him burning with frustration.

Now he was sat here with a new partner waiting to pay for more news. There was a rusty squealing groan as the garage door opened and then Hermes came in, looking even more furtive than usual. He gazed a moment at Keith, the merest smile on his face blackening his mood even further.

"What the fuck happened to you then? Bad day at the office?"

Keith ignored the mockery. "What do you have? Anything worthwhile this time?"

"Oh yes. Definitely worth what I hope you have in that lovely fat envelope there." He seemed to enjoy this more the longer it went on, as he held out a smaller standard white envelope of his own. "Let's swap."

They exchanged, Keith tearing open the paper like a starving animal as Gerry Fox pocketed the money and walked away.

Chapter 14

Recognition

It was a bitterly cold day in December, a lot of snow had fallen and already they were talking about records being broken in Northern Ireland for this time of year. Despite the bone chilling weather Marty had needed to get out, away from the house where he had felt stifled in the crush of well wishers and central heating. It was giving him a headache.

The funeral was over and he wished for everything to get back to normal. He had done his grieving some time ago when he was first told his Ma had a cancer that was going to kill her. He hadn't believed Jimmy at first, although she was now old and infirm she would get better, she always did. Then he had seen her and believed. She was as cheerful as the sunny day he came, even when the coughing racked her wasted frame, but her eyes had a peculiar shine and depth and he knew then for sure.

At the end of that visit he had gone back to his nice South Dublin home and gotten sodden drunk for the first time in years, pouring the stuff into himself to help burst the dam of tears. The grief had eventually come in a saline evening flood, his sobs drawn from a deep well, audible throughout the house. He had been inconsolable and had banished Martina and their daughter Angela to visit elsewhere, not wishing to subject them to this. He wanted to be alone so he could really let go and get it out.

That had been in the summer. He had visited frequently since then along with the rest of the family, now all with kids of their own, Bernie facing her fate with cheerful courage, her joy at seeing all her grandchildren undiminished, Jimmy at her side constantly as they waited for death together. Now it was over Marty felt a renewed grief, but this time it was tempered with relief. The inevitable had come and her sufferings were over, life went on.

He needed some fresh air, which is why he had parked the car and was walking carefully along frozen pavements, wondering again at the changes that had taken place to his native city these last years. The whole place had experienced a massive face lift, the slums were long gone, replaced for the most part by housing of a much better quality, the shops were thriving and the centre especially seemed to radiate an undreamed of prosperity in the peace. A great deal of money had been spent these last years, some calling it a peace dividend; the more cynical called it a bribe. Marty himself was beyond both points of view. He was just glad the violence had stopped as he had become totally and irrevocably sick of it all.

His change had come slowly at first and then accelerated, until at last he had to push himself to action, even the death of Brendan had not been enough. His anger was real, but fast dissolving at the futility of it all, finally at the last moment on a stormy rain lashed night he cut his own personal Gordian knot. He had been arrested and held before he could get away to Dublin, and was sure they would connect him and stitch him up for attempted murder even without proof. There had followed more questioning in the same vein as his last stay in Castlereagh, but to his astonishment no charges. He was released and met by a tearful, joyfully angry Martina at Connelly train station like something out of a film. He didn't know at first whether she was going to kiss him or slap him. He had refused to return north for a debriefing much to their annoyance, but eventually they had allowed him to do it in a slummy flat in the North Dublin. It had passed off without incident, surprisingly easier this time than last, although they wanted to know of course where he had left the gun. He had listened to a lot of bullshit, sitting through their censure of him and orders and the fact they were taking his past record into consideration, so leniency would be shown. It was a serious breach of their rules, he had taken unauthorised action albeit not for personal gain, but the result was that he could no longer be accepted into their ranks. He was dismissed and only just controlled his satisfaction from showing.

Free from any interference, he and Tinks had built a new life. The first years had been fraught with difficulties, financial and emotional. It hadn't been easy finding a steady, well paid job and a lot of the time Martina supported them both, the other thing was getting used to normality. The novelty of a routine life without danger or stress, had for a while turned into a strange kind of boredom at the ennui of everyday existence. It had passed eventually and they married, and after a couple of years were rewarded with a baby girl. Martina progressed at her teaching and Marty found employment wherever he could, things improving as the Irish economy picked up.

The computer age dawned and he found himself with a second chance; he liked and was good with the new technology, and after taking several courses his prized new skills were much sought after. Marty found himself in a unique position of having choice where he worked and the money was excellent. Life had continued like this more or less ever since, a nice house, daughter doing well, holidays and family visits, their past life having to be carefully forgotten in some of the circles they now mixed.

Marty thought about this as he walked along Great Victoria Street. His life had been transformed as much as the city he was born in. As the saying went, time heals, but never totally, the ache was not so strong but occasionally something would happen, an image on the news, out shopping even, or just a smell would trigger a particular memory, bringing it all back for a moment. Once he had even seen Frankie in Dublin as he did some Christmas shopping.

Saunders had given him a frigid hello before walking on, the snobby bastard, as if being seen with the likes of himself was now beneath him. True enough, Frankie was becoming quite big politically, he'd even seen him on the news, bullshitting away with even more gusto than usual. Then he thought of Gerry Fox and how he had just one day disappeared, followed by rumours that he had at first refused to believe. That someone of his standing could become so cynical and give up his own people for mere money was incredible. But there could be no arguing with the facts. He had indeed flown, and evidence came to light later that he had been touting for years for who knew what reasons, even that he had tried to set himself and Martina up. Why, apart from selfish greed nobody really knew.

They had also met Johnno not so long ago on a visit to Dundalk, who much to his amusement was arm in arm with Siobhan. He had temporarily forgotten her real name and almost addressed her as Louis, humming and hawing before Tinks had rescued him. They had a few drinks together, reminisced and toasted absent friends. It was then he got the full story of what had happened that day, surprised but strangely relieved when Johnno insisted that both of the undercover Brits had spoken with clear English accents as they arrested him, his description fitting only one person he had met.

He shoved his hands further into his overcoat and gave an involuntary shiver. God it was cold. He noticed a couple of hardy souls standing outside smoking, their breath hanging in small smoggy clouds and realised where he was, nearing the Crown bar and debated whether to pop in, just to get out of the cold for an hour. The inside was as enticing as always. He had a soft spot for the Crown, despite the name, with its beautiful burnished old world decor and stained glass windows. Everybody loved the Crown, including the tourists of course who had been coming to Belfast in increasing numbers since the ceasefire. Marty felt queasy when he thought about the new tourist trade, some of it had been based on bus tours of famous trouble spots and the hundreds of wall murals that seemed to cover every end house: to him it was similar to someone making money by exhibiting their scars. Thankfully there would be few tourists in this weather. He didn't ever want to hear again the sort of conversation he had recently overheard. An American, obviously drunk and beginning to slur, talking about terrorism and how 9/11 was 'real' terrorism and this 'Irish thing' had just been 'small potatoes'. Marty had told him to shut his mouth and left them staring after him. Arseholes. He went inside.

A few streets away Roy was having almost exactly the same thoughts as he walked through the centre. A group of men passed him, well dressed and chattering in a language he couldn't place, could be East European, but he couldn't tell. They didn't look like tourists though, not at this time of year. Not that he had anything against tourists coming to fish in the lakes or visit the beauty spots of the Mournes and all that, it brought in a lot of cash. No, what he felt a bit sour about were those bus tours of the troubles, thankfully now not nearly as prevalent as when the ceasefire began. The notoriety of the place was at last fading. Thank God. He had found it distasteful to say the least, rather like exposing your Grandfather's corpse to Yank tourists and plastic paddies for a few quid a peep.

He was in a good mood this day, having just bought a beautiful gold necklace for his wife and some earrings for his daughter. His boy Sam would have to make do with a present of cash, not that he would complain. For Roy, the best thing about having money was being able to spend it, but there were worse things in life than not having the latest designer gear exactly when you wanted it.

When Roy left the army he had moved to London and worked in a variety of jobs before he was contacted out of the blue by Helen, who had simply turned up at his Wandsworth flat one day. He was as surprised as he was pleased, and before long they had resumed their relationship, but this time in a normal atmosphere that had been a little odd for both of them. She intrigued him. Despite their history, they found they actually knew very little about each other's background and he had obviously misjudged her in a number of ways, not least the fact that she was keener on him than he had thought. He had assumed her upbringing was much the same as his own, as she had never really spoken of it and her neutral accent betrayed nothing of her roots. He had been amazed to learn she was actually very wealthy, or to be accurate her father was, which was confirmed when after a few months she introduced him at the family home. He remembered laughably now his first impressions of her and that he hadn't been too far wrong. The place wasn't Versailles, but it was a beautiful large mansion, set in its own well kept grounds in the middle of Buckinghamshire. They even had stables. Her mother had died when she was a toddler and her father had never remarried, putting his energy into the hugely successful car business he had been operating since he was in his early twenties: in short, the man was rolling in it. Roy was apprehensive, but to his surprise found her father unaffected and genial, they got on well and it wasn't long before he was married again. At least this time his own parents approved, his Ma especially at his 'good catch'. He would have married her without the money and she knew this, they did after all have a lot of experience together that not many other couples shared. So, he had settled down, set up in London, his hard work in the company met with firm approval. Children followed and life was good.

They still visited Northern Ireland regularly, even more so once the second ceasefire was in place, enjoying the beautiful countryside on summer visits, and they had bought a house recently as a second home and investment. It was in the same village where Major Molyneaux once reigned. Roy turned into Great Victoria Street, putting up his collar as a gust of freezing wind clawed at his exposed flesh. He was always glad to be home, the place even in the darkest days had drawn him back again and again. He thought less about those days now, occasional reminders would pop up in conversation and his imagination and memory would be jolted. Yes, the place had changed. He liked to think he had changed too, another one of his Ma's favourite sayings came to him about leopards never changing their spots. Well maybe human nature in general didn't change, but his own personal experience was that a man's individual reactions to love or pain or any given situation could differ as the years passed. There might be peace of a kind, but he had no illusions that the deep, deep hatred of centuries was still here. It would take a very long time to heal, and he had his suspicions that some people would keep and polish, even cherish, their bitter loathing, their hatred remaining bright and pure as a timeless nugget of gold in the gently flowing stream of history.

Roy checked his watch, debating whether to go straight home or ring Helen and tell her he was stopping for a drink first. Excellent, he would phone from inside rather than standing here on the street fumbling on his mobile with frozen fingers, maybe even have a malt with his pint. Why not? He went inside.

The bar was quiet, the cold and relatively early hour keeping custom to a minimum. A couple of individuals sat on stools at the long mottled red granite bar, with a scattering of small groups in the booths or 'snugs' that helped give the place such great character. Roy didn't bother checking if any of the enclosed snugs were empty, taking a stool at the bar near the door. He ordered a pint, not bothering with the chaser, and taking a small sip turned to marvel at the pubs glorious interior. As far as he knew there was no other pub like this, the windows were stained glass, the tiled floor, the woodwork abounded with intricate carvings and burnished splendour, the pillars scaled like dragon skin. He had once heard it described as more like a church than a pub and would have to agree with that; he had recently visited Italy on holiday and the opulence and colour reminded him a little of a Florentine chapel. He smiled as he took another sip. It might not be a chapel but was certainly a place of pilgrimage for the more discerning of pissheads. He sat in quiet admiration for a few minutes more before remembering to phone Helen. He turned back to the bar and fished out his mobile, fingers now warmed, he thumbed in the number.

Marty sat in the snug contemplating the last few drops of his Guinness before deciding he would have another half before he hit the road. He yawned, pleasantly relaxed now as he took in the surroundings that never failed to please him. He had enjoyed some good nights here in the past. He got up, drained the glass and headed for the bar. It was still pretty empty apart from a few guys sat either end, one an obvious tourist sat facing the snugs, eyes roving admiringly. The other had his back to him as he tapped away on his mobile. The barman came and took his glass, pouring him a fresh one with just the right amount of care.

"Just stopped off for a quick one. What? Yes, I got it. O.K. Bye."

The voice made Marty blink twice, and he slowly turned his head. Roy put his phone away and had another sip, glancing casually to his right and nodding at Marty before again facing the three barrels directly opposite him. Marty stared. Then he saw Roy stiffen and almost owl like slowly turn to face him, his own shock exactly mirrored in those green eyes which widened slightly, flitting over his own face in a second, taking in the features for confirmation before going to his hands resting near his glass. There was a long silence.

"Nice ring. Where did you get it?" Roy asked. Marty took in posture and demeanour, scanning for threat. Roy had done the same and his frame seemed to relax a little as the initial shock left him.

"Beirut, if you must know," he replied.

Roy nodded, not taking his eyes from him as he picked his glass up and took a careful swig. "Aye, I remember now. When were you there?"

Marty was still wary and thought a second before deciding what the hell, none of it mattered anymore. He took a long swallow before speaking.

"The summer of '82." Roy raised his eyebrows as Marty continued. "Aye, my timing was a bit off. Not much of a holiday." Roy gave a small laugh.

"I know what you mean. I was in the Falklands the same time. At least you had it warm." Marty took his turn at raising eyebrows. Roy looked at the ring again in the renewed silence, both of them nonplussed at this unexpected encounter. It wasn't every day you bumped into someone who was once a mortal enemy.

"What are you doing with yourself these days?" Roy asked.

"I'm living down in Dublin," he answered. "It's healthier there," he added with a knowing look. "What about yourself?"

"Just over on holiday, family and that." He glanced at the ring again, remembering it glinting in the dark of a wet night. "I moved to England a while ago, just after leaving the army."

There was another strange silence, both of them drinking up. They looked again at each other, both wondering what the other was thinking, both marvelling at this freakish encounter. They both knew there could be no sudden warm friendship, no hugs and kisses and making up like long lost brothers, their lives too deformed by the times they had lived through. Too much had happened for this type of reconciliation, but like Pandora's Box, at the very last there was hope. They might not pay each other visits or be on each other's Christmas card list, but they had given up trying to kill one another and for the moment they both saw this as more than enough. Roy cleared his throat as he got up to go, both finishing at the same time. There was a scrape of bar stools as he spoke.

"I'd better be getting home."

"Aye, me too."

They walked to the door and exited, stopping for a brief second outside. They looked again at each other, hesitating before Roy spoke again.

"All the best."

"Same to you."

Roy headed one way and Marty the other. Both looked over their shoulders as they went, giving each other a quick final parting nod, not one that contained much in the way of warm amiability but something more profound: an acknowledgement. Recognition.

THE END

ABOUT THE AUTHOR

Lee Watts is originally from Southampton and after studying history at the University of Ulster moved to the Netherlands where he now lives with his wife and daughter. A Stone's Throw is his first book. His latest novel Blue Anchor Lane follows the lives of a group of soldiers during and after the Afghan War of 1879.

Printed in Poland
by Amazon Fulfillment
Poland Sp. z o.o., Wrocław